What the critics are saying...

Synergy:

"...Ms. Douglas knows how to tell a fascinating, humorous, sensual story, while at the same time drawing you deeper and deeper into the story until you are no longer reading a book, but you are living it; You are there with every breath, every tear and all the joy of this love story." - *Sandra Tibbets, Romance Junkies.*

"...This, the fourth StarQuest novel, is both intriguing and sizzling. The passion flares ardently and remains that way through out the story...Synergy definitely has me running to get the previous books by Ms. Douglas." - *Vikky Bertling, Just Erotic Romance Reviews*

Bold Journey

"...Bold Journey is a truly outstanding story that showcases the power and creativity of Ms. Douglas' imagination... A fantastic addition to Ms. Douglas's wonderful Star Quest series, I do not hesitate to add that this is my favourite...From the very first sentence until the very last Ms. Douglas takes the reader on a fabulous journey that should not be missed." - *Larenda Twigg, TRSBlue*

"...Bold Journey is a very fine addition to Douglas' StarQuest series. The hero is one of the next generation and a fascinating creation. Introducing a new world,

Douglas builds a wonderfully imaginative setting for this alien romance." - *Susan Mobley, Romantic Times Book Club*

"…The love scenes are hot, hot, hot and Bolden is yet another of Ms. Douglas' very sexy Miratans…It's a sensual story that will satisfy any reader looking for a terrific sci-fi erotic romance." – *Shelly, Fallen Angel Reviews*

"…StarQuest 5: BOLD JOURNEY is a wonderful science fiction romance and the fifth book in Ms. Douglas's StarQuest series… Their love and devotion is so tenderly sweet your heart will ache - I was moved to tears…Kate Douglas has written a terrific story, one I would recommend to those who enjoy reading science fiction and are looking for something unique and out of the ordinary."
- *Brenda Lee, Romance Junkies*

STARQUEST 2

by Kate Douglas

StarQuest 2
An Ellora's Cave Publication, March 2005

Ellora's Cave Publishing, Inc.
1337 Commerce Drive
Stow, Ohio 44224

ISBN # 1419951459

Synergy © 2003 Kate Douglas
Bold Journey © 2004 Kate Douglas
Other available formats: ISBN MS Reader (LIT), Adobe (PDF),
Rocketbook (RB), Mobipocket (PRC) & HTML

Cover art by: Syneca

Warning:

The following material contains graphic sexual content meant for mature readers. *StarQuest 2* has been rated *E-rotic* by a minimum of three independent reviewers.

Ellora's Cave Publishing offers three levels of Romantica™ reading entertainment: S (S-ensuous), E (E-rotic), and X (X-treme).

S-*ensuous* love scenes are explicit and leave nothing to the imagination.

E-*rotic* love scenes are explicit, leave nothing to the imagination, and are high in volume per the overall word count. In addition, some E-rated titles might contain fantasy material that some readers find objectionable, such as bondage, submission, same sex encounters, forced seductions, etc. E-rated titles are the most graphic titles we carry; it is common, for instance, for an author to use words such as "fucking", "cock", "pussy", etc., within their work of literature.

X-*treme* titles differ from E-rated titles only in plot premise and storyline execution. Unlike E-rated titles, stories designated with the letter X tend to contain controversial subject matter not for the faint of heart.

Also by Kate Douglas

Available in eBook

Lionheart *StarQuest 1*

Night of the Cat *StarQuest 2*

Pride of Imar *StarQuest 3*

More Than A Hunch

Luck of the Irish *anthology*

Just A Little Magic

Synergy *StarQuest 4*

Bold Journey *StarQuest 5*

Ellora's Cavemen: Tales from the Temple I *anthology*

Available in Print

StarQuest *books 1-3*

The Twelve Quickies of Christmas
anthology (contains Just A Little Magic)

Ellora's Cavemen: Tales from the Temple I *anthology*

CONTENTS

SYNERGY
StarQuest Book 4

Prologue

The waiter pocketed a handful of credits left by a slightly inebriated group of soldiers heading out the door. He ran a damp rag across the scarred table, seething with anger and resentment.

Talents, all of them, and so damned cocky with their power. Who the hell did they think they were? Treated him like shit, that's what they did, using kinetics to snatch the drinks off his tray, sailing them across the room, mocking him. Always mocking him.

He'd show them. Would he ever! He glanced up as another group of customers wandered into the rec center, laughing, teasing one another. He turned his back on them and stalked away. When he turned around, he saw them take seats at the long table he'd just cleaned. One young man raised a finger, beckoning him, like he was some sort of servant.

Just then another man entered the building. Dressed in dark, nondescript clothing, he looked as if he'd journeyed long and hard. He nodded briefly toward the waiter, then sat at a table off by himself.

The waiter stared at the man for a long moment before he responded. The muscles in his gut tightened, an odd combination of elation and fear. Ignoring the boisterous crowd at the first table, the waiter headed toward the man in black.

Chapter One

Carly Harris handed a hefty tip to the sexy young cabby with a final, lingering glance, and grabbed the suitcase he handed to her. Too bad she couldn't take him with her on this mini-vacation. She'd fantasized about him all the way from the airport...thank goodness he didn't have a clue what she'd been thinking, sitting oh, so primly in the back seat of the cab with her thighs pressed tightly together and her eyes half-closed.

Especially when they'd crossed over on the ferry. From her position in the back seat, she'd watched him through narrowed eyes, so horny she'd practically come without touching herself. He'd stood on the deck, leaning against the polished railing. The wind whipped that gorgeous long hair around. His broad shoulders bunched and flexed beneath his white cotton tee shirt as he held his balance against the surging waves...damn, he'd looked good enough to eat.

She bit back a giggle and wondered what he'd say if she just asked for a tiny little taste? A second, surreptitious glance told her there'd be no such thing as a *little* taste. His denim jeans couldn't disguise what lay neatly packaged beneath the worn fabric.

Carly flashed him a very proper smile. The young man tipped his cap, swept his long black ponytail over his shoulder and folded his lanky frame into the yellow cab. He gunned the engine. Tires screeching, he roared round the driveway on his way out. Carly sighed as the cab left.

Definitely inspirational. Grinning at her reaction to eye candy most likely half her age, she readjusted the weight of the suitcase, raised the handle and popped the little wheels free so she could haul it behind her.

She held her face up to the sun's brilliance. Thank goodness the odd storm had ended when it did, or she'd be drenched before she got up the front steps. The inn appeared to hover just beyond the drive, surrounded in a shifting layer of silvery fog, all that remained of the near-monsoon rains of only moments ago.

Once again, she wondered if this was the right thing to do. She'd seen the ad for Desire Island Inn purely by accident, and bought her ticket on a whim, once again following the familiar little voice in her head that had so often directed her life.

Did she really deserve a weekend in a gorgeous inn on a mysterious island?

Yes, dammit. She did. With a new resolve, Carly marched toward the entryway.

* * * * *

It was difficult to believe they'd all been strangers just hours before. Now Carly sat with the other guests, laughing and talking as if they'd been dear friends forever. The cognac was wonderful and the ambience of the inn absolutely delightful. She felt warm and relaxed for the first time in years.

They were discussing fantasy. Sexual fantasy. Every woman's favorite topic after a bit too much to drink. The few male guests weren't complaining about the subject matter, either. Carly grinned, thinking of the young cab driver who'd brought her out from the airport.

There was something about younger guys…she sipped at the golden liquor and thought of the gorgeous young cabby, her mind barely focusing on the waves of conversation flowing about her.

Long dark hair tied with a leather thong, brilliant blue eyes hooded beneath thick, black lashes, broad shoulders, smooth, copper-toned skin hinting at Native American ancestry, a lean and healthy body…and his hands. Lord, she hadn't been able to ignore his hands.

Hadn't wanted to.

Long, slim fingers—they'd wrapped negligently around the worn steering wheel as he skillfully guided the car through the raging storm. She'd noticed right away that his nails were clean and neatly filed, the knuckles large, with sinewy veins showing beneath the dark, coppery skin along the back of each hand.

Long arms, long fingers…an artist's fingers, supple and strong. A shiver ran across her abdomen, arrowed down between her legs and settled into a deep, throbbing pulse of frustration. What she wouldn't do right now, to have those long fingers stroking over her needy clit, delving deep inside her wet and wanting folds.

Carly shifted in her chair, clamped her thighs tightly together. Imagined those talented fingers stroking, rubbing, touching…pinching. Sighed a long and shuddering breath, then closed her eyes.

She saw blue. Brilliant, sparkling blue eyes in the face of an angel. A dark angel, framed in waves of hair as black as night. He was looking at her, watching her, and his blue eyes were filled with lush promises and earthy desire.

Damn… Carly shook herself free of the vision, but the sense of the beautiful young man lingered in the after-image behind her eyes. No doubt about it, there was definitely something special about the young ones.

Carly stared at her reflection in the side of the crystal goblet, and sighed.

Fantasy. Why were the good ones only there in fantasy?

* * * * *

Armand Institute, Earth 2104 A.D.

"Hey, Doc! How ya doing?" Tim Riley waved at the Institute's healer across the crowded rec room. Malachi paused, scanned the crowd, then headed toward the table Tim shared with Thom Antoon, the Rebellion's popular leader.

Tim waved to the waiter, kinetically grabbed a cold beer off a serving tray destined for another customer and floated it carefully through the air to Malachi. The waiter scowled, but kept his mouth shut.

Tim chose to ignore him.

"One of these days, Tim..." Sighing dramatically, Antoon dug into his pocket for a handful of credits and handed them over to the waiter before the surly young man had a chance to complain.

"Who is that guy?" Tim nodded his head toward the waiter. "I've never seen him before."

"Must be new. Cheery sort, eh?"

"Any cheerier and we'd all be in tears." Malachi pulled out the chair across from the general. "Thanks for the beer, Tim." He winked at General Antoon and slipped into the empty seat. "Tim, I've been looking for you."

"I didn't do it." Tim laughed and leaned back in his chair, aware he was actually relaxing for the first time in weeks. They'd all lived under the pressure of armed conflict for so many years, it was difficult to accept that, though some dissenters remained, the seven year rebellion had actually ended.

"It was the general." Tim pointed at the older man. "He's guilty."

"I certainly hope so." Thom took a long swallow of beer. "Guilty of what?"

"Nobody's done anything, yet." Malachi leaned forward, his expression suddenly grown serious. "I've had a really strong pre-cog, Tim. You're the star. You and a woman."

"No shit? It's about time there was a woman. Thom's cute, but he's lacking certain necessary physical attributes." Tim jostled Antoon in the ribs, something he'd never have done to the general while they were still at war with the World Federation. Now, though, the relationship between Tim and his mentor had definitely relaxed.

As had their lives. Maybe now he'd finally have a chance for a life of his own. *With a woman?* Damn, he hoped Malachi was right. Of course, the doc usually was.

"Which reminds me." Thom stood up and threw a few credits on the table to cover his tab. "I've got someone with all the correct attributes waiting for me at home. Why am I wasting time with you two?" He took a last swig of his beer and turned to leave.

Tim waved him off, laughing. "She's too young for you, old man...all that sex is gonna kill you."

"Yeah, but I'll die happy." The general tipped an imaginary hat at Tim and Malachi. Laughing, Thom headed for the door. The bounce in his step was obvious.

"He doesn't look fifty, does he?" Tim shook his head, still chuckling. "He's so much fun to pick on since he's been with Jan."

"She's good for him." Malachi finished off his beer. "The pressure of leadership was killing him. Since Jan came into his life, I've seen his old sparkle come back."

"Jan's a year younger than I am, Mal. She's just twenty-four, less than half his age. That's a bit much, don't you think?"

"What's the matter, Tim? Jealous?" Smiling broadly, Malachi leaned back in his chair and stretched.

Tim glanced sharply at the healer. Did Malachi read minds along with his other Talents? *Do you know what I've given up for the Rebellion, Doc? You've never asked me, never considered the cost.*

And why should he? Tim pushed the useless self-pity out of his head. "I don't have time to be jealous," he said, drinking the last of his beer. "I'm too busy keeping an eye on you two old farts."

Malachi sat forward and leaned his elbows on the table. "I really do need to talk to you." He paused, narrowed his eyes. "Is your mother still alive?"

Tim blinked at the non sequitur. "My mother? What's she got to do with anything? She's dead. Mom and my sister died almost eight years ago. Vehicle accident."

Malachi nodded slowly, his expression serious but distracted. "I'm sorry. I knew that." He paused as if to consider something important, then, as if the decision had been made, slapped his palms down on the table. "Come back to the clinic with me. I need to share a precog. It's too noisy here." He didn't wait for an answer, merely shoved his chair back and headed for the door.

Tim tossed some credits on the table next to the change the general had left. He followed the doctor, weaving between the tables crowding the rec center. Why would Malachi be asking about his mom? Tim struggled to repress the grief welling up inside. Damn, he missed her. His sister, Mary, too.

Tim crossed the compound in silence.

"Tim? You okay?" Malachi waited at the door to the clinic, one foot on the threshold. He stared at Tim with concern.

"Yeah. Just thinking about Mom and Mary. It's been a long time. They died in an accident on the way to the Institute—almost eight years ago. I wasn't even injured."

"Tim, I…" Mal paused uncomfortably. "I remember. It's just…" He clamped his mouth shut and turned abruptly toward the doorway. "Come with me."

Silently, Tim followed Malachi down the hall and into the small office at the rear of the clinic. Mal shut the door behind him and motioned Tim to take a seat. Without preamble, he pulled a chair up facing Tim and sat directly in front of him, close enough so their knees touched.

He stared at Tim for a moment, then took a deep breath. "I want you to see this before I explain anything. I want your response to be completely free of my influence."

With his limited telepathic abilities, Tim knew Malachi relied on contact to share a vision with almost anyone but his wife, the Miratan lioness, Sheyna. Curious, Tim leaned forward, touching his forehead to the healer's, resting his hands on Malachi's shoulders.

He was aware of a slight tingling when Malachi's fingertips completed the link, pressing gently to each of Tim's temples. Always a healer, Malachi would be sensing Tim's general health as he shared his vision. Tim wondered if a non-existent sex life might be cause for alarm. If so, Doc's bells would be ringing loud and clear.

Tim was aware of a gentle probing in his mind, the first light touch as contact was established. The image didn't appear all at once — instead, it coalesced out of nothing, a filmy illusion that slowly gained in depth and perception. He saw himself first, the back of his tall, angular frame and long, straight black hair immediately distinguishable. His body partially obscured another person, a woman.

She looked older than Tim, though it was hard to tell by how much. It didn't matter — she was absolutely gorgeous. Her dark blonde hair fell past her shoulders and her eyes were a deep, coffee brown. She was casually dressed in brown canvas pants and a pale blue sweater.

She stared hard at Tim, concentrating intensely as if she were trying to read him telepathically. He felt her inside him, an almost visceral reaction to her inherent sensuality. Without understanding why or how, Tim knew he needed her. Needed who she was and what she represented.

As if staring over his own shoulder in the vision, Tim focused on the woman, on the changing expressions flitting across her face. There was no sound. Still, he sensed urgency and danger and something powerful, dark and frightening. As he absorbed the implications within the image, the woman suddenly whirled around as if in fear. Her mouth opened in a silent scream. A shadow crossed in front of her and she — and the vision — disappeared in darkness.

"Wow." Tim carefully leaned back in his chair, fighting the compelling desire to adjust his throbbing cock and aching balls. He shuddered, shaking off the aftereffects of the sharing, the sudden, overwhelming shaft of physical need. He'd never reacted sexually to a vision before.

The sensation was unsettling.

Malachi nodded his head. "*Wow* is right. Do you feel it? The urgency? The sense of danger?"

"The sex." Tim shook his head in disbelief, thankful the pressure between his legs was beginning to ease. "Damn, Mal. She's the most beautiful woman I've ever seen. Do you know when, what...?"

"No. Not a clue. That's why I shared it with you. I thought maybe you could help me." He laughed. "I take it she's not your mom...I thought of your mother because this woman looks old enough, I think..."

"To be my mom? You're kidding, right?" Tim laughed. "Mom is the last person I think of when I look at someone like her." He took a deep breath, let it out slowly. "So, what's it mean?"

"Precognitive events are strange." Malachi pushed his chair back and stood up. "Sometimes I know exactly what they mean, or at least what their implications are."

"I take it this isn't one of those times?"

"Exactly." Doc nodded. "I haven't got a clue what this portends, merely the very real sense we need to find her, and quickly. Just because the Rebellion has ended doesn't mean we're at peace. We can't afford to ignore warnings, no matter how oblique they may appear. For some reason, I believe she's important. I wish I knew why."

"There's something you need to know, Mal." Tim wasn't sure how he knew, he just did, but he realized this was not a simple precognitive event. "I sense...well, I don't think she's from our time."

"Neither was Jenna." The flat statement hung between the two of them.

"Are you suggesting...?" Tim recalled the night he found Jenna, using his kinetic abilities to lock on to the woman Malachi had shared with him in an earlier precognitive vision. Lock on to her in the early twenty-first century, and bring her forward a hundred years, into her future and Tim's present.

"You did it with Jenna. I think this woman might be from the same time period. The mental signature is familiar."

Anger and resentment warred with curiosity. "Do you have any idea what you're asking of me?"

Malachi nodded. "I'm your doctor, Tim. Of course I know. Every time we share a vision, I feel your frustration. I'm sorry...it's not fair and it's not right to keep asking you to sacrifice so much, but..." He held his hands out, palms up. "There's no one else. You know it and I know it. I wouldn't even consider it if..."

"Okay. It's okay." Tim's palms suddenly felt sweaty and a prickle of apprehension coursed along his spine. "I'd like to see her one more time, get a stronger feel for her signature." He tried to picture the woman as Malachi had seen her. He'd been so entranced by her, he hadn't paid close enough attention to the traits he'd need to search for.

"We can do it now." Mal pulled his chair back into position. "Then I want you to pack some things and go up to the cabin. Sheyna knows what I have planned and she's prepared some food for you to take. The cabin's isolated and private—a good place for you to perform your search and, if you're successful, help ease the woman's entry into our time." Malachi sighed. "It will also give you the chance to assess any danger she might bring with her. I sense Talent in her, but I'm not sure what it is."

"Do you have any idea at all what kind of danger she might represent?"

Malachi paused. "I sense a very subtle link to...you ever hear of the Reverend? He's an itinerant preacher, says that Talent is the work of the devil...he's building a bit of a following of malcontents. Shing Tamura has made a couple of arrests, but..."

A light tap on the door interrupted him. Tim turned just as Sheyna, Malachi's mate, walked into the room. Tall and regal, the exotic features of a lioness of Mirat gave her an alien beauty rarely seen on Earth. Sheyna smiled shyly at Tim, then went to stand close beside her husband.

"Malachi has shared his vision with you?" She tilted her head in question, her amber eyes huge and unblinking, her velvety ears pricked forward.

Tim wondered if he would ever become accustomed to the humanoid lions of Mirat, the cat-like features, soft fur pelts, yet lean, muscular bodies so amazingly human. More so with Sheyna, who lacked the tail typical of most of her species.

Malachi's arm slipped around Sheyna's narrow waist and Tim felt a momentary pang of jealousy. To have someone love him…was it asking so much? Immediately, the image of the woman in Doc's vision slipped into his thoughts.

"He's seen her, my love. Tim's going to head up to the cabin tonight, once I refresh her image for him."

Sheyna nodded. "I've contacted Garan and Jenna. Though they're far from here, they need to know what we're attempting. Especially Jenna, if, as Malachi suspects, this woman is from her time. Sander and Mara have been notified as well, but they'll stay clear of all contact until we know what we have."

"Mal, will you be going with me?" Tim had never told Malachi, not anyone, that he'd passed out after bringing Jenna forward.

At the time, he hadn't realized he'd found her in the past, merely that she'd have to be moved a very long distance to bring her to the Institute. He'd chosen Lieutenant Garan's quarters as the safest place to plant his prize, knowing the effort would leave any kinetic Talent attempting such a feat most likely unconscious, or close to it.

The Miratan officer had first thought Jenna was a spy. Tim wished he could have been a fly on the wall so he could see the big cat's expression when he finally realized his captive was a woman from Earth's past. A woman who possessed more powerful psychic abilities than any other known human or Miratan. Jenna's presence had definitely affected their world.

Would this new woman do the same? Malachi must think so, or he never would have asked Tim to attempt such a risky operation again. Never would ask him to sacrifice so much.

"No."

Tim snapped his head up at Malachi's forceful reply. The healer appeared to be studying a spot on the floor. Even Sheyna looked away. "You need to do this one alone, Tim. I feel that very strongly. Just be careful."

Be careful. Right. Like the blonde wasn't going to be pissed off and scared to death to wake up in what was essentially another world? *If she wakes up at all.*

"You must ease her way into this period, Tim. Malachi and I feel it will be simpler if you are both isolated, away from the curious probing of so much Talent. Plan on at least a few days before you introduce her to the Institute. Make sure she brings no danger to us. If Jenna had decided not to work with us, imagine what she could have done to damage the Rebellion. We have no idea what this other woman is capable of, or how she'll feel when she realizes what you've done."

Sheyna's comment caught him off guard. Jenna was a powerful force, her many abilities still untapped. He hadn't even thought of the potential for danger when he caught her up in the early twenty-first century and deposited her in the present.

"You're probably right, SheShe." Tim sighed, subtly ticking off what little he knew so far. Obviously, this was more important than he'd first thought. Mara had been the Institute's new leader when he'd arrived almost eight years ago. Her contact with the starship captain, Sander, a lion of Mirat, had opened up communication between the two worlds and led to a rebellion of Sensitives and Talents against the xenophobic, anti-paranormal World Federation. It had been Jenna, though, who had proven to be a catalyst for peace, and eventually Earth's amicable resolution between the warring factions.

Jenna had also been part of the new diplomatic unity with the citizens of Mirat. There'd been peace for such a short time. Peace brought by a woman from Earth's past. Sighing, Tim wondered what this new woman might bring to his world.

Chapter Two

Tim stuck the perishables Sheyna had sent with him into the small refrigerator and shoved the rest of the box of supplies up on the pantry shelf without unpacking them. Feeling oddly unsettled, he surveyed the dark interior of the tiny log cabin. Nestled in a narrow canyon in the hills above the Institute, it usually gave him a sense of well being, not concern.

He walked over to the kitchen sink and gazed out the small window at the evening shadows. He loved any excuse to come here. He'd been on a day hike with Malachi and Thom Antoon a few weeks before the Rebellion broke out, when they'd first discovered the dilapidated structure.

They'd spent what time they could making the place habitable, repairing the spring-fed water system, replacing the roof and windows, and clearing away the wild things that had taken up residence in and about the cabin. Now it stood solid and tight against the weather, carefully hidden within the thick woods, a quiet spot away from the constant presence of humanity at the Institute.

Its origins were lost in the last hundred years of war and turmoil, but Tim had enjoyed sitting out on the porch with Mal and Thom, drinking beer and speculating over the cabin's past and the people who had built it.

Tim suddenly looked up from the sink. That's what felt so weird. He'd never been here alone, before. Chuckling to himself over his unexpected case of nerves, he ran the water long enough to clear the pipes and checked the fuel levels for the water heater and gas-fired refrigerator. The sun was almost down, so he lit a kerosene lantern and set it on the table.

The soft glow of the lamp turned the log walls golden, but left the sloped ceiling and corners in shadow. Light caught and reflected off dried specks of pitch on some of the logs. They sparkled like small jewels against the rough wood.

Preparing the cabin had become an old and familiar routine. As Tim swept cobwebs out of the open beams, his thoughts strayed once more to Malachi's precognitive vision. His groin tightened immediately. Whoever the woman was, her effect on him was more physical than anything else, regardless of what she meant to his world's future.

Physical for now, anyway. Tim paused, not at all pleased with the irony of the situation. What a choice…think about her and get a hard-on, or bring her forward in time so he could actually touch her, essentially trading his sex drive for kinetic power.

Shit. He never knew how long it would take to regain his libido. After Jenna, it had been months before he'd even thought about jerking off, much less having sex.

He'd learned about the connection between kinetics and sex early on.

The memories always left him feeling foolish, unmanned, but they crowded him now, forcing their way into his mind. It was before he'd arrived at the Institute. He'd been coming into his power as a teenager, practicing telekinesis in private, not telling anyone his secret. Pushing himself to exhaustion, lifting bigger objects, moving them further.

One night, feeling really cocky about his growing power, he'd gone to a party with some other kids. There'd been a really cute girl about his age—maybe sixteen or so—and she'd come on to him. She'd let him slide his hand down inside her pants, then she'd taken her shirt off. He remembered cupping her small, pointy breasts in his hands, staring at the rosy nipples and wondering why in the hell he didn't feel anything.

He'd seen naked women in magazines and movies and it was interesting to see one in the flesh, but there'd been no reaction. Nothing. He'd been terrified she might want to feel him. He knew all she'd find was a limp dick in his pants and the humiliation would kill him. Praise the gods, she'd been too shy and hadn't done anything but let him touch her.

All the other guys wanted to talk about was how horny they were all the time, how they spent hours jacking off, squeezing their cocks and rubbing on their balls because it felt so damned good.

All Tim wanted to do was move stuff. That damned thing between his legs wasn't good for much more than pissing. It never got hard, never begged to be held. Nothing.

At least he had the power. Fat lot of good it did him then, staring at those perfect breasts, snow white against his long, dark fingers. He hadn't even wanted to lick them or kiss them, hadn't wanted to suckle her perfectly shaped nipples.

He didn't want to hurt her feelings, so he'd told her she was pretty, then he'd slipped his fingers between her legs and felt her thighs clamp down on his hand. He'd rubbed the narrow little slit through soft, downy hair and done some of the things he'd read that women liked.

He remembered feeling as if he were merely following a list—touch here, stroke there. She liked it. She even seemed to like him, but he hadn't felt a thing, even when the girl shuddered in his arms, made little breathy, whimpering sounds and clamped her legs around his wrist. Not until months later when he'd taken a break from using his Talent. He'd awakened one morning with a raging hard-on, memories of those perfect breasts cupped in his hands, and realized what he'd traded for power.

He'd been so careful the past few weeks, hoarding his strength, not using kinetics much at all. Gods, but he wanted to get laid. Wanted to experience what he'd only imagined, that hot, wet, female flesh clamped around his hard cock, the coiling heat in his balls, the out-of-control burst of seed that had to be better than what he managed with his hand. He'd even been afraid to jack off, so worried about losing what little libido he had.

Was that why he'd reacted so strongly to Mal's vision? Was the woman somehow tied to him sexually? He'd felt passion, need, a sense of pure, unbridled lust when he saw her.

He certainly hadn't seen her as a threat. He didn't associate her with anything evil or dangerous, no matter what Sheyna and Malachi thought. He'd known she was okay the minute he'd looked into her eyes. What was that old proverb—*eyes are windows to the soul?* He'd concentrated on her eyes the second time Mal shared the vision. Dark brown eyes framed in thick black lashes tipped with gold. Eyes filled with yearning, with the answers to age-old questions.

Eyes focused completely on Tim. He shuddered, shaking off the vision, the very real, almost visceral sense of her, then opened the door. Stepping out onto the porch, he shook the dust and spider webs off the broom, then stood there a moment, staring at the small meadow in front of him. It was shadowed in dark greens and grays as the last rays of sunlight disappeared from the sky. The varied shades of color might just as well have been cement and asphalt for all he noticed.

She was there, staring back at him, her honey blonde hair waving gently about her shoulders, her head tilted slightly to one side, full lips making sensual promises with her smile. Tim absentmindedly brushed his hand across the heavy denim covering his growing erection, vaguely aware of the ethereal quality of the vision before him.

There was nothing shy or timid about either her stance or her appearance. She looked like a woman used to getting what she wanted, used to taking what was hers. He wondered what it would feel like, to be taken by someone like her? Tim groaned and closed his eyes in frustration. Hell, he wondered what it felt like to be taken by *any* woman. His hand stilled in the act of unzipping his pants.

He couldn't afford the loss of energy. An erection this hard meant his power was at its peak. He took a deep breath, adjusted his jeans to ease the welcome discomfort, and stepped back inside the cabin. He reached for the clean linens Sheyna kept in the cupboards.

Making up the bed was automatic, his swirling thoughts a litany of old grudges and regrets. Growing up Talented meant living as an outcast. It hadn't been an easy childhood for either Mary or himself, much less his mom trying to raise two unruly Talents without a husband.

He'd found acceptance at the Armand Institute, but at what cost? He'd lost the only two people in the world who had ever shown him unconditional love. Tim blinked away threatening tears and knew he had to quit thinking about them. If what Malachi suspected were true, he had to concentrate on the job at hand. For all he knew, he might be summoning more than a beautiful woman—he might be calling forth danger.

The image of the elusive blonde flashed through his mind. He grinned as he tucked the sheets under the mattress and slipped pillowcases on each of the pillows. No way could he equate her with danger! Standing back to survey the neatly made bed, Tim couldn't help but imagine the woman, sprawled naked and wanting, right in the middle of the down comforter, legs spread in welcome, her eyes half-lidded with desire, one finger raised in a beckoning gesture.

Once more his erection threatened to break through his zipper. His breath caught in lungs unable to expand, a steady roar filled his hearing. The sensual vision of the blonde in his bed blurred, wavered…

…flashed out in a wink.

The roaring in his ears dissipated. His balls still ached, but breath whooshed out of his lungs and the pressure on his cock eased a fraction. Silently, Tim turned away from the bed, walking stiffly, awkwardly.

Dammit. She could beckon all she wanted. She could strip naked and beg him to fuck her. Once he used his Talent to bring her here, he wouldn't be able to do a damned thing to her. Of course, getting hard was the least of his problems. A little experience might help.

He'd become a soldier of the Rebellion in a world gone mad, found companionship among other young soldiers, but never love. *Not even sex. Other guys got laid. Why not you, Riley?*

Tim shook his head. He dragged a chair out from the kitchen table and settled down to concentrate on coordinates in time and space for Malachi's mystery woman.

Why not me?

The answer was simple. Only freaks were still virgins at twenty-five. Only freaks could transcend time and space. *Too bad you can't transcend your own fucking libido, Riley.*

Wasn't that exactly what he'd been doing for so many years?

He thought about the night he'd brought Jenna Lang forward in time. He really hadn't thought through what he was doing and he'd paid a tremendous cost. He hadn't expected the enormous physical strain, or the time it would take him to recover his energy and abilities.

He'd been barely eighteen when General Antoon first tapped his kinetic power. Tim would never forget that first rush of success, when he'd discovered the sense of near omnipotence of working in gestalt with other Talent.

The closest bonds he'd ever known, closer even than his relationship with his mother or his sister, had been forged in the fires of battle. Tim stared at his hands, remembering, well aware the battle was over. The bonds had frayed, the friendships scattered, the others had gone on to find lives and futures of their own.

He'd made his choice at eighteen—he'd chosen the Rebellion over any kind of sex life. Now, though, he'd honestly hoped that could change.

Since the Rebellion had ended, he'd backed off on the use of Talent. His libido was increasing—already he noticed a difference in the women he saw regularly at the Institute.

Suddenly they were more than faces and names. They'd become breasts and thighs and soft, sexy voices. They'd filtered into his dreams, taken over his thoughts, left him tongue-tied and horny and wanting so badly to experience what he'd been missing.

He was almost there, almost ready to take a chance with a woman, any woman. Except, once again, Malachi was asking him to give up his personal life for the good of many. Malachi, safe and warm in Sheyna's embrace, was asking Tim to forsake his own pleasure, his own shot at happiness.

Anger surged through him, then just as quickly was extinguished. Malachi had no control over his visions. Neither did Malachi control Tim. He sighed, accepting the truth of the matter. It was entirely his choice.

Like you don't want to find this woman?

Who was he kidding? He could have told Malachi no. Could have refused to snatch an innocent woman from her own time. If he'd refused, though, he'd always wonder. Was she the one destined for him? What if Malachi were right? What if she was preordained to affect his time? To affect him, personally?

The reasons were too compelling to ignore.

Tim rubbed his temples, recalling the thought processes he'd followed when he'd searched for Jenna's particular mental signature, finally discovering it and calling her to him telekinetically.

Damn. Was all this pre-ordained? Had his life's journey been set from childhood, his actions no more of his own free will than those of the woman he'd stolen from her own time? There was no logic, no understanding. Sometimes he felt like such a child, his life at the whim of fate and friends alike.

He looked at his hands again, the fingers long and narrow, nails neatly trimmed, dark veins tracing the copper-toned skin from knuckles to wrist. Definitely not the hands of a child. He folded them tightly in front of him on the worn tabletop and glanced once more about the small cabin. He had a job to do. Leave philosophy to those better suited to it.

This he understood. This action, this search for someone discovered in a dream. He was as ready as he'd ever be. The door was locked from the inside and he held the only key. The windows were tempered glass, though he realized someone desperate enough would be able to break free. Still, Malachi had insisted Tim come here alone, as if that were part of the vision he'd had. Had the doctor held information back? Had he shown Tim merely a portion of the complete vision?

What the hell are you getting me into, Doc?

Somehow, he had to remain conscious when he brought the woman forward, but he knew he'd be weak as a kitten. Pushing himself away from the table, Tim found a length of rope under the kitchen sink. Cutting it into four pieces, he made simple loops at one end of each section. Two he tied to the headboard of the bed.

He left the other two pieces lying on the blanket. With any luck, he'd be able to secure the woman while she was still unconscious, but before he passed out.

He pictured her once again, lying in the middle of the bed, tied this time, her legs spread wide, arms over her head. Pure lust coursed through his veins—lust and need and something more, something that tugged relentlessly at his soul.

Shaking his head, unwilling to pursue such pointless thoughts, Tim grabbed a bottled energy drink out of the refrigerator, then sat heavily at the kitchen table. He stared at the bed, his mind filled with the search for an elusive blonde of the twenty-first century.

He couldn't explain it, even to himself, the manner in which his mind locked on to someone of another time and place. Couldn't describe the sensation, the physical *coming together* of thoughts through time.

Couldn't explain it, didn't understand it...just did it. Felt every muscle in his body tighten, fought pain as the pressure in his skull reached unbearable levels. Searched, touched, held on.

Held on and called her soul to his, then sighed with the answering release, as the woman's mind matched, then melded with his, as her body released its hold on her time and re-materialized smack-dab in the middle of the down comforter, just as Tim had imagined.

* * * * *

A dirty gym sock would taste better.

Carly rolled her tongue around inside her dry mouth as she struggled into wakefulness. The last vestiges of a wonderfully graphic dream floated away with the fading image of the sexy young cabdriver, his hair all long and flowing free, his blue eyes gazing deeply into hers.

Carly's eyes felt glued shut, her stomach rolled uncomfortably, her head throbbed and pounded and if she didn't get up and find the bathroom...

"I really don't remember hangovers hurting quite so much," she muttered, reaching her arms overhead in a slow stretch. Something drew her up short. She jerked awake, suddenly clear-headed and alert.

This was *not* her room at the inn—this wasn't remotely close to her classy Victorian-style room. This was old and rustic, log walls and plank floor, dark and somewhat musty, as if from lack of use. This was Carly Harris, stark naked, tied hand and foot to the metal railings of a large bed. This was not good. It went beyond nightmare, beyond fear...right smack-dab into unbelievable.

She bit back a scream. Her stomach lurched, a precursor to throwing up, something she definitely did not want to do. Fighting nausea, her breath caught in short, hard blasts. Whimpering, she yanked frantically at the ropes, giving in to panic.

A familiar little voice intruded, slipping past her fear. *Calm down, calm down, calm...down...calm.* Carly let her breath out on a shaky sigh, inhaled deeply, then exhaled again. Panic would get her nowhere fast.

That didn't mean she couldn't be really pissed off. She tugged at the ropes, her anger growing with each futile jerk of her hands. *Damn!* Where the hell was she?

Who did this? How the hell did she get here? Where the hell *was* here?

She knew she hadn't left the inn, at least not of her own volition. She'd finished her cognac and sat staring at the fire, listening to the other women talking about fantasy men. She must have drifted off to sleep, still sitting in her chair. Still thinking of the cabby. His image drifted through her mind…long, lean body, straight black hair falling almost to his waist, the seductive look in his blue eyes, affecting her like a drug…

Carly blinked.

Had someone drugged her drink? Drugged her and kidnapped her? What other explanation was there? She started to call out, then thought better. Instead, she twisted around as much as the ropes allowed. The bed was shoved against one wall. Opposite, she saw a small kitchen area, a wooden table with four straight-backed wooden chairs and an unfamiliar styled glass bottle, half filled with some sort of liquid.

An old-fashioned kerosene lantern on the kitchen table cast a soft glow, but it was obviously still night, maybe very early in the morning. The cabin appeared empty, primitive. She twisted her body a bit further until…there! Just beyond her line of vision. A foot?

The edge of one long, narrow foot, a bony ankle, a leg encased in worn blue jeans. Sprawled to one side, as if the person had passed out cold on the plank floor. Carly slid back to the center of the bed to take the pressure off the ropes. *Damn!*

Panting like a terrified dog, she stared wide-eyed at the opposite wall, struggling to organize her thoughts. Her heart thudded in her chest and shudders wracked her arms and legs.

She clamped her jaws shut and took a long, slow breath through her nose. She let it out, took another, felt her heart rate slow just a bit.

Okay…you're okay. You just need to figure out what's going on. You can do this — even though you haven't got a clue where you are — even though you're tied to a bed without a stitch of clothes, you've got to pee worse than you can ever remember and whoever most likely tied you up is either dead or passed out on the floor. Think, Carly!

She banged her head back against the iron bedstead.

Ouch.

Damn, she couldn't even rub the bump. She could, however, feel the rope on her left hand begin to loosen. She looked closely at the knot — the end of the rope had slipped when she tugged at her restraints. It was barely caught within the knot.

She tried to reach it with her teeth. *Crap!* That wasn't going to work. She bent her fingers forward until she could barely flick the end of the rope with her fingertips. It was stiff and she pushed at the end, shoving it as much as she could toward the loosened knot. Suddenly, the end slipped through the loop and the top of the knot popped free.

It took just a moment of wriggling her wrist to loosen the rope enough to slide her hand out. Flush with victory, Carly quickly untied the rope holding her left wrist, then released both feet.

"This is almost too easy, girl…" she muttered, turning slowly on the bed and sitting on the edge to get a good look at her captor.

"Holy shit." The cabby! It had to be the guy who'd brought her out to the inn. Long and lean, the man sprawled across the floor as if he'd been shot. One arm stretched outward, the other lay near his hip. His long black hair was partially untied, the leather thong holding just the last six inches in a loose knot. His back was lean and muscled, his skin a deep coppery gold shade that appeared to be as much from his ethnicity as exposure to sunshine. He wore an old pair of blue jeans. His feet were bare.

Long, narrow feet. She swallowed, suddenly aware she'd stood up and was staring at his feet like they were some sort of sexual turn on.

Your timing sucks, sweetheart.

Tiptoeing carefully around him, Carly glanced toward the door. It was still dark out, she didn't have a clue where she was, and without a stitch of clothes on she certainly wasn't willing to brave the unknown. She dug into the man's ribs with her toe, regretting the stupid move the minute she did it.

That was, until he didn't respond. Was he dead?

His eyes stayed shut, the thick lashes pressed like black velvet against his skin. There were dark smudges beneath his eyes and his jaw carried the shadow of a day's growth of beard, but it didn't disguise the strong line of his jaw or the sensual fullness of his lips.

Intrigued in spite of herself, she leaned over and touched his throat. A slight pulse confirmed he was alive.

Good. Unconscious. But for how long?

Long enough, she hoped, giving in to nature and searching for a bathroom. There were just two doors in the small cabin. One, larger, sturdier, obviously led outside. She took the smaller door.

The bathroom was bigger than she'd expected, given the overall dimensions of the cabin. It was spotlessly clean but old-fashioned, with a wooden water closet high on the wall over the toilet and a chain to pull for flushing. After relieving herself, Carly rinsed her mouth out with cold water and splashed more on her face.

A man's dark blue flannel shirt hung on a brass hook by the door, but there was no sign of her own clothing. The shirt was clean, but held a trace scent of whoever had worn it last, a pleasant soap and man smell that tickled her nostrils.

At least the shirt was large and fell half way to her knees. Buttoning it to just above her breasts, Carly felt a bit more in control. Quietly, she stepped back into the main room.

The man hadn't moved. She recalled the bottle on the table. Was he drunk? She watched him a moment longer, her anger growing by the second. What the hell was going on? Had he molested her? She didn't feel as if she'd been raped, but she felt violated just the same.

"I don't know who you think you are, buddy..." She glanced at the bed, at the ropes neatly fastened to the frame, then back at the unconscious body lying on the floor.

"Your turn," she muttered. Sometimes it paid off being taller than average and definitely athletic.

Feeling more confident by the minute, Carly grabbed the man under his shoulders and turned him toward the bed. It wasn't easy, but considering the fact he had to be well over six feet tall and close to two hundred pounds, she felt quite proud of herself by the time she had him stretched out on the bed.

She tied his hands first, making certain the knots were much better than the ones he'd used on her. She had to make a conscious effort not to look at his chest.

Damn, he was absolutely beautiful.

She turned to restrain his legs. His jeans were unsnapped, though the zipper was still up. A line of dark hair began at his navel, then disappeared in a neat trail beneath the denim.

He'd left her tied to the bed naked. Turnabout was fair play.

Almost giggling with her own audacity, Carly quietly slipped the zipper down on his pants. His cock was flaccid, hidden beneath clean white cotton briefs, but there was no ignoring the fact the package was complete and more than adequate.

I don't believe I'm doing this... With shaking hands, she tugged his jeans down his long legs, fighting the impulse to touch the springy dark hair covering his thighs and calves. She hesitated a moment before removing his underwear.

What the hell... She grabbed the elastic band around his slim waist with more a sense of guilt than she'd expected. Hadn't he done the same thing to her?

The cotton shorts slid easily over his hips, caught briefly on the bulge where his cock sprouted from his groin, then slipped the rest of the way down his incredibly long, well-muscled legs.

Embarrassed now, Carly couldn't even look at what she'd uncovered. Instead, she quickly bound his feet, tying him securely with the ropes fastened at the end of the bed. He was so tall, his feet reached clear to the footboard. She checked all the knots, then stepped back to finally take a look at her prisoner.

Asleep, he appeared so young. She'd thought him at least mid-thirties or so when she'd seen him yesterday...now she wasn't so sure. His lips were full, cheekbones high and sharply defined.

He certainly didn't look like a rapist. It was difficult for her to think of him in that light, especially considering the wonderful fantasies she'd been weaving about him last night— the one she'd awakened to this morning.

He might be sexy as hell, but he'd kidnapped her, stripped her naked and tied her up. She sucked in a hard breath as her anger returned full force. Sexy or not, he'd damned well better have some answers. Carly watched him a moment longer, aware of her body's response to a nearly perfect male in such a vulnerable situation. She couldn't ignore the thoughts creeping through her mind. She could touch him, tease him, make him understand the humiliation of bondage before she left him here and called the authorities.

Or, she could act like an adult and go for the police as soon as the sun came up.

Suddenly, before she could pursue the options, her captive stirred. His dark lashes slowly lifted, she recognized a moment of confusion, then a broad smile spread across his beautiful face.

He didn't seem the least bit concerned, or even interested in the ropes holding him captive. Instead, he studied her far longer than was comfortable.

"Shit," he whispered, almost as if the curse were a prayer. "You're here. You're really here."

Chapter Three

"Of course I'm here, you bastard!" Her brown eyes flashed with anger, her hands were clenched into tight fists and she looked absolutely glorious. "You kidnapped me, didn't you?"

It was all Tim could do not to laugh out loud. She was here, in the flesh, obviously uninjured by the transfer. Damn, she was every bit as magnificent as he'd imagined. He felt a familiar tightening in his groin, the surge of power and heat that hadn't truly left since he'd first spotted this woman in Mal's vision. *Weird.* He shouldn't be getting hard, not after such a huge outlay of power. He almost laughed. There was no denying the surge of blood to his cock, the tingling awareness in his balls.

"In a manner of speaking," he said, struggling to keep his rapidly awakening libido under control. "I guess you could call it kidnapping…it's not like I gave you a choice."

"You're damned right you didn't give me a choice. Why? What were you planning? Rape? Ransom?" She laughed, the sound brittle, frightened. "If it was ransom, you picked the wrong target, sweetheart. The fare and that tip I gave you after the cab ride took just about all my cash."

"Tip?" What the hell was she talking about? *Cab ride?* "When did you give me money? What cab ride?"

She opened her mouth, then shut it and leaned closer to him. The flannel shirt gaped a bit between her breasts. He wanted to stare into the deep shadow separating the full globes, but Tim forced himself to watch her eyes.

Bittersweet chocolate brown, even darker than the coffee he'd first imagined, framed in dark, gold-tipped lashes. Suddenly, a little knotted wrinkle appeared between her eyes.

"You're not the cab driver?" She frowned. "I thought you were the cab driver. I was sure you...well, hell. You look so much like him." She stared at him. "No. Now I see a difference, but you guys could be brothers. Who are you? Why did you kidnap me?"

"My name is Tim Riley. I'm a soldier of the Rebellion...or I was." This was definitely going to be confusing...how could he possibly explain?

The truth never hurt...

"The Rebellion's ended, but I was ordered to bring you forward after our healer saw you in a precognitive vision. We're not sure what your role is, only that you have one in our society."

She opened her mouth as if to reply, blinked and snapped it shut. "What society?" she finally asked. "What the hell are you talking about?"

"I'm talking about Earth in the twenty-second century. You're from the twenty-first, aren't you? I'm not sure, but the mindlink felt familiar. A lot has happened in the last hundred years..." His voice trailed off as she stared at him in disbelief.

Damn, he wished Malachi or Sheyna were here. They'd do a lot better job of explaining. The woman glared at him as if she thought he should be committed.

"You're nuts," she said, confirming his suspicions. "I'm leaving. I'll let the authorities know how to find you once I get to..." She glanced toward the window, where the morning sky grew lighter by the minute. "Well, once I get someplace where there are people to contact."

"That would be the Armand Institute. It's about a half hour hike down the mountain. The trail is fairly well marked," Tim said. "Ask for Doc...that's Doctor Malachi Franklin. He'll explain everything better than I'm obviously doing."

She shook her head. "You don't seem dangerous. Weird, though. Definitely weird." She glanced about the small cabin. "Where are my clothes? My shoes?"

Tim shrugged his shoulders as best he could, tied so tightly to the bed. "I'm not sure. Wherever they were when I brought you forward, I imagine. For some reason, clothing doesn't appear to make the transfer through time. I'm not sure why. It moves through space easily enough."

"Right. Like I believe that."

She looked ready to take a swing at him. Tim thought about that a minute. At least anger was better than fear. He really didn't want to frighten her. He wanted to keep her talking.

He certainly couldn't let her leave. He glanced at his cock, merrily rising to attention. *Amazing…this has never…shit.* She'd really think he was nuts, lying here, staring at his hard-on. He looked up and smiled at her. "My clothes, however, appear to have had some help. Do you want to tell me why?"

"It seemed only fair." She looked in the direction of his face, but her eyes kept straying to her left, obviously checking out his growing erection.

It turned him on even more to know she watched him. "I guess I can agree with that. I know part of me is thrilled." He nodded at his cock, bobbing now as if it had a life of its own.

She turned in slow motion, as if entirely against her will, to stare full on at his penis. He saw her throat convulse as she swallowed. Her eyes widened. Suddenly, she appeared to realize exactly what she was doing.

With a muttered curse, she turned, stalked across the room and grabbed the door. Of course, the handle wouldn't turn. He'd bolted it before the transfer.

She swung around and held her hand out. Anger radiated off her in palpable waves. "Where's the key?"

He nodded toward the jeans. "Check my right front pants pocket. I think it's there."

She marched back to the pants, wadded in a heap on the floor where she'd left them, dug through the pockets and retrieved the key. She glanced up at him, her brown eyes filled with confusion and surprise. "I didn't think it would be there. I thought you'd lie."

"I have no reason to lie to you." Tim tugged gently at the ropes. "Are you going to untie me before you go?"

"No." She stood up, watching him warily. Her gaze slipped once more to his swollen cock, then she quickly looked away. Tim knew he was large compared to most men. He wondered if that appealed to her, if women from her time were as much into a guy's penis size as women now seemed to be.

"No," she said again, taking a deep breath. "I don't think that's a good idea. It's been..." She paused a moment and stared intently at him. Tim sensed regret, almost as if she wished they'd met under different circumstances.

He certainly did. She'd never forgive him, once she realized everything he'd told he was true. Lying might be kinder.

"It's been interesting," she muttered.

"Will you at least tell me your name?" Tim's voice broke slightly on the question. Damn, he just didn't know how to talk to a woman, much less one he was interested in. Trying to carry on a conversation when you were naked and tied to a bed didn't make it any easier.

A throbbing hard-on made it practically impossible.

"It's Carly," she said, pausing in front of the door. "Carly Harris." She sighed, an audible sound in the small room. "Look, I promise I'll send someone to untie you. You didn't really hurt me, so I won't press charges, okay?" She turned the key in the lock and slid the bolt open.

With a telekinetic flip of the mind, Tim slipped it shut.

Carly stared at the door, turned slowly to stare at Tim, then directed her attention back to the door. Once again she unlocked it and slipped the bolt open.

"I really can't let you leave, Carly. I have my orders." He slammed the bolt home, harder this time, for emphasis.

Eyes wide, Carly turned back around and stared at him as if she'd seen a ghost.

Sighing, Tim knew it was now or never. Using his Talent, he untied the restraints holding his hands and feet. The ropes moved like live things, undulating through the twists and turns of Carly's carefully tied knots, slipping free in a heartbeat. For added effect, Tim carefully rolled the lengths of rope into neat loops and placed them on the bed.

All without touching them with his hands.

"That's sort of how I brought you here," he said, turning around and swinging his legs over the side of the bed. At least his erection was beginning to subside. "I'm a telekinetic. In this century, it's not all that unusual to have various Talents. Some people..."

"What did you just do?" Carly's harsh whisper interrupted him. "There's no such thing as telekinesis. I've read about it. It's fake."

"Do I look fake, Carly?" Tim shrugged his shoulders. "I'm as real as you are."

"I don't understand." She looked like she needed to sit. Fast.

Tim stood up and grabbed her by the elbow. She didn't even struggle when he led her to the closest chair at the kitchen table. "Here. Sit down. I'll get you some water."

He detoured quickly to pick up his jeans and slip them on without bothering with the cotton briefs. Then he filled a glass with cold spring water from the tap. When he handed it to Carly, she stared at the clear water.

"It's okay. The water's pure. No contaminants. It's from a spring up higher on the hill. Drink."

She nodded and took a sip of water, her brown eyes gazing blankly at him over the top of the glass. She looked shell-shocked.

"If you want, I can tell you more about what's going on." He swallowed, searching for words that would make sense, words that would make her accept the fact she could never go home, never return to her own world.

His shoulders slumped. He recalled the day he admitted to Jenna he'd been the one to bring her to this time. Remembered the guilt he'd felt, to think he'd...what was the word Carly used?

Kidnapped... That's what he'd done. He'd kidnapped Jenna. Now he'd kidnapped another. He'd made the decision to alter their lives forever. Did Malachi's vision actually give him the right? Tim hoped so. Now he'd seen Carly Harris, he knew he couldn't live without her. Somehow, he had to make her understand.

Then, he had to make her love him.

Chapter Four

She'd had sexual fantasies all her adult life, but never, not in a million years, had Carly ever conjured up one quite like this. At some point she was going to wake up and wonder what in the hell had been in the glass of cognac she'd had the night before.

Right. Don't blame the cognac, kiddo.

Her pending panic attack began to subside. She clutched the water glass like a lifeline. This was not hypnosis, not a hallucination. She was too alert to be on drugs. She swallowed, took a deep breath, let it out slowly…stared intently at the man sitting just across the table from her.

He didn't look crazy. No, he looked good enough to eat. Carly took a deep swallow of the water, then held the cool glass against her forehead. He believed he had brought her forward from her time to some nebulous period in Earth's future. Maybe he had. Right now, she wasn't going to argue.

It was all just too bizarre. She had to accept the fact he wasn't the sexy cabdriver. No, this guy was even better than the one who had starred in her most recent fantasy. She recognized some of the same ancestry in his face and coloring as she had in the cabby, though now she really had a chance to look him over, he was obviously not the same man. Still, the coincidence was unnerving.

This guy had the same beautifully defined muscles under skin so smooth she itched to run her hands across his body. She almost wished she'd taken the chance to touch him while he was unconscious, though that was definitely not her style. Still…

She choked back a nervous giggle and carefully set the glass of water back on the table, aware of his calm perusal of every move she made. He almost acted afraid of her, like he wasn't sure what she was going to do next.

Well, that makes two of us. It wasn't merely the fact he was gorgeous, either. He appeared as likeable as he was physically appealing. Articulate, intelligent, an obvious sense of humor sparkling in those beautiful blue eyes…

If she had half a brain, she'd be scared to death and looking for an escape, but that little voice in the back of her mind, the one that had been suspiciously silent since she'd awakened this morning, merely urged her to stay and enjoy.

Enjoy. It would be so easy, and she'd been alone for so long. Carly knew he shared at least some of her sensual interest — that had been more than obvious from the start. The image of his erect cock flashed through her mind and she sighed. Even now, Tim's moves were smooth and fluid, his hands floating like an artist's when he talked, the long, slim fingers emphasizing his words with supple twists and turns.

How would those fingers feel, stroking, touching her? The brief but vivid image shot through her, followed by a bolt of need. She clenched the muscles between her legs, suddenly wet and wanting, so aware of him, aware of how he watched her with the same intensity with which she studied him.

His hair hung loose, long and black as sin. The strip of leather he'd used to tie it back was still lying on the bed where it had fallen. Now all that beautiful hair draped over his shoulders and down his back in a thick, straight fall. If he were over her, driving into her, his hair would brush like silk across her breasts…her belly…and if he bent to taste her intimately, she would feel the sweep of it between her legs.

The rate of Carly's breathing pumped up and a knot formed in her gut. What if he read minds as well as he moved objects? Considering the images rolling through her brain right now, she knew he would have reacted if he'd had the merest clue.

She tilted her head to study him more intently. His eyes were an anomaly in a face hinting at Native American background—a sparkling crystalline blue framed in dark lashes. His smile, full-lipped and sensual, was almost sweet. In Carly's mind he betrayed a vulnerability she had a difficult time ascribing to a kidnapper. He seemed unsure of himself, as if he feared upsetting her.

So, why wasn't she more upset? Why was she sitting here lusting after a man who openly admitted kidnapping her? She realized she felt more alive than she had in months. Depression had dogged her for ages, a lingering apathy so deep she'd not even cared when her job ended, hadn't been upset when the money she'd carefully invested over the years had dissipated like smoke in the constantly worsening economic climate.

Even the threat of war hadn't altered her life. She might as well have been on autopilot. If what Tim said were true...

It can't be. Stuff like this only happens on late night television. This is definitely not prime time material. "You're asking me to believe that, because someone you know claims he can see the future and saw me in it, you actually searched for me then found me in my time, snatched me out of it and brought me here, to what is, essentially, my future?"

He looked enormously relieved she'd finally said something. "Exactly," he said, his lips curving into a wide smile. "Only Doc's visions are real. They're scary, sometimes. He saw another woman, Jenna Lang, from your time. I brought her forward. I'd never done it before so I wasn't even sure it would work. That was about a year ago. She was needed here. She's the only other person I've ever found in the past. Besides you, that is."

An icy chill raced along Carly's spine. "Oh my God." *Jenna Lang? The same Jenna Lang who...* "A woman I worked with named Jenna Lang disappeared about six months ago," Carly said. She swallowed past a huge lump in her throat, recalling the attractive woman she'd briefly met on a contract job. They'd had lunch together one day when their paths crossed, but Jenna had disappeared before Carly really got to know her.

The headlines had become more lurid as each day passed, then finally disappeared as a new scandal took its place.

"It was in all the papers...on the nightly news. She was in the process of moving to a new job, her household was packed, the new apartment rented. She never showed up. Police questioned a co-worker who was with her the last evening anybody saw her. He was released for lack of evidence. But that was six months ago, not a year ago."

"She's here." Tim spread his hands, as if for emphasis. "The time period I found her in was a little different from when I found you. She's been here long enough to help us end a rebellion that's been going on for seven years. She actually fell in love with a Miratan lion. They've taken off on a StarQuest. She's pregnant, by the way. Carrying Garan's cub...we're pretty excited about it. She and Garan are really special."

"You can't possibly be making all of this up," she sputtered. Good lord, was she lusting after a madman? "It's too absurd."

So was Jenna's disappearance. Absurd. Completely absurd...and unbelievable.

Tim's shoulders lifted with his sigh. "I know. I asked Malachi how to convince you we weren't crazy or dangerous, but he left it up to me. I figured the truth was my best option. Sheyna agreed. She's Miratan, too. You'll really like her."

The truth...what did he say? Jenna was married to... Carly frowned, thinking back over Tim's brief explanation. "What's a StarQuest?" she asked. "What's a Miratan lion?"

* * * * *

Carly's question hung in the air between them. Tim opened his mouth to explain Earth's link with Mirat, then realized his twenty-first century guest needed a future history lesson for anything to make sense.

Briefly and without a lot of detail, he explained the past century of terrorism and war that destroyed governments around the world and ended so many lives, the alien attack that forced the formation of the World Federation but left a decimated world population suffering from severe xenophobia, or the fear of alien contact.

He told her about the late Daniel Armand and the institute he built for the growing number of humans with paranormal talent. He described Armand's daughter, Mara, and her first contact with the starship captain, Sander, from the planet Mirat.

"Why the increase in paranormal talent?" she asked, interrupting him.

"We're not sure. Dr. Armand thought it was humanity's response to almost total annihilation. The doctor was killed by World Federation troops before he could prove his theory, but in his papers he described it as a forced evolution of the senses to help the human race survive. Whatever the reason, the numbers of Talented are growing."

Tim kinetically lifted Carly's empty water glass, floated it to the kitchen sink and refilled it with cold water. Then he placed it back in front of her without spilling a drop.

She stared, unblinking, then shook her head in mute denial. Tim watched her face for a moment, wondering at the myriad questions that must be swirling through her mind. Finally, with a tiny shrug and a sigh, she waved her hand in a gesture that told him he should continue the story.

He glossed over much of the Rebellion. There'd been nothing good about seven years of armed conflict, unless you counted the fact the World Federation now worked *with* Sensitives and Talents, rather than against them.

Carly nodded quietly, taking in everything Tim said without comment, until he described Miratan lions. At that point, Carly finally gaped at him in disbelief.

"You're telling me there is an alien species that looks like lions? Big African lions that walk and talk like people? Yeah, right. This I've got to see."

"Oh, you will. Malachi's wife, Sheyna, is Miratan, though she's from a smaller race than Garan and Sander. Those guys are huge. Have to admit, though, their human wives don't seem to mind they're married to what are essentially big cats. Malachi doesn't mind a bit, either, that he's married to a lioness."

"When can I meet them?"

"In a few days. Malachi said we should stay here awhile, give you a chance to get used to the idea of being in a new time, essentially a new world. A lot will be familiar. You won't find much has changed technologically, at least so it's obvious. A lot of the stuff we use appears much the same as it did in your era, though its function may be more advanced than you recall."

Carly merely looked confused.

Tim couldn't control his foolish grin. She was absolutely gorgeous. "There's been a tremendous amount of upheaval, worldwide, over the past century. The world population is still fairly small, compared to your time. We've found a cure for AIDS and some of the other more devastating diseases, so we're finally back into an era of growth. I imagine the biggest difference for you will be transportation. Vehicles are solar powered or run on hydrogen fuel cells. Space travel is telekinetic, not fuel powered."

He grabbed his warm energy drink and took a swallow, then set it down. "Still," he said, weighing his words, "it's got to be hard, knowing you can never go back." Tim watched her face carefully when he voiced the one thing he hadn't said before. Of course, if she still didn't believe him…

Her eyes were a clear, bittersweet chocolate brown and they studied him with anything but sadness. He felt her sparkling gaze on him all the way to his balls. "If what you say is true—and that's a big 'if,'" she said, "I can only wonder what I would be going back to. I went to sleep last night in a world on the edge of yet another war, with our economy in the toilet, not to mention my own miserable personal life. There's no one to miss me—no family, no job. Like I said—nothing. You're telling me I'm about to start the most exciting adventure I can imagine, and expect me to feel badly about not going back to *nothing?*"

Tim shook his head. "Malachi said you wouldn't believe me, that you'd think I was making this up."

Carly smiled at him and Tim's breath caught in his throat. Her wistful expression lit up her entire face. "I may sound like a gullible idiot, but I am so hoping you're telling me the truth! I grew up on movies about aliens and space exploration. My childhood was filled with characters in books by Bradbury, McCaffrey, Heinlein and Asimov. Losing myself in a good science fiction or paranormal story was pure bliss for me. Those stories were my life. It may sound dumb, but they gave me hope. I *want* to believe you! If I hadn't seen you move things without touching them...well, I might be a bit more skeptical. It's hard to deny what I see, especially when I want so badly to believe."

I wouldn't deny you anything... The movement of her lips hypnotized him. He realized he was concentrating on a tiny spot on her lower lip, the point where her teeth occasionally caught and held, as if she were deep in thought. Tim blinked himself back to what she was saying.

"That certainly makes things easier," he said, feeling oddly out of step with the conversation. He hadn't expected anything like her response. He knew exactly what his own would be— nothing like Carly's! He shrugged his shoulders and prayed she wouldn't realize the effect she had on him.

It wasn't easy, willing his surprisingly lively cock under control, knowing she sat mere inches away, her nude body barely hidden beneath his old flannel shirt. Once again his jeans felt two sizes too small. Strange, though. Exhilarating but strange. So unusual to feel sexual need after using maximum kinetic power.

Action...he needed to do something, anything, to take his mind off her body...off his *own* body. "Are you hungry?" he asked, grasping at straws. "We might as well fix some breakfast. Sheyna packed a bunch of stuff."

Tim pushed away from the table, quickly turned his back and grabbed the box off the pantry shelf. He set it on the table and leaned over to dig through the contents. "There're eggs and some cured ham in the refrigerator," he said, gesturing toward the small unit tucked under the counter. "I've got bread in here, some cereal and..." He reached for a small package and felt himself blush.

"What's that?" Suddenly Carly was standing close beside him, her scent clean and sweet. She looked over his shoulder. Her breast pressed softly against his arm and he felt hot all over.

"Uhm, for some reason, Sheyna packed, uh, condoms."

Carly's laughter surprised him. "Sheyna packed them, eh? The lioness? You're sure you didn't stick them in the box, just in case you got lucky?"

"No! I'd never...I never...I...no." He shook his head, tucking the package back inside the box. "I would never even think..."

"Why?"

He spun around so that he looked directly into Carly's eyes. "Why? Why what?"

"Why wouldn't you think to bring condoms?" Her eyes twinkled impishly. Tim had to remember to breathe.

He swallowed, opened his mouth, shut it and swallowed again. He felt like a damned fish...*out of water, flopping on the...*

"I thought, earlier, you seemed, *uhmmm*..." She drew the word out, then added, "interested." She tilted a glance at him from beneath lowered lashes, and he knew she was thinking of the hard-on he'd had when he was still tied to the bed. She couldn't possibly tell now...no. She couldn't know.

Suddenly it dawned on him. She was flirting. Carly was flirting with him! It was all he could do not to kiss her.

He took a deep, controlling breath. It had absolutely no effect whatsoever. His heart pounded in his chest and he had to open his mouth a couple of times before he could get the words past the tightness in his throat. "I was *interested* the first time Malachi showed you to me in his vision." How could he possibly explain how she'd affected him? "You...you were—are—the most beautiful woman I've ever seen. I..."

She tilted her head and stared at him, a tiny frown drawing her dark brows together. Her lips parted and Tim's hands seemed to rise without conscious will. He cupped her head in his palms, turned her face gently up to his.

Her hair spilled over the backs of his hands like liquid silk and a hot current of pure desire swept through him.

She was tall and strong and still she seemed to melt against his body, coming to him as if they were meant to touch like this. Shivering with years of pent up desire, aching with the most immediate need he had ever experienced, Tim brushed her lips gently with his, explored the soft fullness before risking all and testing the seam between them with his tongue.

She parted for him, welcoming him into her mouth and it was the most natural thing in the world to explore her there as well. Tim sensed a beginning, not an ending, a journey of the senses far beyond his limited experience. Would she know he was a complete novice? Would she care?

Her tongue tangled with his, a sweet battle that banished everything from his mind but the taste and feel of the woman in his arms. She tasted sweet and lush and full of promise. Her hips pressed against his and he knew she wore only his shirt, knew that he could reach down between her legs and touch her there and she would either tell him to cut it out or...

He followed thought with action, holding her with his mouth and one arm wrapped around her shoulders, brushing his other hand down her throat, slipping inside the soft flannel to fan his fingers out over the slope of her full breast.

Oh, gods...skin like silk. She couldn't be real, not real and so soft, so smooth...

She moaned against his mouth and he deepened the kiss. His fingers flipped the top button free on her shirt, then the second and third until the fabric parted down the front. He slipped his hand lower and traced his fingertips along her side, finally touched her rounded buttock and stroked her soft flesh.

He circled her thigh with his fingers and she eased her hips away from his to give him access, an open invitation to his touch. When he found the springy curls between her legs, he groaned. She sighed against his mouth and parted her legs for him.

Hot. She was so damned hot and already wet. It was the most natural thing in the world to slip his middle finger between the damp folds of flesh, to search out the tiny nub of flesh that must be her clit. He stroked it, gently easing his finger deeper with each gentle touch. It was firmer than he'd expected, erect and waiting for his touch. She thrust her hips forward, silently begging him for more. He matched the rhythm of his finger with thrusts of his tongue into her hot mouth.

She whimpered, sucking hard on his tongue, her hips swaying to the music he created with his touch, a rhythm he controlled. Though he'd brought his one teenaged experience to climax, read about sex, watched films, seen pictures in books and magazines, nothing prepared him for this.

Not for the heat, the vibrant life he felt when his finger moved within her body. He slipped another finger inside, then a third, filling her. She pulsed around him, her vaginal muscles clenching tighter than he'd imagined. He found her clit once more, this time with his thumb, and she moaned against his mouth and shuddered.

His cock felt like it was going to explode but he wasn't ready, not yet, and so long as he concentrated on her needs, on touching her body, he seemed to have more control over his own. This was all so new, this chance to explore, something he'd thought about, wondered about for so many years. He still couldn't believe he was holding this woman in his arms, stroking her intimately, drawing deep moans and gasps with each move he made.

She bucked against him and he increased the rhythm, his long fingers filling her, his thumb circling her firm little clit, sliding over tissues all slick and hot from her juices. Suddenly she clamped her legs hard against his wrist, threw her head back and cried out. He kissed the column of her throat, instinctively gentled his strokes between her legs, then quickly withdrew his hand and caught her in his arms when her knees buckled.

Amazed, laughing, body tense as a guitar string, Tim lifted Carly and carried her to the bed. She was all boneless woman, soft and malleable, shivering and sighing and smiling shyly at him.

He couldn't believe it! He'd just brought a woman to climax, felt her tighten around his fingers, inhaled the sweet rush of her breath as she sighed against him. She was hot and shivering and smiling, clinging to him, all warm and needy...needing him!

He wanted to laugh aloud but he didn't dare. Instead, hands shaking with barely suppressed desire, he slowly removed her shirt, sliding the unbuttoned garment over her shoulders and baring the most perfect breasts he'd ever seen — full and round, with deep rose-colored nipples puckered into tight little beads just begging for his tongue. This time, he knew exactly what to do with them. Tim leaned over to suckle first one, then the other, his long hair sweeping across her breasts, over her lips.

Sweet! She tasted so sweet and the feel of that taut flesh against his tongue was like nothing he'd ever imagined. So much sensation, so many new feelings, new tastes. She arched her back, forcing her nipple higher, telling him without words how much she wanted.

Needed.

His fingers raked her sides, touching each rib, slipping along the silky flesh. She was so smooth! He'd never imagined the feel of a woman, the scent, the very essence, would be so unique.

Caught in the sensation of touch and taste, he felt preternaturally aware of the soft, searching touch of Carly's fingers as she worked the zipper down on his jeans. He sucked his stomach in at the slightest brush of her hand and almost bit into her nipple when the cool strength of her fingers encircled his rigid cock.

Ohgodsohgodsohgodsohgods… He didn't want to come, he…*please, just hang on, don't lose it don't…* He leaned away, terrified of losing control, nostrils flaring, his breath ripping painfully at his lungs. "I guess Sheyna knew what she was doing," he panted, backing away from Carly and standing beside the bed.

Quickly he slipped the denim jeans off and left them lying on the floor. His cock jutted out from his body, big and hard and ready. There was none of the weakness he expected, none of the loss of strength that always followed an intense kinetic experience.

He was powerful, his cock was huge and hard and there was a woman waiting in his bed. He wanted to laugh with the wonder of it all, but he flashed a quick grin at Carly, then raced across the room to dig the condoms out of the box of supplies.

He could have grabbed them kinetically without leaving the bed, but what if it messed with his hard-on? He shouldn't be this horny, not after using so much of his power to bring Carly here, but damn, he was so turned on…his hands were shaking so that he could barely get the wrapper undone. Laughing at his obvious lack of finesse, he walked back to the bed and handed the wrapped condom to Carly. She tore the packet free with her teeth.

"Wow…these are different," she said, taking the standard issue condom out of the package.

"How so?" He couldn't believe he was standing here beside a bed where a gorgeous and lusty blonde awaited him, discussing condoms.

"So thin, and clear, too. Condoms are usually thicker material than this." She glanced up at him, then leaned close and suddenly reached for his cock. When her long fingers wrapped around him he thought he'd explode.

Ohgodsohgodsohgodsohgods... He clenched his fists at his sides, tightened his jaw, flared his nostrils to grab each ragged, painful breath. "Technology," he gasped. "I told you it's..."

"Let's just hope it's big enough." She appeared oblivious to his distress as she sheathed him. "That's definitely a material I've not seen before. It's so light it's barely even there and it goes on so easily." She studied her handiwork, then leaned over and placed a kiss on the very tip.

His cock jerked in response. Tim groaned and prayed his knees wouldn't buckle. He knelt over her, enjoying for the first time in his life the pleasurable ache of sexual excitement, the wonder that in mere seconds, if he didn't screw up, he would be burying himself deep inside her wet heat.

Carly spread her legs and arched her hips, inviting him in. Praying for control, Tim knelt between her legs and slowly pressed his cock against her thickened labia. The wetly lubricated flesh parted easily. She was hot, so much hotter than he'd imagined, and tight. His balls ached, the deep, hollow pain a welcome distraction as he entered slowly, fighting the urge to slam into her with all his strength.

He'd waited so long for this experience, wondered what it would be like. It was so much better, so much more...so... *Oh shit*, he really didn't want to lose it now, but she felt so good, so damned good...and hot. He'd never imagined how hot it would be. So hot the damned condom might melt. Hot and wet and he had to go slow, slower or he'd combust.

He couldn't rush things now, not now when he was finally...*oh shit*. She tilted her hips, bending her knees, lifting forward and drawing him deeper. His balls tightened up, the pain in his gut turned to a coil of heat and he was going to lose it, right there, barely inside and he was going to come and make a damned fool of himself and she'd know.

She'd know this was his first time, and she'd know he was some kind of freak and…he pulled back, slightly, and she sighed. The heat was still there, the power and the need, but he'd caught himself, controlled himself in time.

He drove into her again, deeper this time.

He wasn't sure he'd fit. Without anything to compare, he felt he'd literally entered uncharted territory. Mouth slightly open, dragging in great gulps of air, he drove a bit deeper, pulled out, then finally thrust as far as he could. Her muscles stretched and pulsed around him. He clenched his buttocks, tightened his fists around the pillow on either side of her head. Strands of her thick hair caught in his fingers as she welcomed him on a sigh, taking all of him until their pubic hair meshed in a moist tangle and his balls rested against the cleft between her buttocks.

Tim held there a moment, breathing deeply, his chest working like a bellows as he savored the feeling, the sense that all the years of waiting and wondering were worth the pleasure, the sense of coming home he felt with this woman.

The pressure ebbed just a bit, enough to let him sense some control over his raging cock, so he leaned over, brushed his damned hair away from her breasts and took a nipple into his mouth, suckling it hard and deep. The bud tightened, elongated between his lips and he nipped at her with his teeth.

She moaned, arched her back, shoving her breast closer against his mouth. He tilted his hips and thrust once more against Carly. She met him, her hips rising and falling in cadence with his, her breath growing more ragged, the look in her eyes more glazed.

Tim grabbed her up in his arms. He captured her buttocks in both hands, sat up with her clasped tight against him, and leaned back on his heels. She wrapped her legs around his waist and he lifted her with each driving thrust.

He was coming. The coil of power was building and this time there'd be no holding it back. His hips thrust like a driving piston, the heat and friction taking him where he'd never been. Suddenly, Carly tightened, then shuddered in his arms, threw her head back and screamed. She pulsed around him, hot and tighter still, her muscles clenching, holding him, tipping him over into…

Tim cried out, his hoarse shout as much a cry of triumph as release. His hips pumped against Carly. Her arms squeezed his neck, her legs tightened around his waist, holding their bodies together.

Still he came, the orgasm ripping through him with such force he brought Carly once more to peak. She cried out, whimpered and slumped forward until her head rested against his shoulder. Tim had the sudden sensation he was a balloon with all the air let out. His muscles quivered, his lungs felt incapable of drawing in enough air to sustain him. He eased Carly down onto the bed, barely able to support his own weight, much less hers.

Gasping, still locked together in the lingering ripples of release, Tim turned his head to look into the eyes of the woman next to him. What he saw there shook him to the bone. Carly stared back at him through half-lidded eyes, her lips red and swollen from his kisses, her expression one of shock and sated disbelief.

Suddenly she giggled. He felt the little convulsion of her laughter against his cock. He frowned in response and wondered if he'd done something really stupid. What if…?

Carly reached up and brushed his long hair back over his shoulder and giggled again. Her laughter was infectious…Tim fought the urge but he lost it.

Laughing out loud, he leaned close and kissed her on the end of the nose. "Is that all you have to say?" he asked, still chuckling. Good lord, he'd never felt like this in his life! Boneless...absolutely boneless and wanting like hell to do it all over again. What if she didn't feel the same? *What if she knows this was my first time?*

"Do you always laugh at men after sex, or is it just me?"

"Oh, it's definitely just you." She giggled again and her eyes slipped closed. "All I have to say is *wow*."

"Wow works. In fact it works really well." *For a minute there...* Thank goodness, she hadn't guessed. Tim sighed and hugged Carly close. She didn't have a clue he'd never made love to a woman before, much less given her an orgasm...or three.

She snuggled against his side, her warm breath tickling his ribs. "Amazing," she whispered. "Truly, absolutely amazing."

Amazing? Tim tilted his chin and kissed the top of Carly's head, silently thanking her. She didn't know. Had no idea she'd just taken him on the ride of his life. Feeling a bit cocky, he reached down and held the edge of the condom tight against his withering cock as he regretfully withdrew from Carly's warm sheath. She sighed when he pulled out, her sleepy eyes glowing with what appeared to be tears.

The look on her face shook him to the core. Heading for the bathroom to dispose of the condom, he realized his hands were still shaking. When he looked in the mirror a few moments later, he almost expected the face staring back at him to somehow look different, older.

He hadn't changed a bit, at least not so anyone could see. Inside, though...inside, he was not the same guy. Tim studied his reflection as if he were a stranger—deep blue eyes, the dark sculpted face that spoke of his Cheyenne heritage, the thick black hair he grew long in honor of both his mother and sister, women who, like him, carried the blood of an ancient race.

Still the same old face he'd always seen, but now it fronted a totally different guy.

Amazing. He'd heard Carly's soft whisper just before he left the bed. She thought their lovemaking was amazing. He choked back the urge to cut loose with a wild war whoop of triumph. *Not a freak.* No, Carly didn't think he was a freak.

She was right. It was amazing. For the first time in his life, he felt complete. All the battles he'd fought and won, all the successes and triumphs of the Rebellion hadn't left him this satisfied. Feeling like a whole man.

A man with his woman waiting in the next room.

Chapter Five

Carly watched Tim walk across the room and he looked so damned sexy she felt like crying. His butt was perfect, his back was perfect and his long black hair flowing over his shoulders and falling nearly to his waist had to be the sexiest thing she had ever seen on a man.

Not to mention his legs. Long, muscular legs, dusted with black hair — perfect legs. Perfect ass. Perfect...everything.

A perfect stranger.

Her body still pulsed, her skin tingled all over and she'd never, not in her entire life, had an experience quite like the sex they'd just shared.

Sex. Good lord, the best sex in her life and it was with a complete stranger! A stranger who'd kidnapped her, who might, for all she knew, be certifiable. Maybe *she* was, God help her, because she actually believed the crap he'd told her, the stories about a future Earth, wars and aliens, big lions who talked and read minds and flew in space ships.

She was definitely losing it. *But what a way to go,* the little voice in her head whispered. *What a way to go.*

Carly flopped over on her back and stared at the ceiling. Time to think about this. Time to get her priorities straight. She glanced toward the bathroom, but the door was still closed. Was he laughing at her? Forty-five years old, the fresh bloom of youth a thing long past. Was he in there laughing about his charity fuck?

He was so young. Thirty maybe? Thirty-five at the most, but holy shit, he knew how to make love to a woman! She giggled. Couldn't help herself. She knew damn well he'd enjoyed himself as much as she had. The bathroom door opened and Carly bit her lip to control her laughter. Her body had barely recovered from his loving and she already wanted him again.

He stood in the doorway, his cock at half-mast and an adorable grin on his face. He'd pushed all that lovely long hair back over his shoulders, but his blue eyes twinkled and the muscles in his chest rippled. Carly wanted him so much she felt the muscles in her vagina begin to clench in anticipation.

"If we're gonna do this again," he said, laughing, "I need something to eat. Getting you here took a lot out of me. Taking you took even more."

"Taking me?" She bit her lip, grinning at the telling comment. He was younger than she'd guessed.

"Yeah," he said, walking over to the bed and leaning over her, his long, strong arms outstretched and supporting his weight on either side of her. His hair brushed her shoulders, draped over her face, tickled her breasts.

She ducked under his arms, leaned over and quickly grabbed his cock and placed it between her lips.

"Oh shit..." His hips thrust forward and she knew it was a totally involuntary move. So empowering, to know she had this control over him...this power over a man big and strong and so gorgeous he stole her breath away.

His cock was only partially erect when she took him in her mouth and she suckled him deep and hard. Half lying on the bed, she grabbed his firm buttocks and held on tight, controlling his thrusts into her mouth. She kept her lips and tongue in motion while her fingers traced the contours of his ass, touched his balls and tickled the tightly puckered ring of his anus.

He groaned and leaned forward and she went with him, lying on her back with Tim over her, his cock still slipping in and out between her lips, his mouth tantalizingly close to her crotch. He leaned forward to brace his weight on his elbows and his mouth was so close to her pussy she felt her vaginal muscles clench in expectation.

Would he use his mouth on her? Would he find her flavors as exciting as she was discovering his to be? She hadn't expected him to taste so good. There was something almost addictive about him, about the essence of this young man who appeared to honestly find her attractive.

It's been too long, she thought, losing herself in his taste. *Too damned long.*

Oh, gods. He hadn't expected that! Her mouth caught him by complete surprise, the hot, wet suction bringing him erect in a heartbeat. His legs quivered. In the back of his mind he knew he needed food, recognized the chemical imbalance from too much kinetic and sexual exertion and too little fuel, but he'd rather keel over in a dead faint than ask her to stop.

Her tongue curled and licked the full length of his cock and her fingers moved a mile a minute, caressing his balls, sliding up the crease in his ass and teasing him *there.*

Ohshitohshitohshit... She was going to eat him alive and he wasn't doing a thing for her. That didn't seem right, somehow, though for the life of him...

Tim knew his legs were going to give out, knew he couldn't stand here any longer while she did things to his body he'd never even imagined. As if she understood his dilemma, Carly moved over on the bed and he straddled her, his cock hanging down over her mouth, his face delightfully close to her crotch.

Her scent drew him. Like a siren's call, her earthy, womanly scent called him. He knelt over her and rested his weight on his knees and elbows just as she once again swallowed his cock.

He tried to hold back the moan of pleasure, but his chest vibrated with the sound. Her pussy was right there, all springy golden hair and glistening pink lips. It seemed only right to taste her, to run his tongue around that taut little nub at the apex of her thighs, to lap at the fleshy lips pouting just for him.

He wasn't quite certain what to do, but some instinct drove him, some inbred knowledge that she would like it if he suckled her *there*, licked her *here*, put his tongue inside her just *now*.

Damn, it wasn't enough! He buried his face between her legs, lapping at the moisture flooding his lips and tongue. His hair swept over her legs and he pushed it out of his way. He suckled her clit, felt it pulse between his lips, noticed that each time he circled it with his tongue she would jerk her hips, press closer against him.

Her hands and mouth were all over him, suckling his cock, his balls, stroking his buttocks, her fingers pressing against his ass. Hell, he'd never had a clue how sensitive that little hole could be!

Was she...? Did women...? His fingers gripped her buttocks, kneading the fleshy mounds, holding her close against his mouth. With the middle finger of his right hand, he found the tight little puckered opening, pressed lightly against it and felt her moan of pleasure vibrate against his cock.

His left hand was just as busy, his long fingers stroking slowly at the opening to her pussy, spreading the slick moisture along the crease between her cheeks.

Moistening his finger with her juices, he inserted it slowly into her ass, barely breaching the opening the first time, then going deeper with each small circular thrust. His tongue lapped at her clit, then he suckled it hard and fast between his lips just as he buried his finger in her anus.

He didn't expect her to do the same damned thing to him at exactly the same time.

Her mouth clamped down on his cock, her finger breached his ass and all hell broke loose. Tim's orgasm rocked his world. Her fingers clasped the base of his cock, her mouth sucked even harder, as if she wanted to drain him dry.

Fluid gushed into his mouth, hot and salty sweet, and so good. He kept up the pressure on her clit with his tongue, moved one finger inside her ass and pumped his fingers in and out of her pussy. He almost laughed, picturing the two of them all twisted together on the bed, a veritable fucking machine gone mad!

He didn't want to collapse on her. He did the next best thing and fell to one side, his face resting on her quivering thigh. Long moments later he raised his head to look at Carly. She lay there, legs spread wide, one knee slightly bent, a sleepy, satisfied smile on her lips. There was a white smear across her cheek and a look of utter, wanton contentment on her face.

He'd never seen anything more beautiful, nor wanted anyone or anything as badly. It took all the energy he had left to turn himself around and lie next to her. "Okay," he said, brushing the sticky semen off her cheek with the pad of his thumb. "We've had breakfast. Now what's for lunch?"

She raised one eyelid and smiled at him. "Real food, I hope. I'm starving. Damn...Tim, if you're serious about this being a whole new century, all I have to ask is, are all the men like you?"

The question hung there between them. She had no idea what she'd asked, no idea, Tim realized, what a compliment she'd paid him. He leaned over and kissed her very gently on the lips, tasting Carly, tasting himself.

"Not so sure about the men, but if the women of your time are anything like you, I can see why Garan is so totally besotted with Jenna." He kissed her once more, then forced himself to sit up. "C'mon," he said. "You can have the shower first and I'll start something for breakfast. Towels, soap and shampoo are on the shelf in the bathroom."

* * * * *

By the time Carly got out of the shower, the mingled scents of bacon and coffee filled the small cabin. A one-piece jumpsuit of some sort was lying on the bathroom counter. She looked but couldn't find underpants. There wasn't a bra, either, but the suit fit her so well she didn't need one.

The stretchy fabric was a creamy yellow that reminded her of the tights she'd worn for workouts. There was a strange little emblem over the left breast, but other than a pocket stitched across the waist in the back, the garment was seamless and fit like a second skin.

She looked at herself in the mirror, struck a pose and giggled. The outfit reminded her of the costumes worn by busty actresses in old B-movie space operas. Carly had to admit, though, it did wonders for her figure.

She brushed her wet hair back behind her ears but didn't linger long in front of the mirror. Hopefully the satisfied glow of sexual contentment would help disguise forty-five years' worth of living, but she was not going to agonize about what couldn't be changed. She smoothed the sleek fabric of her suit down over her hips and stepped out of the bathroom.

Tim stood in front of the stove, stirring eggs in a big iron skillet. He had his jeans on and he'd reclaimed his shirt, but it hung open and untucked. His long hair rippled, shining and black, once more secured in a neat ponytail with the leather thong.

She thought how wonderful it would be to wake up to something like Tim every morning.

He glanced up and smiled when he saw her. "Wow, that looks great. Sheyna guessed you were about her size. Not everyone looks that good in a skinsuit. They're not very forgiving." He continued staring at her with obvious appreciation.

Carly felt practically naked in the outfit, especially the way Tim was looking at her. She decided she liked the feeling and had to fight the urge to strike a pose just for him. Instead, she brushed her hands along her thighs, absorbing what Tim had just said. This outfit—he'd called it a *skinsuit*—was Sheyna's. That meant Carly was wearing clothing from another planet. If Tim's story was true, her outfit was from Mirat.

She wanted so much to believe.

Tim blinked, as if he suddenly realized he was staring and nodded toward the table. "Toast is ready if you want to put some jam on it. You can slice up the bananas and there's an extra cup by the coffee pot—hope it's okay. I make it pretty strong."

It all felt so…normal. Carly poured herself a cup of coffee then tackled the toast. Tim finished cooking the eggs and carried two plates full of bacon and scrambled eggs to the table.

Carly couldn't remember enjoying a meal more. Tim was funny, his humor often self-deprecating and sweet and he made a killer cup of coffee. He used his kinetic abilities so naturally, Carly realized, that she completely accepted the salt shaker floating across the table, her coffee cup going for a refill and the dropped fork being washed in the sink and returned to her hand, without either of them leaving their seats.

"Tell me about Talent," she said. "How do you know you've got any?"

Tim tilted his head and studied her a moment, as if searching for an answer. "That's hard to answer, actually. Jenna didn't have a clue until Garan forced her to see it. I was so embarrassed by mine, I hid my abilities for over a year. Then I found out my sister was telekinetic, too, so we told Mom. Both of us learned by accident…thinking something and having it happen when we didn't expect it to."

He paused and smiled, as if remembering something special. "My sister Mary knew a girl in school who picked on her all the time. Our father was a drunk and we were kind of poor, so that made us easy targets. Anyway, this girl was teasing my sister, and Mary wished she'd fall into a big puddle. Next thing she knew, the girl was face down in a huge puddle of mud, right in front of her boyfriend and all her snotty friends."

Carly laughed. "Ah, the sense of power…"

"Yeah. I had a similar situation. A couple of guys chased after me. I used to be little and scrawny…might as well have had a big bull's-eye on my butt. They caught me alone after school one day and ran me down. I'll never know what they planned to do, because they both ended up in the river. Kids left me alone after that." He stared blindly past Carly, obviously lost in his memories.

"Where's Mary now?" Tim's face had brightened with the mention of his sister.

Now Carly saw the darkness in his eyes. "Dead. She and my mom died when our car wrecked about eight years ago. It happened so fast we didn't have time to use our Talent to avoid it. One minute they were alive, the next they were gone." He reached out and grabbed both of Carly's hands. "You would have liked Mary. In a way, you remind me of her. You're tough like she was."

He squeezed her fingers before letting them go. "Of course," he added, leering, "I never thought of doing things with Mary like I do with you."

"I should hope not!" Carly laughed as she stood up to clear the table. "You cooked, I'll do dishes while you get your shower."

Tim leaned over and kissed her, then cleared the table kinetically. The dishes and silverware crossed the room to end up stacked neatly in the sink. He shrugged his shoulders. "For some reason, it seems even easier to move things this morning. Usually it takes a little more effort, especially after I've maxed out on my kinetics like I did with your transferal." He stared at her a moment, smiled enigmatically, then headed for the bathroom.

Carly started the dishes, but as he walked away, she sensed the question behind his statement. What did his kinetic ability have to do with her?

Tim felt the excitement building all through his shower. *She can't be, she must be, she has to be, that's got to be the reason...* Carly. His own sweet Carly. A Synergist...a power catalyst, a mind without Talent of its own, other than the ability to passively increase the Talent of others...

He rushed through his shower, growing more convinced with each unavoidable conclusion. He should have known…even during sex. Especially during sex. He shouldn't have been able to get it up, not after using so much kinetic power to bring her to this time. Hell, he'd had so much power, he'd had to control himself. Well, he'd not only gotten it up, big time, he'd needed control not to come and he'd found it. Not on his own…no, he'd tapped into Carly's mind without realizing it, tapped into her power and given it back to himself.

He didn't even wait to dress, merely wrapped the towel around his hips, shoved his dripping hair over his shoulders and barged out into the main room.

"I know!" he shouted. She jumped and turned around, eyes wide, lips parted. "I know why you're here." Tim grabbed her face in his palms and planted a kiss on her lips. "We need to try something, something to prove what I'm thinking. We…"

"What?" She laughed. Her eyes sparkled and she stood there, hands planted firmly on her hips…oh damn, she had the most gorgeous hips, flaring out from that tiny little waist and when he looked at her he was certain he'd known her all his life.

"Good lord, Carly, you're gorgeous." The whispered words slipped out before he had a chance to think. He stood there, feeling as awkward and vulnerable as a child. She was Woman with a capital *W* and he was so unworthy of her, but he knew if she ever left him he'd have no reason to live.

How could this be? Feeling more than a little foolish, he glanced at his wristwatch and realized he'd had her in his time for less then eight hours. She'd think he was nuts. Hell, she already thought he was nuts. He laughed out loud and grabbed her shoulders. "I hardly know you…you don't know me. Carly, I love you. I think I've loved you for all my life."

He leaned over and kissed the surprise right off her face, kissed her until she clung to him, breathless and wanting, her heart beating against his chest, her mind open and free. At that moment, that magical moment when her untested shields were down, he found her mind, found the amazing part of her Talent that let him build and increase his own power exponentially.

Power enveloped him, filled him...limitless power like nothing he'd ever experienced before. Power that was all Carly...all hers to give.

Tim let the rush ebb, controlled the flow that might have knocked another man to his knees. He kissed Carly, brushed her hair back from her face, kissed her eyes, her nose, her forehead. Stunned, he leaned his own head against hers, forehead to forehead, and gave her the words in her mind. *I love you. I truly love you. You complete me. You make me whole.*

She looked up at him with wonder in her eyes. "I hear you," she whispered. "I hear you in my head."

"Only because you've given me the power to 'path the message, my love." Once more he held her face in his hands and kissed her. It was time to explain. Time to tell her just how special she was to his world.

How special she was to him.

Chapter Six

"We'd suspected the concept of synergy for a long time, but not until Jenna showed up did we actually see it in action. Even then we didn't realize what we had. We'd learned to work in gestalt during the rebellion, to blend our powers in order to increase them, but Jenna was a natural. She could take whatever we were doing and increase the power tenfold. Your ability seems to go beyond even that."

Carly stared at him in wonder. He was telling her she had some kind of weird psychic power? Unbelievable. "What good is it, though," she asked. "I mean, I can't do anything on my own."

Tim leered at her and she laughed. "Well, I can do that, I guess."

"You can do so much. I need to let Malachi know so he can be ready for you when we come home." Tim grabbed her hands. "You'll come home with me, won't you? I want you to stay with me. I've got a cottage of my own, and even though I know the rest of the Institute members are going to want you with them I…"

"Wait a minute!" Carly's laughter spilled out over his rush of words. She looked at him, at the face she'd fantasized over, the lips that had kissed her, given her such unbelievable pleasure, and realized she didn't know what to say.

How do you tell a man he makes you whole? How do you explain, without sounding pathetic, that he's the best thing that's ever happened to you and you'd be a fool to leave him? How do you…?

You just tell him, idiot. She cupped one side of his face in the palm of her hand. He nuzzled against her fingers like a puppy and she sighed with the wonder of him. "You're right, Tim. I hardly know you, but I think I've loved you all my life. You have touched something in me that cries out to be loved. You make me whole. You complete me."

The same words he said to me.

Her statement hung in the air between them. *Like a benediction…or a marriage ceremony.*

Tim leaned over and kissed her once, hard on the mouth. "I'm contacting Malachi. With your help, I think I can reach him."

He pulled two of the narrow, straight-backed kitchen chairs together and sat Carly in one, himself in the other. He leaned over and held her head in both his hands, touched her forehead with his.

She watched Tim as his eyes appeared to drift shut, then suddenly she felt a pressure in her skull, a sense of fullness she'd not noticed before.

After a few moments, he raised his head. His lips were curved in a most delicious smile. "I was right," he said. "I've just linked to both Malachi and Sheyna. Mal wants us to head down the mountain right now…Sheyna says to come in the morning, after we've rested. I'm listening to Sheyna on this one. Malachi said he could read me as if he and I were touching. I'm a crappy telepath, Carly. I can't send or read worth beans, but he heard me as if I were right there with him." Tim leaned over and kissed her. "You, my love, are amazing."

"I still don't understand what I'm doing." She kissed him back. "I felt a little pressure in my head and then…"

"That's when I was using your mind as a catalyst for my message to Sheyna and Malachi. It's hard to explain, but you're like a rocket booster for whatever power a Sensitive or Talent runs through you." He tugged lightly on her hand and drew her on to his lap.

She went willingly, snuggling up against his chest, bare and still damp from the shower. She felt his erection growing against her bottom and snuggled closer to his lap. Tim's lips brushed the top of her head, and then he rested his chin where he had kissed her.

"You're going to have to learn some shielding techniques."

"Shielding? What's that?" She licked a drop of water off his chest, just below his collarbone, then went in search of another.

"What?" He chuckled. "Sorry...lost my thought, there. Shielding is when you throw up mental blocks to keep intruders out of your head. I've used your power without your permission because you're not blocked. You need to learn to protect yourself from unwanted visitors."

Her tongue found another drop. She lapped it up, smiled at him, then continued her search. Tim sucked in his breath when she trailed the tip of her tongue from his breastbone to the base of his throat, then across his hard pectoral muscle.

"What if I learned to shield myself, and then blocked you?" She managed to nibble her way closer to his nipple, then ran the tip of her tongue over the tiny little protrusion.

He gasped aloud. "I would be terribly disappointed if you were to block me." His breathing grew more ragged with each swipe of her tongue.

Carly sucked his nipple between her lips and felt him go tense all over. "What would happen if I did?" She licked his hot flesh, then nipped at his chest.

He groaned aloud, and his voice sounded rough and strained. "When I use my kinetic abilities, it usually saps my strength. All my strength. I can show you right now. I'm going to consciously sever the link I've forged between us."

Carly tilted her chin to look up at him. She licked her lips as a warning of what she still had up her sleeve.

"Okay," he said. "I've created a shield on my side, to keep our minds apart." Tim grinned almost sheepishly at her.

Carly realized his erection had totally disappeared. He was soft and flaccid beneath her. She glanced up sharply and he shrugged his shoulders.

"Sex would normally be the last thing on my mind," he said, "but if you'll recall, I was hard as a rock when I was barely conscious and still tied to the bed. You did that, Carly. Not merely your beautiful, sexy body, but your power, as well. I was drawing on you without realizing it. To put it bluntly, there's no way on earth I could have sustained an erection without your power. When we made love, you were giving me strength. When I was afraid of coming and needed control, you gave me that, too. You do complete me, love. You empower me in a way I've never experienced before."

As you empower me, she wanted to add. She didn't, though. She thought about it, but there was something in his voice, a sense of male pride that caught and held her. Was that why he found her attractive? Because of the power she gave him? Guys were like that...into power and physical strength. Hell, she was so much older than he appeared to be. What could he possibly find attractive in her?

He leaned over and kissed her, and her doubts fled like thistledown in the wind. His lips were warm and searching, his tongue almost timidly testing the seam of her lips, then the soft interior of her mouth. She sighed against him, sliding her buttocks close against his cock.

She was aware of a growing pressure in her head, a subtle awareness of Tim's presence as he once again entered her thoughts. Suddenly he was erect and hard against her crotch, his cock fighting the restraints of the towel. His hands worked the seam of her skinsuit and she felt his need, his desire, filling her mind.

Desperation drove her, a sense of urgency overwhelming in its intensity. Hers? Tim's? She didn't know, right now didn't care. His hands stroked her sides, his lips found hers, then traveled farther, along her neck, her jaw, then finally worked their way to her breasts.

He peeled the skinsuit down her arms, lifted her off his lap and stripped it from her body until she stood before him, naked in the shaft of mid-morning light streaming through the cabin windows. She tugged the edge of the towel and he lifted his weight off it just enough that she could pull it free and drop it unceremoniously on the floor.

Tim's cock stood proudly erect. Carly's first instinct was to fall to her knees and take him in her mouth, but suddenly a small packet appeared to fly across the room and flash between them. Tim snatched it out of the air, laughing, and ripped the envelope with his teeth. "I don't think I could walk right now if I tried," he said, removing the condom from the paper wrapper and sheathing himself.

He grabbed Carly by the hips and lifted her easily, settling her over his erection as if she weighed nothing at all. She suddenly realized he was lifting her kinetically so that she practically floated over him. He was hot and hard but she was ready for him, taking him easily inside. She wrapped her legs around his hips, linking her heels to the legs of the chair. Holding herself completely still, she savored the fullness, the sense of completion she found in his arms.

Tim didn't move either, other than to sigh and sweep his hands along her spine in a gentle massage. He rested his chin on top of her head, then rubbed his cheek against her hair. "I just want to hold you like this, feel myself inside you." His whisper ruffled her hair and she felt his words vibrating in his chest.

She clenched her vaginal muscles in response.

His cock jumped, so she did it again, holding the contraction longer this time. Tim's arms around her shoulders tightened, but he kept his hips completely still. She pressed down on his erection, settling her buttocks as close against his muscled thighs as she could.

He swelled inside her and she continued to tighten and release her inner muscles, holding her body still, yet finding a completely internal rhythm. She glanced shyly at Tim, curious as to how he was dealing with such subtle love play, and the dreamy, sensual expression on his face was almost her undoing.

Slowly he leaned forward to kiss her mouth, but the touch of his lips on hers was light and much too brief. He trailed teasing kisses along her throat, bending her back so that he could nip lightly at her breast. He kissed all around her erect nipple, then finally drew it into his mouth, suckling greedily at her flesh, his tongue flicking the hard tip, his lips compressing the full areola.

Carly's pussy found its own rhythm now, clenching and releasing with an increasing pace. She slowly tilted her hips forward to bring her clit into direct contact with the base of his cock and bowed her back, thrusting her breast against Tim's lips.

He abandoned her right breast and moved to the left. Her heart was pounding so hard she knew he must feel it beneath his lips as he drew the nipple deeply into his mouth. There was no gentleness in him now—he suckled hard, his tongue pressing her sensitive nipple against the hard ridges at the roof of his mouth, suckling in perfect time with her rhythm.

Suddenly, his teeth replaced his tongue and he bit down, sucking and biting at the same time as her clit pressed hard against the base of his cock. She cried out, a harsh shout of release. Spasms of pleasure rippled through her pussy and she tightened around his cock. He clutched at Carly's hips, binding her to him.

She felt the pulse and throb of his release, heard his rasping groan against her breast, then collapsed into his embrace. His chest rumbled under her cheek and she realized he was laughing.

She giggled in return, shocked by what they had done—reached a mutual climax without moving their hips, without the thrusting, surging, slapping sexual moves she associated with lovemaking. "My goodness. That was different." She glanced up at the suddenly serious look on Tim's face.

"It's all different." He brushed her hair back from her eyes. "Every time is new." He sucked his lips between his teeth, then made a self-conscious little smacking noise as he blew out a rush of breath. His smile was full of wonder and he stared deep into her eyes for a long moment.

"What?" Carly tilted her head and frowned at his odd expression.

He took a deep breath, sighed and rested his forearms on her shoulders. "It's embarrassing. I didn't want you to know because it seemed so...well, hard to explain at the time but..." He swept his long hair back over his shoulder in an unconscious move. "Carly, you're my first. I've never made love to a woman before you." He laughed, a short, humorless bark that ended in a sad smile. "If I'd known how wonderful it could be, believe me, I doubt I would have waited this long."

"I don't believe you." *His first?* She'd just had mind-blowing sex with a virgin? "I mean...Tim. You. We. Sheesh." At a total loss for words, she stared at him. "Wow. It's absolutely mind-boggling to think what sex will be like once you figure out what you're doing!"

He wrapped his arms around her and held on as if he was afraid she'd try to escape. Laughter bubbled up out of Carly and she hugged him back, raising her legs to wrap them around his waist and her arms round his neck. "How did you manage to go this long without sex? My God, Tim...you're...well, hell. You're so damned sexy. You're handsome and sensual and you make love like you've been doing it forever. How come you haven't been snagged by some predatory female by now?"

"Kinetics." He reached between their legs, managing to fondle her sensitive clit on the way to grabbing the edges of the condom so he could hold it in place. Then he lifted Carly with the power of his mind and set her gently on her feet beside the kitchen chair. She was vaguely aware of the subtle link of his mind with hers during the move, now that she knew what to sense for.

"When I use my kinetic abilities, I lose any interest in sex. My sexual drive is all tied up in my kinetic power and we've had seven years of war, seven years of straining my ability to the max. Before that, I was in hiding with my mom and sister. There was never an opportunity."

He stood up. "Don't move," he said, heading for the bathroom to dispose of the condom. He returned with a warm, wet washcloth for Carly. "Nor was there a handy little Synergist to boost my power and tantalize me with her body." He sat back down in the chair and proceeded to gently cleanse Carly between her legs. The warm cloth was soothing—his touch anything but. She sighed, amazed that, after so many orgasms in one morning she still wanted more of Tim and his lovemaking.

He finished bathing her all too soon, leaned over and kissed her belly then stood up. "It's not something I've accepted gracefully, believe me. I've been resentful a lot of the time. When Malachi asked me to come up here, knowing he was asking me to max out my kinetics to bring you forward, I was angry. I knew you were beautiful, knew I wanted you, but I also knew, from experience, I wouldn't be able to do a thing about it. Luckily I was wrong." He flashed her another killer smile, then carried the damp cloth back to the bathroom.

Carly turned around and plopped her naked butt down on the hard wooden seat of the kitchen chair. *Unbelievable.* The most amazing, mind-blowing sex in her entire life, and the guy was a virgin.

She giggled and clapped her hand over her mouth.

Emphasis on was. Good God!

She hadn't been kidding. There was no telling what he'd be like once he got a little more practice. She sat there, staring at the bathroom door, waiting for him to come back to her. She knew just the woman to help him with his education.

Chapter Seven

He'd never spent a night sleeping with a woman, but Tim decided it was something he could get used to really fast. A couple of times he'd awakened to the soft tickle of Carly's hair around his face or the unfamiliar sensation of a warm and wonderful body snuggled tightly against his chest, one leg thrown over his thigh.

He liked the sound of her breathing, the sense that, for the first time in his life, he could turn to another person in the night and not feel alone. More than once, they made love. Slow, sweet love in the silent darkness, the only sounds her sighs and quiet moans of pleasure, his own harsh intake of breath when she'd come apart in his arms.

She'd whispered things in his ear, things she'd like to do with him, to him. Just thinking of all she had planned made him hard. Thank the gods he'd told her the truth, that he was a virgin. Otherwise, she might not have been so concerned with his education.

That was something he hadn't thought about with their age difference. *Experience.* Carly knew what she liked and obviously didn't have a problem asking for it. Of course he still didn't know how old she was, but she had to be at least thirty. Hell, she could be fifty for all he cared, so long as she loved him. He lay there for awhile, thinking of all the possibilities. Then he fell back asleep, his arms wrapped around the warm and willing body of the woman he loved.

* * * * *

A faint shimmer of light preceded sunrise. Tim stretched his arms overhead just as Carly rolled into his embrace and nuzzled her lips against his chest. Barely awake, he almost laughed aloud at his suddenly erect cock, at the wonderful novelty of a woman in his bed...a woman he'd made love to throughout most of the night. Mentally fumbling for the box of condoms he'd left on the nightstand, he opened the packet and sheathed himself kinetically.

Carly sat back and watched as the transparent film rolled itself over his erection. "You're getting pretty good at that, aren't you? I was going to offer to do it myself, but..."

"Hmm?" Watching her though half-lidded eyes, Tim thought he'd never seen anything more beautiful than Carly Harris in his bed. Her blonde hair fell in a love-tangled mass around her shoulders. Her lips were swollen from a night of kisses, her breasts beckoned to him, begging for his mouth. Heat coiled, sharp and insistent from his gut to his cock as her slim fingers smoothed the condom over him. She gently traced the length of his penis, her touch moving lower to fondle his balls.

She turned and slipped along his body, nipping him with lips and teeth, sweeping her tongue in a swirl around his navel before finally settling her mouth on his cock. With a deep groan, Tim buried his face between her legs, inhaling her scent, tasting her sweet flavors. He drew her clit between his lips, suckling on it as if he'd find sustenance there. She moaned. The sound vibrated against his cock.

"I love you, Carly...love you more than you can imagine." He lapped at her swollen lips until he felt the first tiny quivers of climax, then gently turned her around and positioned her so he could enter from behind. She hugged her arms around the pillow and took him deep inside. He buried himself in her heat, held still for a moment, then slowly withdrew. He reached around her waist and found her sensitive clit with his fingers, stroking in counterpoint to each measured thrust of his hips.

He felt her stiffen, knew her climax was once again upon her, and pulled out. "Not yet," he whispered. "Not yet." She brushed her buttocks against his belly, silently begging. Kneeling behind her, he grabbed her breasts, stroking each nipple to a taut point. His rigid cock settled between the two globes of her butt, slipping and sliding up and down, just enough to tease.

He trapped her legs between his thighs, gliding back and forth against her ass until she whimpered into the pillow. His fingers tugged at her nipples with an occasional foray between her legs, but he stopped each time he felt her body stiffen.

Opening his mind to Carly's, he sensed her laughter, her frustration, her need to come and the fact she was loving every minute of his torment. He nipped at her shoulder and she bucked against him until he grabbed her hips in both hands and entered her hot, wet center.

She raised her hips, inviting him deeper, her body quivering with the need to find release. She raised her hand to touch herself, but he trapped it in his own. "Not yet," he said, maintaining a slow, even pace that was obviously driving her wild. "Not yet."

"Damn you!" Laughing, Carly jerked her hips in a frantic attempt to control the pace, to bring herself to climax. Tim trapped her wrists against the mattress, slipping in and out of her slowly, drawing on Carly's power as he tested his limits and pushed hers. Once more he brought her to peak, held her there, teasing, tantalizing, practically gloating over her growing frustration.

Suddenly she slipped her hand free of his, reached between her legs and cupped him with her fingers, gently squeezing his balls as she thrust her hips tightly against him, her muscles clamping down on his sensitive cock like a molten vise. He opened his mouth in a soundless cry, tried holding himself immobile and failed miserably.

Hips thrusting, cock so sensitive he felt each ripple and pulse within Carly's hot passage, Tim gave up control. Everything he was, all he felt, centered in his cock, his balls, the need to drive deeper, thrust harder. Lungs bursting, he groaned when she tightened around him, cried out with each clenching, pulsing ripple of her climax as she dragged him over the edge with her. Her body stiffened beneath his and she collapsed against the mattress. Almost sobbing, Tim lowered himself on shaking arms to lie atop her back.

After a minute, he felt her body shaking. "Carly? Are you okay? Are you crying? "

"No." He heard her snort, a distinctly unsexy sound. She was laughing, her face buried in the pillow to muffle the sound. He decided she sounded vaguely triumphant.

"You're trying to kill me, aren't you? I was sound asleep and you woke me up just to kill me." He rolled over on his back, bringing Carly with him. She sprawled, face up, giggling.

"Not kill you, precisely…maybe just remind you not to tease? You need a lesson on how not to piss off a woman in bed."

He growled and nipped her shoulder. What else could he do? She owned him, body and soul. Owned his heart, owned his mind…hell, she even owned his damn cock. "I imagine I'll need lots of lessons." Tim smiled into the tangled mass of her hair spread over his throat and chest, thinking of all the lessons he was going to need.

* * * * *

While Carly showered, Tim stripped the bed, packed up the leftover food and cleaned up the dishes, hardly aware of the chores. *Love.* They'd both realized from the beginning they had something special.

He'd known it from the first time he'd seen her, in Malachi's vision.

Did Malachi know? Was that why he'd insisted Tim come alone to the cabin?

Tim held the last dish he was drying and listened to the sound of water beating against the shower stall. Picturing Carly naked, her sleek body glistening with soap and her dark blonde hair streaming over her shoulders, his body quickened once again. Sighing, he quickly brought himself under control.

Gods, would he ever get enough of her?

The pipes rattled when she shut off the water. He fought an almost overwhelming impulse to go to her. Shaking his head over his powerful weakness for one very lovely woman, Tim put the dish in the cupboard and wiped down the counter.

A few minutes later, Carly padded barefoot out of the bathroom. She was wrapped in a soft cotton towel that covered her from breast to thigh. She'd towel-dried her hair and combed it straight back from her face. Once more Tim was taken with her beauty, the classic line of her jaw, the twinkle in her dark brown eyes.

She stopped just in front of him, unwrapped the towel, pressed her shower-damp body close against his and rubbed like a cat in heat. "We need to get going," she said. "Didn't you tell your friends we'd be there before noon?"

He enfolded her in his arms and held her tightly enough to still her motion, rested his chin on top of her head and sighed. "Yeah, but I don't want to go back. I want to take you to bed and fuck like bunnies for the rest of the day." He leaned back so he could see her from top to bottom. "Damn, woman. This is not helping a bit."

Ignoring him, she pressed closer, wriggled her hips against him and kissed his throat. "Fuck like bunnies, eh? Ya wanna know the truth? I'm not trying to help." She tilted her head and looked up at him. "I kept thinking about you when I was in the shower, wondering why you didn't join me. There was plenty of room. It was hot and steamy and I was *so* ready...but, I guess if you're not interested..."

He groaned. The image was much too inviting. Carly turned away. "Witch," he said, laughing. Without thinking, he swatted her soundly on the bottom, harder than he intended. The contact stung his palm. "Oh shit. Carly, I'm sorry—"

She turned and smiled seductively over her shoulder at him. "Hmm, I'm not. Hold that idea for later."

Idea? What idea? A print of his palm on her white buttock slowly appeared. It practically glowed, each finger defined in hot, cherry pink skin. He couldn't stop staring at it, the perfect shape of his hand marking that wonderfully smooth expanse of flesh.

He thought about it all the way down the trail to the Institute. Wondered if the mark he'd put on her still showed beneath the skinsuit covering Carly's delectable ass. It made his palm tingle. Made his cock hard. Made him think of all kinds of things he'd not thought of before.

It also took his mind off the meeting facing them once he introduced Carly to Thom, Malachi and Sheyna.

* * * * *

Carly tried really hard not to stare, but Sheyna was so unbelievably gorgeous, so unique…so *alien*. Everyone else appeared just as normal as dirt.

Handsome dirt, but still dirt.

Thom Antoon, the lanky general, had to be at least fifty, but he looked like an overgrown teenager with his shock of dark hair, slow, southern drawl and ready grin. More reserved, Malachi Franklin was, without a doubt, the best looking doctor Carly'd ever seen.

Though not nearly so handsome as Tim. Every time she glanced at him, the band around her chest tightened. She couldn't love him, not after one day, but how else could she explain his effect on her? They'd made love so often over the past twenty-four hours she'd actually lost count. If they hadn't run out of condoms, they might still be up at the cabin.

There were a dozen in the box. Ohmygod… She blinked and bit her lip to keep from giggling out loud. No wonder her crotch hurt!

Fucking like bunnies.

Tim's assessment had been pretty darned close to the truth. She turned and glanced at Tim just as Sheyna handed him a tall glass of chilled juice. The lioness curled her lip briefly in semblance of a smile. Carly noticed her canines, every bit as sharp and long as her wild counterpart's fangs.

She was amazing. More cat than human, her creamy coat looked soft as mink. Her coffee-colored mane flowed over her shoulders in silken waves. She had perfectly formed cat's ears showing through the thick mane, and a surprisingly sensual, feminine look in spite of her elongated muzzle and the stiff little whiskers at either side of her nose.

Tall and slim, she moved with the elegance and grace of a dancer.

Or a cat.

She'd grasped Carly's hand when they were introduced, her ebony nails carefully retracted, her gaze open and somewhat amused. Carly wondered if Sheyna read minds. Tim had explained the many types of Talent among the members of the Institute. Thom Antoon was kinetic, like Tim, and Malachi was a healer with precognitive abilities.

Sheyna was a healer and an empath. She understood feelings, healed emotional scars as well as the physical.

Now she merely acted the hostess for this small gathering.

"Thanks, SheShe." Tim set his glass on the table and stopped Sheyna with a touch to her arm. Carly barely heard him whisper, "Thanks for packing the condoms."

"You're quite welcome." Her voice was soft, distinctly feminine and filled with laughter. Carly wondered if Sheyna had been aware of Tim's prior lack of experience. Obviously, she'd now know that had changed.

Everything has changed.

Sitting here in Malachi and Sheyna's comfortable living quarters drinking chilled apple juice, Carly might have been in any living room on Earth. Her own Earth. The one she was familiar with in her very own century.

The conversation ebbing and swirling about her felt surrealistic. Talk of empaths and kinetics, telepathy and matter transformation belonged in a science fiction novel, not her life. *This is my life*, popped into her head. Along with, *be careful what you wish for.*

"Do you agree, Carly?"

Tim's soft request dragged her back into the conversation. "Uhm, to what?" She took a sip of her juice, suddenly aware all eyes in the room were focused on her.

Tim laughed, grabbed her hand and squeezed. "Tired? Sorry. Considering what you've been through in the past twenty-four hours, you've every right to be."

His unintended double entendre made her blush. Her mind filled with images of their lovemaking, the erotic excesses of their past hours together. She felt the heat rising along her throat, recognized its mate in Tim's ruddy flush.

"I mean…"

Thom cleared his throat. "We all know what you mean," he said, laughing. "You're projecting like a damned big screen vid."

"Oh, crap. Carly, I'm sorry, I…"

Projecting? That means they see… Mortified beyond anything she'd ever felt in her life, Carly turned and stared at Tim. He flushed deep red and clutched her hand with a desperate grip. She dipped her head, wondering what rock she could crawl under. Everything she and Tim had done last night, every kiss, every sensual touch, all of it in their minds, all of it shared with every other person in the room.

Sheyna leaned over and took her hand. "Nothing will ever leave this room, Carly. You are among friends. You do, however, need to learn to shield your power, just as Tim needs to control his newfound powers of telepathy."

Waves of compassion washed over Carly. A gift from the empathic lioness? Carly clung to Tim's hand, blinked back embarrassed tears and tried to smile.

Malachi nodded in agreement. "Sheyna's right. You're not a natural telepath, Tim, but it's obvious you're so closely linked to Carly right now that you're using her synergetic powers. The scary thing is, neither one of you appears to be aware of it, which is exactly what we were discussing, Carly."

Carly nodded. She slanted a glance at Tim. His flush had faded and he gave her a quirky little smile, then squeezed her hand. "I'm really sorry, Carly."

It was too much. She burst out laughing. "Well, they might not have known much about me before, but they certainly do now." Warm laughter took away some of the humiliation, filling her with a sense of total acceptance. She turned to Malachi. "I don't understand. I don't feel Tim inside my head at all, at least not the way I did yesterday when he contacted you."

"That's because the two of you have formed a synergetic link," Mal said.

"One so in tune you work together without even realizing it," Thom added. "Tim's mind recognizes what it lacks and draws that power from you. You complement one another, sort of a yin and yang of the subconscious."

"Which is a fantastic thing," Malachi said, "once you learn to control it."

"And restrict it." Thom's voice echoed Mal's solemn warning. "I tried tapping in to your mind when you first arrived. Did you notice my intrusion?"

Carly stared at him. Shuddered with a sense of violation. It was one thing to have Tim in her head, but another altogether to have a complete stranger crawling around inside her mind.

Using her.

She scowled at Thom. He held his hand up in apology. "I had to know," he said. "The way Tim described you sounded almost too good to be true. You have even more power than he initially realized. Enough to make you a predominant force."

"Also a very dangerous one," Tim said. "Should the wrong person use you." He took both Carly's hands in his, stared deeply into her eyes.

She heard his voice in her mind, a warm caress across her thoughts.

You need to learn to block, to shield your mind, to protect your power, just as I need to learn to channel my thoughts directly to you without broadcasting to the world how much I love you.

She was vaguely aware of Tim severing some sort of link. "Did you hear what I just said to Carly?"

Both Malachi and Thom shook their heads. "No," Mal said. "I sensed a surge in mental power, but not the words. I wish Jenna were here. She'd be able to help Carly with the block. I don't think any of us has the training to—"

"I do." Sheyna touched her mate's shoulder with one broad, paw-like hand. "As an empath, I can feel what Carly is feeling, sense the type of block that will work best for her, and hopefully teach her to use it." She turned her feline gaze on Carly. "It will require a mindlink. You will have to feel comfortable enough to allow me access to your innermost thoughts. There will be no secrets between us."

"Like I've got any secrets left?" Carly snorted, throwing off the lingering shreds of utter and complete mortification.

Malachi's resigned comment interrupted her. "Are you certain, my love? There is much…"

"I have no secrets from my friends." Sheyna leaned over and nuzzled Mal behind the ear, then turned toward Carly. Her velvety ears pricked forward, her amber eyes twinkled with merriment. "First things, first, though. Carly, why don't you come with me and we'll get some more clothing for you. My skinsuit appears to be a perfect fit, so I'm sure there are other items you can wear."

She turned and practically glided into a back room. Carly glanced quickly at Tim, who merely smiled back. She set her glass of juice down and followed Sheyna.

Definitely surrealistic.

I've just disclosed details of the best sex of my life to a room full of total strangers, I'm following a full grown African lion, only she's a Miratan lion walking on her hind legs and we're going to try on clothes, probably swap girl stories, and then she's going to crawl inside my head and teach me how to keep her out.

With a quick glance back at Tim, Carly stepped into the bedroom behind Sheyna.

* * * * *

"I had no idea." What else could she say? Carly slowly removed her hands from their position at either side of Sheyna's face, stared into the lioness's amber eyes and saw a woman totally unlike the creature she had followed into the bedroom. Now, after a deep link with the young lioness, Carly understood Sheyna on levels beyond speech.

Before linking, they'd spent about an hour looking through clothes, talking, getting to know one another. They'd discussed the curious resemblance between the cab driver in Carly's time to Tim, but had found no explanation other than serendipitous happenstance. By the time Sheyna suggested they attempt a link, Carly knew she was as ready as she'd ever be.

Sitting on two small chairs, foreheads touching, hands pressed to one another's temples, Carly let Sheyna's soft instructions wash over her mind.

She knew Sheyna had protected her from the worst of her memories, but Carly still glimpsed the pain of years of abuse, the sexual assault Sheyna had endured in the waning days of the Rebellion, the final rift between the lioness and her father. She now understood the deep and abiding love Sheyna and Malachi shared, comprehended fully why the human and alien were so perfectly mated.

The moment Sheyna placed her broad palms against Carly's temples, Carly knew her world had truly and irrevocably changed. It wasn't merely the past she would never return to, it was the woman she had been—the woman she would never be again.

Suddenly she understood her power, the ability her mind had to increase the Talent of other Sensitives. A power that could easily be turned from good to evil without the proper shields and blocks—a power that would be coveted by many in this unsettled post-Rebellion period.

By Tim?

Tim is young. Sheyna didn't speak aloud, but Carly heard the words in her mind. Understood clearly the concept of telepathy, now, after her link with the lioness. *He is young but I sense his love is true and binding, that he loves you very much.*

"How young?" Not that it mattered that the young man who had shown her so much, changed her world, changed her life, be too young…be *unsuitable*.

Sheyna tilted her head as if confused by Carly's swirling thoughts and questions. "You don't know? Tim is twenty-five Earth years. On Mirat, we would be peers."

Twenty-five? Carly's skin went hot, then cold, a stark reminder how close she was to hot flashes.

Suddenly his age mattered very much. "He can't be. He's got to be older, he's just…"

"He is what he is. Why does it matter?"

"My God, Sheyna. I'm old enough to be his mother!" Carly stood up, paced across the small room, flung her hands in the air. "I'm sleeping with a child. No wonder he was still a virgin. He's practically a baby, he's—"

"He's a man who has fought a terrible war for seven long years. A man who has seen more in his twenty-five years than many who are older. He has killed, he has lost family and friends, he has suffered many lives beyond his own. This has matured him beyond the number of days he's lived. Carly, my new friend, Tim is an old soul in a very handsome package." Sheyna touched Carly's shoulder softly with one hand, tilted her head in question and asked, "Why would his years make a difference?"

"They do. I don't know why, or how I can explain it, but they do." She flopped down on the edge of the bed. "He wants me to come live with him. I had no idea I was so much older. I can't live with him. It wouldn't be right."

"It would be wrong not to. He loves you. You love him. I feel it in both of you. I'm an empath, remember? His emotions are open to me. As are yours." She smiled and shook her head in dismay. "I am convinced you are sexually compatible—no one in that room would dispute that. Why would you want to hurt yourself?" Sheyna sat down on the bed next to her. Carly felt the waves of compassion and concern wash over her.

Felt the power of that compassion increase as her newly learned shields slipped. She stared at Sheyna, found a target for her anger. "You just tapped into me to increase your Talent, didn't you?"

Sheyna jerked as if she'd been slapped, then ducked her head. "Not on purpose. I'm sorry. I didn't realize what was happening until I felt the surge in my Talent. I didn't mean to do that. It's a violation of every ethical standard we live by, yet I had no control." She tilted her head, studied Carly for a heartbeat. "You act like a magnet, I think. You draw the power to you, make it bigger, more than it should be, and give it back."

"Tim made love to me shortly after he brought me to this time. That's how he discovered I was what I am—a Synergist. How do I know that's not the only reason he loves me? For the power, for what I can do for him?"

"That's possibly one of the things he loves about you. You may never know," Sheyna said, frowning. "Love has many qualities, many facets. It's what we can do for others as much as what they do for us. You give Tim the strength to love you physically. Your power certainly won't affect his emotional desire for you. Is that so bad?"

"It's…" Carly bowed her head. Was it so bad? Her entire world had twisted, warped, wrapped itself inside out. Suddenly, she felt completely overwhelmed by change. "It's too much, too soon." She looked into Sheyna's eyes, saw herself reflected back in their amber glow. "I can't deal with this, not right now. I need more time. May I stay here, at the clinic? Just for awhile, until I learn to block more effectively, learn to control something I never knew I had."

"Of course you may." Sheyna stood up, then turned to stare at Carly for a moment. Her cat's ears tilted back, not quite flat against her skull, but enough for Carly to sense her displeasure. "You will not hurt him."

Carly nodded, but her mind was suddenly clouded and gray. *What about me?* she wanted to scream. *What about me?*

Chapter Eight

"Carly, I don't understand? Why aren't you coming with me?" Tim held her hands in his. The abject misery in his eyes made him look even younger. Carly blinked away tears and shook her head.

"Twenty years, Tim. I had no idea. I'm twenty years older than you. A lifetime. I'm old enough to be your mother, not your lover. If I'd known how young..."

His voice cracked, making him sound even younger, then took on a belligerent, sarcastic tone. "Years, Carly. Just years. Units of measurement...what's the problem? Did my conversation bore you? Oh, maybe we don't like the same music. Why don't you dig up something from over a hundred years ago and see? Or weren't you satisfied with me? Don't I know enough in bed?"

"Enough, Tim." Malachi stepped up behind Carly. "She's been through a lot. This isn't helping. Go home, get some rest. Both of you are exhausted. Give Carly time to adjust to all the changes in her life."

Carly took a deep breath, then let it out. Malachi was right, almost. She wanted to go with Tim, really. Didn't he know how painful this was, this matter of choice? She wanted to tell him she loved him, wanted to throw her arms around him and tell the world to fuck off, she didn't care, she could make him happy, keep him happy...but she knew she'd always wonder.

Does he love me, in spite of my age? Or does he love what I can do for him? Tears thickened her throat and she couldn't speak. Sheyna put her arm around Carly and walked her out of the room. She felt Tim's pain long after the front door had slammed shut, long after the sense of him was gone.

* * * * *

"We're going to the rec center for a beer, Carly. Do you want to go with us?"

Malachi wrapped an arm around her shoulders and squeezed. Carly looked up from the history book she'd been reading on her handheld. She'd always hated history, but reading about what had happened over the past one hundred years was fascinating.

Besides, it took her mind off Tim. Helped her not think of how terribly she missed him, how awful she felt. "I think not, Mal. Sheyna just gave me some new stuff to read and…"

"And you can only absorb so much. It's been two weeks and you haven't left the clinic. All you've done is work on your blocking techniques, build up your shields and read history books. Don't you think it's time to get out?"

"What if Tim's there?"

"Then you tell him hello." Malachi straddled a wooden chair and looped his arms over the back. Sheyna stood patiently off to one side. "Carly, he's miserable. You're miserable." Mal stabbed the air with one blunt finger. "Why are you doing this to yourself? To Tim?"

"He'll find someone else. It's going to happen sooner or later, anyway." Damn the tears! Carly felt her eyes stinging, knew she'd be crying before long.

"Why do you say that?"

Sheyna's soft question startled Carly. "I…I can't imagine him staying. What if he wants children? He's young. I'll be old and gray in a couple of years and he'll just be hitting his prime. He says he loves me, but what if it's just my power? What if he only wants me for what I can do for him?"

"I don't believe that in a heartbeat, but what if that is the reason he loves you?" Malachi snapped his fingers, his frustration obvious. "Get dressed. I don't care how miserable you are. I'm your doctor and I say you're going with us. Think of the beer as medicine."

"He is a very good doctor," Sheyna added, her whiskers twitching with suppressed laughter. "And you are most definitely in need of a beer."

Carly chuckled. She couldn't help it. Whining and moping were definitely not her style. She turned off the handheld and set it on the table. "Give me a few minutes to change my clothes. You win. I haven't got a chance when I'm double-teamed."

* * * * *

The bottle of beer catapulted from the table, bounced off the ceiling and landed in a crescendo of splintered glass and splattered brew in the middle of the empty dance floor. A few surprised shrieks around the rec center, then a scattering of applause met Jan's look of absolute shock. "I did that?" She shook her head. "I'm not a strong kinetic. I'm lucky if I can just make the damned things wobble back and forth."

Malachi held out a handful of napkins. "Yep. That's what we were trying to explain. Carly's Talent, if you want to call it that," he rolled his eyes in her direction, "works like a catalyst to increase whatever power you've got. Now go clean up the mess."

"I'll help." Laughing, Carly grabbed more napkins and stood up. "C'mon, Sheyna. It's always the women who clean up the messes."

"In this case, it's the women who made it." Malachi glanced toward the spreading pool of beer. "Better hurry. Our jovial waiter doesn't look too pleased."

"He is a grump, isn't he?" Jan kissed Thom on top of his head and the three women followed the waiter with the mop bucket.

Thom nodded in Carly's direction. "Tim's a wreck, you know. What happened?"

Malachi just shook his head. "She suddenly discovered she's twenty years older than he is. I guess, in her era, that's an unacceptable age difference for a relationship. Give her time."

"Wonder what she thinks of Jan and me? I'm more than twice Jan's age, but she didn't hesitate when I proposed. She doesn't seem to mind."

"Jan doesn't mind a bit, and neither would Tim. Convincing Carly is the hard part." Malachi leaned closer to Thom. "Off the subject...I'm getting more precogs, something to do with the rec center. Carly's involved, though I'm not sure how. Have you noticed any dissension, any strange behavior around here since Shing busted that group of troublemakers last week?"

Thom shook his head. "Hard to say. There's always going to be an undercurrent of jealousy between those with Talent and those without. I'm not sure how organized it is, though. I've been hearing of some guy who calls himself the Reverend. Says Talent comes from the devil." Thom rolled his eyes. "He's very popular with the un-Talented."

He took another swallow of his beer. "Since the fighting stopped, there are so many new people coming and going, I can't keep track anymore. I used to know all the employees here. Not anymore. The waiters are all new, even the guy mixing the drinks. It's not the same."

"I've heard of the Reverend. Shing's keeping an eye on him. I can handle new faces, so long as the war is over." Malachi leaned back in his chair. "I was tired of the fighting, tired of losing young lives, patching up kids who had no business killing."

He'd barely ended his sentence when the women returned. Laughing, Jan interrupted. "Well, that's the last time I try that!" She plopped down in Thom's lap and kissed him hard on the mouth. "What a mess! I think I'll stick with my standard incompetence, thank you."

"If that's what you want to call it." Thom leered, but the kiss he gave her spoke volumes.

Sheyna and Carly reclaimed their seats. Malachi thought Carly looked happy and relaxed, dressed casually in canvas pants and a sweater. Suddenly the resemblance slammed into his gut—she'd been wearing the same outfit in his first precog. He glanced about the crowded room, searching for anything that might present a threat, then turned his attention back to Carly.

She took a swallow of her beer and rolled her eyes. "We really pissed off the waiter. He did *not* see the humor in the situation."

"We cleaned up the mess. All he had to do was stand there and glower at us." Sheyna touched Malachi's shoulder. "He was radiating hatred. Not merely irritation, but absolute loathing for all of us. You might want to have Shing Tamura keep an eye on him."

Malachi covered Sheyna's hand with his. *Did you notice Carly is dressed in the same clothing she wore in my original precog vision? There was an aura of danger and darkness in what I saw.*

Sheyna's words were loud and clear in his mind. *I'd forgotten what she wore. The significance can't be ignored. We should contact Shing tonight and keep close watch on Carly.* Her fingers tightened, subtly warning him of a new situation.

"Hello, Tim." Jan glanced over Carly's shoulder and smiled.

"Hey, kid." Malachi sent a silent thank you to Sheyna and smiled at Tim, hoping to make him feel welcome among his friends. He stood there, just behind Carly, all the pain and love he felt for the woman so obvious Malachi wanted to shake her.

She stared at her beer, but didn't turn around. Her shoulders looked tense, her face had gone deathly pale.

"Carly?" Tim reached out and touched her shoulder. "We need to talk. Okay?"

She looked up, away from him. "I... Tim, I..." Tears streamed down her face. Sheyna reached for her, but Carly shoved the chair back, twisted past Tim and ran across the center. She almost collided with the waiter at the doorway, pushed past him, and disappeared through the door.

Tim turned to follow her, but Malachi grabbed his arm. "Give her a minute to get herself under control. She's been quietly looking for you all night. I think she'd finally decided you weren't going to come."

"What's going on?" Tim straddled the chair Carly had just left. "She's been avoiding me for two weeks over something I can't change, something that means nothing. Why's she so hung up on our age difference? It's stupid."

"It's not just the age, Tim." Sheyna covered his hand with hers. "It's her Talent. She wonders if you care for her for herself or for the power she gives you. It's very complicated, the way a woman's mind works."

"You think I don't know that?" He grinned ruefully. "How can I convince her I'd love her without her Talent?" He laughed. "Admittedly, the sex wouldn't be nearly so good, but that's not what made me want her the first time I saw her in Mal's vision. Her Talent is part of who she is, what we are. As for the age difference...in my mind, it's not an issue. I guess I just have to convince Carly's mind."

Malachi interrupted. "Tim, she's wearing the same outfit she had on in the precog. Same sweater, same pants. I sensed darkness in the vision. At the time, I thought only of the danger Carly represented to us, not something that might befall her. It might mean nothing, it might mean she faces danger. You better make sure she's okay."

Tim nodded and stood up. "Thanks, Mal. I didn't notice what she was wearing. I'm going after her. I'll keep her safe. This time she's going home with me, so don't wait up."

✳ ✳ ✳ ✳ ✳

The stars spread across the nighttime sky like jewels scattered over black velvet. Once she wiped the tears from her eyes, Carly spotted the Big Dipper and the North Star, right where they belonged. They'd been in the same place a hundred years ago.

One hundred years meant nothing in the cosmos. How could she let twenty years destroy her happiness? She felt absolutely foolish, standing out here in the dark at the edge of the compound, listening to the music and laughter spilling out of the rec center.

Listening to the music and thinking of numbers.

She couldn't get the math out of her head. Jan was twenty-five years younger than her lover. At twenty-four, she was less than half Thom's age, yet she adored him. Tim might be only twenty-five, but his maturity was that of a much older man. She'd thought he was at least in his thirties when she'd first met him. Carly knew that if she wanted to get technical, she was actually a hundred and twenty years older than Tim.

She pressed her knuckles against her lips, not certain if she wanted to laugh or cry. She'd been such an idiot, upsetting Tim, making herself miserable. No one cared about the stupid difference in their ages. Why should she? It wasn't like she and Tim were getting married.

They were terrific together in bed. Just thinking about him filling her, loving her, made her hot and wet and ready. She hugged her arms around herself, contemplating her return to the rec center, the apology she knew she owed to everyone.

Time to eat some crow. She'd been underfoot at Sheyna and Mal's long enough, worried everyone sick and made Tim unhappy for nothing. *What an idiot.*

Almost giggling with relief, she started back across the compound.

They came out of nowhere, dark and menacing, cloths covering their faces, the large fabric sack one threw over her head suffocating her and restraining her arms.

She cried out, but the sound was muffled. She kicked her feet, hoping to at least trip one of her opponents, but he shoved her back and she fell, hard. She heard a loud ripping, realized it was tape being torn from a roll and suddenly the sack tightened around her arms, her throat, across her mouth.

Someone sat on her, wrapped her ankles together until she felt trussed up like a calf at a rodeo. Grunting in frustration, twisting and turning, she struggled to draw enough air through the cloth.

He hit her across the temple, hard. Stunned, afraid, she went perfectly still. Both attackers picked her up, slung her between them like a sack of flour, and, moving at an uncomfortable jog, carried her away from the music, away from the sounds of her friends, away from everything Carly knew.

* * * * *

Struggling for some semblance of control, Tim paced back and forth in front of the table. "I can't find her. I looked all over out there and, unless she's hiding from me, she's taken off."

"Or been taken."

"What do we do, Mal? There's no sign of anything, no sense. I don't know where to start. If she just wants to avoid me, that's her right, but I'm scared to death…"

Sheyna touched his arm. Tim knew it was as much for comfort as to read his mental state, but he didn't mind the intrusion. She cared. They all did. Once again he realized how lucky he was to have such good friends. "Tim, the clinic is locked and Carly doesn't have a key. If she's gone back there, I imagine she's sitting on the front step, feeling really foolish. Look for her there, first. We'll check around the compound, see if we can find her. Try not to worry."

Try not to worry. Right. Tim raced across the darkened compound, his mind open to anything that might lead him to Carly. He hoped like hell he'd find her on the front step, but deep in his heart he knew she wasn't there.

The carpet smelled where she'd been unceremoniously dumped, and the room reeked of cigarettes, unwashed bodies and sweaty clothes. Carly lay on her side, still trussed in the bag. The tape around her face had loosened enough to allow her to breathe, but fear and anger kept her on the edge of hyperventilation.

Two men argued, their voices rising and falling, far enough away that she was unable to understand all of what they said, especially over the rush of her own breathing. Obviously they were aware of her Talent, what little she had. They feared the Talented members of the Institute, but their hatred was stronger.

Carly struggled to slow her breathing. She needed to hear them, needed to understand what was going on.

Footsteps, muted on the carpet, drew closer. "You're sure she can't do anything? She can't, like, set fires or move stuff or read our minds?"

Carly tried to identify the voice. She couldn't.

"Not a thing. I heard them talking. They said she can't do any of that stuff. The bitches thought it was funny, throwing beer and glass all over the place. I made 'em clean it up. All she does is, she makes the others better. If you can lift a little, she makes it a lot."

The waiter?

"How?"

"Hell if I know. I told him about her. Just before I got off my shift. He said he'd pay."

"Told who? Who wants her? What are we going to do with her? I let you talk me into this stupid scheme, but…"

"You idiot. I'm gonna sell her to the Reverend. You've heard him speak. The guy's really sharp—he's got a huge following, bigger'n anyone realizes. He says Talent's an abomination, that it's the devil's work. He's got lots of ideas, lots of plans. I told him tonight about the bitch, how she can make their powers even stronger. He's real interested. I gotta let him know I've got her." He laughed. "I never thought it would be this easy to snatch her."

"How interested? How much money?"

"Enough." Carly heard another bark of coarse laughter, then a sharp jab in her ribs rolled her from her side to her back. Hands groped her legs, tested the tape wound around her ankles and knees. Added new tape around her arms and body. Someone grabbed her breast and squeezed hard. Another hand pressed down on her pubic bone and fingers slipped between her bound legs, touching her through the fabric of her canvas pants. She clenched her jaw and kept silent.

"What's she look like?"

"A babe. She looks good. Later, we'll check her out. Maybe give her a trial run." He laughed again. "Hell, we'll have plenty of time. I won't see the Reverend until tomorrow night. Right now, I need a drink."

"Works for me. Rec center?"

Laughter. "Why not? I'm off for the rest of the night. Besides, if anyone sees us there, they won't connect us with the bitch disappearing."

She heard them walk away, heard the door slam.

She lay in the dark, her heartbeat pounding in her ears, the ragged sound of her breath echoing against the filthy sack.

Tim? Find me, Tim. Please.

Chapter Nine

"I've looked everywhere, Mal. Where can she be?" Tim struggled to control his breathing. Panic wouldn't help Carly. She needed him.

Gods, he needed her. So many lonely nights since she'd chosen her course away from his. He'd ached with wanting her, now fear filled him with pain. He might not be the empath Sheyna was, but he sensed danger, sensed Carly's fear.

Something terrible had happened here tonight.

Malachi grasped his shoulder, steadied him. "I don't know, Tim. We've checked all over the compound, but I really thought she'd be at the clinic. I wanted you guys to have some time together. Shit. I should pay more attention to my instincts. Sheyna, do you sense her at all?"

They stood just outside the rec center, Thom, Jan, Sheyna and Malachi. Supporting him, helping him. Tim watched his friends' faces and realized this was his family, they were the ones he counted on. If anyone could help, these four would.

Sheyna lifted her face to the heavens, composed herself with hands pressed together in front of her chest, palms joined as if in prayer. She bowed her head, concentration obvious in the rigid line of her shoulders, the silence that surrounded her.

A long moment later she spoke. "She was here," she said. "She walked here." Sheyna practically glided across the tarmac surface, eyes half closed, her hands now pressed to her temples. She paused at the small fence separating the rec center parking lot from the rest of the Institute grounds.

"She stood here, not for too long. Her thoughts lie heavy in this spot." Sheyna turned to Tim, a soft smile on her face. "She was thinking of you. I feel happiness, a sense of decision."

The lioness turned and walked back toward the lights of the center. Suddenly she stopped, flinched as if she'd been struck. "Here. Something frightened her. Someone. No...two. There were two men here. Right here. I see only darkness, sense fear, panic even. She can't breathe, her face is covered. The men smell of beer, of stale smoke. There is much anger. A sense of loathing."

Sheyna suddenly looked toward Malachi. "One of them...the waiter. The same hatred I sensed from the waiter, earlier tonight."

"Find him." Thom's voice interrupted, his authority clear. "I'll check the rec center. Malachi, you and Sheyna see what else you can sense in the area. Tim, find out where he lives. He's new here. Jan, get Shing Tamura on this — now. We'll split up and see if anyone knows where the bastard is."

Tim stopped Sheyna with a hand to her wrist. "Thank you," he said. "We'll find her. We have to."

She nodded, brushed his cheek with her fingers, then turned and followed Malachi into the night.

* * * * *

Carly willed her heartbeat to slow, her breathing to grow more even and productive. Her captors were gone, for now. She wasn't certain how long she'd been held, but someone must be looking for her.

Dear God, let it be Tim.

She dropped her newly learned shields. She had no idea how close she had to be for someone to use her power, but with any luck, Tim or Sheyna, or even Malachi might be within her range.

She thought of Tim, of the short time she'd spent with him. All of her arguments seemed so silly, now. What did years matter when your love was timeless? Tim filled an emptiness she'd lived with for much too long. His laughter, his consideration, his love for her.

Who was she to deny her own feelings, much less his? She was forty-five, not eighty-five. If Tim wanted babies, she could still give him children. If he wanted a lover, she knew she could give him everything he wanted and needed. She'd let the fashions of her era determine her actions in his.

She'd not been capable of telepathy, but she remembered the sense of Tim in her mind. She tried now to recapture that, to send out a plea for help.

Nothing.

Still, she left her newly built shields down, opened her thoughts to the night, and waited.

Awareness sharpened. She sensed the hollow, empty feel of the room, felt the despair that lingered here, the anger and hatred. She imagined her mind traveling outside her body, leaving the stink and the loathing, searching for Tim in the quiet stillness of the night.

She floated free, unbound, unfettered. Stars sprinkled the heavens, the grounds of the Institute lay below. There! She spotted Sheyna and Malachi near where she'd been captured. Thom appeared to be heading for the rec center, Jan was running across the compound, headed directly for the security office. Carly wanted to tell them to look closely for the waiter, but her voice did not exist on this plane.

Where was Tim? She floated lower, searching, sending out tendrils of thought to draw him to her. So strange, this floating, flying self. How much was reality, how much her imagination? How much due to the lack of oxygen in her imprisoning sack?

She hovered, part of the air, partly mist, her thoughts as hazy as her appearance. Tim must be close. She sensed him, wanted him. How could this astral body have needs so base and human?

There! She floated down, closer, followed him toward the clinic where Malachi kept records of all the Institute's inhabitants. Tim stepped up on the porch, paused. Looked around, his brow creased with thought. His long black hair had come loose from its customary leather tie. It tangled in disarray over his shoulders. With a look of exasperation, he shoved the dark mass out of his eyes and stared directly at Carly.

Did he sense her presence? She floated closer, closer still until she all but embraced him. Couldn't he see her? Why couldn't he feel her love? She reached out, stroked his cheek, pushed a tendril of long dark hair away from his face.

He stared, wide-eyed, directly at her. His voice was a hoarse whisper, a ragged cry of pain. "Carly? I know you're close. I feel you. Where are you? Oh Gods, Carly. I love you so much. Where are you?"

Crap. She didn't have a clue how to tell him. She reached out and touched his arm. He brushed away what he obviously thought was a bug.

She opened her mind, dropped whatever shields she might still hold. Experienced all the love, the need, the wanting she felt for him.

He looked at her. Directly at her and nodded, as if understanding. She knew he didn't see her, but he at least felt her presence. "Take me there. Take me where they've got you."

Slowly. She had to move very slowly now, drawing her astral self back to the physical, keeping contact with Tim, holding on to the fine silvery thread of her real existence. So new, this method of travel, but exhilarating, wonderful..

Wonder. Wonder that she could be here, so far outside her body, so close to Tim in essence if not substance. He followed her, his senses attuned to hers, his body thrumming with need and life.

She didn't know, actually, where her body was held captive. Merely sensed her anchor, her *self,* lying trapped in a filthy hovel somewhere here in the compound.

She'd found Tim, traveling through solid walls, through buildings, through people when needed. Now she must navigate a way back that would let him follow.

Carly drifted, not really certain of anything but the necessity of reuniting with her body, with that solid core of herself somewhere here in the Institute. Reuniting with her physical self, and more importantly, with Tim.

* * * * *

The air shimmered, as if a fine glaze of quicksilver coated the very molecules of night. The sense of Carly was strong, so dear and close that Tim felt as if he could hold her in his arms. No, here was merely an essence of her beauty.

How much was in his mind? Gods, he missed her, needed her. Wanted her enough to project her image in the very air around him? Like a ghost she hovered, materializing in and out of being. He reached for her, realized there was nothing there, nothing of substance.

Despair gave his voice a rough edge of anger. "Take me there. Take me where they've got you."

The image disappeared, the air shimmered and he felt her frustration—or was it his own? Then the illusion moved, slowly as a sigh upon the breeze, drifting, fading then reappearing like a gossamer wraith, beckoning, begging him to follow.

He crossed the compound, eyes focused on the almost invisible essence that must be Carly.

Had to be Carly.

Suddenly a thought crept unwanted into his mind. Could she be dead? Was this spirit, this astral being merely the remnant of her life? Was it leading him to the remains of her physical self? To her body?

No! Don't go there. Don't even think…

They'd moved beyond the lights, now. Into an older area of the compound, a section of temporary housing set up during the early years of the Rebellion, pre-fab structures now used by the transient population that drifted in and out of the Institute.

Most came, hoping to be tested for powers that didn't exist. Occasionally, a true Sensitive with Talent was discovered, but not always. Those who lacked abilities often floundered, some stayed on, taking work at service level positions.

Like waiters? Kitchen help? Blinking against the darkness, concentrating on the almost invisible shimmer in the air, Tim moved further into the run-down neighborhood. They crossed low fences, ducked under overhanging shrubbery, and with each step, Carly's essence grew stronger in his mind and in his sight.

Her physical self was close, so close, but where? Tim stopped, concentrated on the wraith hovering just ahead, concentrated on Carly. He felt the quickening in his own mind, the blossoming of power that meant she boosted his kinetics.

Boosted his ability to telepath. He called out to her, a mental cry of pain and anguish.

Cried out, and felt her answer, strong and clear in his mind. *Praise the Mother.* He drew on Carly's synergetic power to flash a quick message to Malachi and Thom, received their instant confirmation, then raced past the silent image of Carly, grown brighter now in the night.

The bungalow was little more than a renovated Quonset hut, the metal rusted and stained, but the front door was solid wood and locked. There had not been a lock made that could keep Tim Riley out. He burst through the door and practically stumbled over Carly's prostrate form. Within seconds he'd released her from her bindings, ripped the filthy flour sack off her body and held her in his arms.

"Carly? Carly, wake up!"

The air shimmered, expanded, stilled. Carly opened her eyes, blinked owlishly at Tim, then let out a small cry. She clung to him, trembling, sobbing, her mind a jumble of words and thoughts too confused to understand.

After a moment he sorted them out, and kissed her hard on the mouth. *Don't you ever, ever scare me like this again, Carly*

Harris. I can't take it. You might not think I'm old enough, but dammit, woman, you're making an old man out of me before my time.

I'm so sorry, Tim. I feel so stupid. I love you.

I love you, too, baby. I love you so much it's killing me to be away from you. I've thought about nothing but you for the past two weeks. I figure the only way to make sure you don't pull another stupid stunt like this is to marry you.

Carly's trembling ceased and she pulled back from his embrace to look at him. "Marry me? You want to marry me?"

"Of course I do, silly. What do you think people in love do? Not that much has changed in the past hundred years." He leaned back against the wall, cupped her face in his hands and kissed her gently on the lips. Her tears were salty, her mouth so sweet he wanted to stay there, tasting, touching.

He heard voices outside, the sound of footsteps.

Thom and Malachi raced through the front door. "We got 'em, Tim. Shing's locking the bastards up right now. They're still looking for the Reverend, but at least the two jerks that took her are behind bars. How is she?" Malachi knelt down beside Tim and Carly and immediately pressed his palm against her face.

Tim held his breath while Mal did a cursory telepathic exam. He finally exhaled when Malachi sighed with relief.

"You're okay, right?" Mal brushed Carly's hair out of her eyes and smiled reassuringly at her, then turned to Tim. "How'd you find her?"

"She found me." Tim shook his head, smiling. "Carly does have a Talent. She just didn't know it."

"You mean I wasn't imagining all that?" Her voice still sounded shaky, but there was definite excitement behind her question.

"All what?" Thom sat down on the filthy sofa. "What did you imagine?"

"I wanted to find Tim," Carly said, scooting onto Tim's lap and laying her head on his shoulder. "I was sure he'd be looking for me. I was terrified, but I forced myself to be calm and just pretended I was leaving my body, flying over the compound, searching for him. Suddenly I could see him. I saw all of you, but I couldn't talk or communicate." She touched Tim's jaw with her fingers. He turned and kissed her palm.

"Astral projection?" Thom threw a speculative glance at Malachi.

"Exactly," Tim said. "Astral projection. I've heard of it, but don't know anyone who can do it. You, my love, have a very rare Talent."

"Amazing," Thom said. "We've been searching for someone with the ability to project. I never would have guessed."

"The thing is, once we find someone with a particular Talent, they can often teach it to others." Malachi stood up as Jan and Sheyna entered the room. "Everything okay?"

"Those two are locked up and Shing's picking their brains," Jan said. "You okay, Carly?"

"Now I am. I was so scared!"

Tim wrapped his arms even tighter around her and she snuggled down against his chest. He felt her heart beating close to his and almost wept with the pleasure. This felt right, so perfectly right.

"You don't need to be frightened anymore," Sheyna said. "Once Shing Tamura gets involved, problems tend to be resolved. These two are just a couple of two-bit crooks without a full brain between them. The Reverend's long gone. I doubt he'll be back, now that he knows we'll be watching him." She held her hands out to Carly and Malachi. "C'mon. I would suggest we find a cleaner place to converse. This is disgusting."

"I've got a bottle of good cognac back at the clinic." Mal took Sheyna's hand and she tugged him to his feet. "For medicinal purposes only, of course."

Carly reached for Sheyna's other hand. "Cognac? That's what I was drinking the night I got into all this trouble." She gave Tim a knowing look, more invitation than reproach. "Are you absolutely certain it's safe?" She grinned at Tim and held out her hand.

He took it, felt the connection, felt the love and pure acceptance in her touch. "Cognac sounds good to me. Then I'm taking you home."

Chapter Ten

Off-center and self-conscious, Carly followed Tim through the doorway into his bungalow. In the two weeks since she'd known him, she'd never been inside his home. She opened her mouth to say something, anything, to ease the tension between them.

Tim pressed his fingertip to her lips. "It's okay. Whatever has happened, it's over. We're starting today and everything is new. Gods, Carly, I've dreamed of bringing you home with me since the first day we met." He hauled her into his arms, his body tense as a bowstring. His thoughts filled her mind, a confusing jumble of words and phrases and feelings that stunned her with their passion.

"I'm so sorry, Tim. So sorry. I feel like such an idiot, to put you through this, to cause so much needless trouble…"

I love you, Carly. Love you more than you can possibly know. I need you. Right now I need you so much I feel like I'm going to die if I can't make love to you.

Then what are you waiting for? Carly added a mental shout of laughter as Tim swept her up into his arms and carried her down the dark hallway. A single bedside lamp glowed softly in the bedroom. He lay her almost reverently on the downy spread, then leaned over and kissed her very gently on the mouth.

Her body blossomed beneath his touch. Tim tugged Carly's sweater over her head, then carefully slipped her sandals off her feet. She lay quietly, allowing him to undress her as if she were a child. He unzipped her pants and pulled them down. Her bra was next. He leaned over and kissed each breast as he uncovered them. Finally, slowly, he removed her silk panties, peeling them over her hips, revealing each inch of flesh as if he uncovered priceless treasure. His eyes gleamed — lit by blue fire.

When she was totally nude, he sat back on his heels and stared at her. The hunger in his eyes made her squirm in anticipation. His smile was slow and seductive as he carefully removed his shirt, one button at a time. His chest rippled, all lean muscles and smooth, dark skin. His hair hung long and sleek to his waist, parted over his shoulders and black as night.

Carly pictured the ebony strands draped over her breasts, flowing across her thighs as she imagined him kissing her, licking the hot fluid already gathering between her legs. She shared the image with Tim, testing her growing ability for telepathy. He groaned in passionate response, then kicked his shoes off. Kneeling between her parted thighs, he slowly unzipped his jeans.

His cock bulged against his plain white cotton briefs. Carly licked her lips and reached for him. He backed away, smiling. "Not yet," he said. "I've waited too long to rush this."

Still wearing his briefs, he leaned over and pulled one taut nipple between his lips. Thick strands of his hair cascaded over her breasts, tickled her lips. Carly groaned and once again she reached for him. He backed out of reach, laughing. "I was afraid you wouldn't behave."

Chuckling to himself, Tim turned and glanced at the open closet door. Suddenly, a hanger of brightly colored neckties floated across the room. "I always knew these would come in handy some day. Don't move a muscle."

"Why is it I have the idea you've been planning this?" He flashed her a look of such boyish innocence, Carly laughed out loud. Then she dutifully held her hands up over her head and spread her legs wide.

He grabbed a handful of the ties and bound Carly's hands to the headboard, then turned and, spreading her legs even wider, tied her feet just as securely to the foot posts. "I've been imagining this since even before I brought you forward," he said, kneeling once more between her legs. "I imagined you bound and naked in the middle of the bed up there at the cabin, but I knew I wouldn't be able to do a damned thing about it. I still wanted you badly enough, I was willing to give up my libido, any chance at loving you physically, just to be able to bring you to this time so I could have you, love you. Period. You. Not your Talent, not what you can do for me. That wasn't part of the deal because I didn't know about it."

He stroked her thighs, running his fingertips along the sensitive skin until it quivered. He looked away, as if struggling for words, but when he faced her once again, he was smiling. "Carly, when I said I love you, that you complete me, I meant every word. I mean them even more, now." He leaned over and kissed her belly, just below her navel, then sat back on his heels, laughing. "That doesn't mean I'm not going to fuck you crazy tonight...and, I'm going to make you pay for what you've put me through."

Carly squirmed against the ties, the anticipation of Tim's form of vengeance driving her temperature through the roof. He'd bound her so securely, though, she could barely move at all. He leaned over once more and kissed her belly, swirling his tongue around inside her navel, but this time he didn't stop there. He trailed kisses along her groin, nipped at the tender flesh of her inner thighs. Swept his tongue just once, oh so briefly, through the damp center between her legs, then suckled the swollen lips. He nuzzled her clit, barely touching it with the tip of his tongue.

Each infinitesimal stroke of his tongue blasted through her like a shot of electric current. His hair, just as she'd dreamed, swept across her breasts, trailed along her thighs, pooled in a silken mass over her belly. Still his tongue continued to flick ever so lightly over her clit. She forced herself to lie perfectly still, so afraid he'd stop. He reduced the pressure, merely hinting at the pleasure he could give. Carly's chest tightened, the muscles in her legs quivered, her entire body begged for release.

Oh God, Tim. Don't stop, please...more, please? I'm so close! She felt his laughter in her mind, experienced his growing arousal as if it were her own, waited for him to take her over the edge. Instead, he reached up and plucked at her taut nipples with both hands, fondling and rolling them into tight, painfully sensitive little buds. She arched her back, silently begging for more, pleading for release, for the intimate invasion of tongue and teeth and lips.

The minute the thought entered her mind, he stopped. Carly flattened her body against the mattress, gasping for air. She watched him through half-lidded eyes, wondering how long he intended to continue his long, slow seduction.

Tim leaned back and slipped out of his briefs. His cock surged free, hard and erect like she'd never seen it before. He wrapped his fist around the thick base, stroked himself a couple times just to irritate her, then guided himself carefully between her legs. Carly's breath caught on a sigh of expectation, only to whoosh out of her lungs in total frustration when he merely swept the solid tip lightly over her throbbing pussy.

Once more he teased her with his cock, gently probing but not entering, tantalizing without fulfilling. Bucking in frustration, sobbing and laughing at the same time, Carly flailed at the bonds holding her. "Tim," she wailed. "What are you *doing?*"

"Reminding you how good we are together. Showing you how much more we can be." His voice had grown deadly serious now. He knelt over her, his knees between her spread legs, his forearms resting on either side of her face. She felt the heavy weight of his cock against her belly. Her vaginal muscles clenched in frustrated anticipation.

"Open your mind to me, my love." His voice was a harsh whisper, a sensual invitation to even more passion. "Open completely and let me in. I want to be part of you. You've linked with Sheyna. You know how it's done. Link with me. Love me. You'll never doubt my love again."

Carly blinked back sudden tears. She understood the depth of trust a link required, knew what Sheyna had risked, what Tim now offered. "Untie me first," she said, knowing nothing would ever be the same again. Not *wanting* anything to be the same. "I want you to know I choose to link of my own free will, not because you've tied me to the bed. Not because my need for release is all that drives me."

She felt the surge in her mind as Tim drew power from her for his Talent. The ties fell away, leaving her hands and feet free. *My body may be free, but my heart will always be tied to you. Tim. You are my love.* Carly opened her mind and her body, felt the heat as his cock slowly filled her, felt the love and overwhelming sense of rightness as, just as carefully, he entered her mind.

The moment they linked, sensation increased tenfold. She felt the clenching force of her vaginal walls, the muscles pulsing around his cock, experienced Tim's passion and coiling need, the tightness in his balls, the hunger. She knew the control he wielded to keep himself from thrusting hard and fast and deep, the concentration it took for him to link them both, body and mind. Most of all, she knew Tim. Knew the parts of him he would never speak of, the loneliness, the misery, the pain he'd experienced throughout his unusual life. Felt his loss, knew his triumphs.

Even more, she knew love. The forever and ever, till death do us part kind of love, love like she'd sought but never expected. She clutched at his shoulders, clinging to him, her anchor, her lifeline. Body trembling, shivering uncontrollably, Carly gave in to sensation, so immersed in passion she'd lost all control. Tim's love filled her mind, his raging cock filled her center and turned her core molten.

She wrapped her legs around his waist, clinging to him, sobbing each breath as she rode higher with each driving thrust, caught in the fusion of Tim and Carly, Carly and Tim, a maelstrom of heat and light, all shared, all one single surge of love.

It blossomed and grew, bursting within like a fireworks display of monumental proportion. His cock was a driving force, thrusting harder, faster, taking her into a lush and thrilling plane beyond anything she'd ever known…a climax of the soul, an orgasm of the spirit, mirrored by each tremor and pulse, her pussy, his cock, all one and the same.

It seemed a long time later before conscious thoughts made sense. Tim's mental touch was almost tentative at first, his approach shy but filled with love.

I had no idea…no idea you loved as strongly as I do, needed as much as I need.

Nor I, my love. Carly gazed into the crystalline blue eyes, so close to hers, smiled at the mouth she'd grown addicted to as he lowered his head to kiss her once again. If they hadn't linked, she never would have believed. Not in a million years. Now she felt his cock growing hard once more, sensed the passion in Tim just as he would be feeling hers.

Will it always be this way? This sharing of sensation, of passion? Will I always be able to hold you in my mind?

Always. Whenever you want me, I'll be here. Part of you. Always part of you.

* * * * *

"Jenna and Garan will be home Wednesday night, so they'll make it in time for the wedding this weekend. Jenna you already know from your time, but I can't wait for you to meet Garan. He's a trip and a half, an arrogant son of a bitch if ever I knew one."

Carly sprawled naked across Tim's lean body. She'd felt completely sated just moments ago after a long morning of lovemaking, but there was something about the way his toe was rubbing the back of her calf, the soft caress of his fingers along the side of her breast, the gentle link of his thoughts mingling with hers…he rolled her nipple between his thumb and forefinger, then gently pinched the turgid flesh and she gasped.

Sated never lasted with Tim. Her nipple stood at attention and once again she felt the sweet rush of desire coursing through her veins. Carly nuzzled his chest then licked the smooth skin. "An arrogant son of a bitch? And I'm supposed to like this guy?"

"You can't help yourself. He's so head over heels in love with Jenna..." Tim's voice trailed off into quiet laughter. "Garan used to scare the crap out of me, but he's all bluster and show when Jenna's around. He gives the term 'pussy whipped' an entirely new definition."

"Hmmm, pussy whipped. I like that idea. If I'm going to be the older woman in this soon-to-be marital relationship, I think I'll demand full obedience. You may address me as Mistress Carly. I think I like the sound of that, don't you?"

She raised herself up and away from his chest and smiled down at him. The twinkle in his blue eyes was pure devilment. With her budding powers of telepathy strengthened by their link from the night before, she knew exactly what he was thinking—the image of his dark red hand print on her snow-white butt filled her mind with the clarity of a three dimensional photograph.

"That's not quite what I had in mind," she said, shoving away from him.

He grabbed her wrist, swung his legs over the side of the bed and flipped Carly over his knees. She squirmed and giggled and managed to position herself perfectly. The flat of his hand came down harder than she expected. She jumped at the contact, but before she had time to say anything, he swatted her again...and again, his wide palm finding a most amazing rhythm.

"Ouch...that hurts!" Except it didn't really, at least not as much as it should have. She squirmed against his legs, against the heat where his hand steadily smacked her heated butt, against the growing agitation between her legs.

She felt him rising under her belly, his cock hard and thick, and the spanking took on a new rhythm as he stopped every few swats to rub her buttocks, soothing the tingling flesh with his touch, then slipping his fingers down the crease between her legs, teasing her clit, spreading the moisture that gathered there, so slick and hot.

She was close, so close to coming, but he pulled his fingers away from her, leaving her hanging by a thread. Carly wriggled against his lap in a vain attempt to ease the torment, and he swatted her again, hard and fast until her flesh burned and her breath exploded, ragged and harsh.

She was desperate, so desperate for release. Each slap against her buttocks brought a new rush of desire, until she screamed in frustration, bucking her hips, laughing and crying while he simply drove her insane.

Suddenly, the spanking stopped. "Had enough?" Chuckling like an evil despot, Tim let his fingers drift idly across her overly sensitized skin, barely dipping between her legs but avoiding the one spot she wanted him to touch. "Willing to admit I'm in charge?"

"You are making me crazy!" She tried to break free, but he held her tightly across his lap, his fingertips still making those lazy circles, teasing her swollen labia, quickly flicking her clit, dragging the moisture from front to back without ever coming close to taking her over the edge. Laughing, squirming, she fought his gentle control, but no matter how much she struggled, he held her too tight to break free.

"Only because you made me crazy. Two weeks of crazy! Do you have any idea how I suffered? My gods, woman, I was ready to come over and steal you away in the dark of night. You will never, ever, put me through anything like that again. Do you understand?"

"I... I'll think about it." She giggled, daring him, anticipating, shivering with excitement.

He growled in mock displeasure and followed it with another swat. The next hard smack with the flat of his palm sent a combination of pleasure and pain rocking through her body. Before she had time to react, Tim lifted her off his lap, bent her over the edge of the bed and drove into her from behind.

Hot, wet and ready, she grabbed at the tumbled blankets and climaxed with his first hard thrust. His love poured over her, filling her mind, her heart as completely as he filled her body.

She came once more when Tim cried out with his own release. He fell forward, wrapping his arms around Carly, pressing his body over hers. He nuzzled the sensitive skin behind her ear and kissed her. She felt him inside her, felt the hot rush of seed and the final pulsing of his climax.

A flicker of surprise, elation, then remorse filtered through her thoughts.

I forgot to use a condom.

I know. She smiled into the blankets, loving the weight of him resting on her, loving even more the thought of his child. *You didn't use one last night, either. I'm only forty-five. I can still give you a child if you want.*

What do you want?

For once in her life, Carly knew exactly what she wanted. Tim Riley and, if the gods and goddesses of this new world agreed, she wanted Tim's child.

I gave up on ever being a mother because I never met a man I wanted as my child's father. At least, not until I met you. I'm not too old...

No, my love. You are not too old. You're perfect.

We're perfect. It just took me awhile to figure it out.

She felt him growing hard and solid within her once again. To think she'd been stupid enough to believe she could give this man up? "I guess you're never too old to learn, my love."

"Or too young." He nipped her shoulder and loved her once again.

Epilogue

"You weren't kidding when you said he was arrogant, but he's most definitely a pussycat. I really like him." Carly pushed her lacy veil back from her eyes and sipped champagne as she watched Garan, the huge lion of Mirat, carry a plate of fruit across the room to his mate.

Amazing. Absolutely amazing.

She couldn't wipe the grin off her face. Didn't want to. Would she ever grow accustomed to this new Earth? Huge, upright lions intermingled with humans, dancing, talking, laughing. The occasional glass of champagne or hors d'oeuvres occasionally floated from plate to person, and the conversations flowed on in the minds of her guests as much as they were spoken out loud.

Her telepathy was improving. She and Jenna were working on the many nuances of astral projection. Since the link, Tim had learned to stay tapped in to her mind, no matter how far apart they were, without affecting her blocks and shields. It essentially protected her from unwanted intrusion but allowed him to share his abilities — and his constant love — with Carly.

Loving Tim was amazing. Telekinesis was definitely a hoot.

No, she would never, ever grow tired of all the surprises ahead.

Tim's fingers wrapped tightly around hers. He lifted her hand to his lips and kissed the gold ring he'd just placed on her finger. "Any regrets?"

Carly stroked the long, silky black hair flowing freely over his shoulders and looked into his brilliant blue eyes. She studied the face she loved more than any other, and shook her head. "None. You've given me love, a new life, a whole new world. I lost nothing. I gained everything. Not many women have their fantasies turned to reality."

"Not many men, either." He leaned closer and kissed her very gently on the mouth. She tasted him, the sweet effervescence of his kiss as intoxicating as any champagne. The night couldn't come soon enough.

Familiar voices pulled her regretfully away from Tim's mouth.

"Congratulations, you two." Malachi and Sheyna raised their glasses of champagne in a toast. Mal took a swallow, then suddenly stopped and blinked in surprise. He stared blankly into space a moment, then smiled brightly. "Tim, I need to talk to you. I keep having this precog..."

"Oh, no you don't." Tim held up his hand, fingers crossed as if to ward off evil. Carly covered her eyes in mock terror.

Sheyna just shook her head. "Come along, dear." She grabbed Malachi by the arm. Protesting, laughing, he followed her across the room.

BOLD JOURNEY
StarQuest Book 5

Chapter One

He was large and almost human, his golden eyes catching the light from the small campfire and sending it back to her in potent flashes of heat. She stood before him, a captive of his need as much as her own.

Swaying with the hypnotic dance of the flames, Cené slowly untied the laces holding the tunic closed across her small breasts. As she pushed the soft folds of beaded blue leather to her waist, she felt his presence in her thoughts.

Need. Want. Now.

A powerful yearning ripped through her soul, a sense that this alien creature was the mate she'd been promised in her dreams.

Cené examined him as intensely as he studied her. Sitting quietly, his long, muscular legs folded, ankles crossed, he followed her movements with the flickering glance of his eyes, the tight clenching of his strong jaw.

His need washed over her, a silent craving to touch, to taste—to mate.

Cené's knees almost buckled in response. She took a deep breath and prayed for strength.

Where was the familiar surge to her power?

Goddess? My Lady? I don't understand? Silence met her plea for answers. Breathing deeply, acting purely on instinct, Cené softly palmed her breasts until the dark red nipples budded into sensitive peaks. She felt his desire grow stronger.

Her pussy wept, her inner muscles contracted tightly against an imaginary penis.

A low growl echoed across the campsite. Startled, she glanced up. Hunger glittered in his amber eyes.

Empowered, she slipped the tunic down over her hips, standing naked in the flickering light. Her blessing bag, hanging from a woven thong around her neck, rested between her breasts.

Suddenly he stood before her, his broad chest heaving with barely repressed desire, his cock straining against the strip of leather covering his loins. His left hand reached out, the fingers long and broad, the nails thickened, sharp and oddly curved, reminding her of cat's claws.

He closed his hand around her blessing bag, compressing it lightly within his huge fist.

Something squeezed her heart. She faltered, gasped in surprise as much as fear.

His other hand encompassed her left breast, his thick fingers golden against the ebony depths of her skin. She moaned, unable to move away, barely able to breath.

He leaned over and kissed the sensitive flesh beneath her ear, then drew his unusually abrasive tongue across her jaw line. The rough texture left a trail of longing in its path. Cené twisted her chin to one side, allowing him better access to her throat. She heard him growl again, a deep, guttural vibration that rumbled up out of his chest.

The sound sent shivers racing the length of her spine.

His right hand still kneaded her breast, the other held her blessing bag, as if he held her life in his big, broad hand. His tongue, rougher even than the coiling tongue of the nightcats that roamed her village, scraped once more along her jaw line. She answered him with a cry of pleasure and a deep coil of wet heat between her legs.

Need. Want. Now

Was that his thought? Was it her own?

She moaned and arched against him, offering herself.

Suddenly, he opened his jaws against her throat, his sharp teeth inhuman, the long, pointed canines sinking easily into the tender flesh, sinking into the deep artery that carried her life's blood.

Tearing and rending, he bit savagely into her throat, ripping the blessing bag from her neck, his claws sinking into her breast until, with a final scream of agony, Cené awoke.

* * * * *

Bolden glanced at his solar receiver, noted the full charge and lack of messages, then turned and watched in disgust as the briding party swept down upon the unsuspecting village. He'd thrown in with this motley band of savages more out of boredom than need, but this vicious attack of theirs was way over the top.

Two years...it had been almost two years now, since his starship had been caught in some sort of space storm, tossed into this unfamiliar solar system, the craft too badly damaged to maintain life. None of the others in the small crew had survived. He accepted the fact that pure luck and the grace of the Mother had allowed him to access the only working rescue pod and make it to the planet's surface once he realized his friends were gone. He still didn't have a clue where he was, what sun warmed this planet.

Hell, he still didn't even know what this world was called. When he asked any of the indigenous population the name of the planet, they looked at him like he was nuts. "She has no name. She just is," was the best answer he could get.

She who?

At this point, it didn't matter who these people were. He just wanted to go home, to see Earth again, and Mirat, to ease his parents' worry over the loss of their only son. As if that was ever going to happen. At least these humanoids had accepted him without too much difficulty. They'd been curious about his alien features, but appeared too dull and disinterested to be judgmental.

He'd ignored questioning glances his entire life. One of very few inter-special children born of Earth humans and Miratan lions, he accepted the fact he combined the best of both species—he was irrefutably male, with facial characteristics and the smooth skin of his mother's human race, the thick mane, retractable claws and long, rough, feline tongue of his father's people.

As a small kit, he'd wished he had a tail like Garan's—he'd settled for the physical strength and massive size of a lion in his prime. At least the aboriginals he traveled with had been greatly impressed. He bit back a chuckle, recalling the first time any of them had seen him without his loincloth.

He'd often wished they were more interesting companions, but after almost two years on this Mother-forsaken planet, he'd been desperate for anything even remotely close to human companionship.

"Not this desperate," he muttered under his breath. The villagers didn't stand a chance. They fell quickly under the massive swords and battle axes wielded by the barbarians, their young women separated from family and friends and hauled off as prizes of battle.

Already, male bodies of the unarmed villagers littered the trampled ground as the remaining survivors scattered before the marauders. Screams of the captive women pierced the air. Triumphant shouts and curses added to the cacophony as briders fought over the spoils of war, roughly dragging the women from one man to the other.

Bolden held back on his pony, tugging at the corded reins even as the shaggy beast reared to join the brief battle. As much as he missed the warmth of a woman's arms, this was not the way Bold intended to find himself a mate.

No. Rape and savagery were not his way. He'd never needed force to bed a woman. Besides, he wouldn't need a mate here, not once he figured out how to get the hell off this damned primitive world and back to Earth. Lush and beautiful it might be, but it would never be home.

"Ho! Bolden!" Tarn, one of the younger warriors, called to him, pointing toward the sharp cliffs behind the village.

Bolden squinted against the sun's glare. There, near the top of the rugged white cliffs, he spotted her. Even from this distance he recognized a decidedly feminine figure scrambling up the narrow trail.

Tarn raised his sword and raced toward the base of the cliff. Seban and Jarde followed, their hunting cries echoing over the screams and shouts of a decidedly one-sided battle.

Disgusted by the behavior of the savages he'd ridden with, Bolden checked to be certain his receiver was well secured within his pack, then followed the three younger men. Possibly he could protect this one lone female from the lusts of the three warriors, maybe even help her escape.

Anything would be better than witnessing the rape of innocent women and girls.

Anything.

* * * * *

Bolden grinned as he studied the single footprint in the sand. This chase had become a welcome challenge, one that brought him awake each morning with a sense of adventure he'd not known for many turns of the strange blue-toned moon orbiting this planet.

Seban had been the first to drop out of the hunt. Hungry and disgusted, he'd turned back on the trail in spite of the teasing from his mates.

Tarn might have remained had Jarde not broken his wrist in a fall. The brothers had reluctantly quit the chase just two days ago, leaving the field clear for Bolden.

They'd glimpsed their quarry only once in all these days, a dark sprite of a female scampering just far enough ahead to keep her pursuers forever scrambling for sign. Now Bolden sensed her drawing close, knew she had finally decided to face him rather than continue trying to evade his pursuit.

He might have started out on this quest with the best of intentions. He should have gone back when his companions abandoned the chase, but Bold couldn't bear to give up when his goal was almost within reach. He'd felt more alive while pursuing this woodland creature these past few days than in all the long months since he'd been marooned on her world.

Alive, yet strangely on edge in the darkness of the forested plateau. His dreams had taken strange turns, the nights pulsing with sensation and need such as he'd not experienced before. He shifted his tumescent cock within his loincloth, marginally aware he'd remained at least semi-erect most of the time since entering this silent forest. There was little birdsong and not much chattering of small creatures or stirring of insects to distract him...only the pursuit of one dark feminine nymph through the thick undergrowth, and the residual effect of nights filled with hauntingly sensual images hovering just beyond his consciousness.

Crouching low on the narrow trail, Bolden's mind opened to the gloating thoughts of the woman perched just above him. She carried a dagger. He sensed the steel, knew it was spelled and warded though he didn't recognize the power behind the spells.

There was other energy as well. Something he'd perceived before on this world, a feeling of some subtle omniscience beyond the mere thoughts of the inhabitants, almost as if the planet itself were alive. If only Garan and Jenna were here! His sire was much better at reading the shifts and nuances of psychic power and there was no creature known to exist who was more psychically powerful than his birth mother, Jenna of Earth.

The image of his parents flashed through Bolden's memories, leaving a lingering sadness behind. Would he ever see his family again?

Bolden put his questions aside and feigned interest in the trail below. He sensed his quarry drawing near, and prayed to the Mother he would know the moment *before* she struck.

* * * * *

Cené grasped the knife tightly in her fist and crept silently along the narrow ledge of rock to a point just above her target. She struggled to control her labored breathing, clenching her teeth and inhaling through flared nostrils rather than gasping for the oxygen her lungs demanded.

Swallowing her fear, she dropped to her belly and stretched out along the sun-heated granite to peer over the slightly raised edge of rock. She automatically fondled her blessing bag, tied about her throat.

Filled at her birth by a shaman of the village, the contents were known only to that holy man, dead these past nine years. Cené had not opened the bag. She would not dream of such a sacrilegious act.

The contents of the blessing bag could only be shared with her one true mate, her lifemate, should she choose one. Shared, and then added to, as her mate placed a sacred item of his choice within the pouch and tied it around his own neck.

Until that time it would keep her safe.

Safe! Ha...! How safe could a female be, alone in the Dream Forest, pursued by a randy male twice the size of any normal man?

Cené closed her eyes. *Goddess, I beg you, give me strength.* Aware of a subtle shift in her energy levels, she silently gave thanks to the Lady before continuing to inch toward the edge of the cliff.

There! Her quarry, hidden by the outcropping until now, balanced motionlessly on hands and feet as if to leap from the rock below hers, a huge predator searching the narrow trail beneath his perch, awaiting his prey.

If he only knew. Cené almost laughed aloud at her own audacity. Hidden just above him, she fought a growing desire to stand up and shout *Here I am, you fool! Catch me if you can!*

His prey had become predator, his victim, slight and feminine though she might be, empowered by the warded steel blade grasped in her hand and the blessing bag tied about her throat.

He'd trailed her through the Dream Forest for days now, his tenacious presence a constant threat to her freedom, pursuing her by day, ruling her dreams with passion and fear by night.

He'd traveled with a small band at first, finally pressing on alone when the others had gone back. She must admire his persistence, if nothing else.

She'd been aware of his quest from the beginning, from the day almost half a moon ago when the vicious band of seasoned warriors raided her village.

Luckily, she'd been on her vision quest to the Dream Forest, the monthly journey taken by the single women of the village when their menses was upon them. Closest to the Goddess at that time of the month, it had always, in the past, been a time of peace and renewal.

Cené's dreams had been anything but peaceful. She'd started back early, wanting to ask the village shaman for a dream speaking, when suddenly, she'd heard them—shouts and screams, the strangled cries of battle. She'd raced down the narrow trail, almost reaching the village before she realized the nature of the attack.

Briders! The bride-hunting party was small but well armed. The men of her village hadn't stood a chance. In fact, from what Cené could tell from her hiding place on the trail, they'd been naught but cowards, practically throwing the young virgins at their huge adversaries.

Cené would not be the spoils of war. Her goddess gave the power of choice over to the woman. The thought of being taken forcibly by some barbarian had leant wings to her feet. She'd quickly scrambled back up the face of the cliff.

She'd almost made it. Almost, until the warriors spotted her. A shout had gone up. Those men without a woman thrown across the saddle had left their ponies and pursued Cené on foot.

Of the four, only this man remained. One relentless bastard among the entire band.

Fear had been her companion these past twelve days. Fear and loathing and the knowledge that if he caught her, she would never see her home again.

Not that there was much she'd miss. None of her family survived. She'd been alone for almost five years. She had few friends. The only good thing she could think of was the fact home was familiar.

Much as her persistent predator had become familiar.

Now, though, for the first time, Cené truly saw him. His shadowy presence had merely hinted at the man whose leonine majesty now stole the air from her lungs. Her breath caught in her throat—this was the same man who filled her dream time with passion—and terror.

Perched motionless on the trail below her, he reminded her of a sleek nightcat stalking its prey. His broad palms pressed flat against the hard packed earth, blunt fingers spread as if he prepared to leap. His toes dug into the ground, knees bent, one drawn forward almost to his chest.

Cené's gaze traveled over the taut muscles of his narrow hips and powerful thighs barely concealed by a simple loincloth. There was a leather traveling pack slung across his back. The long, tawny mane of wind-swept hair emphasized the breadth of his shoulders, the strength of his muscular arms.

His dark golden skin, burnished by sun and wind, glistened with the sweat of his pursuit. He turned slightly, and for the first time she saw the face of her enemy. Though his thick hair covered much of his profile, there could be no doubt. He was definitely the same man, the one sent by the Goddess to bedevil her dreams. She studied him closely—dark brows hiding his eyes, a strong jaw, the unexpected hint of a smile on full lips.

She touched her throat, felt the pulse where she'd dreamt his teeth had torn her flesh, and stifled an urge to flee, to escape deeper into the woods. Her fingers tightened on the leather-bound handle of her blade and she searched his face for answers.

Why did he follow? Why, when the others abandoned their useless pursuit, did he continue? Even more unsettling—why didn't she just slip away into the forest she knew better than any, slip away from this intriguing adversary who would take her freedom, her life, her very soul?

Caught between desire and fear, Cené hesitated a moment too long.

Suddenly, the man pushed up with those broad hands and sinewy arms, rising to his feet in a single, catlike leap to face her. In that one, brief moment, caught in the light of his amber eyes, Cené knew the battle was all but lost.

Chapter Two

She had expected rape. He'd merely tied her hands and bound her to a tree with enough rope that she could stand or sit, or lie on the bed of soft boughs and mosses he left for her.

He would beat her.

Instead, he offered water from his flask and a stick of dried meat for her to chew on.

She refused both, then salivated with hunger while he prepared his simple meal and ate alone.

He finished eating, then offered her a bowl of the food he'd cooked. She turned her head aside, feeling like an utter fool, but not certain how to accept gracefully.

Night fell quickly. The fire crackled, close enough to hint at warmth, far enough away to leave her chilled and shivering. The lingering scent of the spicy stew made her mouth water and her stomach grumble in protest.

She watched him through half-lidded eyes, feigning sleep while her captor moved silently about their camp. Catlike, he moved with a graceful silence and economy of motion that fascinated Cené. He ate sparingly, cleaned his utensils in a small pot of water by the fire, then quickly bathed his gleaming body in the rushing stream near the campsite.

She continued watching as unobtrusively as possible while he carefully dried himself with a soft looking cloth he took from his pack, standing tall and proud in the flickering light of the fire. With his back to her, Cené noticed his body was shaped differently than that of the men of her village, different even from the barbarians who tended toward a swarthy, stocky build.

This man stood tall and lean, his shoulders broad and thighs heavily muscled, hips narrow and buttocks taut. His hair grew thick, the color of old bronze, brushed back from his high-swept forehead to fall in thick tangles over his back and shoulders. A narrow ridge of hair followed his backbone, then faded away above his buttocks. Lean muscles rippled across his back with each movement he made.

His pale golden skin fascinated her.

The image of their bodies pressed together suddenly, unexpectedly, filled her mind. Her skin as dark as night, his the color of autumn grasses.

Before she had time to consider this strange direction to her thoughts, he turned slowly in her direction. Cené barely held back a startled gasp.

What form of man was he?

Expecting his manhood to hang down between his legs, Cené was shocked to see his held close against his belly, encased in a soft furred pouch that seemed to grow right out of his groin. His balls hung below, similar but still different from men she'd seen. A thick pelt of bronze fur covered his entire genital area, followed a line to his belly then spread out over his chest. She found the pattern oddly seductive, unusual. She frowned, wondering what tribe he might have come from, wondering why she'd not heard of his kind before.

Though yet untried, Cené was not innocent to the shape and size of men. *Normal men.* This man was unlike any she'd seen before. She studied him, especially fascinated by his unusual cock. Everyone knew how a man should look.

Suddenly, Cené realized she'd been staring at him much too long.

She raised her eyes and shivered.

The man was looking directly at her.

She did not bow her head. No, Cené would not bow to any man. She stared back at him, acknowledging him as her captor.

Slowly, as if with respect, he nodded in her direction, covered himself with his loincloth, then knelt beside the fire.

What manner of man was this?

* * * * *

Bolden stared into the leaping flames, his nightly prayer for rescue running through his head. Now, after so many months on this world, the words were as familiar as his own name.

Bless the Mother. I, Bolden of two worlds, son of Garan a lion of Mirat, child of Jenna, a human of Earth, thank the Mother for saving me, for giving me succor on this world. I ask for your forgiveness of past sins. I ask for your blessing. I ask for your grace on those who were lost. I ask for rescue, that I might return to my home.

Home. He'd learned not to dwell on thoughts of home, whether it be the mountains and valleys of Earth or the golden savannas of Mirat. Neither world held all of his soul—both held a piece of his heart.

Just as well, he thought. Just as well there was no one waiting for him to return, no kit crying for its father, no wife bemoaning her empty bed. Only his parents. Garan and Jenna must be heartsick, but with all traces of his ship blown to smithereens in the cluttered orbit of this planet, there would be nothing to tempt them to search for their son on this Mother-forsaken rock.

His shoulders slumped briefly before he caught himself. No lion of Mirat ever gave up. No man of Earth would submit to despair. He shrugged away the sadness with a wry grin. As a creature of two worlds, he had the weight of much history resting upon his shoulders.

Bolden studied his captive through the flickering light of the fire. Dressed in a short leather shift, she could be a tiny dark elf for all the size to her. Barely five feet tall with close cropped, black hair and emerald eyes filling her heart-shaped face, she had the look of a child but the attitude and strength of a woman his own age.

Her skin was black. Not the chocolate brown called *black* on his mother's home world, but black as a shard of obsidian or a starless sky, more like the sleek panther race of Mirat, but smooth, essentially hairless. When he'd bound her, Bold had fought an almost visceral need to touch her skin, to go beyond the brief contact he allowed himself as he knotted the ropes about her slender wrists.

She'd felt like satin. Skin so smooth, so silky, he'd curled his fingers against his palms to keep from stroking the length of her arm.

The people of this strange world appeared every bit as human in appearance as his mother's people. They came in many hues and shades, but his captive was the first he'd seen with skin so dark.

Or with eyes so green. He looked up, well aware she watched him study her. Her emerald eyes met his, unflinching, steady. He sensed her curiosity, the bundle of questions hovering behind the wide set eyes.

Did she know he could see into her mind, should he choose that path? Searching another's thoughts without permission was forbidden, but rules of behavior were easily put aside when one was lost and alone.

Not so alone. She wants you. Her body is ripe for yours.

What? Bolden tilted his head and listened to the silence. The voice, soft and seductive, had flitted through his mind in less than a heartbeat, though the message remained strong and clear.

It hadn't come from his captive. Who spoke to him, tantalized him with possibilities?

It had been well over two years. Too long for a man to go without a woman, but none on this planet had attracted him. For that matter, there'd been few on Earth he'd been close to, other than his flight school roommate, and theirs had been merely an affair of convenience.

He studied his captive with a new eye. She sat now, her back against the tree, and stared directly at him, her gaze unflinching, her full lips shining and ripe for his kiss. Without conscious volition, he focused on the dampness where her tongue had recently swept across her blood red, full lower lip. Firelight glinted briefly, then cast her face once more in shadow.

Her breasts were high and firm beneath her shift, her body, on casual inspection, even more humanoid than his own. Ever aware of his leonine heritage, Bolden wondered if she found him at all attractive or if the look of the beast frightened her.

The voice caressed his thoughts once more.

She's wet. Hot, wet and wanting, waiting for you to give her a sign. Why do you delay?

Bold shook his head, dislodging the intrusive yet seductive words. He glanced around the campsite, wondering who spoke to him, seduced him. Even more important, was the voice right? Did his captive want him? Was that a look of seduction, or mere curiosity? Was she afraid of him, of the beast in him? The questions scattered when she took a deep breath, raising her breasts higher, parting her lips on a sigh. With a silent prayer for forgiveness, Bolden dropped his shields and let his mind find hers.

His first tentative foray into her thoughts startled him. This was not the mind of a dull primitive. She was nothing at all like the men he'd ridden with. Instead, she practically sparkled with intelligence. Bolden sensed her fear, but even stronger, her curiosity sparked with need. Her exact thoughts were foreign to him, so he searched the part of her mind where language resided and learned her words, a complex language well beyond that of the savages he'd met so far on this strange world. Her vocabulary was extensive and highly evolved.

Entering another's thoughts without invitation went against all he believed. Throwing another quick prayer to the Mother for forgiveness, Bolden silently greeted his captive, allowing her the option of asking him to leave.

He knew the moment she sensed him in her mind. Her eyes widened, frightened at first, then narrowed in concentration. She leaned forward, lips slightly parted in wonder. Obviously no longer so afraid of him, she stared long and hard at his face.

He felt her attempt at contact, her timid venture into his mind with her own untried thoughts. Bolden opened to her, stepping closer to make the contact that much easier. He knelt down and touched her temples with his huge hands, staring at them as if, by wishing it, he could make his leonine paws with their retractable claws less threatening.

She accepted his touch without recoiling. He sensed her fascination with his alien appearance.

Once she spoke aloud, said the words so that he would understand their correct pronunciation and sound, they would be able to communicate verbally. He attempted to tell her as much with his mind.

She didn't even hesitate. "You mean me no harm?" Her voice was soft, the language lilting, almost musical, but he understood her words.

"No harm." He swept his hand very lightly along the side of her face, unwilling to break even that small physical contact. She didn't flinch at his caress, but her eyes remained wary.

"You have pursued me into the Dream Forest. Why?"

"At first for sport," he answered honestly. "Then to protect you from my companions. I had much respect for your tenacity, your ability to elude us. I did not want you to fail."

"Yet you have tied me, taken my freedom?"

Bolden studied her a moment, her skin like black velvet, her eyes as green as spring grass, and shook his head. "I was afraid of losing you." He chuckled, still feeling the effects of the challenging pursuit through this odd forest. "You intrigue me," he said, smiling. "I would know more about you."

"Untie me." It was as much a demand as a request.

Bold nodded and slipped the knots free from her wrists. She appeared surprised it was so easy to gain her freedom. Once more she studied him, her green eyes glinting in the firelight.

He clasped his fingers tightly into a fist, so strong was the need to touch her skin, to stroke the fine line of her jaw. Even on his knees he towered over her, but for some reason felt almost childlike beside her, as if she knew all the secrets that had long been denied him.

Suddenly, she stood up and held her right hand to her chest. "I am Cené of the Katerí, a single woman empowered by the Goddess. I serve her and bow to no one but my Lady. We are in her forest, walking upon her sacred ground. I ask for her protection, that you not defile my virginity. Only the makáo may take me."

Makáo? "I'll not take any woman against her wishes." Bolden stood up, then bowed slightly to her, a woman half his size who was in all ways his captive. "I promise, I won't harm you." He grinned and reached out to tip her chin up. "That does not mean, however, that I won't do my best to seduce you."

Cené frowned, then smiled as if she finally understood his intent. "Ah, that of course is an entirely different matter." She stepped back, out of his reach. "I would eat now, then find my rest. The makáo await. We have come far into the Dream Forest and this is their haunt."

"What are these makáo you speak of?" Without asking again if she was hungry or not, Bolden reached for the pot he'd left on the fire and ladled some of his stew into a bowl for the woman.

She took the bowl from him with all the grace of an elfin queen, curled her legs beneath her and sat to eat. Holding her spoon like a baton, she jabbed the air in his direction. "They dwell here. Have you not met them in your dreams?"

Frowning, Bold allowed himself to delve into the disturbing dreams that had followed him through this forest. He'd been long without a woman, but these past few nights had been filled with sensual dreams of a most seductive nature.

"I've had dreams," he admitted, unwilling to disclose their content. He certainly wasn't going to tell this woman how he'd awakened the past few mornings, his loincloth sticky from his own ejaculate after erotic dreams such as he 'd never experienced in his life.

"Ah," she said, nodding and smiling. "As have I. You come in these dreams? You find the great pleasure?" She took another bite of her stew and smiled at him, obviously expecting Bolden to answer.

He coughed and turned his head. No way was he going to discuss wet dreams with a complete stranger, especially one beautiful enough to inspire a few on her own.

Her small hand found his wrist. Her eyes were somber, her lips unsmiling. "It is not a reason to be embarrassed. We are in her forest. She rules the passions, the makáo merely do her bidding. Tonight, when they come, do not fight them. Enjoy. As I intend to."

She finished up the last of the stew, then carried her bowl to the stream to wash it. She set the bowl near the fire and glanced over her shoulder at Bold. "I will not run away. I merely need a private moment."

Bold nodded his head as she slipped into the thick undergrowth downstream from their camp. She was gone for just a few minutes, but returned with her hair freshly washed and her tunic damp from her bath.

He added a few pieces of wood to the fire, then spread his one blanket out for Cené. "It is not necessary," she said, slowly stripping her tunic from her head, revealing the most perfect body Bolden could recall seeing in his thirty years' existence. "The nights are warm, and this is all the bedding I will need."

Bold choked back a groan and closed his eyes. He could still see her against the darkness behind his lids. He clenched his fists so tightly his extended claws dug into his palms. The smooth line of her buttocks, the pear-shaped curve to her breasts, her nipples the color of dark cherries against black velvet. He'd barely glimpsed the pouting lips between her thighs, partially hidden in a nest of black curls. She'd been a deep red there, as well. Would she taste as sweet as the cherries she reminded him of?

Unable to completely stifle the groan that forced itself from his throat, Bold stretched out on his own blanket and turned his back on Cené. His balls ached and his cock throbbed, swollen well beyond the covering of his foreskin. Thank the Mother he'd at least put his loincloth back on.

Did the woman have any idea what the sight of her naked body did to a man? Breaking his rules once again, Bolden briefly searched her mind.

Damn it all! Somehow, the little vixen had already learned how to throw up a shield to protect her thoughts.

Probing her mind, he met nothing but static and the faintest hint of laughter.

Chapter Three

The dream was clearer tonight, the images of the dozen or so women of various sizes surrounding him so real he thought he might touch them. Bolden sighed and rolled over onto his back, stretching his arms and legs wide. He felt no fear—this was, after all, not a nightmare but a most seductive dream.

Pale and ethereal, they swarmed over his body, touching, kissing, stroking. A nip here, a lick there. He reached for one lithe beauty, but his arms were heavy, so heavy they felt glued to the damp earth.

He looked to his right and saw a tiny woman, no larger than a house cat, straddling his arm. Another clasped her thighs around his left wrist. He felt the moisture between her legs as she pleasured herself against his arm, so his dream self curled his fingers as far as he could to touch her smooth backside.

Before he could fully appreciate how good she felt, small hands tugged at the tie holding his loincloth in place, then pushed the garment aside. Warm lips brushed over his cock, long hair swept across his thighs. He tilted his chin to see what imaginary being suckled him and grinned. This woman was larger, almost as big as Cené, but as pale as Cené was dark. She licked and sucked his cock, taking all of him into her mouth, swallowing him completely until her teeth scraped the base.

She held him there a moment, then her lips slipped along his shaft. He felt her tongue press solidly against the back side of his cock and her cheeks hollowed with the force of her suckling.

Closing his eyes against the pleasure, Bold slowly raised his hips as she found her rhythm with him. His buttocks came down on the palms of two smooth hands, another set of warm lips found his balls and an agile tongue explored his sac.

More fingers rubbed his thighs, stroked his chest. Hands squeezed his buttocks and fingers found their way to his ass, softly penetrating him. He tried to open his eyes again, but this was a dream and now they were so heavy he could no longer lift the lids. Somehow, he felt he needn't know who pleasured him, only that he felt pleasure.

Lips plucked at his nipples, followed by the sharp pinch of teeth. More hands stroked him. He tried to raise his hips as the mouth suckling his cock drew him deeper, harder than before. He opened his mouth to draw in a breath of air and a breast teased his lips. The nipple tasted sweet. He imagined Cené's, cherry red and swollen with desire, and clamped his teeth around it, stroking the tip with his tongue.

No part of his body was left untouched, no opening unfilled. Fingers and lips, teeth and tongues—all were employed to bring him pleasure. The dreamlike quality persisted. Bolden tried once more to open his eyes, attempted to force himself awake, but the sensations increased, the tactile bombardment of his senses grew more intense, his need greater.

Gasping, feeling the tight coil in his gut building to a point of no return, yet unable to move so much as an eyelash, he suddenly remembered Cené's strange comment from the night before—*Tonight, when they come, do not fight them. Enjoy. As I intend to.*

What had she called them? *Makáo?*

This wasn't a dream!

Reaching beyond sensation, Bold drew on the power of both his parents—the physical strength of his father, the psychic mastery of his mother. He called out to the Mother of all, his silent shout commanding the creatures pleasuring him to be gone.

He sensed it, then, the deep burst of feminine anger reacting to his order. Not the makáo. No, they simply disappeared, leaving his body thrumming with unspent passion, his cock hard and throbbing, his balls aching. The anger was something more, something almost visceral — as if it belonged to the air he breathed and the dirt his body sprawled upon.

He lay there a moment, gasping, willing his raging libido under control. His eyes opened easily, now, and the first thing he noticed was his loincloth, untied and hanging loosely from one thigh. He knew it had been securely tied when he went to sleep.

The fire had burned down so that only coals glimmered under the starlit sky. There was no sound but the deep rasp of his own breath, echoing in his ears...the rasp of his breath and the soft, lush moans coming from the far side of the fire pit.

Bolden raised himself groggily up on one elbow and blinked slowly, adjusting his cat's eyes to the darkness of night. Cené writhed and twisted upon her wrinkled tunic, her hips arching to the touch of unseen hands, her nipples an even deeper red than they'd been the night before. Like Bold had been earlier, her arms and legs were spread wide apart.

Though he saw no one, Bolden sensed the makáo, knew they pleasured Cené, swarming over her body just as they had taken him. Somehow, he had to...

No. What had Cené said the night before? *Enjoy. As I intend to.*

He clenched his hands. He had no right to interfere. This was Cené's world, her culture...her pleasure. She hadn't been afraid of the makáo. No, she'd described them with a sense of anticipation. She wanted this!

The pledge of all who searched the stars echoed bitterly in Bolden's heart — *our mission is to study, not to change. To learn, not to teach. To observe, not to involve.*

Like Sander before him, the Miratan lion who'd crashed to Earth and been the catalyst of rebellion against the corrupt World Federation, Bolden had unwillingly become a part of this new world.

That didn't mean he had to like it. It did mean, however, that whenever possible he must honor his pledge. He retied his loincloth, stretching it over his raging erection and moved closer to Cené, prepared to help her should she need him.

Right. She certainly didn't appear to need anything from Bold. A purely carnal smile twisted her mouth. Her tongue darted out to lick the lush fullness of her lower lip and Bolden felt his balls contract. Her fingers clenched, her hips twisted, then began a rhythmic up and down motion, as she fucked her unseen lover. Her pussy lips glistened, deep red and pouting, the fluid covering her inner thighs, thick, inviting him.

Bold groaned. His cock was hard as steel, his balls drawn tight between his legs. Hardly aware he was even touching himself, he raised up on his knees and untied his loincloth, then wrapped his fist around his cock and stroked in time with Cené's undulating hips.

She moaned. Her stomach rippled, her buttocks lifted off the ground. She held the arch, fingers digging into the damp earth, knees spread wide, an offering of pulsing flesh and streaming fluids. Suddenly, she lifted her hips even higher, her mouth opening in a silent scream.

Writhing now, hips swaying against an invisible lover, head thrown back, she climaxed. Virgin or not, her unrestrained orgasm, the pure animal eroticism of the moment stunned Bold, took his breath and left him with an ache in his gut like he'd never felt before.

He had to touch her, had to taste her, he...he couldn't. Could not break his pledge.

His hand moved faster on his cock. Cené wasn't through. Her breath was choppy now, her hips rising and falling faster, as if keeping time with Bold's right hand. The fingers on his left hand practically trembled with the need to delve between her legs, to bury themselves deep inside her and experience the clenching contractions of her orgasm.

Instead he grabbed his balls, squeezing and rubbing them in counterpoint to each stroke along his cock. Kneeling beside Cené, watching her sleek body writhe and twist beneath an unseen lover, Bold lost himself in the erotic sensations created by his own hands and the vision before him.

Cené's chest trembled with each ragged breath, her fingers grasped frantically at the soft earth at either side of her hips. Her eyes were still tightly shut but her legs spread even wider, as if now she took a lover almost too large for her small body. She grunted, held very still as if adjusting to size, then sighed. A hedonistic smile tilted the corner of her lips as she once again caught the rhythm.

Lost in his own haze of sensation, his hands pumping furiously, Bold opened his mind to her thoughts. There were no shields now to hold him out.

Neither were there swarming masses of horny little men pleasuring Cené, as Bold had imagined.

Only one. One very large, very male lover. The makáo between her legs, the creature bringing Cené once more to explosive orgasm, was an identical copy of Bolden.

Drawn too far into lust to feel even shock, trapped in Cené's sexual explosion, Bold felt every ripple and spasm of her climax, felt his lungs burn as her scream ripped from her throat, shuddered as she crested once, then again even higher...he felt her vaginal muscles clenching, seizing the cock of his double, the makáo that had given her pleasure. Felt his own explosive climax as he pumped his cock, not into her slick, wet heat, but into the callused fist of his own Mother-be-damned hand.

Legs quivering, balls practically exploding, Bolden came, his ejaculate splattering all over Cené's velvety black breasts, his milky sperm a desecration of her dark beauty.

Faintly, as much in his head as in the silent air around him, Bold heard the tinkling, derisive peal of feminine laughter. He lacked the strength to even raise his head to search for the source of the sound. Instead, he leaned forward, catching himself with his hands pressed to his trembling thighs, the air rasping from his throat.

Humiliated beyond belief, he couldn't even look at what he'd done to Cené. Somehow, he had to clean his seed off her breasts without waking her, clean her off and hope like hell she didn't have a clue what disgusting thing he'd just done to her.

Clenching his teeth, Bold willed his ragged breathing to steady, brought his still raging libido under control, took a deep breath and opened his eyes.

Cené stared reproachfully back at him. "You?" she asked, her brows knit tightly together. "It was not the makáo?"

"Sort of. A little..." *Oh crap.* This was worse than anything he could imagine. "It took my form. It looked like me."

She didn't seem the least bit offended. In fact, if anything, she looked relieved. "Ah...I see. The makáo take the form of your desire. I desired you."

"What?" His voice cracked. He cleared his throat, trying to recall the women who had taken him. None had looked even remotely familiar. He only remembered breasts and lips, buttocks and soft thighs, tongues...all the things that gave him pleasure.

Suddenly Cené's admission, if that's what it was, settled into his brain. "Me? You desired me?"

She laughed and sat up, bracing her weight on her elbows. Only then did she seem to notice the globs of sperm on her breasts. "Only as a fantasy. I am yet a virgin. What's this?" She ran her finger through a white smear on her left nipple, then brought it to her nose and sniffed. "What is this stuff?"

Oh shit.

"I, um...lost control a bit."

"The makáo did not pleasure you?"

Bold shook his head. "No. Of course not. I stopped them. I felt as if they were doing it against my will, for someone else's pleasure. I didn't like it."

Now she looked offended. Cené drew herself into a sitting position. "Well of course it was for someone else's pleasure.

151

How else do you think the Goddess experiences passion? She must take it through the makáo. They are her breasts, her vulva, her cock. We are in her forest and that is the price of our passage. You must have angered her very much." She looked around almost fearfully. "I hope we'll still be safe." Her hand went to the little bag she wore, tied to a thong around her neck.

"Oh, I think your goddess found her pleasure." His cock still ached from his own hand. As embarrassing as it had been, to lose control like that, it had felt spectacular. This was truly a strange world.

He stood up and grabbed a handkerchief from his pack, dipped it in a cup of water warmed by the fire, and carried it back to Cené. "May I?" He held the cloth against her chest. She nodded, a wary expression in her eyes, as he carefully washed his sperm from her breasts, playing close attention to her deep red nipples.

They tightened and peaked at his soft caress, but he pretended to ignore Cené's reaction. Instead, he cleansed her entire chest, encircling both breasts with the soft cloth. She tipped her head back as he bathed her, thrust her breasts forward and closed her eyes.

"Your touch feels better than the makáo," she whispered. Her legs parted just a bit, enough that Bold caught a glimpse of her nether lips, the pouty vermilion flesh still swollen and glistening with moisture. Without thinking, he bent down and touched the very tip of his tongue to her mons, licking at the soft, springy curls.

She gasped, but instead of warning him off, she tilted her hips forward, silently asking for more. Emboldened, he stretched out between her legs and ran his tongue along the damp flesh, lapping gently at her sweet fluids. She tasted differently than the women of Earth, different as well from a Miratan lioness. Cené's essence was almost fruity, a sweet, addictive flavor that had Bold's cock immediately standing at attention once again.

He carefully slipped his rough tongue inside her pussy. The passage was tight, the muscles gripping at his tongue as he tasted her. She had claimed to be a virgin. He proved it with the tip of his tongue, teasing the taut barrier of intact flesh.

She moaned and arched her hips. Bolden quickly withdrew. He didn't want to risk breaking what she had so far managed to protect. How had the makáo bedded her? He'd seen the damned thing, Bold's doppelganger, drive his huge cock up between her legs, thrusting hard and fast as he brought her to climax.

Bold sat back on his heels. Cené raised her head, her disappointment obvious. "Why did you stop?"

"How can you still be a virgin?"

They both laughed, talking over one another. Bold stroked her thigh. "You're intact. How? I saw that thing take you."

"Ah, the makáo. He is all essence and thought, not real at all, other than what he can do for the Goddess. I feel him thrust his huge cock between my legs, but it isn't a real cock. You were not fucking me, yet that's the image we both saw, what I felt. All a fantasy. My feelings, though...my passion? That is real. That is what the Goddess wants. I give it freely."

She shrugged her shoulders, as if her explanation made perfect sense.

"If I were to bring you to orgasm, not your precious makáo, would your goddess feel that? Would she experience your passion?"

"I don't know." Cené glanced at him out of the corner of her eye. "You are certainly welcome to try, but only if you can do it without entering my passage. I save that for my lifemate."

"So long as you remain intact, I may do as I please?" Gazing over her perfect body, Bolden figured the possibilities for pleasure were endless.

Cené nodded. "I have never lain with a man. I have only been with the makáo on a few occasions. I would like to experience this passion with a real lover." She looked him over carefully, as if evaluating him. "I feel I can trust you, but the night is short and we have not yet slept. Tomorrow will be soon enough for passion."

Bold glanced down at his cock. The damned thing practically begged for a taste of Cené's passion. He willed it back to parade rest and regretfully moved away, to lie down on his blanket.

Cené might think the night was short, but Bolden imagined the few hours left would probably be some of the longest he'd ever spent.

Chapter Four

Her song awakened him. Dawn was but a hint on the horizon, the pale lavender sky practically lost behind the dense forest canopy. Cené's pure voice pulled Bolden from the most restful sleep he'd experienced in many long nights.

There'd been no dreams — merely sweet oblivion once he'd reached his blanket. He'd fully expected a night of wanting and frustration. Instead he felt rested and refreshed.

He strained to hear the words and realized Cené was singing a prayer to her goddess, a prayer of supplication. She was asking the goddess to accept their offering — the gift of their passion.

He bolted upright. It was time to end that particular idea. No way was he going to have sex for some voyeuristic goddess. He blinked against the pale dawn, his mind awash in Cené's sweet song. Awake, now, reason intervened. Bolden sat, shoulders hunched, and accepted the fact that Cené's goddess was very real to her. Plus, he was the one who had brought the idea up last night. Now was not the time, and this was not his place to intervene.

Instead, he spent a few moments checking his supplies and organizing his pack. The charge was down on his solar receiver, so he set it in full sunlight near the fire. He stared at it a moment, then flipped it open to check for messages. Of course, there were none. It would only receive from someone either orbiting very near this planet, or with a direct link. No one had a clue where he was, so there was no way to establish a link. They'd been way off course when the ship failed, so there was no reason for anyone to look for him here.

He wasn't sure why he continued to look for the message that never showed up. It hadn't happened in the past two years. He didn't really expect it to happen now. Still, he kept the damned receiver fully charged, if only to maintain the saved files on it. If he ever was rescued, he had a complete star map of this section of the galaxy.

If nothing else, he'd be able to make a detailed report for his Quest, even find his way back to this world...as if he'd have any reason to want to return to this Mother forsaken lump of rock.

Cené's song drifted in the still morning air. Bold had to admit, the planet looked a lot better today than it had at any time over the past couple years.

He bathed as unobtrusively as possible, loathe to disturb the hypnotic melody echoing in the quiet forest. As he scrubbed himself clean, he watched Cené where she knelt on a large, flat stone near a small waterfall. Her ebony body, darker even than the shadows, swayed with the rhythm of her song. Her only adornment was the small leather pouch she wore hanging from her neck.

Her hands lifted high in worship, her eyes closed. Her voice flowed as gently as the stream, crossing more than one octave in a song that was more hymn than melody, hypnotic in its spiritual strength and beauty.

Bold felt the timbre clear to his core, the deep resonance when she found the lowest notes, the sharp sense of need when she softly touched the highest, moving almost beyond his range of hearing at both ends of the scale. He dried himself as he watched her, wrapped his loincloth around his hips, then stoked the fire to heat water for their morning meal. When all was done, he sat back on his blanket, immersing himself in Cené's song of prayer.

The tempo suddenly changed, increasing as the morning light found Cené. Still kneeling, she stroked her sides with her fingers spread wide, rubbed her breasts, pinched at her nipples. Singing her words strong and true, her song now gloried in her own body, her own needs.

Bolden leaned forward, drawn to the erotic scene before him. Cené's head tilted back as one slim hand plucked at her nipple and the other slipped along her smooth belly, the fingers disappearing through the tuft of tightly curled black hair into the soft tissues between her widely spread legs.

Still she sang on, but her voice grew choppy, the words beginning to lose form as she stroked herself. Bold realized he'd moved closer to her, was suddenly directly in front of her, kneeling almost near enough to touch. Something held him back, some unusual power kept him rooted to the soft earth before Cené's stage of stone.

It truly was a stage. The mote-filled beam of morning sunlight broke through the leaves and caught her sensual twist and sway full in its glow as she pleasured herself. Her song cascaded down the scale, then drifted into a series of moans and soft grunts. Her back arched so that her head almost touched her heels.

She raised and lowered her hips in rhythm with her fingers, now fluttering across the crimson lips, then rolling her protruding clit. From Bolden's viewpoint, it appeared her thighs and waist were controlled by the strings of a puppet master, her long fingers playing a sensual rhythm over her most sensitive tissues.

Bold realized his own short breaths matched her rhythm. His cock strained against his loincloth, but the compulsion he'd felt last night to relieve his own need was missing. Instead, he reveled in the lush sensations of throbbing cock, aching balls— found strength in the power he kept barely checked.

Suddenly, Cené's fingers tightened around her swollen clit and stayed there. The other hand pinched her brilliant red nipple, tugging it to a hard point. She cried out, a long, keening wail that raised the hair on the back of Bold's neck. His breath caught in his throat as he watched her orgasm, shared the wave of her sensual pleasure with each beat of his heart, each pulse of her swollen tissues, spread before him as if for his pleasure as much as hers.

Suddenly her fingers went into motion again, sliding back and forth over her clit and streaming labia. A second climax lifted her, pulled a scream from between her parted lips. This too, Bold felt, from each staccato thrust of her hips to each choking cry torn from her throat.

Still, he didn't come. His cock throbbed, his balls practically twisted with wanting, but he held his hands fisted at his sides, his attention totally riveted on Cené.

She lay slowly back, knees bent and pressed to the ground, her unbelievably limber body stretching backwards like a contortionist's, so that her sleek buttocks touched the stone between her heels, her shoulders pressed against the heated rock. Slowly, her left hand slipped from her pussy, her fingers covered with her juices.

The restraints holding Bolden in place seemed to fall away. He leaned closer to Cené, took her hand in his and raised her fingers to his lips. While she watched through half lidded eyes, he carefully licked her syrup from her fingers. Sweet, addictive, the taste filled his senses. He took great care, sweeping his long tongue between each slim finger, trailing it along her wrist, then suckling her middle finger between his lips in a parody of fucking.

More fluid gushed from between her legs. As if caught in a dream, Bold leaned forward and lapped like a kitten at a bowl of cream, drinking in her sweet flavors, carefully bathing the swollen tissues with his long tongue.

Her fingers clutched at his thick mane, weakly tangling in the thick hair falling across his shoulders. He thought she might push him away, but instead she pulled him closer, pulled his face down tightly between her widely spread thighs.

He reached underneath and lifted her buttocks with his hands, careful to keep his nails sheathed. She raised her hips even more and slowly straightened her legs out from under her, stretching them along either side of Bold, raising up to give him greater access to her swollen pussy.

He laved her with his tongue, worshipping her satiny skin, nipping and tasting as he bathed her from ankles to belly, breasts to throat and back between her legs.

He could tell when her arousal began to grow, when she suddenly went from sated to wanting. Her labia thickened, her small clitoris protruded from its protective sheath. She bucked beneath him, begging him silently with each thrust of her hips, each soft moan that slipped between her parted lips. He felt her need grow beneath his hot tongue, grow until it spilled out in a mental cry and filled Bold's mind with her hot desire.

She wanted him, wanted him deep inside her virgin passage, wanted the hot thrust of his cock tearing through that thin membrane she'd guarded so carefully for all her life.

Hands grasping at his thick mane, lips pleading incoherently, she practically wept the words. Bold ignored her, girding himself against her pleas, well aware her goddess ruled her passions. He would give her release, but he would not take something Cené was not ready to give of her own free will.

Her true life's mate was to receive that gift. Not an alien castaway whose strongest wish was to leave this planet and all it contained, leave this lost and primitive world in an unknown part of space and find his way home once again.

Anger drove him, anger and loss and the fear he might never see Earth again, might never walk the golden plains of Mirat. Bolden grabbed her swollen nipples between his fingers, twisting and tugging, pinching them into hard, vermilion points. He thrust inside her streaming pussy with his tongue, touching but not sundering the fragile barricade.

When she arched against his mouth, attempting to force his entrance, he withdrew and concentrated on her clitoris, swollen and pulsing free of its protective sheath, large enough now in her excited state for him to wrap his sandpapery tongue around it, to suckle on her clit and drag it across his sharp canines.

Cené screamed, her body stiffened. She thrust her vulva hard against his mouth. Lapping, licking, suckling her sweet release, Bold took her over the edge. He sat back on his heels, dragged Cené's hips up to his mouth and lifted her legs over his shoulders. Without letting up his sensual attack, he brought her back to an even higher peak, his tongue sweeping between her legs, licking across her firm buttocks, tracing the crease from backbone to belly, over and over as she cried out and shuddered against him.

She went completely limp, her only response left, the residual quivering tremors against Bold's tongue where it pressed between her hot, wet folds.

More. I want to feel more.

Bold raised his head, blinking himself back from the blinding haze of lust that consumed him. He stared hard at Cené. Her eyes were tightly shut, her fingers curled into claws and grasping at nothing. Her body was slack, her legs hung loosely over his upper arms so that her pussy was completely visible, pulsing dark red in the aftermath of orgasm, the copious fluid slick and shining on her inner thighs. She appeared totally sated. He knew her dark skin hid multiple scratches from his abrasive tongue. He'd not meant to be so rough, never intended to allow passion to rule him.

Please. More. I need more.

Bold opened his mind, ignoring his throbbing cock, the pain in his groin, the tight agony in his balls. Opened his mind to the commanding yet obviously feminine voice that was not Cené's.

Who are you? What do you want?

I am...

He sensed the hesitation behind the words, as if whoever said them hadn't really considered exactly who or what they were.

I am...everything. I am the rocks you walk upon, the trees that shade you, the water in the creek that satisfies your thirst. I am this world. I have always been...since time began, I have existed, though not always so alone. Now, I am always alone. I do not speak to my people like this, cannot make them understand my true words. Nor do I feel such passion, such a sense of being, not even with the makáo. I want...more. I must feel...more. I hunger for communion...please, I have never been able to make myself understood...except to you. What form of man are you?

Praise the Mother...the voice Bold had heard since entering this strange forest finally made sense. It was Cené's goddess. Bold's breath caught in his throat. Cené's goddess *was* her world.

This lush but primitive planet was sentient.

* * * * *

Cené felt as if she were swimming from the bottom of a dark pool, swimming as hard as she could, struggling to find the surface. She wanted to open her eyes, to see how far she still had to go, but it took so much effort, so much of the strength she needed to fight her way to the top.

Finally, she drew a great gasp of air and realized she'd not been underwater at all, merely somehow away from her body, a body that still pulsed and throbbed with the most unbelievable sensations she'd ever experienced.

Whatever Bolden had done to her, she wanted again. If she hadn't felt so lethargic, Cené might have laughed aloud. Oh Goddess, yes, she definitely wanted to do that again. Her pussy still throbbed and pulsed, her breasts tingled, both nipples ached, her buttocks and vulva stung with the most exquisite abrasions from his even more exquisite tongue.

She must learn more about that tongue of his. Whatever tribe he hailed from...the thought drifted away. No, there couldn't be more like him or she would have heard. He was unique among men, of that she was certain.

Her body thrummed, sated yet still filled with desire. She felt wanton and sensual and very feminine. If only her eyes would obey. She quit fighting the need to open them, concentrating instead on the odd buzzing in her head, as if voices spoke just beyond her reach in that most unusual mindspeak Bolden had shown her.

Bolden. Such an unusual man. Such an *amazing,* unusual man. He still held her flat on her back, her legs spread wide, draped wantonly across his broad arms, which meant all her feminine secrets were secret no longer.

She had no shame with this man. There could be no shame in what he made her feel. The Goddess certainly hadn't minded. Cené had felt her Lady's presence throughout her song, even stronger once Bolden joined her. One day, soon, maybe the Goddess would give her permission to take him inside, to finally break that fragile barrier she'd protected for so long.

Until that time, Cené figured she'd be quite satisfied with what Bolden could do to her.

What could she do for Bolden? Cené knew she wanted more even after finding the great pleasure, but what pleasure had Bolden found? She'd not felt his essence upon her belly this time.

Now when she tried to open her eyes, she found she once more controlled her lids. Blinking against the morning light, she smiled up at the huge man still holding her.

His gaze was unfocused, his mind obviously not on Cené. "Bolden? Are you all right?"

She shoved herself up on her elbows, then freed her legs from his light grasp. He turned her loose without acknowledging her presence. Instead, his brow wrinkled and the corner of his lip curled, as if he snarled.

For the first time, Cené noticed his canines, the eyeteeth longer, sharper. Again, she thought of the nightcats in the village. Semi-domesticated carnivores standing almost to her waist, they seemed to have much in common with this man. Then, just as suddenly, images of the dream returned. He'd torn her throat with those teeth. Torn her throat open and ripped her blessing bag away.

Wrapping her fingers tightly, protectively around the bag at her throat, Cené backed away, scooting across the sun heated rock where she could watch Bolden from a safer distance.

He sat, unmoving, obviously concentrating on something. Cené tried to enter his mind, much as he had hers, but she heard only that mild buzzing noise, nothing she could understand.

Well, she could be patient. She would wait for him. While she waited, she would watch him. She liked looking at him, studying him. His appearance pleased her. He was much like the men she had seen, but again, very much different. His hands, though they looked like the paws of a big cat, were capable of such amazing gentleness.

She sighed, thinking of what he had done to her with those amazing hands...and that tongue. *Dear Goddess*, would she ever get enough of that tongue? When he was through, she would pleasure Bolden, much as he had pleasured her. She must not fear him. He had shown her only kindness...kindness and much pleasure.

It was only fair.

With that thought comforting her, Cené sat back in the sun to wait. To wait, and to wonder what Bolden might want from her.

Chapter Five

He knew Cené was consumed by curiosity, but Bold had nothing left to share. His cock still pulsed, hot and swollen within his loincloth, but it no longer seemed of great importance. He must sleep, if only for a brief time. Sleep and try to understand what this world wanted of him. He crawled back to the campfire, now merely cold ashes in the morning sun, and lay down on his blanket.

Cené crept up beside him, as if to comfort him. He held his arm up and she snuggled close to his chest, lying very still against him. Soothed by her warmth, Bold closed his eyes and willed his mind and body to relax.

* * * * *

He walked in a dream that wasn't a dream, through a small village, even more primitive than Cené's, yet alive with activity. Women cooked over open pits outside their stone houses, children ran naked and free in the morning sun. Old men sat and smoked strange looking pipes made of bone that curled almost to the ground. A smoky haze hung in the air about them.

Cené walked beside Bolden, her bright blue leather tunic shimmering with each step. She held tightly to his arm, as if terrified of losing her grip on him, but she smiled bravely.

No one appeared to notice their passing. Though the village was unfamiliar, Bold realized he knew exactly where to go. With purposeful steps, he walked toward the largest building on the square, a huge edifice of white stone with large carved lions guarding the gates.

Lions, carved in stone, exactly like those he'd seen on Earth guarding the estates of the very wealthy, one vicious paw upraised, mouths wide with teeth gleaming and tongues curling. Lions that looked much as his father's people had once appeared, in their long-ago primitive beginnings.

Suddenly a scream broke the peaceful setting. A beautiful copper-skinned young woman, barely in her teens, ran past them. She cried and held her hands to her belly, stumbling as she ran. An older man, his face contorted with rage, pursued her. He held a thick leather strap in his hand.

Bold stepped forward to block his path, but the man passed directly through him, as if he were nothing more than mist. The man grabbed the sobbing girl, flailing her viciously about the face and shoulders with the strap, kicking her repeatedly in the abdomen and chest when she finally fell, barely conscious, to the ground.

Distraught, unable to affect what happened in the dream, Bold and Cené watched in horror as the man brutally beat the young woman. Barely moving, she no longer tried to avoid the blows.

A crowd gathered, but no one offered to help the girl. Unconscious now, her body lay still beneath the savage attack. Suddenly, a lanky teenaged boy broke through the group of onlookers and raced to the girl's side. He raised a knife in one hand as if to strike the older man.

The man turned, his rage apparent, his lust for blood obviously not satisfied. Screaming in rage, he swung a meaty fist toward the teen, who chose that moment to strike. The man's fist barely deflected the sharp blade. Instead of burying the knife in his target's heart, the boy sliced cleanly across the older man's throat.

Blood gushed from an opened artery, shooting out like a fountain, splattering across the stunned onlookers. Gurgling, a look of surprise wiping away the rage, the older man fell to his knees. He grabbed futilely at his gaping throat, held his hands out as if surprised at the blood, then fell forward over the body of the young woman.

Sobbing, the boy pushed him roughly away and gently lifted the girl. Carefully carrying her through the crowd, he marched with dogged steps to a stone bench beside a small well where he dampened the handkerchief he'd worn round his neck.

Holding her across his lap, he slowly and gently bathed her face, sobbing anew with each bruise he uncovered. Her lips were parted and still. No pulse beat at her throat.

Suddenly her body gave a long, ragged shudder, then went completely still. A look of horror crossed the young man's face as he stretched her out on the rock wall, parted her legs, reached beneath her bloodied tunic and drew forth a tiny, perfectly formed fetus.

Covered in blood, the babe was dead, the umbilical cord torn from its body, its skull shattered from the brutal beating. Holding his child, for there was no doubt in Bolden's mind this *was* the young man's son, the boy stood up and faced the silent crowd standing around them.

His voice was ragged but strong, the anger and tears evident in every word he spoke. "You allowed this to happen. You, the people who should have protected her, protected our child, you allowed this! You have brought Evil into this land. You and our Goddess have failed me. I curse you. Curse all of you. I beg the Goddess for forgiveness, but I curse her as well. She was the one who freed Evil. She is the one who damned us."

The crowd drew back. Fear quickened their pace and they quickly dispersed, stepping around the bloody corpse lying in the square, giving the body of the man who had once ruled their village no more than a passing glance as they scurried away.

The young man knelt beside the body of his beloved and placed the baby against her breast. He took the girl's lifeless hand in both of his and kissed her fingertips, sobbing quietly, whispering against her lips. "I will always love you, but our love on this plane has been denied. Please, wait for me."

He stood up and raised his fist to the heavens, shouting, his voice rich with anger and despair. "I curse you, Goddess! May you know pain. May you never find love, never, ever know the peace you have taken from us."

Weeping, he slammed his fist against his side. Lightning flashed. Thunder rolled in the distance, growing closer, louder. Clouds gathered, huge, boiling black clouds roiling and spreading at supernatural speed across the heavens.

Unafraid, the young man stood beside the body of his woman. A scream, inhuman, powerful, frightening yet filled with despair, split the heavens. The man, no longer an untried boy, raised his arms, a look of fierce determination on his face.

Even though he knew nothing in this realm could touch them, Bolden pulled Cené close against his side and stepped away from the well. They'd barely moved when a huge bolt of lightning exploded over the village square, just above the well. Shielding his eyes, Bolden grabbed Cené against his chest and turned away, protecting her.

When he looked back, the young man, the woman and the babe were gone. Only a smoking pit remained where the well had been, and water, foul and putrid, boiled and steamed within its depths.

What remained of the body of the older man, bones, burnt flesh and the remnants of clothing, smoked and sizzled on the cobblestones, but as Bolden and Cené watched, the clouds just as suddenly rolled away, the sun came out.

Birds sang close by.

Blinking, unsure exactly what they had just witnessed, Bolden led Cené away from the scene of misery and destruction. As they left the village, the ground began to shake beneath them—a rumbling, crackling noise echoed about the valley. Bolden looked back, just in time to see the large white stone building fall to the ground. Only the carved lions at the gate remained.

He grabbed Cené's hand and raced for the outskirts of the village, no longer quite so sure they would be safe. The buildings around them collapsed, the ground split, huge flares of flaming gasses burst forth.

Eyes tearing, lungs burning, Bolden and Cené finally reached the edge of the village, raced across a small clearing and on into the deep, green forest. Here the air was still, the sounds of destruction no longer audible.

Holding Cené in his arms, Bolden collapsed on the thick green carpet of moss and fell into a deep sleep.

✳ ✳ ✳ ✳ ✳

Cené's lips pressed against his chest were the first thing Bolden knew when he awoke. The pressure of her lips and the warmth of her small body snuggled close to his. The noonday sun was high overhead, but the air was cool and there was enough shade to keep them comfortable.

He lay there a moment, inhaling her sweet scent, recalling the dream that was obviously so much more. Did Cené share the same vision? He wanted to know, but was loathe to wake her.

Bold's stomach growled, a reminder they'd not eaten this morning. Cené raised her head, her short hair tousled and mussed from sleep, and smiled at him. She quickly frowned and pulled away.

"Did you...?"

"It wasn't a dream, was it?"

She stared at him a moment, shook her head and sat up. "I've long heard this story of the curse that locks our Goddess, in fact, our whole world, in misery. That's why she has the makáo. They are the only way she can experience the love denied her. Some say it's why our world doesn't prosper, because our Goddess is cursed. I've heard the story, but never experienced it quite so...graphically."

She stood up and held out a hand to Bold. He took it, surprised at her strength as she tugged him to his feet. When he finally stood, he towered over her.

"Your goddess spoke to me," he said. "I will admit, I didn't believe she was real, before. Then she spoke to me, and I understood." He spread his hands wide, encompassing everything around them. "She *is* your world, this goddess. Your world is the goddess. They're one, a single entity."

"I know." Cené smiled, obviously pleased he'd finally figured it out. "She is everywhere, everything. Omnipotent. That is the way of gods and goddesses everywhere, right?"

"Generally speaking." Bold figured Cené wouldn't catch his dry cynicism, but she surprised him, laughing.

"Well, our Goddess is special. Especially to me. The Lady feels close to me because I've long been one of her chosen, though I've never actually conversed with her. Still, she is always near. You say she speaks to you?" Cené tilted her head, as if in wonder, and smiled. "What does she say?"

Bold thought about the conversation he'd had with Cené's goddess, remembered the sadness he'd felt in her, the isolation. "She said she wants more...more passion, more communion. I think she wants to know what it's like to feel love again. To be human. I think your goddess is lonely."

Bold reached into his pack for dried meat and fruit, but he watched Cené for her reaction. Other than a thoughtful frown on her face, Cené merely grabbed the small pot and rinsed it in the stream. Quietly, they went about preparing a meal. Finally, after they'd eaten and cleaned up without speaking, Cené gestured to Bolden to join her by the creek.

"We must ask the Goddess exactly what she wants. Then, if it's in our power, we must give it to her."

"No," Bold said, shaking his head. The idea had been rambling around through his brain all morning long, even before they'd been given that most disturbing, graphic dream. "I've got a better idea. Not *give* it to her...trade her for it. There's something I want that she may be able to grant me. I would ask your goddess to help me go back to my home world. In return, I will try and give her what she wants."

Cené studied him for a brief moment then bowed her head. "Ah, now I understand. I wondered if you might be from somewhere far away. I had no idea you were actually from a different planet. You would not want to remain on a world so poor as ours. There is nothing to hold you here."

Bolden experienced her pain as if it were his own. He hardly knew Cené, yet he felt a bond to her stronger than with any woman he'd ever met. There was no question in his mind that he wanted to know her better. "I would take you with me," he said. "*If* I can ever go home." He reached out and lifted her chin, forcing her to look him in the eye. "I would not want to leave you."

"I know that," she said, with total conviction. "But I can't abandon my world. The Lady needs me." She turned away, breaking the physical contact. "That doesn't mean I can't be with you while you're here. It merely means that when you finally go, you will go alone."

Chapter Six

Cené sketched their location in the smooth mud near the creek. She marked an X for her village, drew a large, misshapen circle to denote the Dream Forest, then jabbed the stick into the center of the forest. "Somewhere, here in the very middle, is our Lady's temple. Generations ago, long before I was born and long before the curse, my people worshipped there, making a yearly pilgrimage to pay homage to our Goddess and to thank her for her blessings. Her temple is where the people could ask the Goddess for a favor. Nothing was beyond her power. If she was pleased with the offering, she would grant the petitioner's request. The old tales say ours was a peaceful planet, the people healthy and strong. I imagine their needs were not much. They had everything, then."

"You describe what my mother's people called the Garden of Eden. This may not be Paradise, but your world seems fine to me, now." Bold spread his hands wide. "Other than the briding party and a few small skirmishes I witnessed between tribes, it's a beautiful world."

"When I say peaceful, I mean that in every sense." Cené rocked back on her heels. "There was no war, no killing. That's why the father's murder of his own daughter and grandson was such an abomination. I don't know the story behind his act, why he felt such rage. Maybe the evil was even then breaking free. It had long been held prisoner in the Goddess's blessing bag."

"Her blessing bag?" Bold reached out and touched the small pouch hanging at Cené's throat. "Like yours?"

"Yes. Legend says, the Goddess found a man she wanted to take as her lifemate and she loved him with all her soul. When she pledged herself to him, he, as custom dictates, opened her blessing bag to add a sacred object of his own. Instead, he stole the precious gems he found there. The Goddess, realizing she had been duped, killed her beloved before they were ever intimate. She turned him into a small, black stone and placed him in the pouch to guard over him. He was Evil, but she wore him in the bag about her neck, controlling him. It is believed that, somehow, the bag was lost or stolen. He escaped from the Goddess's control, released by the power of the young lover's curse. Evil is still free, though he knows her power is greater than his and usually behaves himself. Still, we have all suffered ever since."

Bold shook his head. In many ways, her story paralleled the basic allegorical legends of every world he'd visited, including Earth and Mirat. He found it as difficult to accept this story as anything more than legend, yet Cené certainly believed. He couldn't deny the dream they had both experienced.

He stared a long moment at the rough map she had drawn in the mud. "Do you think you could find this temple? How far is it?"

"I don't know." She stood up and erased the drawing with her bare foot. "The Dream Forest is huge and I've heard it grows darker as you near the center. I've only been in a small part of it. This journey, as I ran from you and the other hunters, has taken me deeper into the forest than I've ever gone before." She looked around the small clearing and shrugged her shoulders. "We can always ask the Goddess to lead us to her, though she may ask for an offering from us first."

Cené smiled. Bold knew exactly what the Goddess would demand in return, the horny bitch, not that he wasn't all that willing to comply. The more he'd thought about it, the more he'd come to feel there was something invitingly erotic about sharing their passion with a third party, even though that party was the actual ground they walked on, the trees they sheltered under.

Now he knew this goddess actually existed, the thought of her taking part, if only vicariously, in their lovemaking had a certain prurient appeal. "How do we get her attention?" Laughing Bold grabbed up his pack and slung it over his shoulder. "Yell, 'hey, Goddess? You there?'"

Yes. I am here. I am always here.

"Shit." Bold glanced sideways at Cené. She blinked in surprise, grinned, then laughed aloud.

"Oh my," she said, shaking her head. "That seems to work. I heard her that time. I've never actually heard her speak before."

"We seek your temple, where I would ask you a favor. Will you show us the way?" Bold spoke aloud, unsure which direction to look.

What do you offer?

Bold glanced at Cené. She nodded her approval. "We offer ourselves. Our passion. Sensuality. No makáo. Just two real people. There will be no penetration. That is for Cené's lifemate, whomever she chooses. Will that be enough?"

We shall see. You are many days' walk from my temple. Remember, she is a maiden, so your passion must remain chaste— within the boundaries of her beliefs. Should you not satisfy either Cené or me, you will not be able to find my temple. If you do not find it, I will not grant you your wish.

"So, we'll just wander around in the woods until we starve to death, right?" He shrugged his shoulders. "Like we have a choice?"

You always have a choice. However, once you reach my temple, should you find it, I require three more days of passion before I will consider your request. Three full days and nights of whatever carnal delights I desire. Me. Not the woman beside you. Are you willing to give so much of yourself? Will you bed a goddess, mortal, for the chance to see your home again?

Bed a goddess? Now that's a story to tell the guys...as if anyone would believe it. "Whatever you say, Goddess. You keep your end of the deal, I'll keep mine."

A sudden thought stopped him. *How does she know what I intend to ask?* He hadn't said anything to the Lady about wanting to go home. He'd only told Cené.

Wondering if he'd just made a deal with the devil, Bold checked to make sure his pack was secure and his receiver safely stowed. Then he motioned to Cené to lead out. A narrow pathway suddenly opened through the dense foliage. Without hesitation, Cené led Bolden into the forest.

✷ ✷ ✷ ✷ ✷

"Are you thinking about what we're going to do tonight, Cené? Is your Lady giving you any ideas?" Bold bit his lips the minute the words were out of his mouth. What good was it doing to bait the girl? Of course, following Cené's petite form for hours on end was enough to turn any saint into a sinner. Bolden realized he'd been walking with a painful erection for so long he'd almost begun to ignore the discomfort. Knowing what lay ahead once they made camp kept him edgy and horny.

Cené stopped and looked at him, her lips parted in a half smile, her eyes wide and inviting. "Of course I think of it, Bolden. I think of it every step of the way. I wonder what you will teach me tonight." Then she turned without another word and headed up the trail.

Bold swallowed back a retort and watched her sway her little butt back and forth with each step. Praise the Mother, but he wanted to wrap his palms around her tight little ass and squeeze, wanted to suck the smile right off her lips. The problem was, she was as guileless and innocent as they came. Hell, she was still a virgin, and it was his duty to make sure she stayed that way.

Shit. Bold adjusted his hard-on within his loincloth and followed after Cené. It was going to be one hell of a long afternoon. Other than the usual song of birds and occasional rustling of small woodland creatures, the hike was long and uneventful. There was no sense of position, of direction or distance, so deep and dark had the forest become. It looked impenetrable, but the path continued to open just steps ahead of Cené. Bold figured they must be making excellent time, wherever the hell they were headed, but it wasn't fast enough for him.

There were no beams of sunlight, no shadows within the woods, so dense were the trees and vines. They rarely saw even a glimpse of sky. He forced his mind away from thoughts of Cené and her perfect butt, and wondered about the charge in his solar receiver. There'd been no chance to set it in sunlight for many hours now. Of course, there wasn't much point in worrying about it, not when there was no one near enough to contact him, but he didn't want to lose the maps and files. They were the purpose of his Quest, not this hunt through a dark forest.

He pushed that thought from his mind as well, and concentrated instead on the thick timberland around him. Rather than feeling oppressive, the forest was a thing of beauty, filled with waxy looking flowers and oddly shaped and colored plants that constantly tempted Cené to pause and study.

"I am not a healer, " she said, after one such stop, "but I've always wanted to learn more about the medicinal and even magical qualities of plants. There are many here I've only heard of, others that are totally new to me." She turned and smiled at Bolden. "Are any of the plants like those on your world?"

"Yeah, there are, and it's really weird." Bold had noticed the similarities between this world and others he'd visited, many times over the past couple years. Flowers, trees, grasses...things that should have been totally alien to him were hauntingly familiar.

One more thing to add to his report, should he ever return from his Quest.

Thank goodness Cené was showing some interest in the forest around her. Their conversation helped take his mind off her softly rounded behind and the long slim line of her legs. His hands ached from clenching his fists more than once, imagining her small, firm breasts within his grasp.

Tonight. You will touch her tonight.

Would you quit doing that? Shit, it was bad enough knowing the damned goddess was going to be playing the voyeur tonight. Having her inside his head when he was fantasizing was carrying things a bit too far.

He stopped and glared around him, accepting the fact she was everywhere. *You're going to have to keep your mouth shut when I'm with Cené. Do you understand that? I'm not going to make love to this woman with you yammering in my head.*

You would talk thus to a goddess?

Bold almost chuckled at the confusion in her mental voice. She obviously wasn't familiar with anything but total adoration. *Yes. I would talk to you this way. I have agreed you may experience our passion. I'll even fuck you myself when we get to the end of this trip, but I don't want to be reminded you're watching every move I make. If you keep popping in and out of my head, I won't be much good to Cené – or to you. Okay?*

Oh. I didn't realize...okay.

Suddenly, as if she'd never existed within his thoughts, all sense of the goddess disappeared. Aware of conflicting emotions of relief and expectation, Bold caught up with Cené.

She paused near a small pond. There was no inlet, which meant it was most likely spring-fed. Soft tendrils of steam rose from the clear water. "We should camp here. It's a hot spring. I never imagined we'd find one in the Dream Forest."

Cené cautiously dipped her fingers into the water. "Perfect. I can't believe we're so lucky! The Goddess has truly blessed our journey today." She sighed and folded her legs as she sank to the ground. "I'm exhausted. There's no way to tell, but I bet we've walked many miles. Soaking in a hot pool sounds wonderful."

"Well, whether or not she's blessed the journey, at least your goddess has led us to a decent campsite."

Cené glanced coyly in Bolden's direction. "She knows what we've promised her. I imagine she wants both of us freshly bathed, our bodies as perfect as we can prepare them, before we find our pleasure." She slowly ran her hands along her sleek sides. "I know I've spent the day imagining things I'd like to try." She stood up once more and stepped closer to Bold, ran her hand lightly over the bulge barely concealed within his loincloth. "Now that I have permission to explore without fear of losing my maidenhead, I am eager to learn as much as I can."

Bold gasped, sucking hard on an indrawn breath. *Praise the Mother*, he thought his heart might pound right out of his ribcage as Cené's unschooled fingers slowly traced the ridge of his cock through the smooth leather. He swallowed, almost choked and swallowed again. He stared at her slim fingers, imagined them enclosing his cock, squeezing it in her tight little fist. Mesmerized, his vision clouded as every nerve in his body reacted to the subtle sweep of her fingers.

His cock twitched, practically begged the woman to squeeze it. Bolden's testicles contracted tightly between his legs and he closed his eyes as he struggled for control. She didn't squeeze, didn't increase the pressure, just continued that slow, gentle, teasing caress. He sure as hell wasn't going to beg. Not yet, anyway. "Bathing sounds like a great idea," he mumbled, backing away from Cené's seductive touch. Anymore of her exquisite fondling and he'd make a complete fool of himself.

"First we'll need a fire." His voice sounded choppy, the words clipped. He hoped she didn't realize she'd nearly taken him over the edge. Before he shot his seed all over himself, Bold turned his back and began gathering wood, all too aware of the sounds of the woman behind him building their sleeping area out of boughs and bracken fern, then covering them with his blanket.

✱ ✱ ✱ ✱ ✱

Cené removed her tunic and slipped quietly into the steaming water. She bit back a sigh of pleasure, unwilling to draw attention to herself right now. She wanted this moment to reflect, to commune with her Lady, to find the inner peace that had eluded her all day. There was much she should consider, yet all she'd had on her mind today was the huge male following closely behind her. She'd heard him breathe, sensed his desire, his need for her, even smelled a faint, musky aroma that made her think of sex, of the lush tangle of limbs, of kisses and touches she'd never experienced. This was all new, this awareness, this passion.

She found a rock just beneath the surface of the pool where she could sit with the warm water lapping about her chin. She scooted her bottom around until she found a comfortable spot and thought about passion, about desire and the need that kept her pussy throbbing and wet throughout the long walk they'd made today. All the while, she watched Bolden as he carefully built a campfire. He seemed to take an inordinate amount of time at the simple task.

Suddenly she realized the big, self-assured warrior was not nearly so sure of himself as she'd believed. He wanted her. She didn't doubt that for a moment. Wanted her even beyond his need to find his home once again. Her fingers still tingled from tracing his hard cock beneath his loincloth. It had practically doubled in size when she'd stroked him. He wouldn't have been so hard or so big if he didn't want her, but somehow, for some reason, he now acted intimidated by her.

Was it knowing the Goddess would be there, sharing their passion that unnerved him? Maybe he didn't understand what an honor had been given to them. An honor she must prepare herself for. Cené looked down at her body and wondered if she were truly worthy of sharing love with her Lady, if this simple, peasant's body, unusually colored as it was, would suffice.

She licked her lips. They felt fuller than usual. More sensitive. She rubbed her palms over both her nipples, raising them to brilliant red peaks against the black flesh of her breasts. Their outline wavered beneath the clear water, appeared almost mystical. She felt the connection between her breasts and her pussy, the coil of sensation that looped back in upon itself.

She plucked at the vermilion tips, rolling her nipples back and forth, relishing the sensation zinging from each turgid peak to the pleasure point between her legs. The sensation was far beyond anything the makáo had given her, though not nearly as nice as what Bolden could do.

The moment she thought of Bold, her desire increased. Her breath grew choppy, the grasp of her fingers more intense. She smiled, her eyes half closed as she suddenly realized she truly was preparing herself. This wasn't merely pleasuring herself for pleasure's sake. No, she was preparing herself for Bold's touch. Making her body ready for the goddess to feel her passion. Of course, Bold couldn't penetrate her. He had already promised not to breach her maidenhead, and she had complete faith in his honor, but he'd also hinted at untold pleasures beyond mere coupling.

Cené trailed the fingers of her left hand from her breasts to her belly, finally to the nest of curls guarding her pussy. She slipped one finger between the thickening folds of her labia, rubbing over the extended tip of her clitoris before sinking into her tight passage.

She wondered what Bold would do, how far he would take her. Pretending her slender fingers were Bold's thicker, longer ones took a real stretch of imagination, but her eyes slowly closed and she imagined him deep inside her, his cock tearing past her fragile barrier and filling her completely.

Her vaginal muscles clenched around her middle finger just as a deep growl ripped her away from her fantasy. Cené glanced up sharply, her fingers still buried between her legs, practically touching her maiden's barrier.

Bolden stood over her, his hands clenched in the knotted leather cord that held his loincloth about his powerful hips. His big body practically quivered and the sinews and tendons across his chest and neck looked so taut they might snap. His claws were fully extended, his knuckles almost white from the tight grasp he had on the cord at his waist.

Cené licked her lips, waiting for him to remove the covering. He hesitated a moment longer, then with a huge sigh, untied the cord and dropped the strip of leather to the ground beneath his feet.

Cené blinked. She slowly withdrew her hand from between her legs, then looked at the size of her slender fingers and back at the rampant erection thrusting out from Bold's groin. The strange foreskin that usually held it close to his belly had slipped back along the base, freeing his cock from confinement.

Thank the Goddess, he had agreed not to penetrate her, because there was no way that thing was going to fit. Cené almost giggled her relief as Bold slowly stepped down into the warm water, walking out into the center of the pool where it was deep enough to cover him to his chest.

He stared at her a long moment, as if weighing what to do next. Finally, he leaned his head back, took a deep breath and his nostrils flared. "Do we need to formally invite your goddess to join us?" His voice rasped harsh, but the tone was soft, almost reverent. Cené nodded, pleased to see he recognized the importance of what they were about to do.

"Goddess?" Cené lifted her hands skyward. "Be with us, a part of us, join us as we willingly share our passion. We invite you to be one with us, in whatever way you choose."

She closed her eyes and opened her heart. There was a surprising sense of fullness, of two hearts beating in counterpoint before finding their rhythm. When her heart beat once more as hers alone, Cené nodded and her breath caught. She'd never imagined this, not once since they'd struck their bargain. Never dreamed of such an honor.

"We may begin," she said, smiling broadly. "Bolden, I don't believe this, but...my Lady, the Goddess has chosen to become a part of me rather than merely to observe. She says you are uncomfortable knowing she would be watching. Now, she won't have to observe, she will instead participate. You will touch both of us, pleasure us as one—just as you will allow us to pleasure you."

She looked down her slim legs and wiggled her toes, held her fingers out in front of her face, touched thumb to fingertip. *So long!* She'd not held corporeal form in such a long time, not since before Evil was set loose on her world.

To feel again, to hurt. To experience the warm water lapping against her breasts, to know the physical responses of desire, the pulsing between her legs, the taut coil of heat and need deep within her belly.

Thank you, Cené. Thank you for the generous sharing of your body, your soul. Your desire.

She felt Cené's silent acknowledgment. The core of the woman had slipped aside, unselfishly made room for the goddess. There was no guile in her, merely the desire to please the one she worshipped, to please the man she was beginning to love.

Love. She'd loved once. It had brought only pain, loosed the Evil upon her peaceful world. She would not make that mistake again. The price had been much too high.

Sighing, testing the synapses and senses of this most glorious body, she ran her palm over the dark red nipple on her left breast. Unusual, this cherry red color against flesh as black as night. She'd not seen a woman colored such as this before, not once among her own people.

Was Cené someone sent to her for a purpose? Was fate moving in its own inexorable manner, controlling even a goddess?

Ah, even immortals must sometimes wonder. She sighed, licked her lips and looked at the man standing beside her. Looked at him and wanted.

Without understanding exactly how or why, Bold knew the moment the goddess joined with Cené. Rather than feel intimidated by her immortal presence, his cock immediately responded. He had thought her beautiful before, but now she defined the concept of beauty. Her eyes were greener, her skin blacker, the red of her lips as ripe and inviting as cherries. Her breasts seemed fuller, her demeanor more regal yet, unbelievably, more appealing, almost vulnerable.

Forgotten was the reason behind his seduction, forgotten the deal made or bargains promised. Bold only knew he must give Cené pleasure, must bring her to ripe fulfillment without penetration. He would protect what she had entrusted to him. Protect her and show her love.

He watched a moment as she held her fingers out and studied them, palmed her swollen nipple and sighed. The goddess appeared to be enthralled with her borrowed body. What was it like, to have suddenly taken on form and substance?

Bold only knew he desired her beyond anything he'd ever felt. Desired her and wanted to please her.

She was a woman first. He would have to see her as a woman, not a goddess. He almost laughed aloud. He was not the most sexually experienced of men. Who was he to think he could satisfy an immortal?

Then she turned and looked at him, her green eyes almost hidden beneath thick, sooty lashes, her lips red and swollen, shining where the very tip of her tongue dampened the lower one. He watched as she licked slowly across her upper lip and realized he was licking his own in response.

The water rising against her body shivered with tiny ripples. The Lady Cené trembled. Was it desire or fear?

Either emotion drew him to her, took away whatever sense of inadequacy he might have felt. She looked at him and trembled. Immortal goddess or needy woman, she was one and the same.

She was Cené, no matter what entity resided within. She was the woman who wanted him.

He reached for her lithe body, lifted her away from her submerged rock and positioned her in front of him, her back against his belly, stroking his hands almost reverently along her sides, her sleek flanks, sweeping his palms across her breasts to barely touch the firm nipples.

He cupped her breasts, holding each one separately, feeling the warmth spreading through his hands. She practically purred beneath his caress, her body growing more pliant with each stroke of his hands, the trembling giving way to sensual undulations of her hips as she searched, then found a rhythm to her own song of need.

He slowly turned her around and lay her back upon the water. Buoyant, she barely broke the surface of the heated pool. Spreading her legs wide, Bold brought her glistening nether lips to his mouth, supporting her back with his broad hands so that she floated there, an erotic feast spread out before him.

He knelt in the smooth sand at the pool's bottom, close to the far side from their camp. The water lapped softly about his chin. He stared at her a moment, mentally devouring the sweet, fleshy lips, imagining his tongue parting the tender folds. He projected the thought, letting Cené see his fantasy, see herself as he saw her.

She moaned. Her buttocks clenched tightly and her hips swayed in response to the images he shared. Ripples spread in an ever-widening circle around her. Grinning, Bold slipped quietly out of her thoughts and licked lightly along Cené's inner thighs. Her dark flesh felt like satin beneath his tongue. Her legs hung loosely over his shoulders, her hands paddled in lazy circles beside her hips as he nibbled and tasted his way closer to the pouting lips.

He was very careful with his tongue, knowing just how abrasive it could feel against tender skin, but a flick here and there soon had Cené clenching her fingers into tight little fists rather than slowly moving through the water.

The spring must have been filled with minerals because the water tasted mildly salty to Bold. The closer his tongue came to Cené, the sweeter the water as her fluids blended with the pool. He had to fight the lure of her pussy. He wanted to lap slowly at her soft labia, drinking up her sweet juices, but at the same time, he wanted to take her higher, farther than she'd ever imagined.

Bold worked his way slowly along the tender flesh between her legs, nibbling and licking as far as the crease between thigh and groin. He managed to completely avoid the soft lips between, choosing to tease her all around instead. He worked from side to side, with just the lightest touch, a bare brush against her swollen clit, an almost accidental caress to her pussy. Here she was the sweetest of all. He bit back a groan of need and forced himself to back away, to tease her even more.

His hands massaged her back, then her buttocks, then merely supported her back again. He couldn't get enough of her satiny skin, the firm muscles rippling just beneath. She moaned, spread her legs wider in wanton invitation, but still Bold teased. The flicks to her protruding clit might come a bit more often, the nibbles to her inner thighs occasionally reach the fleshy lips, his tongue might even enter that hot, dark entrance for the briefest of tastes, but it was all merely an accident, not the direction he intended.

Or so it seemed. Cené reached out and grabbed at his dark mane, pulling herself even closer to his mouth. Practically sobbing with frustration, she rubbed her wet pussy against his lips and jaw, searching frantically, demanding relief.

Laughing, Bold sat back on the submerged rock and wrapped his arms around Cené's body, drawing her close and sucking hard on her clit. He licked between her legs like the big cat that was so much a part of his heritage, savoring the sweet taste of her. He pulled at her vaginal lips with his teeth, licked and suckled, finding exactly the right spot, exactly the perfect pressure, penetrating just to the very edge of her virgin's barrier, then retreating once more to tease her swollen clit, finally to press his lips around that sensitive bit of flesh and suckle it like a baby at his mother's breast.

Cené's back arched, her limbs went rigid, her knees clamped tightly to the sides of Bold's head. She screamed, a long, drawn out wailing cry of release, of surrender, of unimaginable passion. Screamed once again as he continued to suckle at her clit, then run his tongue gently over that moist and tender bundle of nerves.

Her chest heaved with the effort to draw air into her lungs. Finally, after a last sweep of his tongue, Bold turned her in his arms and carried her to the edge of the pond. He stretched her limp body out in the soft sand, then trailed his fingers along her smooth skin. She shuddered, still caught in the aftermath of orgasm, her fingers grasping limply for Bolden as he sat back on his heels.

He laughed out loud. He tried to dampen his mental shout of triumph, but it wasn't easy. Knowing the haughty goddess had just been rendered speechless almost compensated for the raging hard-on that continued to bump against his belly.

There was something to be said for an abundance of testosterone. "I take it both of you enjoyed yourselves?"

Still gasping for air, Cené raised one eyelid at his smugly self-satisfied comment, glared at him a moment, then let it fall shut. Bold saw her throat convulse as she swallowed, watched as her breathing slowed and returned to its normal cadence. Finally, she opened her eyes and glared at him. "It was okay," she said, only her voice wasn't really Cené's at all. "It's been awhile. I'd forgotten."

"In case you hadn't noticed, Goddess, it's been awhile for me, too." He gestured toward his fully erect cock, wondering at her reaction. The woman grinned, and it was Cené this time, though he knew the goddess was somewhere in there.

Her fingers reached out, almost tentatively, and she touched him. His cock jerked in response. Cené jumped. Then she grinned, as if realizing her feminine power for the first time. Slowly, she sat up and scooted close to Bold. He sat back on his heels, his cock standing fully erect, veins distended, the smooth head marked by a tiny drop of semen. He knew if he didn't find release soon, the damned thing would probably explode

Cené touched him again, but she was obviously prepared for his reaction, because her slim fingers suddenly tightened around him and held on.

Bold groaned and thrust his hips forward. Cené licked her lips. He watched the pink tip of her tongue as it swept a damp trail across her full lower lip, then watched even closer as she lowered her head and licked the very head of his cock.

Oh Mother...that slightest of touches, the bare hint of heat from her slick tongue almost sent him over the edge.

Her fingers tightened until she managed to completely encircle his girth. Holding him immobile, she leaned closer once again and drew the thick head into her mouth, slowly wrapping her moist, firm lips around the very end. Trembling, much as she had trembled earlier, Bold forced himself not to move, not to thrust his cock down her slender throat, no matter how loudly every nerve in his body screamed for him to find release.

Instead, he held his hips rigid, even when Cené's other hand suddenly reached down between his legs and gently cupped his sac. He bit back a groan as she began to slide her wet lips back and forth over the sensitive head of his cock, finding a rhythm with one hand squeezing and stroking the shaft while the other gently fondled and lightly caressed his balls.

In, out, up, down...

His breath caught in his throat. He forgot to breathe, forgot everything...his entire being focused on pure sensation, on Cené and her magical mouth and fingers. Bold know if he made any sound at all, it would most likely be a terribly unmanly whimper. He clenched his teeth while his unsheathed nails left deep trails in the damp sand.

Cené's suckling grew more intense, her lips moved farther along his shaft until she had taken almost a third of his length into her mouth. Bold watched her, fascinated to see this petite creature swallow more and more of him each time she raised and lowered her head, her cheeks hollowing as she drew him into her mouth.

She slowly shifted her position, stretching out in front of him, taking him even deeper, then sliding him out of her throat to lick the length of his cock, her small tongue leaving a trail of wet heat and pure sensation wherever it touched.

Sound caught in his throat—a moan, a gasp, a most unmanly mewling cry as Cené wrapped her lips more securely around his cock and gently squeezed his sac. Bold threw his head back, silently begging for control. Where was the Mother, now he needed her?

Cené hummed against his weeping cock, sending vibrations all the way to his balls. He heard and felt the sound, echoing in the dim recesses of his beleaguered brain, sending a ripple of sensation from the tip of his cock to the base, then all the way to his testicles.

She deepened the song, dropping down an octave, reaching longer, stronger vibrations. Her tongue never stopped licking and twirling, her fingers squeezing, the humming rising and falling as she shredded his control, shredded him, took him beyond any sensation he'd ever experienced.

He couldn't take much more...couldn't take *any* more. A brief thought flitted through his mind...*What is the protocol for shooting one's load down a goddess's throat?* Before he could carry the thought even a step further, Cené swallowed his cock completely, taking all of him, clamping her lips about the base of his penis, her tongue stroking the underside while the fingers of both her hands grasped his balls almost to the point of pain, caressing, squeezing, driving him insane.

Over...over the top, too much, too...

His seed burst up and out of his sac, following the convoluted trail toward ejaculation before he even realized he was coming. Cené held him tightly in her mouth, though he tried to pull free. Groaning, Bold grasped the sides of her face as gently as he was able and filled her mouth and throat with his seed.

Instead of backing away, she took him greedily, suckling his pulsing cock throughout his entire orgasm, her fingers gently massaging his balls as if milking him for every last drop.

Bold shuddered, unwound his cramping legs from beneath him and stretched them out so that Cené still lay between his thighs, her lips clamped tightly around his pulsing cock.

Legs shaking, his breath rasping in his chest, Bold lay back and closed his eyes to the sweet sensation of Cené's tongue licking him clean, of her soft lips compressing the now flaccid length of his penis. He thought of trying to enter her mind, realized he didn't have the energy for it, and merely let his remaining shreds of consciousness float beneath her ministrations.

Long moments later, she pulled herself up along his chest. Her lips glistened, and when Bold pulled her close for a long kiss, he knew he must be tasting himself.

Odd, he'd never thought about what his semen would taste like, never imagined the combination of salt and sweet and spice, like cinnamon. Combined with Cené's sweet taste, it was almost intoxicating, tasting himself on her lips.

She ended the kiss and snuggled close against his chest.

"She's gone."

He lifted his head to stare at Cené. Her face was pressed against his chest, right where his heart beat at a rate beyond what had to be healthy. "The goddess?"

"Yes. She thanked us both and said she'd be back later. I think we surprised her."

Bold lifted her chin with his fingers. "Well...you certainly surprised me."

"Me too. That was the goddess's idea. I've never done that before. Didn't know you *could* do that." She looked shyly at him. "I like the way you taste. I want to do it again."

Oh Mother. Grinning, Bold wrapped his arms around Cené and drifted in the pleasure of her scent, the soft warmth of her small, lush body against his. He wasn't at all sure he could take it again.

At least not for a few minutes.

No bed partner had ever taken all of him in her mouth. Never had he allowed a woman to swallow his seed, yet Cené — or the goddess — had held him close and not allowed him to pull out.

He rather liked the feeling of a dominant woman. Liked it a lot. He realized he liked everything about this woman who was now more than just the person he'd pursued through the forest, more than an exciting challenge. Somehow, she'd found a way into his heart just as she'd pleasured his body. Bold lightly stroked Cené's shoulder, reliving the sensations of his climax.

Her fingers caressed his belly, occasionally trailed across his cock, explored his sac as if all her touches were mere afterthoughts. The complete and total indifference excited him.

Damn. Praise the Mother, he was growing hard once again. Did she mean it? Would she take him in her mouth again? He shifted his hips in the warm sand, trying to find a more comfortable position, one that would at least bring his cock into contact with Cené's warm thigh.

Now that's the desire of a desperate man. He sighed and wrapped his arms around her. She nuzzled his chest. Little Cené, an innocent if ever there was one. A woman grown, but without the goddess as part of her, still almost childlike.

Then he thought of the merry chase she'd led him on as he'd pursued her through the Dream Forest. No, not a child. Merely a very pure and guileless woman. A woman who managed to take his entire cock down her throat and bring him to his knees.

Of course, it was the goddess's idea. His cock throbbed and pulsed, semi-erect now. His balls ached and he'd never felt so sated in his life...or so needy. The slight form of the woman snuggled against his chest made him feel comforted and protective at the same time.

Her fingers stilled, wrapped lightly around his tumescent cock. Her other hand rested against his heart, her breathing grew soft and even, her body limp. She slept. Bold kissed the top of her head, nuzzled his lips in her short silky hair. His arms tightened around her. He rested his chin on top of her head, wondering.

Which woman did he want to protect? Which one comforted him? Cené or her alter ego, the goddess, the essence of a world, immortal and powerful beyond imagining?

The one who would send him home. The only one with the power to let him see his loved ones again, to grant him favor. Was that the woman he was beginning to love? He'd not felt this way just for Cené, as much as he enjoyed her company and her touch, had not felt this depth of caring, of need, of desire beyond physical.

No, it had taken a goddess to give him a teasing glimpse of his future, one he had no chance of claiming.

Chapter Seven

They bathed in the small pool, then ate. Bold spooned up the last bit of stew from the pot and added it to Cené's bowl. "I'll need to hunt in the morning. There are birds in this forest that I recognize. Will the goddess let us kill any of the creatures here?"

Cené nodded. "She is within me once more. She understands our need for sustenance. You may hunt. She trusts you to kill only what we need."

"How does that feel, having someone sharing your head as well as your body?" Now that he was looking for it, Bold did see a difference. Almost a sense of royalty, of hauteur that was usually notably lacking in Cené.

"I like it, actually." She grinned shyly. "I feel more self-confident. More aware. I understand things I normally wouldn't even wonder about. I think each time she is with me, I will feel even more a part of her, more as if I *am* her. I also feel more need, more desire." She stared down at her bowl a moment, then back at Bolden. "I want to be with you again, something I would hesitate to ask if I were just Cené, knowing that our intercourse, for you, at least, is so incomplete. With the goddess giving me confidence and strength, I have no problem telling you that I want to do more with you again...soon, though not tonight."

Bold cleared his throat and set his bowl down. His cock had immediately leapt to life at Cené's off-handed comment. "Trust me, what we did tonight was complete enough for me. You gave me much pleasure. Is this, *ahem*, wanting to do more, hypothetical, or are we talking the real thing?"

Cené laughed and set her bowl down as well. "Oh, most definitely the real thing. As real as we can get without taking my true virginity. Tonight, though, I want to sleep. I want to think about what we did today, how it made me feel. Tomorrow, after you hunt, we will walk once more toward my...toward the goddess's temple. Later, I want to try something different, something we haven't done before."

"Something without penetration."

She glanced slyly in Bold's direction, and he was well aware she had picked up the resigned sound in his voice. Hell, he couldn't help wondering how it would feel, to finally drive deep inside her, feel the tight clenching as her pussy wrapped around his cock. He'd even fantasized what it would feel like, coming up against the fragile barrier of her virginity, breaking through it.

After experiencing the most amazing oral sex he'd ever had, he couldn't help but want more. His vivid imagination kept him hard most of the time now. Whenever he looked at Cené he imagined touching her, being touched by her. Taking her.

"Well, not penetration of my virgin's passage," she said, bursting into the bubble of his fantasy. "The goddess tells me there are other passages where we may find pleasure."

Bold blinked, then stared at her. He could only think of one other they hadn't breached. He swallowed, letting a new fantasy take him. He hadn't tried that one before. Not that he hadn't thought of it...he'd just never had a partner he felt intimate enough with, close enough to, to even suggest it. He stared hungrily at Cené's slight frame. "I wouldn't want to hurt you."

Laughing, Cené stood up and walked toward the pool. Her soft blue leather tunic clung to her hips, slipping and sliding across her rounded behind with each step she took.

She turned and glanced back over her shoulder, her stance flirtatious, enticing. "Neither would I enjoy pain. That's not something I find exciting. I do, however, have a great deal of curiosity about many things I've not known of before. The goddess has given me much knowledge. Of course, the knowledge my Lady passes on to me is, as you say, purely hypothetical."

Totally unselfconscious of her nudity, Cené slipped the tunic over her head and stepped into the water. She moved slowly through the steaming pool. Bold stared, fascinated by the perfect shape of her buttocks. He watched as she moved into deeper water, hiding her bottom from view, then moving to a spot deep enough to cover her breasts. Bold immediately followed her.

She said she didn't want to do more tonight, but she certainly appeared to be leading him into temptation.

He wasn't really disappointed, he told himself later, when all Cené did was bathe. She even offered to wash his back, but there was no seduction behind the offer, merely good manners.

Once again he gave his blanket to Cené. She covered herself, turned her back to him and promptly fell asleep.

Bolden lay wide-eyed and staring into the dying embers of their campfire, Cené's concept of curiosity keeping him awake long beyond nightfall and into the early hours of the morning. It was nearly time to rise before he finally fell asleep. Then, however, his thoughts were no longer on seduction, but on the woman Cené had become, now that she was also a goddess.

* * * * *

"You are quiet this morning, Bolden. I would think, since your hunt was so successful, you would be more animated." Cené smiled back at him, glancing over her shoulder as she led the way along the trail. Her eyes glimmered with more than her usual native intelligence, her smile was seductive and ripe with hidden meanings.

Bolden could only grunt in assent as he followed her, silently acknowledging it was the goddess who teased him, not the guileless Cené. There was too much roiling about his head this morning, too many questions and uneasy thoughts colliding with a monumental headache from his poor night's sleep for him to make even the simplest conversation.

Somewhere, deep in the nighttime hours, he had accepted the fact he was more involved with Cené than he had ever intended. She ruled his thoughts, his dreams, even his damned cock. She was the last thing he thought of when he closed his eyes at night, she ruled his heart and mind when he awakened in the morning.

The woman fascinated him, but which woman was he courting? For that matter, was he courting, or merely lusting? Was it Cené, the sweet and innocent yet tenacious young maiden he had pursued for days through the Dream Forest, or was it the mysterious goddess who now shared her form, the unknown seductress who had already begun planning their next tryst?

He found both of them fascinating, wanted each one, separately and alone. Instead, they were bound together, one so much a part of the other he wondered if even *they* knew where Cené began and the goddess ended.

Bound together for now, but not forever. At some point, he would leave this primitive world, leave the goddess and all she represented. Possibly, he could convince Cené to come with him, but was Cené the woman he really loved?

It was all so confusing. Maybe he didn't love her at all. Maybe he was just so damned horny he couldn't think straight. Maybe his cock was in charge after all. With the promise of new delights when they finally made camp tonight, Bold figured his cock would most likely remain in charge.

He practically salivated, watching the perfectly round little ass in front of him as Cené followed the mystical trail through the deep forest. He ignored the beauty around him and studied instead the slope of her trim waist along the sleek line of her hip. He imagined that smooth flesh quivering beneath his tongue as he bathed her. The thought of licking her all over, of spending hours tasting and exploring that perfect little body actually made him salivate. She carried so much lush promise in such a tiny, feminine package, all of it barely hidden beneath a soft leather tunic that clung to her dark skin like finest silk.

His cock ached, straining against his loincloth. He licked his lips, imagining her taste, her sweet response. Grunting in frustration, Bold adjusted himself, hoping to relieve the discomfort, realized there was no way he'd find comfort, not with the enticing vision of Cené's perfect bottom leading him along his way.

Definitely no argument at all. His cock was truly in control.

It was a rather demeaning admission to make to himself. He huffed out a deep breath of impatience, shifted the pack and the bagged game birds over his shoulder and stared at the lithe figure moving away from him. He'd never let a female confuse him so much in his entire life.

No...not a female. Two females...and one of them is immortal...all tightly packaged together, just to confuse me. Shaking his head, he followed Cené down the trail. With two of them, he didn't stand a chance.

* * * * *

They camped once again by a woodland pool. Not warm this time, but refreshingly cool and clear. Cené had stopped many times during the journey to gather plants, flowers and various herbs. Tonight she simmered them slowly over a small fire.

"Is this part of our dinner?" Bold placed the two cleaned fowl on a flat stone near the fire pit, and gestured at the steaming pot. Whatever she cooked smelled musky, more earthy and seductive, not at all like something he would like with his roasted fowl.

"No." Cené shook her head, smiling somewhat mysteriously. "It's for later. Here..." She handed a long, sharpened stick to Bold so he could skewer the birds over the fire, and continued stirring whatever potion she prepared.

He watched her, mesmerized by her dark beauty. The goddess was strong in her today, so that everything about Cené was *more*. He realized he liked her this way, then felt guilty for preferring the goddess to the simpler woman.

He didn't feel her in his mind, but still he knew she heard his thoughts. Cené glanced over her shoulder at him. "I am who I am," she said. "No more, no less. Just as you are who you are." She flipped her fingers in front of her, emphasizing her point. "You have said you are a man of two worlds, a mixture of lion and human. That mixture makes you complete, makes you who you are. Cené has always served the goddess, has always been a part of the goddess. Now the goddess is a part of Cené. We are one and the same."

"Yes, but not for always." Bold concentrated on the birds cooking over the fire, searching for the right words. "The goddess only borrows Cené's body. You share her mind and her thoughts, but at some point, you will leave and go back to doing whatever it is that goddesses do. What will that leave Cené?"

"Stronger than she was before. Wiser. She will always retain much of my thoughts, my history...my needs and wants. Goddesses are not so unlike mortals, you know. We love. We lose. We feel pain and sometimes, with luck, great happiness. We want and need just as you do. Very rarely, though, do we have our desires fulfilled."

"What of the makáo?" Bolden waved his hand, encompassing the surrounding forest, now fading into darkness. "They've not visited since you took on your human form, but they are there for your pleasure, right?"

"I've not needed the makáo." She glanced over her shoulder, as if watching for her pleasure-seekers in the woods. "Yesterday, with you, was better than anything the makáo can do for me. Tonight will be better still." She stirred the small pot a bit more, then set it away from the fire. "This must cool before it is ready. Is there anything I can do to help prepare the meal?"

She could have been any gorgeous woman from any one of a number of inhabited worlds. Why was it, Bolden wondered, that the one who fascinated him the most, the one who tugged at his heart, was someone totally unacceptable, someone completely out of his reach?

"No," he said, shaking his head. "I've got it covered. I'll call you when dinner's ready."

* * * * *

The meat from the birds Bolden had cooked was tender and juicy, the evening warm and the conversation between man and immortal easy and entertaining. Though she was the sentience of her world, the woman who was goddess accepted how little she knew of the thoughts and desires of man. She *was* the world, the solid, growing, living, breathing planet on which the race existed, but still she was apart, separate.

The goddess within Cené stared at her dark fingers holding the bits of meat, relishing the taste of food, the mere act of eating, something she'd not done for millennia. Had she once held human form? If so, it was lost in the dust of history, a barely tangible memory too far removed to be recalled as more than essence, of possibility.

Everything about this body fascinated her. Even the soreness of her muscles after the day's long trek, the aching in her feet, the bug bites on her arm that itched...she'd forgotten—or had she even known—the satisfaction of scratching, the pleasure of rubbing her fingers over the raised bump and feeling the itch go away.

Such simple pleasures long denied a goddess.

The man sitting across the fire from her pleased her even more. More than that, he made her feel, made her want. Reinforced the knowledge she'd been able to bury for so very long, just how lonely she was, how ineffectual the makáo really were in bringing her satisfaction.

She wanted, no, *needed*, a consort. She sighed, accepting reality. What man of his own free will would give up life? No, immortality wasn't at all what it was cracked up to be. It was just damned lonely. Too filled with responsibilities.

Even now, as she anticipated the night ahead, she must remain alert for the ever present sense of danger that had followed them through the forest. *Her forest.* This should not be. Bolden was unaware of the entity that shadowed them, Cené only marginally aware something wasn't quite as it should be.

Well, she wasn't a goddess for nothing. She'd held Evil at bay for eons now, ever since that damned curse had set it all back in motion. Not that it was easy, and not that she'd been a hundred percent effective, but she'd done her best.

Not only that, she'd done it alone. She only vaguely remembered her one love that set Evil free on her world. Memories such as that were best lost in the dust of time. She had been alone since the beginning. Alone, with her people and her world.

Just as she would continue, long after Bold had returned to his home, long after their deal was fulfilled, and she was alone once again.

"Cené? Are you all right?" Bold's amber eyes were shadowed with concern. She must have been woolgathering, to make him look at her so. Before she could answer, he cupped her chin in his hand. She leaned into his callused palm. It was warm. Alive. Comforting and so very strong.

"What you mentioned yesterday. What you wanted to try? If you've changed your mind, you know I'll not force you."

Ah. So he's been thinking of that all day! The knowledge made her giddy, made her even more aware of herself in this pleasing woman's form. She'd wondered how much, how graphically he thought of her, but bowing to Bolden's ethics, she'd not go, uninvited, into his mind. At least not about matters of a sensual nature. Those he appeared to hold private, deep inside where they were not easily read.

Now though, he opened himself to her. She saw his desire, his curiosity, even sensed his concern over harming her in any way. She found his worry disarming and very touching. She was a goddess and immortal, after all. Very little could harm her.

While she dwelled within this woman's body, it was protected as well.

It felt good to flirt, to tease one such as Bold. "Ah," she said, using her most superior goddess's voice, "but what if I wish to force you?" She slanted a smile his way, hoping to dispel any of the darkness that seemed to hover closer to their camp. His answering chuckle warmed her even more.

"There is nothing you could do that would displease me." He leaned closer and kissed her. His lips were full and soft, the rough promise of his tongue a sensual counterpoint to their searching, questing caress across her mouth.

She groaned, sucking the sensation of his touch into her heart, deep into her immortal soul, drawing him in and filling as many empty parts of her as she could find. It would have to last her forever.

If only she'd not sworn to return this body to its rightful owner! It would be so easy to forego her duties to this world, to strip her sentience from the planet, abandon the world and all its trials and leave, choosing life, no matter how brief, within this warm and willing woman's body.

Honor, of course, would not allow it. Honor and duty might be all she had that kept her whole, but she would not renege.

She felt Cené stir within her mind, heard the woman's voice.

My body is yours, Goddess. You would do me great honor, should you choose me, to be your host forever.

Bless you, child. Your offer is without equal, but I will only borrow you for awhile. You please me, much as the man pleases me. You have my thanks and gratitude, but I have a world that needs me.

Bolden's lips covered her mouth, his kiss lush with promise. Cené's thoughts faded into the background of her soul. Even goddess's were allowed short vacations from responsibility.

She lost herself in his kiss. Bold leaned over her, his huge body compelling, the warmth from his flesh heating her, practically burning through her barriers with a need more intense than she'd thought possible.

She wanted him. Cené wanted him. Her maiden's barrier was nothing more than a bit of flesh, something easily broken, something...something irreplaceable.

But, as she'd said to Bolden last night, it was the *only* passage denied them. She twisted lightly out of Bold's grasp, stood and took him by the hand. The sleeping pallet was already made, a soft bed of branches, bracken fern and moss covered with Bold's blanket. The lotion she had prepared sat cooling in a pot nearby, a powerful aphrodisiac among its properties.

Not that she needed anything to increase her desire.

Already her heart pounded in her chest and her woman's parts were swollen and wet. She felt the fluid there, knew it readied a passage Bolden's honor wouldn't allow him to breach.

Ah, but as Cené had reminded this man—there were other passages. Pulling Bolden down onto the pallet beside her, the goddess gave into passion and became one with Cené.

Chapter Eight

She was quicksilver in his arms, so slight and feminine, her body still taut with the power of her immortality. For awhile there, as they'd eaten, he'd not sensed Cené at all. No, he'd just shared his rough meal with a goddess.

Now, though, she was all fluid curves and wanting woman, her breathing choppy, her hands sliding frantically over his flanks, across his chest, through the pelt of fur that ran down his belly, then tugging his loincloth loose. His breath caught on a gasp as her slim fingers reached beneath the leather and gently encircled his hard cock, then slipped away as he pressed into her grasp, caressing his balls, then almost timidly tracing the crease between his buttocks, trailing along the sensitive ring of muscle around his ass.

Oh Mother! He'd meant to touch her, there. He hadn't dreamed it would feel so good for her to touch him! Never before had he wanted so much to know more. How does a mortal please a goddess? Hell, he'd rarely had the opportunity to pleasure *any* woman, between his schooling, his duties, his long space voyages. There was so much he wished he knew.

He let her know, admitted his lack of experience, his worries about pleasing her, but her only answer was a disbelieving and totally un-goddesslike *snort*. Then she sighed when he stroked her flanks, whimpered and arched into his touch when he slowly and gently brushed his broad hands along her buttocks, under her breasts.

At least it appeared his instincts were good. Bold lifted her tunic over her head, nibbling at each breast as he uncovered it. She arched her back and cried out, so he licked at her nipples, hoping the abrasive texture of his tongue would bring her pleasure.

Something warm and musky trickled across his buttocks. A sensual perfume filled his nostrils. The stuff she'd been cooking...some kind of lotion? So that's what she'd been making. He'd worried about that, wondered what he could use as a lubricant, afraid the sex she'd wanted from him wouldn't work. Now, though, her soft hands were working the scented cream into his lower back, rubbing it around his butt and inspiring him to do the same to her.

Still suckling at her turgid nipple and flicking his tongue over the tip, he scooped a handful of the warm cream out of the small pot and smeared it across her belly. Cené arched against his touch and practically purred as he rubbed it into her thighs and over her smooth stomach.

She continued touching him, her fingers running between his buttocks, trailing along the sensitive crease, pressing at the tight ring of his anus. *Oh Mother.* He paused, unwilling to move away from the sensation, then practically whimpered as she penetrated him with one slim finger, sliding in and out with the smooth flow of lotion.

If she kept this up...he didn't want to lose it, not now, not when she wanted him, needed what he could give her.

He turned her nipple loose with a wet popping sound, then sat back on his knees, putting his ass out of the reach of those delightful fingers of hers, and began to massage her with long, deep strokes of his hands. She groaned in pleasure as he worked over the entire front of her body, lavishing her with the sweet, creamy lotion. It left her skin smooth and glistening, her nipples pointed into sharp crimson peaks. Her eyes were closed, her lips parted, but he could practically see her heart beating in her chest.

He paid close attention to the crease between thigh and groin, then dribbled warm drops of the sweet-smelling cream between her legs. He used the pad of one finger to slowly rub it in to her protruding clitoris. Carefully pushing the tiny protective hood back, he touched her there. She jumped in response, then sighed when he added more lotion and slipped his fingers lower between her legs, rubbing the swollen lips without entering her pussy.

He stroked her, sliding slowly back and forth, barely scraping at her clit on each pass, until she trembled with his caress.

Knowing she hovered close to the edge, he left her there, lightly massaged her belly once more, then carefully flipped her over on to her front. Cené sprawled wantonly on the soft bedding, her round bottom so perfect, the skin as smooth and silky as black satin. Almost afraid to touch her, Bold sat back and just stared at her for a moment. Could such perfection really be meant for him?

He grabbed her by the wrists and stretched them up over her head, planting them there. "Don't move your hands." She nodded, clasping her fingers together as if her wrists were tied. He leaned over and touched her left hip, barely grazing it with his fingers. When she sighed, he repeated the gesture, dragging his fingertips over her right hip. She tilted her bottom, just enough to offer more of an invitation. Bold opened his hands wide, extended his claws and, barely touching her silky flesh, dragged the pointed tips from waist to thigh.

When she moaned and writhed, he repeated the motion, each time exerting just a bit more pressure, each time drawing closer and closer to the crease between her buttocks.

She whimpered, but she didn't move her hands. He felt her need, her desire, like a hot shaft in his mind. He grabbed more of the lotion and spread it over the backs of her thighs, across her buttocks and up the length of her spine, soothing the invisible scratches he'd made, carefully rubbing it in until only the dark sheen of her skin glistened in the firelight.

He scooped up more cream, gradually aware of a tingling sensation on his palms, even along the cleft of his own ass. "Ah, Cené, " he whispered, spreading the lotion in small circles over her soft bottom. "This is more than a mere lubricant you've made, am I right? Something in this magic potion of yours is making me even more aroused. Does it do the same for you?"

Her soft chuckle sounded strained. She projected the sensation, sharing with him the tingling, burning, cold/hot sensation along each fine line of her ass where his nails had scored. Bold's cock immediately responded and he clenched his own buttocks tight.

Then he ran his finger slowly along her cleft once more, slipping down between her legs to flick softly over her clit. She moaned and rubbed her belly against the bedding, almost forcing his finger inside her.

He carefully withdrew, unwilling to risk penetration of the one place forbidden him. "Aren't you going to answer me?" he asked. She moaned again, more of a sigh this time. He spread her cheeks wide with his thumbs, and applied more of the lotion, taking a moment to press his finger lightly against the pink puckered ring of her anus.

She raised her hips, inviting him. He pressed harder and she moaned again, so he took his cock in his fist and swept it through the lotion, dragging the pulsing head from her clit, over her anus and on to the end of her spine, then back again.

He added more lotion, both to Cené and to himself. The tingling along the length of his cock was a thousand tiny fingers touching, teasing, making him throb with sensation.

Cené raised up on her knees and elbows, her hands still clasped tightly together. Baring herself completely for him, she lowered her head to her crossed arms, and waited, submissive, ready, her body trembling beneath his gentle massage.

Not from fear. No, Bold recognized passion and need in every shiver he raised with his touch. He rubbed gently, massaging the lotion deeper into her skin with his left hand, concentrating on the ever-softening ring of muscle around her anus with his right, finally pressing just a little bit harder, slipping through the tight ring and probing deep within her with one thick finger.

"More!" She cried out and bucked against him, pleading with each small whimper as he stroked one finger slowly in and out, easing the way. Withdrawing his finger, he added more lotion and this time inserted two fingers. She whimpered again, her breath choppy, her hips undulating with his gentle thrusts. The path was easier now as he slowly worked in and out, stretching the tight muscle, turning her on even more.

He felt her deep shudders, heard her panting breaths. He reached down between her legs and dragged the fingers of his left hand through the thick juices flowing down her inner thighs. They were sweet and slick, and he brought his fingers to his nose and inhaled deeply, then licked the sweet syrup from one hand while he slowly fucked her with the other.

It was almost too much. Bold realized his own breathing was growing uneven and harsh, felt the tight coil of need deep in his loins and knew that if he didn't find release within her tight passage it would soon happen most ingloriously all over her gorgeous backside.

Kneeling behind her, he added more of the lubricating lotion to his cock for good measure, then slowly pressed the smooth head against her anus. She moaned and spread her knees wider. He felt the tight ring of muscle give just a bit, and withdrew. Once more, he pressed against her, only this time he rubbed the pad of his finger lightly across her clit.

She shuddered, as if she didn't know which sensation to pursue—the soft rasp of his finger between her legs, or the persistent pressure of his cock against her ass.

Groaning, she lifted her hips higher just as he pressed forward. He felt the tight ring of muscle release, then squeeze down once more behind the head of his cock.

Oh Mother. Never, not once in his life had he ever felt anything remotely like this! Thighs quivering, balls contracting up so close between his legs he thought they might continue the journey and crawl right on inside, he slowly, so slowly, pushed forward into this most virgin passage of all.

Cené's breath huffed out of her now in deep gasps. Her thighs trembled, her smooth buttocks quivered as he seated himself completely inside. Her tight little anus grabbed at the base of his cock and his thick pubic hair rubbed against her buttocks. He couldn't imagine what this felt like for her, only knew that what he felt was beyond any pleasure he could imagine.

Suddenly, Cené was there in his thoughts, sharing the lush fullness of his cock buried tightly in her ass, sharing the overwhelming sensation of the rough tangle of his hair abrading her sensitive, lightly scratched buttocks, even the pain that was more pleasure, of his unsheathed claws digging into the flesh along the sides of her hips.

At this thought, Bolden guiltily sheathed his claws. Cené laughed aloud, so he reached down between her legs and stroked her clit once more, his fingers slipping through the sweet fluids.

She sighed, then moaned her pleasure and her thoughts slipped away from his. Bolden understood. It was too difficult, trying to make a coherent connection to another mind while experiencing sensations only imagined.

Not even his imagination had been this good.

He withdrew just as slowly as he'd entered, then pushed his way in again. With each stroke, entry was easier, the sensations even more pleasurable. He and Cené found their rhythm as she lifted her hips to each thrust of his. Bold kept his thrusts slow and steady, rubbing lightly at her clit with the fingers of his left hand, plucking and tugging at her turgid nipples, one after the other, with his right.

She whimpered again and lifted her hips higher, pressing harder against him. Her thoughts filled his mind, jumbled, tumbled with passion, spilling over with desire. *More, I want more...this feels...it feels...deeper, please, Bold. Harder. Please...*

He wanted this to last forever. He wanted to know this wonderful pleasure would go on and on, but the coil was tightening in his gut and her mental pleas were filling his mind.

Bold knew he couldn't hold onto the slim shreds of his control much longer. Cené's breath huffed out in great gasps, her slick fluids covered his fingers and it was all he could do to make one more long, hard thrust into that amazingly tight passage.

He buried himself as deep as he could and held his body rigid, reveling in the sensations of heat and pulsing woman all around him.

He captured her clit between his fingers, rolling it like a miniature cock, rubbing the foreskin back and forth over the tiny bundle of nerves, tilting his hips, lifting her on his cock.

Cené arched her back and screamed, her muscles clamped down like a damned vise on his cock and he couldn't control the speed, couldn't help but pull back out and slam into her, hard and deep, again, then once more as she climaxed about him. The muscles deep in her bowel tightened around him, hot and grasping, squeezing him like a fist, tighter than he'd dreamed possible, holding him immobile.

Time, for one brief moment, stopped. Bold threw his head back and roared, the full-throated cry of a Lion of Mirat in his prime, then emptied himself deep inside Cené. The pulsing, clenching pleasure-pain of orgasm was more—hotter, tighter, unbelievably intense. Cené's knees gave out and she lay flat against the boughs, hands tightly clasped together, with Bold still buried deep inside. He sprawled across her trembling body, peripherally concerned, somewhere in the back of his mind, that his weight was too much, but she didn't protest so he stayed where he was.

Not that he could have moved, even if he'd had to.

The spasms holding his cock in place seemed to go on forever, as if her climax had no intention of ending. It suited him just fine. So fine, in fact, that he felt himself harden, lengthen, return to his almost fully erect state, still buried deep inside the hottest, tightest channel he'd ever known.

Once was wonderful. He didn't think she'd want him again quite so soon. His cock lengthened, hardened, until he knew he must once more find pleasure or retreat. Regretfully, Bold began to slowly withdraw. Cené unclasped her hands, reached around behind her and grabbed his wrist.

"Don't you dare," she said, though there was no real threat in the words. She was, however, speaking in the voice of the goddess. "Again. I want you again."

"At your command, my Lady."

He felt, rather than heard her giggle, felt her body relax, as if something went out of her. "No, I'm Cené, now. The goddess just made her demand and left. She said she has much to consider, but wanted us to continue to enjoy ourselves. Personally, I think we wore her out."

Groaning, Bolden nuzzled against Cené's smooth back. "She's not the only one."

"I don't believe that. I feel you grow large once more inside me. It feels wonderful." Her voice was muffled in the soft blanket, but Bolden still heard the invitation in her words. "We have a long night ahead of us," she said, wriggling her hips beneath him.

"I wonder how much farther to the temple?" Bold asked, not really expecting an answer. Cené giggled, fully understanding the question.

He wanted more nights of this. More nights with Cené. She wriggled once more against his huge weight, and when he gave her the room, shoved her bottom up against him and knelt between his thighs, buttocks thrust high, her head lying on her crossed arms.

This time he would take it slow. The reality of their relationship was something he pushed to the back of his mind. He was pleasuring Cené — and the goddess — in the hope she might see fit to send him home. He wanted to go home, wanted to see his family again.

Cené said she wouldn't leave her world. Bold missed his own, missed his family. Plus, there was the small matter of completing his Quest, of making his formal report to the Academy.

How, though, would he go a lifetime without Cené? Or her goddess? No, he wouldn't think about that. Not now. He would think only of Cené, of giving her pleasure—and of satisfying her goddess.

Her muscles clenched tightly around his cock as he thrust slowly in and out. He savored the sensation, each tiny ripple of her warm and clasping body, each small moan and whimper he drew from her. Who was he kidding? Bold shivered with the overwhelming pleasure he found within Cené's dark heat. *Praise the Mother*, he never wanted this to end.

Chapter Nine

Once, during the darkest hours just before dawn, Bolden sensed the makáo near their bed. Male and female, the figures hovered just beyond his consciousness, barely visible as wraithlike shadows in the feeble glow of the last few burning embers in the fire pit.

Had they been closer? Had Cené invited them for her pleasure?

The shaft of jealousy that crawled over him at the mere thought of her taking pleasure, even from creatures of the mist, shocked him.

Cené stirred, then rolled closer to Bold. He wrapped his arms around her, as if to protect her from the makáo. She'd once welcomed them to her bed...did she still need them? Did the goddess? He hoped not. He could no more sit by and watch his woman with one of those slimy...

Idiot! What right did he have?

None, really. Of course...the little monsters haven't been around much, lately.

No, they hadn't returned since he and Cené had first found pleasure with one another. The goddess hadn't mentioned them, other than in passing. Maybe the little beasts were forbidden now.

The thought pleased Bold tremendously.

Maybe he and Cené gave the goddess so much pleasure, she didn't need the makáo. Then another thought intruded. Could the creatures feel jealousy? Might they be a danger to Cené?

As if sensing Bold's concern, Cené nuzzled her cheek against his chest. Bold felt her soft breath lifting the pelt that darkened the area between his nipples. His cock tightened. No matter how innocent her touch, she had an immediate, sensual effect on him. Sighing, he forgot the makáo, forgot the goddess and his quest, forgot everything but the feel of Cené held safely in his embrace.

* * * * *

She was the trees, the rocks, the very boughs they slept upon, everywhere, every thing. Not the makáo, though. Never the makáo. They gave her pleasure, foolish ephemeral beings that they were, but she'd not created them, though she knew that was what her people believed. No, the makáo just *were*, much as she herself *was*.

They had appeared after the *great deceit*.

Odd, how she could think of it now without so much rancor. She once fell badly and paid a terrible price. He had been Evil. Greed, envy, malice...all the sins of mankind, wrapped into one beautiful male body that promised her pleasure.

She'd fallen hard. Thank goodness his true nature had shown itself before it was too late. If she'd actually given herself, let him take her maidenhead, he would have won. Evil would rule and she would be naught but a barren world.

Still, she felt Evil stirring again. Automatically, she reached for her blessing bag, but of course it was gone. Lost in time over the millennia, possibly stolen, though she'd never guessed who might have taken it. Who would steal from a goddess, other than Evil?

Impossible. He was imprisoned within the bag...he couldn't steal himself. Misplaced...merely out of sight, lost but not forgotten. It would be comforting to know exactly where Evil lay, but the blessing bag would hold him prisoner, wherever it might be...hold him securely, trapped within the stone, the stone within the bag.

She was everything. Silently, she let her senses flow, experienced the night air on this side, the sunshine heating her world/body on the far side. Rain fell, giving her cool relief where the sun had once burned, her winds ruffled the leaves of ancient forests.

I am. I exist. I am everything. How could she have misplaced her blessing bag upon herself? A question like that might keep her mind active for eons. Ah, she should have guarded it better, held on tighter, but the blessing bag with the essence of Evil was gone.

Hopefully, dropped somewhere deep within her forest, at the bottom of an endless canyon, maybe in the ocean. Who was to say? Gone for so long she'd almost lost the habit of reaching for it.

Almost, but not quite.

I am. She concentrated once more on the lovers. The man pleased her. The woman's body pleased her. Both let her focus on living, not just on being, on feeling more than merely existing.

I am. So different, now, fully immersed within her immortal state as world, not woman. No emotion, no real sense of need or desire, merely the memories of those feelings. Memories stirred each time she focused on Bolden and Cené.

The makáo scampered around their dying fire, drawing close but not touching the sleeping lovers. She watched the creatures dispassionately, ignoring them as she usually did unless they served her.

Suddenly, the wraiths stopped, holding perfectly still—as if they listened? She used all of her senses, but there was no sound. Merely the sighing of her branches, the rustle of her grasses, the soft chatter of night time creatures finding their nests for the coming day.

Then, as one, the makáo drew close to Cené, stroking her thighs and caressing her breasts. One slithered to a spot between her legs and placed its mouth over her clitoris, sucking like a baby at its mother's breast. Cené moaned, but it was a sound of fear, not pleasure. An edge of fear laced with dark desire seemed to enfold the entire camp, but the makáo continued their sensual assault on Cené's sleeping body.

Odd, how they appeared to not just ignore, but to avoid the man. He slept, unaware as they serviced the dark woman. Her hips writhed as if she tried to escape, but still she slept. Another fearful moan escaped her lips.

Suddenly, Bolden sat straight up, his fists clenched, eyes wide and mouth curved into a snarl. The makáo dissolved into tiny threads of energy and melted into the forest.

Bolden shook his head, as if he'd awakened from a disturbing dream. Cené slumbered on, calm now, seeming unaware the makáo had touched her. Bold leaned over and gently kissed her lips, brushed his palm across her cheek, then lay back down and wrapped his strong arms around her, protecting her.

The goddess sighed, touched by his gentleness. There was no fault to find in that damned cocky male. She'd tried. She wanted so much to find something, anything that would make it easier to see him go. She'd been marginally aware of him since his burning ship had spit him on to her planet in that small metal sphere, aware as she was of all the creatures in her element, but not until he captured Cené within the Dream Forest had the goddess really taken notice.

He was a truly beautiful creature. An intriguing combination of man and beast, with the strong, upright physique of a man, the musculature and strength of a nightcat in its prime. The thick mane of hair was intriguing, though not nearly so intriguing as that wondrous cock he'd used so beautifully on her human self, or even that most amazing tongue. She remembered shivering, crying out and practically begging for more of his magic when he'd licked and kissed her.

Sighing, a soft breeze of sound, she wished things could be different. She would truly hate to see him go, though she must honor his request to return to his home world, just as he had honored her request for passion.

Ah, the passion. She still had at least one more night. Two if she turned the trail a bit more, made the way just a little more convoluted. No matter...what was one day in forever? A day of memories, another day of experiencing passion...even love? How much longer could she keep him here before fulfilling her part of the bargain?

She would still have her three days, once he reached her temple, but he must return to his own world, eventually. She'd promised him his boon, should he fulfill his end of the bargain. Still, she hated to think of her world without his presence.

It would once more be so lonely. The goddess settled down into the world that was her true self, wondering.

She sensed the makáo, once more near the sleeping pair. *Odd.* They had not been summoned, not by herself and definitely not by Bold or Cené. She'd experienced nothing when they attempted to pleasure the woman, had sensed only disquiet, even fear. *Very odd.*

They hovered even now, just beyond the lovers.

The makáo existed for her pleasure, and hers alone. Who directed them this night? It was obvious Cené had not invited them into her dreams. Whatever being they bowed to must be powerful indeed, for the makáo were the essence of dreams and fantasy, acting at the whim of the goddess and no one else.

Or so she'd believed.

* * * * *

"The way is not as smooth as in the past." Cené paused at a twist in the trail and struggled with a knotted vine that blocked their way. The ropey plant was bigger around than her slim arms. After a moment's struggle, she threw her hands in the air in frustration. "Why do you think the Lady delays us?"

"Ask her." Bold set his pack on the ground and set to work on the vine. It practically fought him as he ripped it back and opened up another small portion of the trail. Then he smiled at Cené and gestured for her to proceed. She glared at him, then shoved on ahead. She took this journey so seriously, intent on finding her Lady's temple.

Bold threw his pack over his shoulder and fell in behind her, grinning broadly at the stiff set of her shoulders. The journey itself had become his goal, not the temple. All he could think about was the pleasure he was going to find at the end of the day. He'd developed an amazingly powerful attraction to her perfectly shaped backside. His cock twitched every time he thought of the night he'd spent with Cené. They had truly and most satisfactorily breached the last passage available to them.

Well, not totally. She'd hinted to him it was a passage they shared. Though he was certain it wouldn't be nearly as pleasurable for her to penetrate him in such a manner, Bold had discovered a new awareness of his own ass.

Was it Cené's idea, or the goddess? She'd not made her appearance yet this morning, though he'd sensed her all about them, almost as if she protected them.

But from what?

"Bold? Did you hear that?"

Cené paused, held perfectly still, then pointed off to the left. He listened, heard nothing unusual and shook his head. "No. What was it?"

"I'm not sure. A rustling, something that felt like it didn't belong." She shrugged her shoulders and pushed the thick plant fronds aside.

The trail was definitely more difficult to follow today. Bold moved closer to Cené and searched the surrounding foliage. "Maybe the goddess doesn't want us to find her temple," he said. "Maybe the sex is so good she wants us to stay."

"I will stay. You are the only one who will leave."

"You could come with me." He'd pursued this line of thought for the past two days.

Her answer was always the same. "You know I cannot leave." This time, though, Cené didn't just drop it. She turned and stared at him. Her green eyes glittered, not from tears but anger. She flipped her fingers to empathize each word. "You know I must stay. I am as bound to this world as is our goddess. Why do you insist? What is it about this world of yours that draws you more powerfully than mine?"

"It..." He sighed. "It's my home. My parents are there. They probably think I'm dead. It tears at me, knowing how they must grieve. I'm their only son, the only child to survive. My mother lost two other young. It's not easy for a human woman to give birth to a Miratan cub. It's not fair she should lose me, too, especially if there's any chance at all I can return. For that alone, to ease their minds, I need to go home. Then there's the duty of my Quest. I have a report to make. I made an oath to do everything in my power to fulfill the tenets of my Quest."

Cené bowed her head. "I'm sorry. I didn't understand. It's just..." She looked up at Bold, her eyes filled with tears. "I...my goddess, will miss you." She sucked her lips between her teeth, then turned toward the trail.

The way suddenly lay clear before them.

They camped early by a small pond. Once more the pool steamed in the cool evening air. Cené ran her fingers through the water and sighed. "Warmer than the last one. It will feel wonderful when we bathe."

"After we eat," Bold said. He'd fished today, spearing several small fish that looked like fat trout. As was the way since he'd first been marooned here, the planet provided exactly what they needed. Today, the question weighed heavily on him—did every world have its own sentience? Was the *Mother* they prayed to on Mirat actually that world's true self? What of the *God* on Earth?

No...that god claimed to rule the universe, something Bold found quite unacceptable. Here, though, he sensed the goddess all around them. Now he knew the planet was sentient, he was even more aware of her presence.

Today, though, she'd not appeared even once as Cené. He missed her.

Sitting cross-legged by the fire, Cené wondered at the thoughts in Bold's mind. She'd almost tried to read them, then realized that was unacceptable without his permission. How could she survive once he left her? His world was so advanced compared to this one, so far away, she couldn't imagine him ever coming back to hers.

Her pussy throbbed with need and she was already wet between her legs. Her maiden's passage had been preparing for Bolden ever since they'd met...truth be told, since he'd continued pursuing her when his companions had turned back. She'd been impressed then by his tenacity, his perseverance when the others quit.

She missed the goddess. Today she'd not felt her presence, other than as a silent witness to their trek. Cené sensed her sadness, wondered if she was going to miss Bolden as well.

Goddess? Will you join us tonight? She'd not had to ask before. Tonight there was no answer. Cené frowned and glanced at Bolden. He watched her through half-lowered lids, his amber eyes glinting in the firelight. Were they still free to experience one another's bodies? Wasn't that the only reason they made love — to give the goddess pleasure?

Last night was for our pleasure, and ours alone. Cené felt the heat rising in her face, just thinking of the things she and Bold had done, long after the goddess departed. Her bottom had felt a bit sore this morning, but the memories kept her hot and wet all day long.

To think that huge cock of his actually fit inside her that way! She closed her eyes and sighed, recalling the surprising sensitivity of that uninspiring part of her body, the sense of fullness, the slow stretching of her small opening when the slick, smooth head of his cock pressed against her, then his complete entry. The combination of his fingers toying with her clit and the slippery *in and out* thrust as he filled her made her even wetter now. She'd felt his seed emptying into her, so hot and deep within her own heat it made her skin flush even now, remembering. She squirmed a bit, rubbing her clitoris against the bare heel of her foot and realized it was already slick with her juices.

She'd taunted Bold with the idea of making love to him, just as he'd done to her, though of course she lacked that marvelous cock of his. She'd been teasing, but the way Bold watched her, especially now their meal was ending and the night growing close, told her he'd thought quite seriously of her proposal.

She still had some of that wonderful lotion the goddess had told her to make. She'd not forget the ingredients of that one! Smiling, Cené stood up and held her hand out to Bold. The goddess hadn't arrived, but there was no reason to delay.

Chapter Ten

"Tonight is your turn."

Bold blinked and, without thinking, reached out to grasp the small hand Cené held out to him. "My turn?" He looked up at her. The half-lidded eyes, full lips and secretive smile promised an exceptional evening. His cock twitched in anticipation. He willed the damned thing to be still, then rose to his feet and let Cené lead him to the pool.

She glanced over her shoulder, smiled enigmatically, then slipped the leather tunic over her head. Her rounded breasts seemed fuller, the nipples a darker red. Bold swallowed deeply, gave up trying to control his recalcitrant cock, removed his loincloth and followed her into the warm pool.

The water was hot and the scent of minerals strong. He bit back a sigh of pure pleasure as he sank slowly down in the still pool. Steam spun and swirled just at the surface. Bolden drifted to the far edge where Cené had already found a seat. There were stones around the edge, smooth and perfectly placed at a depth that allowed them to sit with the mineral-laden water lapping at his chest and her chin.

He sat close to her, their sides pressing together from the length of his thigh all the way to his underarm where she snuggled close against him. She stroked his belly lazily with one small hand, her fingers drifting perilously close to his erection.

"I've called to the goddess, but she's not joined with me tonight."

"I know." Bold kissed the top of her head, nuzzling his lips through her hair. She wore it short. It was black as night, with the texture of soft mink. He'd not seen her cut it, but the length hadn't changed in the three weeks since he'd first seen her. He recalled other women on this world with every length of hair imaginable.

Only Cené's was so short.

She was, as usual, unique.

"I've learned to sense when the goddess is with you," he said, bending to kiss her just below her left ear. If anything, the skin there was even smoother, silkier, than anywhere else...anywhere except the soft expanse at her inner thigh, or that perfect curve beneath her breasts, or...Bold grinned, touched the whorl inside her ear with the tip of his tongue, then pulled back far enough to look at her. "Tonight, you are yourself. I like this, just the two of us, as much as when she's here." Cené raised her face to his and he kissed her waiting mouth. Slowly, exploring taste and sensation, using the very tip of his tongue, he traced the outline of her lips much as he'd just explored her perfect ear.

She smiled against his mouth, tilted her head and used her own tongue to part his lips further. They stayed there, tongues mating, bodies held in stasis by the warm water steaming about them. Bold raised his hand to caress her breast, thought better and merely rested his huge palm on her shoulder.

This was all mouths and lips, teeth and tongues and a communion as intimate as the act of sexual intercourse. She thrust her tongue deep inside his mouth, then withdrew it, mimicking the act of love. Bold tightened his lips around her tongue, suckling her sweet flavor, compressing her tongue as she entered and retreated so that she fucked his mouth, her lips close to his, their breath mingling with each parry and thrust.

Cené withdrew and Bold followed, so that now his tongue filled her mouth. Carefully, well aware of the size and abrasive texture of his compared to Cené's, he made love to her mouth. She moaned against his lips, tilted her body closer and thrust her pussy up against his thigh. He lifted her so that she straddled his leg, both he and Cené still almost completely immersed in the warm pool.

She was hot between her legs, hotter even than the water, and slick where her juices spilled from her swollen pussy. Grasping her buttocks, Bold held her close against his thigh, matching her rhythm as she rubbed her protruding clit against him, timed to each thrust of his tongue deep inside her mouth.

Suddenly her lips compressed around his tongue and her hips stilled. Her legs tightened around his and she pressed hard against his thigh. He grabbed her buttocks in his broad hand and held her there, immobile, as her orgasm claimed her.

He felt her legs contract around his, felt the spasms ripple from her nether lips to his leg as she arched her back and let her climax take her. Her mouth opened in a silent scream, releasing him as she stiffened, gasped for air, and shuddered in release.

She giggled when she finally collapsed against his chest. "Oh my." She gasped for a breath of air. "I hadn't counted on that. I only meant to kiss you. This night's supposed to be for you."

"That's all we did," Bold countered. "Kissed." He stroked her shoulder. She still trembled in the aftermath of orgasm. "Kissed really well. I love what you just did. Believe me, there is nothing I can imagine that's more exciting than watching you come."

"Ha." She looked away, as if embarrassed. Her voice was a bare whisper. "You have way too many tricks up your sleeve, my friend."

Bold tapped his foot and bounced her slowly against his thigh. She giggled again, then trailed her fingers across his stomach once more, easily evading his straining erection.

Her hands drifted closer and closer to him, bumping into his cock as if by accident, then skittering quickly away, but always returning for one more brief touch. Finally, her fingers gave up all semblance of rubbing his belly. Bold sighed as she settled back down beside him and stroked his penis, running her palm along the upper side, rolling across the top where she paused a moment to rim the tiny hole with her fingertip, then tracing the strong vein along the bottom. She didn't stop there. Her fingers discovered each hard nut within his sac, rolling first one, then the other with great care.

Bold scooted his back against the earthen bank and spread his legs wider so that he floated just beneath the water's surface. His cock broke through, like a swollen flag pole marking the spot.

Grinning, Cené continued her exploration, floating around so that she stood between his legs. The water lapped against her breasts. She reached under Bold's hips and lifted his taut buttocks in her palms, then leaned over and took just the head of his penis between her lips.

He forced himself to relax so that his natural buoyancy allowed Cené to raise and lower him at will. She suckled him, moving him in and out of her hot, wet mouth with her hands on his ass. Her tongue kept busy, pressing and licking, her cheeks hollowing with each deep, sucking pull against him.

Praise the Mother...so caught up in the sensations overwhelming his cock, Bold almost missed the early exploration of her fingers, edging closer and closer together, deep in the cleft between his buttocks.

Suddenly, her fingertip found his anus, pressing, then retreating, pressing again, a little deeper this time, then retreating, raising and lowering his hips with just the pressure of that one finger.

He clenched his buttocks tightly and she squeezed back with her palms, still suckling his cock, still raising and lowering him in the warm water. He wanted to grab for her, but knew she wanted control. There was no goddess, this time. No large male calling the shots. This was Cené making the night special for Bolden.

He let go and the rhythm took over, closed his eyes and gave himself to Cené. She was all lips and hands, warm, seeking mouth and slim, searching fingers. He reached over his head and grabbed onto a clump of twisted roots at the edge of the pool, anchoring himself. Locking his hands in place.

Her fingertip gained entrance to his ass and he moaned. Between her firm lips, his cock twitched in response as she slowly circled the taut puckered ring of muscle, pressing inside then returning to tease him before entering again. *In, out, in...out...his cock in her mouth, her finger in his ass...two fingers...two in his ass, circling, probing, deeper...in then out, in, in deeper...pressing, pressing deeper and swirling about, finding, finding...oh Mother!*

Whatever Cené found, Bold hoped like hell she'd find it again. He gasped, on the edge of coming, his cock hard as stone, her lips rubbing slowly over the tip, his buttocks clenching her fingers, squeezing down on them as they slowly circled then retreated to rub just within the rim of his ass.

He hung on to the tangled tree roots, anchoring himself firmly as Cené once more dipped her head over his groin, lifted his hips in her slim little hands and swallowed his big cock down her throat.

Cené...not the goddess. His little Cené was doing this all on her own. Legs trembling in the warm water, Bold struggled to control his raging libido. Cené let most of his cock slip free and grinned at him, then once more took him in her mouth.

He felt her tongue sweeping the backside of his cock, one hand stroking his taut balls, the other fingering his ass once more, *pressing, pressing, deeper...one finger, two...deeper, deeper, pressing harder, slipping further inside, just...there!*

Ohshitohshitohshit!

Arching his back, his buttocks clamped down tightly on Cené's hand, on her finger tips massaging him deep inside. Grasping the twisted roots of the tree, he opened his mouth in a silent cry that ended in a full-throated roar. Water splashed as he bucked his hips. Cené sucked even harder on his cock and he filled her mouth with spurt after spurt of his seed.

Gasping, lungs screaming for air, trapped in pure sensation, he arched his hips and clenched his buttocks as hard as he could, clinging to her fingers. Cené massaged his balls with one hand, while the fingers still inside him continued their gentle pressure against whatever organ she'd discovered. Shocks riveted through his gut, twisted his loins, sparked the length of his cock. Even his nipples puckered and tightened, his entire body thrummed with sensation.

Cené continued her rhythmic pressure and massage, licking his cock clean, holding him in her mouth long after his orgasm ended. Slowly she withdrew her finger from his ass, but continued to gently massage his balls, creating a mere whisper of sensation now, all of it awash in the warm water, the gentle lap of waves against his thighs.

Practically whimpering with pleasure, Bolden shuddered and gasped once more for air. His fingers clenched spasmodically at the tree roots. *Praise the Mother*, that had to be the most exquisitely painful, overwhelmingly pleasurable orgasm he'd experienced.

Cené crawled up beside him and wrapped her arms around his waist. Bold draped one limp arm over her shoulders and held her close. Tendrils of steam wafted about them as the ripples in the water slowly dissipated.

They lay there for a long time, or so it seemed to Bold. The water stayed comfortably warm, Cené dozed against his chest and the night sounds blended, one into the other around them.

Still, the goddess had not joined them, though he'd been almost certain he'd sensed a presence near the pond.

The makáo? He'd dreamed them last night, he was certain. Uneasy now, Bold tried to remember if the makáo had actually pleasured Cené or not. He knew they hadn't touched his body. He would know if they had.

Something brushed the side of his face in the dark, startling him. Bold raised his hand and felt only himself, his wet and tangled mane floating out around his shoulders in the pool.

Still, he felt uneasy now. As if their campsite was not quite so secure, their privacy not nearly so private. Slowly, so as not to disturb Cené's slumber, he stood with her small body in his arms and walked to the edge of the pool.

The fire cast very little light, but the embers still burned hot. Bold lay Cené on top of their makeshift bed and covered her with her tunic. Then he built up the fire, adding from the stack of wood they'd gathered earlier. He took a moment to check his pack. The charge was low on the receiver, but they'd hardly seen the sun since entering this deep, dark part of the forest. He carefully repacked it, wondering why he even looked anymore. There'd be no messages from home. At least he'd managed to store coordinates of the visible stars in this world's solar system. Some day, he would come back here.

He glanced at Cené, sleeping so peacefully now. When awake, she was such a bundle of energy, her body always in motion, her expressions changing with each word she spoke, each thought that crossed her mind. She never bored him, always excited him. He couldn't imagine life without her in it. Yes, he would definitely return to her world. He was sure of it.

He added more wood. The flames flared up brightly. The snap and crackle of dry wood catching fire awakened Cené. She sat up, rubbed her eyes and smiled at Bold. "It has been a most pleasurable evening," she said.

Bold chuckled as he pushed the coals closer to the fire with a long stick. "I would say that. Thank you."

"You don't really think we're through, do you?"

His balls still ached, his cock had practically gone into hiding, but the moment Cené hinted at more, he was instantly on full alert. "Oh?" He turned and moved closer to the bed. "Just what did you have in mind?"

"I have all this wonderful lotion left...we didn't use it tonight."

"No, we didn't, did we? Bold leaned over to kiss her, when a sudden movement just beyond the fire caught his attention.

Makao! A whole group of the ephemeral little beings, massing almost as if for attack.

"Do you see them?" Bold leaned over and whispered to Cené, taking a pose as if he were going to kiss her. "Why are they here now?

"I don't know." She scooted up into a sitting position. "They are creatures of passion, of dreams...of the night. I've not called them. They're not of my imagining." She grabbed Bold's arm and hung on. "Why are they here?"

"Call the goddess. She'll know."

Cené lifted her head and closed her eyes. Her lips moved, but there was no sound.

Suddenly a bolt of light crossed the campsite. There was a howl of pain, a loud screech, and the assembled makáo disappeared into the forest.

Leaves rustled in their path. The ground looked trampled where they had waited.

Bold stared at Cené, well aware the goddess now resided within. "What's happened to your little pleasure-seekers, Goddess? For creatures of imagination and desire, they've suddenly developed quite sturdy little bodies...I've never before seen creatures of the mist who left footprints behind."

Cené's head hung in shame. The goddess's shame. "I know. That's why I've not been with you today. Someone is controlling the makáo. Someone evil. I believe Evil is free once again on my world. I was so sure he could not escape." She raised her head, determination evident in the thrust of her chin, the glint in her eyes. "I must be strong. I cannot let Evil win my world from me."

Guilt swamped him. He never should have been so sharp with her. Bold reached out and gathered her into his arms. She went, willingly, no longer merely Cené, but Cené just the same. Holding her tightly, he wondered once more about the future, wondered where this journey might take all of them.

Chapter Eleven

Bold stood guard most of the night, the first night since entering the Dream Forest he'd felt such a need. Cené slept fitfully beside him. Though the goddess had no need of rest, the woman's body was tired.

Bold sensed the goddess all about their campsite, as much a part of her world as of Cené.

The makáo didn't return. Bold added more wood to the fire, as much for heat as for light. His cat's eyes had little need of the extra light. He sensed Cené stirring, knew she was awake.

"How far, Goddess, before we reach your temple?" He wasn't thinking of going home. No, there was a battle to be fought, a woman to protect. He hoped the temple offered protection from whatever followed them.

He waited, but she didn't answer.

No matter that the woman he wished to protect was a world unto herself. Bold shook his head and grinned. *Who the hell do I think I am?*

A goddess had no real need of a mere mortal. Or did she? He sat down next to her on the bed and brushed his palm across Cené's hair. She snuggled against him and sighed. Her eyes remained closed, but she seemed more peaceful now.

He wanted her. Need for her kept him awake, thinking of her at any time of the day or night left him aroused. Obviously, she didn't have the same problem.

No, even Cené would survive quite well without him.

Will I survive without Cené?

Even now he wanted her. With all their lovemaking, he still wanted the ultimate connection, the chance to love her as a man should love a woman. Not merely the act of copulation. Bold wanted the act of love. Penetration of her virgin's barrier had nothing to do with sex and everything to do with Cené—and her goddess.

More than anything, he wanted to leave a part of himself inside her, impossible though that might be. Could a mortal impregnate a goddess? Not likely.

Maybe.

Would Cené choose him as her lifemate? Would he consider staying here, on this world, never to see his family again? Never to ease their grief over his loss? Would he knowingly break his oath to return at all costs from his Quest?

Over the past couple days, Bold realized he'd put thoughts of going home almost completely out of his mind. Only when he answered Cené's questions about Earth or Mirat did he think of his dual homeland...and his parents. Only when he thought of staying here forever, of staying with Cené, did he remember the reason they made this journey.

The only reason—to ask the Lady to send him home.

Well, he'd found this world once. He could find it again. He would do as he'd planned and ask the goddess to send him back to Earth.

Then he'd merely come back to this world, whatever it was called, and claim the woman he feared he'd grown to love.

How does a mortal claim a goddess? Sighing, he lay down beside Cené, still alert to the night around them.

* * * * *

Bold wasn't certain what he'd expected a goddess's temple to look like, but the vine covered pile of stones Cené now approached with reverence certainly wasn't it.

They'd find no protection from the makáo or the power behind them, here. The walls, once at least ten feet high, were now nothing more than piles of rubble partially hidden in ferns and twisted vines. One huge tree grew out of the middle of what had once been some sort of building, its roots wrapped and twisted about the massive stones so that they were a part of the tree as much as the tree had become part of the structure.

Bold looked up, his gaze traveling over the rough bark, reminiscent of ancient Sequoias on earth. Shreds of long, red bark hung in tattered strips. The trunk, at least fifty feet in diameter, disappeared into the leafy canopy above them where the first thick branches stretched high overhead.

He hadn't realized the turmoil he'd experience when they finally reached their destination. Cené paused beside him and studied the ruins, then reached out and took his hand. Her fingers squeezed his. She tilted her chin and looked at him, her eyes filled with sadness. "I can't believe we're actually here," she said. "I wondered if we'd ever find this place. It has been the stuff of legend. I feel her power here, though the temple is fallen and there is little left of the grandeur I expected."

"I know." Bold drew her into his arms. She came willingly, her small frame fitting against his larger one as if they'd been created as a pair from the beginning. Made to be one. He brushed her hair with his palm, then cupped her face in both his hands. "Many times, I've hoped we would wander the forest forever, making love, touching, talking. This journey with you has been a most amazing experience. I'm almost sorry we've arrived."

Cené stood up on her toes and kissed him on the mouth, then turned and walked directly up to the tree, stretched her hands out in front of her, placed her palms flat against the giant and shut her eyes. Bold held back, sensing the goddess strongly within the woman, the power emanating from her slight frame a tangible thing in the still ruins.

Suddenly a glow appeared to spread out from beneath her palms. As Bold stared, a doorway opened into the tree and light spilled out of its depths. Cené stepped through the opening. Bold grabbed up his pack and followed her. The moment he crossed the threshold, the door behind him closed.

He barely noticed. *Praise the Mother, what manner of temple is this?*

Gasping like a fish out of water, he finally remembered to breathe. Instead of a rough hewn cavern within the tree, they stood now in a palace stretching in all directions. This one room was the size of a sports arena. Many doors led to other rooms. Richly furnished, hung with tapestries and lighted with a thousand candles, this room alone was so far beyond the realm of anything Bold had expected, it left him speechless.

His pack hit the floor with a loud *thud*. Cené turned around, her eyes as wide as saucers. Obviously, from the look of amazement on her face, the goddess was no longer within her. "I've heard of the riches of this place, but I never dreamed..." She swept one hand, encompassing all around them. "It's beyond anything I have ever seen in my life."

Bold just shook his head. "To think I was worried about finding protection in that wreck of a temple. I have a feeling this place is about as safe as it gets. I don't imagine the makáo will bother us here."

Cené giggled. "I have no idea where she wants us to go. This is so big, so..."

"Yeah." Bold grabbed up his pack and took Cené's hand. "I wonder if we're still on your world. This place is obviously *not* inside the tree. Maybe the doorway took us into some other dimension. There's got to be an explanation." He dragged Cené, still gaping at the opulent beauty around them, across the huge room. They stood before a tapestry that stretched for at least a hundred yards along the wall. Exquisitely woven of finest silk, it was covered with many colorful scenes, like a huge woven mural telling a story.

Bold set his pack down, frowning. "I've seen something similar, though not nearly so large, in one of the temples to the Mother on my father's world, Mirat. It's the story of creation, only the creatures on the Miratan tapestry are all feline or leonine." At Cené's curious glance, he added, "...of the cat family. Like my father." He pointed to a scene on one end.

"See...this scene in a bountiful garden, possibly your world's version of Earth's Eden, or Mirat's Paradise. The creatures here look like you, only their skin is of many hues, their features more primitive. It's almost as if they're growing out of the ground...as if they've been planted here. In the Miratan tapestry, the creatures are feline, but they're doing the same thing...rising up out of the ground."

He walked the length of the tapestry, dragging Cené with him. "Here, they discover language, and here, fire. Do you see?"

"This is the way we learn, what the goddess teaches us of our beginnings. She taught us these things, the use of fire, of language. Our history. You learn the same from your world, don't you?"

"Yes and no." It would explain so many things, the idea forming slowly within his mind. "Cené, I've told you when my ship was destroyed, I was on my Quest. It's something the people of my father's world do. We explore other worlds, searching for not only our own beginnings, but the reason behind the commonality we've found on all worlds. Look at me." He held his arms wide for Cené's perusal. "I shouldn't exist. I am a creature of two totally different species from different planets, yet my parents' mating created a viable offspring. Not only viable, but fertile. I was tested by doctors at the Academy who were convinced that a child of two species shouldn't be able to reproduce. My sperm is fine. They're just as healthy as can be. They shouldn't be, but they are. My parents aren't the only ones to have a child of two worlds. Our scientists have done extensive tests that show our DNA, the stuff that makes us unique, is so similar we can mate and produce live young with people from other planets. That should not be."

"I'm not sure I understand." Cené frowned, so obviously lost in Bold's explanation he wasn't sure where to start. "You and I, were we to mate, would most likely have a child, wouldn't we?"

"If all holds true, we probably could, but we shouldn't be able to, not if our species evolved independently on each of our worlds. The fact that all of us, all races on all known worlds, are essentially similar, no matter how dissimilar we appear, shouldn't be. We *should* be totally different, not so much alike that my sperm and your egg would be compatible."

Cené slanted her gaze and looked coyly at him, suddenly taking all thought of scientific discourse out of his mind. "I would like to try sometime, letting your sperm meet my egg. If you were to stay on my world...choose to be my lifemate...?"

His shoulders slumped. She'd never, not once, asked this of him directly, though he'd thought of it often enough. *Praise the Mother*, he would stay if he could, but now, so close to the chance of actually seeing his parents, letting them know he lived...he cupped her face in his palms. "I would, if I could. You know I can't. I intend to ask the goddess to send me home, but I promise you, I'll return. I'll ask her to bring me back. If she refuses, maybe I can somehow retrace the coordinates that brought me here..."

Cené bowed her head. He felt the splash of a single hot tear on the back of his hand. "No. The Goddess will send you to your home. That's the bargain she struck with you. She will send you there, but she will not bring you back. You must choose to stay here forever, or leave forever. That is her decision."

Bold dropped his hands from Cené's face and straightened. Anger toned his spine, tightened his hands into tight fists. He'd never dreamed she would forbid him to return. In the back of his mind, he'd figured he would somehow retrace his voyage and find this world again, no matter how long it took him.

"Cené, I ask you again. Will you come with me?"

She gazed up at him through tear-filled eyes and shook her head. "You know I can't. I am as much a part of this world as is the Goddess I serve. I have pledged my life to my Lady. If you stay, I would forego that pledge and ask you to be my lifemate, knowing I could still serve the Lady. If you choose to leave, I will remain in her temple, her servant always, in all ways."

The finality of his choice sat like a weight in his chest. It truly lay with him, to stay or to go. Cené obviously felt she had no choice. He must honor her wishes and beliefs in this. Standing here, now, looking at her sweet face, her beautiful green eyes swimming in tears, he felt his heart might break.

"It's not a decision I can make quickly. Will she give me time?"

Cené smiled. "Of course. You have plenty of time. Don't you remember her original bargain?"

When he frowned at her, she giggled. "Three days, Bolden. She has three days and nights of passion still due her. Three days when the goddess takes you to her bed. She wants memories, Bolden. Memories of passion, of desire, of feeling. Those memories will stay with her once you are gone. They'll stay with me, as well."

Praise the Mother, he'd totally forgotten that part of their deal, he'd been so enraptured by Cené, in the feelings that had been growing for her—and her goddess—each day they spent together.

But loving the goddess alone? Without Cené? It twisted what they had shared. Turned their loving exploration of one another's bodies into something tawdry, cheapened the feelings that had been growing between them.

"How can I do that, Cené?" He grabbed her hands and held them against his chest. "How can I make love to the goddess if you're not the one I see, the woman I hold? I know she's been with you these past days, but at least you were still there, too. It wouldn't feel right."

Smiling, Cené bowed her head. "My Lady will, for the next three days and nights, *be* Cené. My thoughts, my feelings, my love for you. Much as it has been along our journey when she's joined with us, but at those times, she remained mostly in my background. When I give her permission to enter me this time, the Cené you know will become but a small kernel of existence within the heart and mind of the Lady. I will experience everything with you, even feel what she feels—but she will be Cené, a woman, not a goddess, for the first time in her remembered existence."

"Do you allow her in of your own free will? I can't let you do something..."

"Oh, Bolden! This isn't your choice to make. You can be so thick, sometimes!" Cené wrapped her slim fingers around his wrist, her voice harsh with frustration. "Don't you understand what honor she gives me? These past few days when she joined with me, became part of me for those brief periods, I..." She swiped her hand across her streaming eyes and glared at Bolden. "I never dreamed I would be singled out for such honor. Think of it, Bolden—to share my body not only with the man I love, but my beloved Lady as well! I would do anything, *anything* at all for her. Now she grants me my greatest desire, to take you inside my virgin's passage in a most holy coupling. I choose the goddess as my lifemate, should you decide to leave. I choose you, should you stay." She grabbed his hands, squeezing them between her own.

"Are you sure, Cené? Of your own free will, are you saying we can make love? Once that tissue is broken, you're no longer virgin. You've kept yourself inviolate for so long, I don't feel right, knowing I may not..."

"What I said...remember? This isn't your decision." She laughed, her smile free and untroubled. "Ah, Bolden, whether you realize it or not, you love the Goddess, my Lady, as much, if not more, than you love me. You don't say the words, but you show them in everything you do. You may choose to go when the three days are ended, but you will leave both my Lady and me with memories of passion and love. You are free to make that choice, to go or to stay, just as I am free to make mine. The deal was set when you first asked the Goddess for favor."

She touched the side of his face, as if memorizing his look. Her chest rose and fell with a deep sigh. "Good-bye, Bolden of two worlds. I go now, that the Goddess may take her place within my body and my soul."

There was a brief flickering within her deep green eyes, a sense of power quickly dampened, and once again, before he had a chance to consider all the ramifications of Cené's impassioned speech, the goddess stood before him. She held out one slim hand, Cené's hand no longer.

He wrapped his big fingers around hers, looked into her eyes and realized Cené had known more than she realized.

As much as he loved the woman, he loved the goddess more.

Chapter Twelve

"I ask one thing of you." The goddess who was Cené pressed her finger lightly against Bolden's lips. "There will be no talk of your leaving, no talk of the makáo and the threat that lies outside these walls. There will be only you and me. I am Cené, the woman you love. That is all I ask, that you honor my fantasy. That you give me three days."

Bold stared down at Cené, reminded once again how tiny she was, how fragile, yet strong. He would do as the goddess asked. He could do no less. His cock, solidly pressed against his loincloth, had obviously already agreed.

He parted his lips and sucked her finger into his mouth, compressing it with his tongue. Cené moaned and pressed her body close to his. He grabbed her wrist and pulled her finger from his mouth, then kissed the tip. "As you wish, my lady. Whatever you desire, whatever I am able, I will do."

"Love me." She stood on her toes and wrapped her arms around his neck. "Love me as a man loves a woman. In all ways. There are no barriers between us."

He looked into her deep green eyes, saw passion and need and something he'd not noticed before, not when the goddess joined with the woman. He saw fear and vulnerability beneath the blatant desire.

Fears that echoed his own. Could he be what she desired? He slipped his hand beneath her hips and lifted Cené to his chest. "There must be a bed somewhere in this temple of yours. Just point."

Laughing shyly, she gestured toward a door at the far end of the room, then pressed her face against his throat. As Bold walked across the long stretch of the main room, he wondered if she felt his heart pounding in his chest, wondered if she knew how terrified he was of failing her.

Three days. He practically groaned aloud, wondering what he and this woman might discover over the next seventy two hours.

* * * * *

She'd expected desire. She'd not been surprised when her pussy practically wept with need the moment he sucked her finger into his mouth, wrapped that marvelous tongue of his around it.

She'd not expected fear. Not even considered the fact she might consider herself inadequate. That thought certainly hadn't entered her mind when she'd shared Cené's body, but now that the young woman had retreated so far within herself as to barely be noticed, the goddess suddenly wondered if she, by herself, could please this man.

He'd grown comfortable loving Cené. Would he respond as well now Cené was gone? Certainly the body was every bit as appealing, but the personality, the sweet loveliness of the woman, would be lost beneath her own powerful persona.

It had been so long since she'd thought at all how she appeared to humans. They existed on her world and so, revered her. That was as it should be. They prayed to her and she answered their prayers when she could or when she felt they were deserving.

She'd not had to worry if she pleased them. She worried only about keeping them safe. The thought flitted through her mind that this was selfish, this three days out of time she'd asked for herself. Evil walked abroad, the makáo appeared to have taken on form and substance, powered by something unknown. They were just outside the temple, even now. Surrounding the huge tree, wondering how to find entrance to her sanctuary.

Let them wonder. She must deal with them, and deal soon, but for now she wanted this time, this man. She was a goddess, immortal. She would please him, and herself. Somehow.

She pressed her face against the soft hollow between his throat and shoulder. Even here she could hear the steady rhythm of his heart. It was an oddly comforting sound. She'd enjoyed the feel of the woman's heart, but hadn't really thought what it would be like to hear the man's so close. Hadn't considered the thrill of anticipation...or the fear.

There was that word again. *Fear. A goddess does not fear. A goddess is. A goddess...no, a woman. I am a woman...being carried off to bed by an amazingly sensual, virile man.*

She closed her eyes and absorbed the sensations...*his muscular arm behind my back, another beneath my legs. The swift beat of his heart, the rhythmic sway of his body as he carries me so swiftly across the room.*

The harsh intake of his breath when he first sees the sleeping chambers, the very soft pressure of his lips against my forehead as he lays me on the downy blanket covering the bed.

She sprawled within the softness, legs spread ingloriously wide, and stared up at him, seeing him through Cené's eyes as if for the first time. He loomed over her, huge, a powerful man who was as much the beast as he was human. The strong line of his jaw, the thick mane covering his shoulders, spreading across his chest and following a narrow line to the edge of his loincloth, even the sharp canines when he smiled and the sharper, retractable claws at the ends of his blunt fingers...all exciting, mesmerizing, terrifying, even to a goddess.

She licked her lips, slowly running her tongue over both her bottom and upper lip, and knew at once it was an invitation.

He carefully untied the loincloth and let it fall to the floor. His erect cock was gorgeous. Huge, dark, pulsing with life and need. The foreskin was completely drawn back. She reached out to touch him, once again amazed at the contradictions in texture. Smooth as silk yet harder than any stone. The thick veins that fed it pulsed with life. The tiny opening at the end wept a single drop of creamy white fluid.

She stroked the length of him, then ran the pad of her thumb lightly over the head, smearing the liquid across the bulbous head. His cock jerked, his hips thrust forward, a slight movement that displayed his frayed grasp on control.

She raised up on one elbow, leaned over and took him in her mouth. The pleasure of the act drew a moan from her throat as she tasted him, the salty sweet flavor hinting of some exotic spice. *Addictive.* She could suckle him forever and never grow tired of the taste.

His broad palms came down lightly on the sides of her head. She felt them trembling as he held her, gently directed her rhythm. She wrapped her tongue around him, licking from base to tip as she drew him into her mouth.

He groaned and shifted his position slightly, as if afraid his knees might buckle. She grinned around the huge cock in her mouth and looked up at his face. His eyes were closed, his head thrown back, a grimace that might have been pain twisting his lips.

The tendons where his neck joined his shoulder were rigid bands, the muscles across his chest bulged with his effort. She knew he struggled for control, but she wanted him to lose. Wanted to taste his seed, feel his hot semen filling her mouth, so she raked her fingernails lightly over his sac. He jerked and his hands tightened on her head.

She fondled his sac once more, this time rolling the hard testicles lightly between her fingers, massaging the sensitive perineum behind his balls, then slowly running her finger along the cleft between his tightly clenched buttocks until she found the puckered ring of muscle.

His hands shook as he slowly worked with her, following her pace as she suckled his cock slowly in, then out of her mouth. She pressed slightly at his anus, finding resistance for a brief moment before her finger slipped inside, beyond the clenching muscle.

Bold's hips jerked to a complete stop, his cock so far down her throat she was forced to swallow him or choke. She squeezed his balls with one hand, thrust her finger deep inside his ass and compressed her cheeks and tongue as tightly as she could around his cock.

She felt the first pulsing in his balls, heard the deep throated roar as Bolden climaxed. She felt a ripple run the length of his cock, knew it took all the control he possessed not to shove deeper down her throat. Instead, she held him immobile, sucking as hard as she could, milking him with her lips and tongue and the pull of her cheeks. His hands slipped from the sides of her head to the edge of the mattress and he leaned over her, his huge body trembling, chest heaving, cock still pulsing in the long release of his climax.

Holding him in her mouth, she withdrew her finger from his ass and tugged lightly on his balls. Taking the hint, Bold practically collapsed beside her on the bed. She kept his penis between her lips, suckling gently now, licking and cleaning him of the very last drops of semen.

"I came in here with the intention of making love to you," he said. His voice was barely above a whisper, the words slipping out between each deep breath. "You didn't give me a chance."

She smiled and slowly dragged her lips the length of his penis, planted a kiss at the very tip and scooted up on the bed so that she faced him. When he cocked his eyebrow at her in question, she leaned over and kissed him. Their tongues twisted together, then he drew hers into his mouth, sucking it hard. She knew he tasted himself on her. Knew how much it excited him.

Slowly, so slowly she ended the kiss. "You'll get your chance," she whispered, licking at the corner of his mouth. "You just looked terribly needy...and absolutely delicious. I had to taste, to see if you were as good as I remembered."

Once again he cocked an eyebrow at her.

"Yes. Even better. That's something I could never grow tired of."

"Me either." He laughed, a harsh sound to her ears. "I think I've become addicted to you. To what you do to me. Who you are."

She sighed, then ran her hand through the thick tangle of mane cascading over his shoulders. "And who am I, Bolden of two worlds? What am I to you?"

"You are Cené. You are her lady. You are, together, the woman I love. You are the only woman I will ever love." He touched her face, cupped her jaw in his palm. "I ask the same question of you. What am I to you?"

She turned her head and kissed his palm. The skin was leathery, deeply callused. She knew this hand could be as soft and gentle, or as fierce and strong as need be. He was truly a man of two worlds, just as he was a man of many sides.

"You are my lover, the one I would choose for my lifemate, should that be possible. You are all things to me, but most of all, you are the only man I want, the only man I will ever desire. You complete me. I desire you in all ways, without barriers, without reservation. You are my love."

It felt like a marriage, as if the quiet vows they made to one another were binding for all time. Bold looked into the eyes of the goddess and saw Cené, saw his future, though he knew that could never be. She was, first and foremost, a goddess. Immortal. He would grow old in what, for her, would be a mere heartbeat.

Still, she had asked him for passion, for love, for memories to sustain her. He wanted the same. He couldn't imagine ever loving again, not like this. He brushed his hand through her short, silky hair and leaned over to kiss her. She tasted of his seed, her lips shiny with his essence, the subtle cinnamon flavor he had discovered was so much a part of himself. The eroticism of tasting his ejaculate on her sweet lips coiled into a pool of heat in his gut.

He licked lightly at her lower lip, then kissed her eyes, her cheek, the tender flesh beneath her ear. Straddling her with his knees on either side of her hips he kissed her just beside her blessing bag, deep in the V of her breasts. Trailing kisses, following the hem up her thigh and across her belly, he slipped the tunic off her slim body. She arched her back, presenting herself to him, but he ignored the pouting lips between her legs and concentrated instead on her navel, filling it with the tip of his tongue, circling 'round and 'round until she screamed and bucked her hips as if trying to throw him off.

He moved on, finding first one breast, then the other. Palming the turgid nipple on her right breast, he suckled her left. Her heartbeat pulsed against his lips, speeding up when he encircled her nipple with his tongue, lapping at it until he figured his sandpapery tongue had probably left it raw and stinging.

He switched to her other breast. Once more his tongue swirled around and around, scraping at the tender, sensitive nipple. It rose hot and tight against his tongue as he lapped and licked it into a hard knot of sensation. As he licked her, he swept his hand along the silky underside of her breast. There was no place more erotic, no flesh so soft and sweet as the deep curve where her breasts joined her slim ribcage.

Like caressing silk...warm, live silk.

He sat up, holding his weight on his knees, his balls resting in the nest of silky curls between her legs, his cock once more erect, pointing directly at her face. She panted. Her hands twisted the blankets and her hips writhed beneath him. He scooted back all the way to her calves, pushing her legs down and trapping them close together beneath his weight.

Her clitoris protruded at the juncture between her thighs, swollen and red, the small, protective hood stretched back, exposing just the tip. Bold leaned over and ran his tongue roughly along the crease between her legs, tracing the cleft from her knees, ending just before touching her clit.

She cried out, tried to raise her hips, but his weight held her in place. He chuckled and repeated the motion, stopping just short of licking her where she most wanted his attention.

He grabbed her buttocks in both his hands and squeezed gently, massaging, rubbing, lifting her hips just off the bed. She moaned and her limbs seemed to loosen, lose some of their tone. Still massaging her buttocks, Bold shoved one of his knees between hers, spreading her legs apart. When she had them opened wide, he knelt between her calves.

She lifted her knees, presenting him with a perfect view of her dripping pussy, the lips engorged and deep red, her virginal opening barely visible. Almost reverently, Bold leaned over and licked her.

Sweet. She was so damned sweet, like tasting syrup on waffles in the morning. He licked her again and she whimpered, so he lifted her hips up, dragging her across the bed to bring her pussy to his mouth. She was all languid and loose woman now, her legs draping over his upper arms, her hands grasping the soft downy blanket beneath her.

Knowing what awaited them gave Bold the patience to drive her right to the edge. He suckled first one, then the other swollen lip into his mouth. He licked her from just behind her pussy to just before her clit, then suckled her thick labia again. Her whimpers sounded more desperate now, her leg muscles tightened over his arms. She raised her hips, silently begging.

This time he nuzzled her clitoris, then suckled it gently between his lips. His tongue pressed lightly against the underside, then slipped lower, slowly entering her virginal passage, pressing lightly against the tissue barrier.

He'd been denied this for so long. Lifting his head, Bold looked at the woman in his arms. Her eyes were closed, her lips parted, her breasts were swollen and her nipples looked almost raw from his suckling and licking. Bold swallowed, thankful she'd already made him come at least once, or he knew he wouldn't have the control this moment demanded.

"My love, are you sure? Once breached, your maidenhead is gone forever. I have to know this is what you really want, what Cené wants."

She opened one eye and smiled at him. "I love you. I will always love you. You are the man I choose." She flipped her hand at him, in mock dismissal. "Go now. Get on with what you were doing."

Laughing, Bold dipped his head and once more stroked between her legs. He licked again, sliding over her clitoris, taking her right back to the level of arousal where he wanted her.

This time, when he entered her passage with his tongue, he pressed harder at the tissue blocking his way. There was just enough room for the tip of his tongue to find entrance. Slowly, as carefully as he could, he pushed his way through.

It would be easier this way, with his tongue, than to enter her the first time with his cock. Press, retreat, press again, retreat. His upper lip rubbed lightly over her clit as his long cat's tongue slowly stretched the fragile tissue.

She bucked against him, wriggling her hips in a blatant invitation for more. Holding her buttocks tightly in his hands, he pressed her close against him, at the same time forcing his tongue completely inside her pussy.

He tasted blood, the salty, metallic taste that, even in his highly evolved state, still made his own blood boil, brought forth the beast in him. He knew her climax was close, knew the pain must be negligible or she wouldn't be pressing her mons so hard against his mouth. It was time and she was as ready as he could make her.

He swirled his tongue gently inside her, cleansing her of any blood from the torn tissue, soothing her as best he could. Then, quickly laying her back on the bed, Bold grabbed his cock in his fist and slowly entered her. She raised her hips, her whimpering cries sounding need, not pain, desire, not fear.

He felt the tight walls of her pussy clutching at him, felt his cock swell in response. Slowly, so very slowly, he pushed inside her. Just as slowly, he withdrew. The next time he went further, deeper, and when he withdrew she lifted her hips, as if trying to follow him.

Her juices flowed, easing the way. Bold pushed inside, harder this time, until he bumped up against her cervix just as the thick tangle of his pubic pelt nestled in her damp curls.

He rested there, held himself perfectly still, savoring the experience, the fact he was more deeply, tightly embedded within a woman than he'd ever been in his life. She was hot, practically burning him with her heat, and the tight clenching grasp of her vaginal muscles rippled around his cock. He sighed, slowly tilted his hips and seated himself just a bit deeper.

She opened her eyes, looked at him and grinned. "I wondered if that thing would fit," she said. "You're much larger than the men of our world. This body isn't really designed to accommodate one of your size."

"This body is designed perfectly for me." He leaned down and kissed her. As he entered her mouth with his tongue, he pressed his cock against the mouth of her womb. Withdrawing his tongue, he pulled back against the sucking clasp of her vaginal walls.

In and out, making love to her mouth as well as her pussy, filling her body, claiming her soul as he released his own into her care.

She'd not even dreamed how this would feel, this joining of bodies that was more intimate than anything they had experienced since she had first joined Cené on the trek to her temple. Though they'd come close when he penetrated her before, they'd not faced one another then, not shared kisses as well as this amazing sense of connection.

No wonder the people of her world would do anything for this. She realized now what a pale imitation the makáo truly were. They were sensation without emotion, sex without passion.

This man loved her with his heart, his soul, his body. His perfect, powerful body, connected to her, held tightly within the clasp of hers. She realized she could control the muscles holding him, could tighten them even more around his swollen cock so that the look of pleasure and pain that crossed his face excited her even more.

This was not the power of a goddess. No, this was the power a woman had over a man who loved her. The power of a woman in love. He pressed into her harder, faster now, his cock banging against her womb with each thrust, his pubic bone rubbing against her swollen clit.

She felt it coming, the climax she hadn't expected so soon, the deep yearning, burning, clenching spasms that ripped from her throat to her toes. She opened her mouth to cry out and there was no sound. She arched her back to hold him close, and he pressed home, filling her with a hot rush of seed, pumping into her like a battering ram, his mouth twisted, his eyes closed, every tendon and vein in his body and throat distended, pulsing with life and passion.

Rocking against her, his breath hot and sweet, his arms trembling as he held his weight off of her, Bolden still filled her, slower now, his thrusts bringing her down, easing her off the peak, the pulsing, shimmering peak he'd taken her to.

Finally, as if his strength had failed him, Bold lowered himself to one side, his cock still filling her throbbing pussy, one heavy arm draped across her breasts, one muscular thigh holding her to the bed.

"I have never..." He gasped, shook his head and said no more.

"Nor have I, obviously." She ran her fingers along his shoulder, touched the side of his jaw, traced his full lips. He kissed her fingertip as it swept across his mouth, but his eyes were closed, his nostrils still flared, his chest expanding with each great breath he took.

What did one do now, she wondered. What was the protocol of humans after lovemaking such as this? Suddenly, her very human stomach growled.

It took her a moment to recognize what the sound meant. Then she giggled. "We should probably eat something," she said, still trailing her fingers through his tousled hair. She certainly wanted him to keep up his strength. This body of Cené's required sustenance as well, something she'd have to remember if she wanted to have all the energy she'd require for the next three days.

Three days...she knew how quickly three days would pass. She wanted him forever. *Impossible.* He was mortal. She wasn't.

No, she would not think of what she couldn't have. Only of what was possible. Only of this time, this place in her world. Smiling, she brushed the thick hair back from his face and kissed him. Luckily, the possibilities appeared endless...at least for the next three days.

Chapter Thirteen

Somehow, Bold had expected food to magically appear at the goddess's command. He certainly hadn't pictured her washing vegetables in a sink, slicing them into a large pot hanging over a fire pit, adding bits of seasoned fowl and pungent spices, or covering the dish with a deep, red wine.

Nor had he considered how erotic it would be, to watch her perform the simple task of preparing a meal. She'd covered herself in a short silky sarong, woven of fabric the same brilliant green as her eyes. The glistening material wrapped under her arms and around her chest. A large jeweled brooch held it closed between her breasts. The stone caught the dancing light of the fire with each graceful move she made, glinting in every color of the rainbow.

While the aromatic stew simmered over the low fire, Cené washed and prepared some type of red fruit. They reminded Bold of strawberries, though larger, with smooth skins. Cené bit into one after she'd removed the stem and leaves. Her eyes closed in pleasure, her tongue swept her lower lip, catching a drop of the red juice.

She offered the other half to Bold. He leaned over and, with his lips, took it from between her fingers. He caught it with his tongue and slipped the piece of fruit into his mouth. Immediately his mouth was filled with flavor, a burst of sweet and tart at the same time. The seeds were small and soft, tasting vaguely like vanilla. The fruit itself reminded him of something between raspberries and kiwi.

Cené continued cleaning more fruit, shyly glancing at Bold as she worked. He realized he was focusing on the deep red of the fruit and comparing it to the red of her lips, the darker red of her nipples. Wondering what it would taste like, to lick the sweet juice off her body, to fill her pussy with fruit and find each tangy bit with his tongue.

He let his thoughts flow, projecting the lush image of suckling the bits of fruit from between her legs. Cené's eyes sparkled as she saw his vision. Bold felt her hot rush of desire, sensed the wet heat in her pussy. He let her experience his growing erection, shared the deep coil of need as it built inside him. He'd not been able to share so easily before, when Cené was the dominant force within her body.

Now, though, with the goddess in control, his thoughts and hers flowed easily back and forth.

Thoughts and feelings, sensations and need. Caught up in Cené's overwhelming desire, Bold suddenly found himself standing behind her, his hands on her breasts beneath their smooth silk covering. She arched her back, tilting her face up to his. Her hands were still filled with the small paring knife and the fruit, the kettle bubbled behind them over the fire.

Bold's stomach growled this time. Cené snorted, a terribly un-goddess like sound. "Okay. I get your message. Eat first. *Then* we feast."

Bold slipped his hand over her torso, spread his palm across her belly, pressed his fingers through the fine silk to find her clit. He stroked her slowly, up and down. The fabric darkened where her fluids soaked through. She moaned and twisted her hips, bringing his searching finger up hard against her clit.

"What are you doing? I thought you were hungry."

"I am. For you...I just wanted to make sure you wouldn't forget me while we eat."

"As if I could." She smiled up at him, then twisted out of his arms. Her expression was suddenly serious, almost sad. "I will never forget you, Bolden of two worlds. Never." She turned away and busied herself with finding plates and silverware, implements very similar to what Bold would have used on Earth.

At any other time he might be fascinated by the similarities of the three worlds he was most familiar with—Mirat, Earth and this unnamed planet. Now, though, he put all thoughts of his Quest behind him. Part of their first day was already gone. "You weren't going to speak of my leaving," he said, touching her lips with his finger. "Only of what we can do for each other now."

Cené nodded her head, smiling. "I can feed you. Our meal is ready."

"Is that all you're thinking of?" He ran his finger along the side of her face. "I'm more concerned about dessert."

"Ah. I have a most wonderful fruit prepared for you." She ladled some of the stew into a bowl as she spoke, then placed it in front of Bold. "But dessert comes later."

She wasn't certain, but Cené didn't think the men of her world helped with the women's chores. Bolden, though, grabbed up the dishware and quickly washed everything while she put the leftover food away in the cool case. She'd almost forgotten all the wonderful implements this sanctuary held within its magical walls. There'd be food whenever they were hungry, a small chilled closet to keep things fresh. Somehow, she wished she could give these things to her people. It would make their lives so much easier.

Bolden wiped the last dish with a soft cloth, then turned his attention on her. She shivered, as much with desire as anticipation when he set the cloth and plate to one side and walked across the room. His eyes glinted, fired by his own light. She knew he saw her, and only her.

Did he see Cené? Did he lust for the goddess or the woman?

Did he want both? That thought pleased her most, the idea that this man could want not only the human woman, his companion these past days, but the essence of immortality that was her true self.

She blinked when he stopped right in front of her. His big hand brushed her shoulder, trailed along her arm. Her knees practically buckled, knowing what power lay behind that gentle caress.

He leaned over and brushed the sensitive skin beneath her left ear, kissing, then nibbling at her earlobe. She moaned, swayed, tucked her shoulder to her ear to protect herself.

He laughed. She loved the sound of his deep laughter, loved knowing she could make him this happy. Suddenly, he swept her up in his arms and held her close against his broad chest. She struggled, just enough to make him hold her even closer. He leaned down, still pressing her tightly against him, grabbed up the bowl of red fruit in one hand and set it on her belly. Then he kissed her full on the mouth.

She drew his tongue deep inside, sucking him into her mouth. She'd never, not in all her days, get enough of that amazing tongue. Abrasive as rough stone, amazingly mobile, he seemed to know exactly how to direct it, where and how hard she wanted him to touch her, no matter where he licked her body.

Right now it brushed the roof of her mouth, swept along her teeth, then tangled with her tongue. She was no match for him. Moaning, pressing her mouth against his, she opened to his gentle, teasing onslaught, offering him everything.

Suddenly he was stretching her out on the bed, their mouths still connected, tongues still waging mock battle. She felt the clasp between her breasts release, then the silky shimmer of fabric sliding over her breasts, catching on her turgid nipples. He grabbed the material in his fist and rubbed her belly with it, then slowly pulled it completely off of her.

Eyes still closed, she raised her hips, offering herself once more.

Something touched her breast, something warm and moist. Whatever Bolden held in his fingers left a trail from one nipple to the other, then circled across her breasts again before slipping the length of her torso.

Something soft and squishy filled her navel just as Bold ended the kiss. Blinking, Cené raised her head, just in time to see Bold lean over and lick the juice from her nipple, then from her belly. He lapped slowly like a big cat, cleaning her, licking slowly across her flesh until he found the bit of fruit in her navel.

This piece required much more diligent work to retrieve. Squirming and giggling, she writhed against the bed as Bold searched and probed her navel with the tip of his tongue.

Bold raised his head, looked at her and laughed once more. "You have to hold still for this to work." Then he dipped his head again and nibbled at the bit of fruit. He placed his lips over her navel and sucked, tickling the very center with his tongue until she thought she'd fly to pieces.

Then he sat back on his knees and spread her legs wide apart. She scooted up on her elbows, watching, wondering. He studied her seriously, but there was a grin curling the corner of his lip. He took one of the ripe berries and put it between her legs, then leaned over and shoved it in with his tongue.

"Wha...?"

"Be patient. I'll tell you in a minute."

He looked so serious, as if he were a scholar studying something very important, that she decided to watch and see what he was up to. He took another piece of fruit and pushed that one between her legs. He repeated the process until she was completely filled.

He grabbed a pillow and shoved it gently under her hips. Then he leaned over and slowly shoved his tongue inside her pussy, crushing the soft fruit the deeper he went, so that she felt the cool juices running out of her pussy, running along the crease in her ass. He withdrew his tongue and licked her from ass to pussy, catching every drop. His rough tongue swept over her clit, then went back inside. He nibbled the fruit, nibbled at her, licked and sucked until she thought she might come apart.

His tongue went deeper, the juices flowed, he licked and bit, lifting her hips up to his mouth as if she were a goblet filled with rarest liqueur, just for him.

His chin was stained with the sweet juice, with her juices, and still he feasted, his long tongue curling deep inside her, the soft fruit slipping about as he retrieved each and every piece.

When they were all gone and she was panting, trembling, moaning with each lap of his tongue, each kiss from his mouth, he began to slowly lick her inner thighs, her hips, the line along her ribs, bathing her from shoulders to knees with that most amazing tongue.

She cried out, her flesh so sensitive that each touch was a shock, each caress another level of lush sensation. She writhed beneath his searching tongue, her nipples peaked into hard knots, her belly rippling and flexing. There was no part of her he didn't lick, no bit of skin that was safe from that abrasive, searching tongue. He found the soles of her feet, each individual toe, then lapped his way along her calves, paying particular attention to the bends of her knees.

When she bucked and writhed, he flipped her over on her belly, laving her thighs and calves, the tense muscles of her clenched buttocks. His tongue was sandpaper, back and forth across her butt, licking and lapping, now down between her legs, then along the crease of her ass all the way to her waist.

He held her down. She shrieked. Giggling, cursing, fighting to get away, but she let him see her thoughts and he knew she loved everything he did, every lap of his tongue, every nip of his teeth.

Her skin was fire, tingling wherever his tongue had scraped her, burning and freezing, all hot and cold and prickling. She wanted...she needed...she raised up on her knees and put her head down on her crossed forearms as his tongue found a steady rhythm across her buttocks, between her legs, into her streaming pussy.

He knelt behind her and suddenly she was filled, his cock finding entry into her waiting pussy, pressing deep and solid with a single thrust that took him all the way to the mouth of her womb.

She arched her back, cried out, bucked against him, taking him deeper, harder, so that he rode her with all the strength that was in him.

There was no gentleness now, no playfulness. There was only aroused male and wanting woman, the hard thrust of his hips and the needy sway of her hot flesh. He reached down between her legs, found her clit with his thick fingers and rolled it roughly. His claws were extended. The rough pads of his fingers, the smooth edge of his claws, tugging, rolling, exciting her clit beyond all imagining.

Cené felt the heat coiling in her middle, felt the pressure between her legs as he took her deeper, harder than she'd imagined possible. Suddenly he found her nipple, the one just over her heart, found it and squeezed it between rough pad of finger, smooth steel-hard nail of claw. Pain, indescribable, pleasurable, thrilling, exquisite pain...she arched her back, raised her chin, stared blankly at the silk hangings surrounding the bed with her mouth wide open and cried out, a long, low wail that rose in pitch to a screaming crescendo as he drove into her hot depths, raked the sides of his claws across her tender clit, grasped her turgid nipple and squeezed it between finger and ebony steel.

He stiffened, then thrust hard and solid deep inside her, slamming against her buttocks with his thighs, pounding into her. His hips continued pumping and thrusting, his cock was still hard, but she knew his seed filled her, knew he'd found pleasure within her hot center. Her pussy clenched and rippled around his cock, tightening even as he lost his tumescence, even as the veins collapsed, the hard strength of him reduced and relaxed. Finally, his thighs pressed solidly against her hers but his once noble cock was merely an afterthought, barely filling her wet, hot center.

She tightened her muscles around him, though, and he thrust once more against her. She felt him rise, felt the surge of heat, knew he'd only rested.

His arms wrapped round her torso, his heavy head rested solidly on her back. She held him up as best she could, so lost in the quivering tremors of her orgasm she wasn't sure how long her legs would work.

"Thank you," she said, surprised her voice would even work. "I thoroughly enjoyed dessert."

"My pleasure, Lady...but I'm not through, yet."

Before she could react, Bold pulled out of her. She felt the hot, wet slide of his cock, waited for the gush of fluids that would spill along her legs.

Instead, he carefully rolled her over on her back and spread her legs wide. Suddenly, she felt his tongue. Softer, lighter this time, he licked her thighs, between her legs, cleaning her pussy of the remnants of the fruit juice, of her own fluids, of his seed. Her stomach clenched and tightened with each soft, cleansing sweep of his tongue. Mostly human he might appear, but a big cat ruled his libido, ruled his very nature. He bent her knees and pushed back close to her body, licking her thighs, her ass, her pussy. Driving his tongue deep inside.

Cené felt her desire rising, felt the deep satisfaction of knowing this man loved her so much, loved her enough to purify their love, to cleanse her as he would a kit...or a mate.

He found her clit, his touch so gentle, so light, she felt only warmth and moist pressure, enough to take her once more over the edge. Her climax this time was slow and easy, a rolling surge of desire that turned her legs to jelly and made her eyes heavy.

Bolden lay down beside her, wrapped his arms around her shuddering body and pulled her up close against his own. She felt his cock, solid and hot, settle moistly in the crack between her cheeks, his thighs pressing against hers, his arms holding her securely against his chest. He rested his cheek against the top of her head and his lips placed a feather light kiss on her ear. "I love you, my Lady. I would stay, if you would let me. I would be your life mate, for whatever life is left me. Only you can make that choice. I beg of you, Goddess. I don't want to leave you."

Stunned, Cené thought her mortal heart might break. He couldn't stay. He must go at the end of their three days together. Go, and never return.

It was the only way she could save him.

The makáo grew stronger outside her temple. Evil walked by night and now threatened the bright hours of sunlight. Her strength was not a match to His, this she knew. A battle loomed. A battle even a goddess might lose.

No. She would send Bolden home and forbid him to return. How could she tell him, she might no longer exist on *any* plane by the time he found his way back to her?

Bold was mortal. She might, by some strange twist of fate and the strength of her existence, survive. Bolden would never survive a battle with Evil. He would be swept aside as if he were nothing more than an irritating insect.

Cené felt the unfamiliar pressure in her chest, the stinging in her body's eyes. *Crying.* She knew what tears were, knew her people sometimes wept. She'd not suffered such pain before. Of course, she'd never known this kind of pain, this twisting in the heart, this desolation of the soul. No, not ever, even when Evil first deceived her.

Her choice was simple and irrevocable.

She had two more days to love Bolden. Then he must leave or die.

Chapter Fourteen

Bold lay awake throughout most of the night. Why hadn't she answered him? He'd spilled his guts, begged her to let him stay, pleaded in a most unmanly way for her to love him as he loved her. He'd known she was still awake, felt the sudden shift in her body when he spoke. It wasn't a request lightly made. He ached, thinking he might never see his parents again, would never be able to put their minds to rest. He was even choosing to dishonor his oath to the Quest. Yet she'd not answered him.

Bold sighed and nuzzled the short, soft hair behind her ear. His decision was purely selfish, motivated by his need for the woman in his arms. *Woman! Ha!* Immortal, literally a world unto herself. As sweet and loveable as Cené was, he loved the goddess more. Now, even as she ignored his plea to stay, to be her consort for as long as he might, he knew he desired her for all time.

How does a man love an immortal? In every way, in all ways. He shifted her closer until her lithe body melted into his like warm putty. His cock rose hungrily in its bed, pressed tightly along the valley of her ass. He tilted his hips, slipping back and forth in the tight crease without waking her.

She moaned and snuggled closer. He searched with his thoughts, but her mind was blocked, whether in sleep or a conscious need to shield herself, to hide her true thoughts. Still, Bold was almost certain she loved him. Hadn't she said she did? She wouldn't lie to him, would she?

He tried to pin down the differences between the women. The body was the same, but Cené and her goddess were nothing alike. Was it the attitude? He almost laughed, thinking of the haughty, imperial woman that was only a small part of the goddess.

There was definitely something that drew him, made him want to stay on this primitive world for whatever days remained to him, knowing he would grow old while she would be forever young.

How does one love a world? It was ludicrous, really, to think she might feel as much for him as he did for her. Sighing, his cock still solidly clasped between her warm cheeks, he finally felt his eyelids grow heavy, his heart beat steady and slow.

He let himself drift in thoughts of the morning, of loving the woman he held in his arms, as if they had forever.

* * * * *

She brought it up first. "We will not talk of your staying. It is not possible."

Bold blinked, coming up out of sleep and dreams as if he'd been somewhere far away. Sunlight spilled through windows he'd not seen before. The walls around the room were rough hewn, the furniture not so opulent as when they'd made love last night.

He sat up, scooting back against the carved headboard of the bed. He was covered to his hips in a many-colored afghan, knit out of simple, homespun yarn. Cené perched on a tall stool near a table. She sliced strange looking fruit into an earthenware bowl.

"Where are we?"

"My temple. Or what is left of it. It was once a huge edifice of stone, polished and new, but that was long ago, in what was essentially a different world. Remember the tree we entered?" She gestured about the walls of the large room. It was at least fifty feet across, about right as far as Bolden could recall, if they were truly inside the tree that grew from the stone ruins.

"What about the huge room, the tapestries, this...?" He shook his head, reminded quite forcibly exactly who and what this woman really was.

"Ah, you saw what was, what existed before Evil had his way with my world. I can still bring it back, but it takes much out of me." She hung her head, as if ashamed, then looked up, her smile once more in place. "It is foolish to waste my power, merely to impress you. I would save it for other things."

Still blinking himself awake, Bold let his mind wander on to other things. The erection that rarely seemed to subside when he was near this woman, leapt once more to life.

He stretched, twisting his back and shoulders against the soft pillows. "Is there a place to bathe in this tree of yours?" Cené looked freshly bathed, her hair still sparkling with droplets of water.

"Yes. It's just outside the door." She gestured toward a cut in the wall, held shut with a crude latch. As Bolden slid his legs over the side of the bed, Cené frowned. "Be careful, though. I fear the makáo are close by, and I don't know what their powers might be during daylight."

"I thought they were merely creatures of the night." Bold stood up and reached for his pack. The sunlight reminded him he hadn't charged his solar receiver in a couple days.

"They were." She smiled when she looked up at him, but her eyes were troubled. Bolden chose not to pursue the question. Right now he needed a bath and a chance to refresh himself. Unless he could get the lady to change her mind, they only had two days left. He didn't want to waste a minute.

* * * * *

He found the pool close by the twisted roots of the tree, a stone grotto formed by the fallen blocks of the ancient temple, lush with ferns and dark orchid-like flowers growing about. A beam of sunshine fell across the surface, catching the rising steam in a brilliant shaft of light. The water was not only warm, it appeared to be fed by an underground spring that bubbled and pulsed with jets of pressure.

Bold slipped into the hot water with a long, low sigh. Immediately he felt his muscles begin to relax. Every muscle but his damned cock. That thing seemed to work according to its own agenda. Bold willed his errant body part to retreat back within his foreskin, and almost laughed at the slow return to its slightly tumescent state.

He could have asked Cené to join him, but it was just as well he was alone with his thoughts.

There was much to think about.

His receiver sat on a rock near the edge of the pool. He'd activated its camera for a timed snapshot of the sky overhead. Since first landing on this world he'd stored graphs of the stars in all the seasons, but this picture would better pinpoint his location. It might be the only thing to help him find this world, should Cené make him leave. In spite of the brilliant sunlight, it would still find the constellations. Bold stared at the receiver, comparing the advanced technology that give him such marvelous instruments, to this world of Cené's.

He sometimes forgot just how primitive it was here. Hell, this world didn't even have a name! When he'd asked the goddess what the planet was called, she'd looked at him as if he were nuts. "There's no name," she said, sounding perplexed. "I have no name. I am Goddess, the lady of this world. I *am* this world. I am Cené while I share her body, but only for this short period of time. None can name me."

She'd laughed as if he were a damned fool. Bold shook his head, feeling foolish. How could he love someone so different, so unique, so totally unobtainable.

So perfectly unsuitable.

So perfect.

His cock twitched.

Point. Counterpoint. Did his damned cock rule his mind? There'd certainly been enough jokes over the centuries regarding the amount of blood it took to run either the cock or the brain, but neither at the same time. As hard as he'd stayed while near Cené or her goddess, he'd had little time for rational thought.

He bathed, enjoying the pulsing jets of hot water against his stiff muscles, soaking up the hot rays of sunshine that found so few breaks in the heavy foliage. He rested his head on the mossy bank at the edge of the pool and let his mind drift.

He wasn't certain how long he'd dozed, how much time had passed, but Bold suddenly realized he wasn't alone.

The sense of *other* was faint, at first. The sense someone watched him from within the thick cover of forest, studied him. He felt the weak probing at his shields, the mental thrust and twist as something, or someone, tried to read his thoughts.

His first reaction was to stand and challenge. He forced his adrenalin charged, quivering muscles to relax, willed his breathing to remain steady. He studied the questing thoughts, took them apart one by one and examined them.

Not human. No, not familiar at all, though definitely of this world. The makáo? He'd not thought them capable of intelligence. Hadn't Cené said they were creatures of fantasy? Ephemeral beings brought to life to fulfill her sexual desires?

Ephemeral beings didn't leave footprints. Nor did they enter a man's thoughts with intent. Evil intent. He sensed it now. Felt the dark tendrils gain power, push at his strong mental shields.

Cautiously, as if completely unaware of the searching mind, Bold strengthened his shields further, rose from his bath and grabbed a soft towel. He dried himself, all the while sending out searching thoughts through the surrounding woods.

The source was here, there...everywhere. Whatever searched his mind, surrounded the pool, in fact, the entire temple. Nonchalantly, keeping his mental shields strong and intact, he leaned over and retrieved his receiver, grabbed up his loincloth and walked back to the entrance cut into the tree. When he pressed his palm to the center, the door swung open.

He made certain it was tightly closed behind him, then turned and faced Cené. As if she knew what was on his mind, she carefully set the knife on the countertop and folded her hands in her lap.

* * * * *

He must not know her fear, must not realize how precarious was her own existence, once Evil made its move. She found strength in the knowledge he would be safely away from her world by the time Evil was ready. Knowing he would survive gave her the strength to remain composed in the face of her own possible end.

"Did you like my pool?" She smiled and held her hand out, inviting him.

He stood where he was, one hand still on the door, and shook his head. "The pool is perfect. The temperature just right. It's the audience that concerns me."

"Pay them no mind. The makáo merely study you. They are curious. You are the first ever to deny them."

"Creatures of fantasy and thought shouldn't feel curiosity. Not unless they have sentience of their own...or unless they are directed by someone of a curious nature." He stepped closer, as if he challenged her to say more.

His loincloth was still tucked under his arm, along with his pack. He'd thrown the towel over his shoulder and faced her now completely unclothed, his powerful legs and broad chest all muscle and sinew and thick pelt. His mane of hair spread out over his shoulders in a damp tangle that framed his beautiful face. His huge cock was sheathed within its foreskin, but he was still huge, partially erect.

Masculine perfection, so far as Cené could tell. Masculine, and growing impatient with her lack of response.

She couldn't lie to him. Neither could she tell him the entire truth.

"I sense Evil. I've told you that. I believe it directs the makáo. I am still more powerful and can keep them at bay. I will deal with them later. For now, I anticipate our next two days together."

She stood up and walked slowly toward him, her hips swaying, breasts thrust against the tight beaded tunic she wore. He watched her, dissatisfaction with her answer written all over him, evident in his controlled stance, in his expression, but as she drew closer to him, touched him, she saw the change come over his face, felt his cock rise against her belly, and knew she'd dissuaded his questions for at least a few more hours.

Ah, the power of this body! Cené hadn't had a clue...nor had she, for that matter. To think she could touch him, move her hips for him, press her mouth against that flat, copper colored nipple just over his heart, and whatever concerns had troubled him suddenly fled.

She heard his pack drop to the floor with a soft *thud*. Felt his arms snake around her and knew she'd won this round. His mouth came down on hers with a gentleness that was almost her undoing.

He knew. Knew perfectly well she'd used her body to avoid his questions. Knew the answers must come soon, as this ploy would not work again.

His broad palm slipped down to the hem of the tunic, then slowly shoved the soft leather up along her hip. He tugged it over her head and tossed it aside. His lips found hers, his fingers found the cleft in her buttocks, stroked between her legs, shoved slowly in and out of her wet pussy.

His tongue was hot and searching, filling her mouth with slow in and out thrusts. She moaned against his lips, suckled his tongue deeper, felt the hot rush of fluid between her legs, the tingling, almost painful tightening of her nipples.

How could she react so quickly? She'd been preparing breakfast when he walked into the room, her thoughts nowhere near lovemaking. Suddenly she was wet and ready, her pussy spasming with each thrust of his fingers, her breasts growing heavy and full, nipples hard and tight.

Cené gave herself over to his touch, gave her heart and body to Bold. Gave a long, low sigh and surrendered to his tongue, his fingers, his solid cock that rested hot and heavy against her belly.

Her eyes slowly closed, her breath grew ragged. Awash in sensation, she knew only Bolden, felt only his touch, until...*no. Not here. Not now.*

At the very edge of her consciousness, she sensed something, someone, probing at her mind. Testing the shields she'd left in place.

Testing her here, within the sanctity of her temple.

Evil grew stronger. The makáo walked in daylight.

Bold lifted her hips, wrapped her legs around his waist, and thrust his cock into her waiting pussy. She gripped him, a moist velvet glove encasing each solid thrust, grabbing onto him, tightening around him.

All thoughts, everything other than Bolden, what he did, how she felt, disappeared into a maelstrom of sensation.

Cené arched her back, forcing him deep inside. Sucked his tongue into her mouth, then kissed his shoulder, biting at the muscle when he leaned down and dragged his tongue across her breast. His lips found her nipple, his teeth grazed, then bit down on the sensitive, swollen flesh.

She tipped her head back and screamed.

A subtle sense of triumph. A sense someone else intruded in her desire, experienced her climax.

She tensed, then lost herself once more to sensation.

Bold's hips pumped, each savage thrust lifting her, filling her, forcing the intruding thought from her mind and filling her with pulse after pulse of blinding pleasure.

She screamed again, her head thrown back, mouth wide open as her second climax engulfed her. Wave after wave of rippling, writhing sensation, so intense, so unbelievably hot, the perception as much pain as pleasure. Still he thrust into her, his hands clasping at her buttocks, squeezing her tighter, lifting her against his cock.

He was hard as a rock, solid and long and filling her, sliding easily in and out of her streaming pussy, his thighs trembling against hers, his big hands lifting her as if she weighed nothing at all.

Sobbing, grasping his shoulders and feeling the rise of pleasure streaking through her body once again, Cené opened her mind and grabbed for Bold, found his thoughts, his mind full of sensation, of the hot wet glove that was her pussy, holding him, clenching around him, of the scents and sounds of their sex, the all-consuming pleasure and pain of his impending climax.

She felt his balls tighten as if they were her own, cried out at the coiling spasm, the tightening pressure deep in his gut that sent his seed shooting the length of his cock, filling her hot passage, pumping into her...all of it. She felt it all, experienced it all, again, and again as he thrust into her, sensed his anger, his confusion, but most of all, she felt his love, felt hers and knew, at the very peak of fulfillment, this was the best she would ever know, the finest joining she would ever, in all her existence as goddess and human, experience.

As her body shuddered in his arms, as his legs trembled with the effort of holding her body close to his, she sensed something else.

Something dark, deviant and frightening, a parasitic connection, entangled within their minds, feeding off their passion.

Gaining strength from their love.

Something disgusting and dark, breaking free of their mental link just at the peak of climax, breaking free but taking the sense, the power of their passion, the inherent energy of their orgasmic release, stealing a part of their experience to hold on to as his own.

Shuddering, shivering with release, Cené grabbed tightly on to Bolden, pressed her face against his chest, listened to his heart pounding a staccato beat. How could this have happened? Here, where the goddess lived, where her rule was inviolate?

Evil had penetrated the sanctity of her temple, had violated the sacred bond of their love. Cené felt a need to bathe, to cleanse herself, not from Bold's touch, but from the disgusting essence left behind by their trespasser.

Their deviant voyeur. A thief.

Evil had found release, taken pleasure in her lovemaking with Bolden. Much as the goddess had used the makáo. Was this, then, their revenge?

She slowly let her legs slip along Bold's trembling thighs. He helped ease her body down, his hands still clasping her buttocks, his face buried in the soft flesh at her shoulder.

He didn't look at her. His mind was closed to hers.

He knows. He knows we were not alone.

Ashamed, head bowed, legs still shivering and pussy wet with their shared essence, Cené found her balance and took a deep breath. It was not easy, not for a goddess, to ask for help. Suddenly, though, she knew she could not do this alone.

"We must strengthen the barriers to secure the sanctuary." Her voice sounded hesitant, unsure. This would not do. She must be strong. She had to be strong, at least while Bolden was still here with her. Still vulnerable to Evil.

"You've lied to me, Goddess. You've not told me the truth of their strength." Even though his breath still came in deep gasps, his voice was strong, steady. He reached under her chin with one broad finger, lifting until she had to meet his amber eyes. "What is the true risk to your world? To you?"

She stared long and hard into his eyes. It would be so easy to tell him, to burden him with the short and horrible future she saw. Easy, and unfair, not when he lacked the ability to help, to change anything.

He was mortal. She must remember that. "I've not lied, my love. Merely not wanted to speak of things so unpleasant. Once the three days are ended, I will once more pursue Evil. As always, I will be victorious. Now, though, he is merely a nuisance. If we strengthen the power that protects this place, he will not bother us further. None of them will."

Bold looked at her, as if weighing her words. Finally, she saw his jaw clench, the rise and fall of his chest as he took a deep, cleansing breath. "All right. I'll help where I can to shield your temple against him. Then we'll talk. I want to know how I can help. I've asked you to let me stay. I do not intend to leave you here alone to do battle with something so powerful, so vile. Remember, my Lady. I felt him in my mind just as you did. He is no weak spirit, out to irritate and pester. He exists to do evil, to kill, to destroy. I believe he takes energy from our passion, builds on it, grows with it. That much I sensed, and our touch was brief. I will not leave you to fight him alone."

He tilted his head, leaned down and kissed her very lightly. There was no passion in his kiss.

Merely a promise. A promise Cené knew she could not allow him to keep.

Chapter Fifteen

She watched him sleep for a very long time. With his intense amber eyes closed and the dark crescent moons of his long eyelashes resting against his face, he looked almost childlike — sweet, even vulnerable.

One paw, for that was what his hand resembled when curled tightly with the nails tightly sheathed, was tucked beneath his cheek. He held the other folded up under his chin, hidden in the dark mass of his tangled mane. His full lips were barely parted, his chest rose and fell in a regular, restful pattern, and Cené wanted him more than she'd wanted anything, ever, in her life.

The goddess hovered beside her, mere essence in the air, apart from Cené, though very real. Cené felt her indecision, sensed her sadness. "You have done all you can, my Lady," she said, brushing her hand lightly through Bold's tangle of dark mane. She knew he slept soundly, understood the power of the goddess's spell that kept him blissfully unaware of all that was happening outside the temple.

I asked for three days. I promised him that. It has been barely two, but I can no longer keep Evil at bay. The makáo grow stronger by the hour. My power is weak when I keep human form, weaker still when I am lost in passion, drugged by his amazing love. Is it so selfish of me to choose life for this man? I must send him home now, send him away from here before it's too late, while I still have enough power to move him so far

"How can it be selfish, my Lady, when you want him to stay even as his deepest wish, beside his love for you, is to see his family once again? You have chosen your world over your love for one mortal." She brushed her fingers across his cheek and sighed. "Still, I will miss him greatly."

Go with him. I will send both of you to this world, Earth.

Cené shook her head, one hand trembling against Bolden's shoulder, the other stroking the side of his face. He was so terribly dear to her. So amazing. He had shown her more than she could possibly ever imagine, had given her passion and desire, desire for Cené, a simple handmaiden to the goddess.

She accepted from the beginning he loved the goddess more. Was that so difficult to understand? Even Cené loved the goddess more. That was the way of immortals. They demanded all, though Cené would ever be grateful for the generous nature of her goddess, a being so willing to share this man's love.

No, she would never, not in all the days remaining to her, forget this man. Even after he was gone from her world, he would be her lifemate.

Cené slowly lifted her blessing bag from around her neck and slipped it over Bold's head. He stirred, but didn't awaken. Cené clasped the familiar bag in her hand, closed her eyes, and passed the strength of its power to the man who wore it now.

"I choose Bolden of two worlds as my lifemate, though you send him away, to his home world. I choose you, my Lady, to serve until my days' end. Though I love the man with all my heart, I love you more. For whatever time remains, I will remain your handmaiden, your devoted celebrant."

Do you understand, my child, that you may indeed be choosing death? I cannot protect you, should the makáo enter my temple. I'm not even sure I will be able to save this world from the Evil that seeks to control it. You would not survive, should Evil rule. I fear what the makáo would do to you.

Cené merely shook her head. Her decision was made. She had no intention of changing it. "Will he remember us, Goddess?"

Yes, unfortunately. I have not the power to make him forget. I wish I could.

"What if he comes back here? What will he find."

Nothing, I am afraid. I doubt he can find us. We are but a small world among many in a galaxy far from his. No, when I send him home, he will be lost to us forever.

"We'll have our memories, for whatever time remains." Cené leaned over and kissed Bolden on the mouth. Even in sleep, his lips pursed and he kissed her back. When she raised her head, forcing herself to move away from him, one of her tears fell on his lower lip. His tongue slipped out and caught it, then swept across his lip as if searching for more. He sighed and rolled over, still sound asleep.

Cené stood up, grabbed Bolden's pack from the floor beside the bed and slipped the strap over his arm. Her fingers lingered on his shoulder. She ached to touch him, to stroke her hands once more across the smooth muscles of his chest, to feel his passion, his desire.

She would forever dream of the hard palm of his hand gently cupping her breast, of the spicy, salty-sweet taste of his essence when she took him in her mouth. She licked her lips, remembering the feel of his mouth on hers, of that most amazing tongue stroking her lips, licking her breasts, delving between her legs.

She was no longer a maiden. She smiled against the pain of losing him, and thanked the goddess once more for giving her the freedom to know total love from this man.

Suddenly, Cené felt the goddess enter her once more. She sighed and closed her eyes against the pleasure. To be one with her Lady, to touch the man she loved...there was no greater feeling, no desire more powerful, no passion so magnificent.

I needed to feel him once more, to touch him with a woman's hands, to kiss him with real lips. Please, my friend, do not be angry.

"How could I be angry? You honor me, my Lady."

Cené, as the goddess, leaned over and placed a warm, moist kiss against Bolden's mouth. His eyes fluttered open for just a brief moment. He smiled, reached for her.

Energy seemed to swell from deep within her heart. Cené raised her arms overhead but the goddess spoke, so that the words of power Cené cried out were those of an immortal.

Bolden's hand lifted, his fingertips reaching for her, his eyes wide with surprise. His voice rose barely above a whisper. "No."

Just a single word.

No.

Then he suddenly disappeared.

Cené felt her knees buckle, sensed her Lady's misery as she retreated, becoming one once more with her world. Wind howled outside the temple. Thunder crashed. A tree fell somewhere, not far away. Shrieks and screams filtered through the thick walls as the makáo made yet another rush at the temple.

Cené crumpled to the floor, sobs tearing at her chest. He was gone. Forever gone. Death did not concern her. Fear found no place within her heart.

It was full. Filled to overflowing with grief too crushing to contain.

✳ ✳ ✳ ✳ ✳

The steady *beep, beep, beep* of his solar receiver brought Bolden awake. He hadn't heard the incoming message alert in so long it took him a few moments to recognize the once familiar tone.

Lifting himself up on one elbow, he groaned. There wasn't a part of him anywhere that didn't hurt. Moving slowly, he fumbled through his pack until he found the unit, flipped it open and hit the receive button.

His father's voice. The deep timbre of Garan's words brought tears to Bold's eyes. He thought he'd never hear the sound again.

My son. If you able, please reply at once. This message is on an auto play loop, broadcast galaxy-wide at six Earth-hour intervals.

Where are you Bolden? Your mother is frantic...as am I. I miss you, my son. Please call.

"Good question, Dad. Where the hell am I?" He pushed himself to his feet and brushed the leaves and dirt away from his legs. The air was clean and easy to breathe, the sky a familiar blue. He was in a mixed forest, surrounded by oak and pine trees. Sunlight filtered through the bright green leaves of early spring. The flowers looked familiar, but he was unable to see any landmarks that would place him.

It felt like Earth. *Impossible.* Yet he looked at the receiver in his hand, at the print out of the message he'd just heard, and knew it was true. The goddess had lied to him. She'd promised him three days and sent him back before even two had passed.

Sent him back though he'd begged to stay. Why?

Later. He'd figure it out later. For now, he felt like he was coming off a two week drinking binge. His head ached, his muscles felt as if they'd been stretched and contorted in every direction. He arched his back and felt something drag across his chest.

Cené's blessing bag! How had that ended up around his neck? She'd said it would only go to her lifemate, her one true love. He wrapped the soft leather in his palm, the way he'd seen Cené hold it so many times. He felt the objects inside, odd shapes that made no sense to him.

His lifemate. Cené and the goddess, one and the same. But where? How far away was their world? Sighing, he ran his fingers through his tangled mass of mane. Later. He'd figure it all out later. Right now, though, he had to call his parents. First he needed to figure out where he was.

He opened the receiver and hit the GPS. Immediately, the screen cleared and refocused, showing him a map of the nearby area. *Amazing.* Somehow, she'd managed to place him near the old cabin, the one where his father's friend Tim Riley had taken him camping.

That meant he was only a short hike from the Armand Institute. Bold studied the map a bit until he had his bearings, then returned the unit to his pack. Unless they'd moved, his parents were no more than fifteen minutes' walk away.

He found the cabin, and from there the trail. He stood there a moment, clutching his pack against his side, taking deep, cleansing breaths of air. Earth's air. It seemed impossible, but he was truly home. Home after two years.

He imagined his parents' faces when they first saw him. His mother would cry. She cried when she was happy, when she was sad...he hated to think of the tears she must have shed while he was gone. His father would be more reserved. Damn, Bold felt his eyes tear up. He missed Garan and Jenna more than he'd imagined.

He started down the trail at a brisk walk. After a couple steps he broke into a lope, then a full run. Two long years. Were they even still alive? So much could happen. There'd been political unrest, as usual, when he left on his Quest. Were they once more at war?

His bare feet pounded the grassy trail. His pack bounced against his back. War. What about the world he'd just left? Was the goddess even now at war with Evil? Who the hell was Evil, anyway? She'd never explained. He'd never really asked. They'd spent all their time making love, as if they had all the time in the world.

Dammit, they still had almost a day and a half! Why the hell had she sent him home? His thoughts took up the rhythm of his feet, the pounding in his heart, the pain in his chest that was, for now, anyway, dampened by the fact he would see his family once again.

He wouldn't let himself think about Cené. Neither the woman nor the goddess. Not yet. There would be time to figure out a plan. Now, though, he was almost home. He sent out a thought, a question to Jenna and Garan.

Are you there? Are you close, my parents? I'm coming. I'm almost home. I'm sorry to have worried you. I love you both.

* * * * *

"Bold? Bolden, is that you?" Jenna, mate to Garan of Pride Imar, bolted upright. She'd been dozing, swinging slowly back and forth in the old porch swing, letting her mind drift lazily after a long morning of working on the books for the Armand Institute.

She shook her head, blinking away tears. No, it wouldn't be her son. Not now, after two years. If he could have contacted his parents, he would have done it long before now. She raised her arms over her head and stretched.

Suddenly Garan slammed the front door and raced out on to the porch. His mane stuck out in all directions, as if he'd been caught napping as well. His long tail twitched and skittered back and forth, a sure sign of his agitation. "Bold? He's here? Where is he?"

"You heard it too? I thought I was dreaming." Jenna stood up and grabbed her mate's arm. Garan gathered her close. Both of them projected, searching for any sign of their son, any flash of his thoughts.

They didn't have to look very hard. "Mom? Dad? It is you!"

Jenna saw him first, racing down the trail from the woods, his long legs carrying him through the green grasses at a full gallop. He wore a primitive loincloth and the pack over his shoulder was of an unfamiliar design. His mane was much darker than when she'd seen him last, the hair across his chest and belly a thick mat that reminded her of his father.

Garan raced down the steps, vaulted over the wall to the compound and grabbed his son up in his arms. Crying, sobbing with more emotion than she could even hope to contain, Jenna raced after the two of them.

She didn't even attempt the vault, but instead merely projected herself to a spot next to her son.

"Praise the Mother...I never thought we'd see you again." She wrapped her arms around him, feeling his strong young body close to hers, the same body she'd carried for the full term of gestation, the body she'd raised from tiny kit to full grown man.

Her manchild held both his parents tightly, crying in great, gulping sobs, his huge shoulders shaking. She realized Garan cried as well, her big arrogant lion who never showed his emotions unless he was showing his love for her.

Other members of the Institute were running across the compound, called by the overwhelming rush of emotion the three of them broadcast. Jenna felt the joy, the relief, the unbelievable jubilation over their son's return.

For just this moment, this wonderful joyous moment, she had both her men to herself. She'd dreamed of this, prayed to the Mother, to Earth's gods, to every deity she could think of, yet she'd never truly dreamed she would one day hold her child in her arms.

Suddenly they were surrounded. Bolden raised his head, the tears still streaming down his face, his beautiful amber eyes alight with joy, and greeted his friends. Questions flew but no one heard the answers. For now, it was celebration and a time of thanks.

Later, Jenna knew, would come the time for stories. A time to find out where her only child had been for two of the longest, saddest years of her life.

Garan's arm tightened around her waist as Bold's friends welcomed him. Garan smiled down at her, not even trying to hide the tears that coursed along his cheeks. She reached up and touched his face, dearer to her than even the child she'd just welcomed home.

For over thirty years, he'd been her best friend, her lover, her protector. Still strong and fit, well into his seventieth year, he had been badly shaken by his son's loss. Now, it was as if the mantle of age she'd recently noticed in him had been shed. He stood tall beside her, his arm warm and comforting.

Once more, Jenna felt complete. She'd missed that since Bold's ship was first reported missing. "Where do you think he's been?" She didn't take her eyes off her son, but Garan heard her soft question.

"We'll find out later. For now, he needs to celebrate his return. They need to, as well." Garan leaned over and nuzzled the top of Jenna's head. "He looks good...healthy, but there is something bothering him. Something deep, heartfelt."

Jenna nodded. "I sense it, too." She brushed her hand across her face, wiping away the tears. "Whatever it is, it doesn't matter. We have him home. Our son is alive."

Garan grabbed her hand and they walked back toward the compound, following Bolden and the others. She felt the confidence in her mate's stride, the arrogance in the set of his shoulders. Slanting a look at him, she almost laughed out loud. Her big cat was grinning. An ear to ear, canine flashing grin.

Bolden is home. Our son is finally safe. She hugged Garan's hand against her side and walked with him to the house. Shielding her thoughts, she allowed the one truth she'd found finally come to light. *He's home, but not for long. Whatever world he has found, has taken his heart.*

Damn. Sometimes she wished her psychic powers hadn't just gotten stronger with age. There were a lot of things mothers really shouldn't ever learn about their sons.

Chapter Sixteen

"So, that's it. Somehow I have to go back. She needs me, even though she doesn't want to admit it."

"It's not that she doesn't want to admit it, it's that she wants to keep you safe." Jenna placed her hand on Bold's knee. "Look at me, Bold." She laughed when he raised his eyes to her as if he were six years old and waiting to find out what his punishment was going to be.

"You've said she's immortal. No matter what befalls her world, she will live on. You would die. In this case, a man's strength is not more than a woman's."

"Your mother taught me not to assume I was the strongest a long time ago, Bold." Garan carried three glasses of cognac into the room. "How would you be able to help this woman...this goddess? Your mom's raised a good point. Cené's immortal. She can only be with you when she takes on mortal form, right?"

"I don't know how I can help, only that I have an overpowering sense that I should be with her." He grabbed the leather blessing bag and held it in his palm. "She must have given this to me before sending me home. This is Cené's blessing bag. It was given to her at birth, filled with objects by the shaman in her village, objects meant to direct and give meaning to her life. She's never opened it. In a formal bonding ceremony, we would have opened it together. We would study the contents, find their meaning, and then I would place something of mine inside."

Jenna reached out and touched the bag. The beaded leather was warm from her son's skin, but she felt power in it, too.

"Should you open it now? The contents might tell you something, give you a sign of what your next step should be."

"I have nothing to put in it." He stared down at the leather pouch, then looked at his father. "What would you do, if you were in my place?"

Garan rubbed his chin a moment, studying the bag. He reached over and touched it, stroking the leather with one callused thumb, let it fall back against his Bold's chest, then slowly nodded his head. "I think your mother is right. There's definitely power here. Very old power. Open it, son. There might be a message inside, something to tell you what direction you should take. Where your destiny lies."

Bold took a sip of his cognac, then slowly removed the bag from around his neck. He closed his eyes for a moment, searching for Cené, for any sense of the goddess. His Lady didn't answer, but he really didn't expect her to. The distance was too great. For all he knew, even time had shifted when she sent him back.

He pulled a small wooden table from the side of the couch and slid it around in front of him. Jenna spread a linen napkin out, to catch whatever was inside the bag. Bold held the pouch in his hands, his eyes closed as if in prayer.

Jenna reached over and grabbed Garan's hand. She respected whatever choice Bold might make, but she feared his choice, as well. Whatever he saw within the small, beaded leather pouch might be enough to take him away. This time, she knew, he probably would not return.

Bold stared at Cené's blessing bag for a long moment. He thought of her soft touch, her bright, emerald eyes, the full red softness of her lips. He remembered the strength of the goddess within her, and the tenacious, yet guileless woman when she served her goddess as a mortal.

She'd worn this bag since she was an infant. Now she'd entrusted it to Bolden's care, giving it to her lifemate. He wondered if there were words he should say, a prayer to be spoken. He asked the goddess, but heard only silence.

Praise the Mother, how he missed her. When he finally reached for the bag, his hands were shaking. He almost laughed aloud, to think he could feel this much emotion, this great a sense of loss.

He'd been with Cené, made love to the goddess, mere hours ago. With any luck and the grace of the Mother, he might yet see her again. With trembling hands, he carefully worked the intricate knots loose. They were tied very tightly, yet practically fell apart beneath his fingers, the woven strands parting as if by magic. He looked up at his mother.

Jenna sat with her hands folded almost prayerfully over her breasts. She nodded when Bold glanced at her. "Yes," she said. "There is much power within this bag. I sense it, a feminine power unlike anything I've felt before. It's amazing. May I?" She reached out, as if to touch.

"Of course." Bold pulled his hands away. The pouch tipped over but remained closed.

Jenna held her hands just above the leather, closed her eyes and held motionless. Bold had watched her do this before, knew she drew her power about her in order to pick up whatever essence the items before them might hold.

"I sense no evil in this, nothing to fear." She tilted her head and smiled at Bold. "Unless it's the fear that whatever you find inside will take you away from us again."

"Mom, I..."

Garan reached out and clasped his son's shoulder. "Your mother only speaks what we both feel, Bold. Your choice is entirely up to you and should be made with a free will. We would never hold you from your destiny. If what this little bag has inside it is...well..." He nodded, curled his lip around his sharp canines and sighed. "You'll make the right choice. You always do."

"Thank you, Sire, Mother." Bold bowed his head to both his parents. He couldn't remember ever feeling more love or more respect for either one of them. He'd been blessed with a childhood filled with love and laughter, the knowledge that, though he was unique among people, he was always loved, always a source of pride to his parents.

He hated the thought of leaving them. Hated even more the thought he might never see Cené again, might not ever hold the goddess in his arms. What if she needed him, even now? What if Evil attacked? No, he really had no choice. None at all. Bold grabbed the small bag and carefully emptied the contents out on the soft linen cloth his mother had spread on the table.

The first item to roll out of the bag was a large, white tooth, a scimitar shaped canine from the mouth of a large carnivore. Bold lifted it, studied the shape and sharpness and looked at his father.

Garan reached out and took the tooth, weighed it in his hand, then handed it back to Bolden. "Do they have lions on this planet of yours?"

"No. Only nightcats, felines not much larger than a medium sized dog. They're domestic animals, fairly intelligent but nothing more than a dog's level. They live in the villages, hunt creatures similar to our rats and mice. This tooth comes from a much larger animal. A wolf, perhaps?"

Jenna laughed quietly. "No, my son. Not a wolf. A lion. It is definitely a lion's tooth. Look at your father and see if you have any doubt. Or, look in the mirror." When Bold glanced at Garan, his father curled his lip back, exposing an identical canine. Bold carefully placed the tooth back on the linen cloth.

His mother reached out and touched his hand. "What else is in the bag."

Bold shook it again. A shiny black claw slipped out of the pouch. He picked it up, held it in the palm of his hand, compared it to his own claws. This one was a perfect match, broader than Garan's, exactly like Bold's.

He looked at his parents faces. Both of them were smiling, but he saw the sadness in their eyes. The acceptance. The undeniable love.

He stroked the bag with his fingers. There was one more item inside, the largest piece. He had to reach into the pouch to pull it out, a perfect miniature of one of the stone lions that had guarded the gate in the vision he and Cené once shared. Carved from a golden piece of amber, it was finely detailed, right down to the raised paw with extended claws. The tail curved around the back feet, one paw rested on the ground. The mouth was wide open, showing fierce teeth, sharp as needles. The entire carving was barely over an inch tall.

In the chest, where the heart would be, was a deep red ruby captured in the fossil. When Bold stared at it, the heart almost appeared to beat.

Jenna's voice broke into his mesmerized stare. "You really don't have a choice, do you?"

He shook his head. No, he had no choice other than this. Somehow, he must find his way back to Cené. He was the guardian lion. His was the tooth, the claw, the guardian soul she'd lived with all her life. Now was not the time to desert her. How, though? How would he ever find his way back to a planet so far from Earth?

Bold's mother took the carved lion out of his palm and held it in her hand, stroked the smooth surface, touched her fingertip to the chest, just over the heart. Her voice broke when she whispered, "Somehow, we have to find a way to send you back." Jenna turned to her mate. "Garan? What about Tim Riley? If he worked off of Carly, using her powers of synergy, and if I were to add a kinetic boost, I imagine we could safely transport Bold to his world...so long as we know where it is."

Bold lifted his head, suddenly realizing he had what they needed. "What about the star charts on my solar receiver. I took readings from the planet's surface. Could Tim work from those? Do you really think it would work?"

"I don't know why not." Garan's deep voice rumbled up out of his chest. "Tim managed to bring both your mother and Carly forward in time, working from images in Doc's mind. As far as the actual kinetic sending itself, I haven't known your mother to fail at a single thing she's set her mind to. I would suggest you sleep, first, then give a full report on the world and the results of your Quest to Thom Antoon. He's keeping our records now, while Malachi and Sheyna are on Mirat."

"Mirat?" Bold frowned, surprised at the news. "I didn't think Sheyna would ever go back to Mirat, not after what Gard did." Bold had heard the story of Gard's long-standing physical and sexual abuse of his daughter. It wasn't easy to imagine the dignified lioness, Malachi Franklin's beloved mate, enduring such treatment, but her quiet strength had always impressed Bold.

Garan waved his hand dismissively. "Gard's dead. He was murdered while in the prison colony—no great loss, in my estimation, even if he was my father. The worlds are better off without his perversions. Sheyna's taken a post to teach at the university in Heáz, the capitol. Malachi's there with her as a visiting professor, as well as to keep their kids in line."

"Anything else happen while I was away?" Bold slanted his eyes at his mother.

Jenna laughed. "It *has* been over two years. Two very long years. When you go, this time, we will know where you are, set up some form of contact. I don't want to lose you again, Bolden." She grabbed both of his hands in hers. "The contents of this small leather pouch tell me you are pre-ordained to take a part in this world's history. I would never keep you from your destiny. However, as your mother, I do want to keep track of you."

Laughing, feeling the weight of two years' of regret and guilt, Bold leaned over and kissed his mother's cheek. She was still beautiful, still young looking even though he knew she was in her sixties now. For some reason, the Sensitives and Talents on Earth rarely showed their age, as if time, for many of them, stood still.

Bold stood up just as Garan also rose to his feet.

His usually undemonstrative father clasped Bold in a tight embrace and kissed him solidly on the mouth. "I have missed you, my son. Missed you more than you can know. It is good to have you home, if only for so brief a time. Very good."

Suddenly he broke the embrace and quickly left the room. Bold stood there, practically in shock. This was not his father as he remembered him. Not the Garan who was arrogance personified, reserved in emotion, quick to anger and just as quick to forgive. He glanced at his mother.

She smiled and wiped tears from her eyes. "I always knew you would come back to us. Your father, pessimist that he is, thought you were dead, Bold. For him, you've come back from the grave. Garan loves you more than life itself. The fact you're here, safe and alive, is a miracle, the most wonderful gift you could have given him...to both of us. We're going to miss you terribly, but you are right to want to return. It is your destiny." She laughed, smoothed her hand across the small amber lion. "I feel yours is a powerful destiny, and we would be so wrong to try and stop it."

She stood up and drew Bold into a tight embrace. He felt her tremble and wrapped his arms around his mother. She'd always been a powerful, beloved figure in his life. He'd never thought of her as vulnerable.

Now, realizing the sacrifice his parents made to so generously give him up once more, Bold finally understood the meaning of unconditional love.

He hoped he was worthy of their faith. He prayed to the Mother of all that he not fail any of those he loved.

Not his parents. Not Cené. Not the goddess.

Sleep was a long time coming. He worried about Cené, wondered if the makáo had breached the temple. Wondered if he would have the strength to save the women he loved. Most of all he wondered about the contents of the blessing bag, tied once more around his neck. Cené had never opened it, still did not know the contents.

She never realized he was pre-ordained to protect her. But, was it Cené he was meant to protect, or the goddess who resided within her body?

Somehow, he would learn the answer. Tomorrow he would make his report, then he would meet with Carly and Tim Riley. With the world's most powerful synergist, the best kinetic and his mom, whose power still appeared limitless, there was nothing that could keep him from the woman he loved.

Smiling as he imagined explaining all this to his beloved, Bolden finally found peace in sleep.

Chapter Seventeen

Cené leaned against the rough-hewn wall of the temple, her sword clasped in her hand. She'd never known this kind of exhaustion, never felt such despair. Bold was gone. Her beloved Bolden of two worlds. Sent away forever, he'd never know how she died.

That bothered Cené more than she'd thought it would. Though she knew he truly loved the goddess, Cené knew Bold loved her as well. Somehow, she wished he would also know that she fought well, that she'd not allowed the makáo to take her, no matter how seductive they'd become.

It was hard to believe those evil creatures had once been welcome to her bed at night. Now, though, the ephemeral beings of fantasy and desire had taken on form and shape. The males had sharp little teeth and enormous, perpetually erect penises. The females sported big, floppy breasts and oversized labia, their sex organs blatantly oversized, their lips huge and greedy, tongues long and snaking out of their mouths.

They practically oozed evil, a nasty, oily sense of *wrongness* they'd not had before. The goddess helped keep them away, but their numbers seemed to increase exponentially. Cené wondered about the rest of the people on this world. How did they protect themselves from the creatures that now spread out to ravage an unsuspecting populace? Where once they'd been confined to the Dream Forest, now they traveled with impunity throughout the land, raping and pillaging unsuspecting villages at will.

The attack on her own village, the rape of the briders, had been one of the first manifestations of Evil. Even Bold hadn't suspected. He told Cené he'd been disgusted by the barbaric behavior of his companions, but he'd not realized their behavior was, even then, controlled by Evil.

The goddess believed the creatures drew power from their sexual excesses, power they transferred to Evil. The victims of their deviant passions unknowingly fueled Evil. Somehow, the makáo siphoned the emotional energy, whether it be rage, desire, fear or hatred, then passed it on to Evil.

Much as they had once shared passion with the goddess.

If only they'd known. If only the goddess had somehow understood, before she'd helped provide the power to set her nemesis free.

Cené sank slowly to the floor. She was tired. So damned tired. The goddess gave her succor when she could, but now she was a part of the world around them, protecting her people as best she could. Only Cené guarded the temple, the last refuge for the goddess in human form.

She held the sword across her knees, her eyes wide open but barely aware of anything around her. All she could think of was Bold. Was he safe? Did he think of her, of the goddess? Would he miss this world once he returned to his own?

She hoped he found his mother. His father, too, for that matter. Cené's parents had died when she was young. Her memories of them were fleeting, not filled with a deep and abiding love as Bold had for his kin. She envied him that bond. Everyone should know that kind of love, at least once.

Cené smiled. She'd known that love. Knew it now with her goddess and with Bolden. He was a kind, honorable and generous man, and she knew he'd loved her. She thought of him, picturing his rippling muscles, his lean strength, the soft pelt of fur covering his chest, trailing down his belly and on to his groin. She shivered, recalling his huge cock, watching the supple foreskin sliding back as his erection grew, freeing the huge penis it barely contained. To think that wonderful monster fit inside her!

She would never forget the sensation of his loving, of that massive cock filling her, of his love surrounding her. That love gave her the strength to wait here, to guard the final sanctuary of her goddess. To hold a sword she had no idea how to use. To be willing to give her life to protect the one she served, no matter what.

* * * * *

Dressed now in his regulation skinsuit, his feet covered in soft boots for the first time in over two years, Bold sensed the bittersweet aura that surrounded this meeting of the governing body of the Armand Institute. This was his family, these were the ones who knew him best. They were also the people with the power to decide his fate.

Once the Rebellion ended, the year before Bolden was born, the original members of the band of Sensitives and Talent that had openly defied the powerful World Federation, had settled back once more into the place that had long been their home.

He glanced at the group seated at the long director's table and the memories came rolling back through his mind, swirling about his heart. Seated at the far end were Mara Armand and her mate, Sander, who had been the ones to set the original rebellion in motion. Thom Antoon, the lanky kinetics expert who led the fighters through seven long years, aided by Shing Tamura and Tim Riley, all of them sitting together along the side opposite Bold.

Bold smiled at Tim, nodded to Tim's wife, Carly. She was as beautiful as when Bold first remembered her, still youthful, still so much in love with her much younger husband. Bold swallowed back the huge lump that suddenly filled his throat. Would he ever be able to look at his own mate, so many years in the future, and find the same contentment he saw in Tim and Carly's eyes?

Just about the only ones missing were his own contemporaries. Mara and Sander's daughter, Kefira, was studying on Mirat. The ever faithful Tad Barton, son of a past president of the World Federation and long her admirer, had followed her off world. Jenna said Kefira was ignoring Tad, as usual, but she didn't expect her studied indifference to last much longer. Both Kefira and Tad had applied for a Quest.

Mara herself had suggested sending the two of them on the same ship.

Bold wished Malachi and Sheyna could be here, if only so he could tell them good-bye. Of course, with any luck, Earth, Mirat and Cené's world might some day establish regular contact. Stranger things had happened.

Thom looked up from his recorder. "Your report is excellent, Bold. This is the first evidence we've had of a sentient planet. The fact the sentience can take up residence in a willing humanoid figure is nothing short of amazing. If we can do a successful transfer and get you back there in one piece, I look forward to learning more about it. Interesting, though, that the planet hasn't got a name. It sounds as if the population is sophisticated enough to call it something, if only to name their goddess." He shrugged. "Well...I've already forwarded your report on to Mirat. I'm sure we'll hear from them within the day."

"They think of the planet as their goddess," Bold said. "Since she does actually communicate directly with them on occasion, they speak of their world as 'she' or 'my Lady.' It's a totally unique relationship, as far as I can tell. I look forward to returning so that I can learn more as soon as possible."

He just hoped they realized how soon that return needed to be. Bold felt his shoulders tense as Sander looked him directly in the eye, looked to his wife as if for confirmation, then took the floor.

The big lion nodded his head toward Bolden. "Garan has spoken to me regarding the need for your prompt return. We should probably make the attempt to send you back without waiting on word from Mirat, don't you agree?" His steady gaze swept the others in the room.

Bold felt his shoulders tense. His life, possibly the lives of Cené, of his goddess, of the people of her world, depended on the decision made here today. How he was going to make that change, Bold didn't know. He clasped the blessing bag in his huge paw, wrapped his fingers lightly around it and begged the Mother to intercede.

Amazingly, he felt the pouch grow warm beneath his fingers, felt a shift in power as if his prayer had been answered.

As he looked up, he realized everyone in the room was nodding in agreement with Sander's comment. He was going home. They were going to send him back.

* * * * *

Tim and Carly Ryan were the only ones to accompany Bolden, Jenna and Garan back to his parents' bungalow. Bold could practically feel the power emanating from this small group of Talents. He knew he was, quite literally, in the presence of greatness.

He opened the door and held it for the two couples. Tim and Carly could be any middle-aged couple. The same could be said for Jenna. Only Garan, with his imposing size and leonine strength stood out among them.

Yet, of the four, his powers were the least impressive. Tim had the ability to move people through both time and distance, his wife was a synergist, her main talent that of increasing exponentially the talents of those around her. Carly was also adept at astral projection, one of the first of the Sensitives to show that particular ability.

Of all of them, though, Bolden knew his mother wielded the strongest psychic power. Even Garan stood in awe of his wife's abilities. There was no explanation for her power. Born over a hundred and fifty years ago, she'd been brought forward in time by Tim when he was hardly more than a kid.

Bold knew the stories, how Jenna had taken his father to the home world of Mirat to find a way to heal him after a traumatic attack destroyed his mind, how she'd stood up to Gard, Garan's father, a cruel and perverted monster.

How she'd stuck by Garan, loved him, borne him three kits over the years, only to watch two of them die at birth. Only Bolden, the first son, had survived.

Yet, for all her amazing powers, Jenna, mate to Garan, mother to a gangly half-breed cub, was still just Mom. She'd loved unconditionally, taught him to not only accept his differences but to show pride in his unique abilities, his unconventional appearance. She'd taught him well. From his mother he'd learned love and forgiveness, strength of character and honesty.

Ah, but his father. Bold looked at his huge parent and couldn't hold back a grin. To think he'd sprung from that creature's loins! He loved his dad, admired everything about him, even prided himself on showing a bit of the leonine arrogance that cloaked the big cat. He would never be Garan's physical equal—the human genes within his make-up were much too strong—but he prided himself on inheriting his father's quick wit, good mind and sense of justice.

Jenna brought out cups of coffee while they all made themselves comfortable. "I know you're in a hurry to go back, but we need to know more about this world before you leave." She grinned and set her cup down on a coaster. "Besides, I would like to know more of the woman who has stolen my son's heart."

Bolden laughed, leaned forward and dropped his hands between his knees. "Well, everything you need to know about the world is in the report I gave to Thom. I'll leave a copy of it with you. As far as the woman? How does one explain a goddess?" He laughed again, and shook his head at Tim's grin. "No Tim. I'm not calling her a goddess just because she's hot. She really *is* a goddess. I've fallen in love with an immortal."

✳ ✳ ✳ ✳ ✳

"I know it's time, my son. We have no right to hold you. Not any longer." Jenna stood up and took the tray with their sandwich plates and coffee cups into the kitchen.

Bold recognized the square set of her shoulders, knew how deeply she hated to see him leave. At least now, with any luck, they would make contact once he returned to the planet.

If he returned. Tim had spent the past half hour studying his solar charts gleaned from Bold's receiver, comparing them to known systems. He was almost certain he'd found the proper world, *almost* sure he could relocate Bold. Between Carly's synergistic abilities and Jenna's telekinesis in gestalt with Tim's, there was little the three of them could not accomplish.

So long as they sent him to the right world. He'd be arriving without an oxygen pack, without clothing or adornment of any kind. He wondered if the blessing bag would make the transfer? It seemed to be a life unto itself. Hopefully, it would remain a part of Bold. It had certainly still been on him when the goddess sent him to earth.

Of course, his loincloth had come, too. He glanced down at the regulation skinsuit and boots. The idea of arriving bare-ass and buck naked, possibly in the midst of a battle, definitely lacked appeal.

He stood up and headed for his bedroom. With any luck, his mother hadn't tossed the well-worn loincloth.

* * * * *

He hugged his mother, got a surprisingly tearful kiss and bone-crushing hug from his father, then stood in the midst of a triangle made up of Carly, Tim and Jenna. The three held hands and surrounded Bold. He wore his loincloth and blessing bag, his pack was securely tied over his shoulder. He felt apprehension, but no real fear.

He looked directly into his mother's eyes, saw the love, the regret, the power in their depths. He knew that Tim searched out the proper coordinates, fixed them in his mind and shared them with Jenna. The sense of tightly leashed power within the enclosed space grew.

At exactly the instant Carly opened her mind with its synergistic boost, Jenna and Tim unleashed their kinetic thrust. Combined, they produced a powerful force, centered directly on Bold.

His world went black.

There was no sense of movement. No pain. No light or sound. He simply *was*, one moment.

And then he wasn't.

Chapter Eighteen

Cené blinked, frighteningly aware she'd fallen asleep. Even more aware she was no longer alone. Her body was slumped against the rough wall of the temple, in the shadows close by the fire pit. Someone moved just beyond, on the far side of the softly glowing coals. She blinked, grabbed her sword up off the floor and held it steady in her hand. Then she waited.

Bolden? No, it couldn't be. He was gone, sent back to his world by the Lady, bless her. Just in time, since so much on her world had gone horribly wrong the past couple days.

The figure stood up, the familiar looking massive shoulders and sinewy legs catching flashes of reflection from the fire. He was nude, his heavy cock still partially encased in its foreskin, his chest unencumbered by her blessing bag. Somehow, he must have lost it in his travels.

She automatically reached for it at her throat, but of course, it was gone. It saddened her, to think it might be lost forever. The goddess had lost hers. Cené knew the Lady still occasionally reached for her own bag when she shared Cené's body.

At least Cené had had the satisfaction of knowing hers was with the person who rightfully should carry it—her lifemate. Now, though, if this were truly Bolden, he appeared to have lost it.

The figure seemed to hesitate, as if confused. His face remained in the shadows, but she sensed his needs, his wants. His desire.

She dare not move, barely took a breath. Whoever he was seemed dazed, as if awakening from a long sleep. He shook his head and a large mass of dark hair tangled about his face.

He turned, looked directly at her. His hands were clenched into half-fists, the dark nails long and sharp. His amber eyes stared at her...through her.

His need washed over her, a silent craving to touch, to taste—to mate.

Bolden! Yes, but different, somehow. Distant, as if coming out of a long sleep. Cené rose slowly to her feet, let her thoughts flow free without barriers or shields.

He studied her, but his thoughts were tightly shielded. She sensed no essence of his true self. There was a dreamlike quality about him, about this. Cené searched for the goddess, but her Lady was nowhere near. She held her hand out. Stepped away from the shadows, into the light. Her fingers trembled. "Bold? Is that you?"

He saw her then, his beautiful head turning, his eyes boring into hers. The corner of his lip curled up in what could have been a smile but for the fierce canines it exposed. He took a couple steps, faltering just a bit, as if his legs would no longer hold him.

He had traveled far. The Lady said his world was very far away. How did he come back? No ship could return so quickly, that much her goddess had assured her. The journey must have been difficult. She could only wonder at how it worked, how a body could be suddenly transported across great distances of space and time.

Suddenly he took two quick steps and stood before her, his broad chest heaving with barely repressed desire, his cock jutting stiffly out from his groin. His left hand reached out, the familiar fingers long and broad, the nails thickened, sharp and oddly curved, reminding her of cat's claws.

He pressed his palm against her heart. The heat from his hand almost burned her flesh. She faltered, gasped in surprise as much as fear.

Bolden?

His other hand encompassed her left breast, his familiar fingers golden against the ebony depths of her skin. She moaned, unable to move away, barely able to breath. Oh Goddess, how she had missed him!

He leaned over and kissed the sensitive flesh beneath her ear, then drew his abrasive tongue across her jaw line. The rough texture left a trail of longing in its path.

*Yes! Bolden...*Cené twisted her chin to one side, allowing him better access to her throat. She heard him growl, a deep, guttural vibration that rumbled up out of his chest.

The sound sent shivers racing the length of her spine.

His right hand still kneaded her breast, the other still pressed against her heart, as if he held her life in his big, broad hand. His tongue scraped once more along her jaw line. She answered him with a cry of pleasure and a deep coil of wet heat between her legs.

Need. Want. Now

Was that his thought? Was it her own?

She reached up with her hands and wrapped them around his neck, drawing his head down to hers.

Suddenly, instead of the kiss she'd prepared for, he opened his jaws against her throat, his sharp teeth inhuman, the long, pointed canines sinking easily into the tender flesh.

Tearing and rending, he bit savagely into her throat, his claws sinking into her breast, his steel hard cock pressing against her pussy. Cené screamed in agony as something foul, hot and oily washed over her soul.

Evil! Here, in the goddess's temple. She cried out, her mental shout as loud as her scream.

Bolden! Help me! My Lady! Save me. Save me, please!

* * * * *

Something pulled him from sleep, a sound, a sense of danger? Bold blinked wearily, suddenly coming alert. He took a deep breath when he realized he lay in the soft mosses near his Lady's temple.

It worked! He sent a silent prayer of thanks to the Mother, then rose to his feet. His pack lay in the grass beside him, his loincloth was still securely tied about his waist, but most important, the blessing bag hung securely from the woven thong around his neck.

A scream! He heard it this time, as much in his mind as in the air about him. Cené! He raced toward the tree, searching frantically for the doorway hidden in the rough bark. Finally he sensed the opening, said a quick prayer to the goddess that parted the door, and stepped inside.

A nightmare. It had to be a nightmare. No reality could be this horrible. Cené's torn and bloody body lay on the ground. There was no movement, no sense of life about her. The makáo stood over her, the one who looked exactly like Bolden. Blood dripped from his jaws, his hands were covered in the stuff. His cock jutted obscenely out from his body. He turned and snarled at Bold. His teeth were red with Cené's blood.

With a frenzied scream borne of unimaginable grief, Bold leapt across the fire pit and tackled the makáo. The beast skidded across the floor, clawing and biting, his foul breath burning like a noxious gas, his eyes blazing in red fury.

Empowered by rage, Bold tore at the beast's throat, clawing and biting like the wild animal that was so much a part of his heritage. The beast fought back, more powerful than Bolden, fighting for its very existence, its massive strength hampered only by its lack of familiarity with the body it had created.

Bold managed to flip the thing over on its belly. He clamped his knees down on the creature's hips, then grabbed it by the chin and hair. Pulling its head back, stretching the neck until he was sure it should break, Bold poured his anger, his hatred, his lust for blood into every move he made.

The creature howled, but the sound choked off as Bold pulled its head back even harder. "Break, damn you. Die!" The tendons stood out on the creature's throat, the muscles across its back bulged and its fingers scrabbled uselessly against the stone floor.

Suddenly it grabbed hold of a table leg, wrenching the small table behind its back, hitting Bolden squarely across the face. Stunned, Bold's hands fell away from the creature's hair and face and he slipped to one side, landing heavily.

Roaring, finding strength it hadn't yet learned in this unfamiliar body, the creature twisted around and came down hard on Bolden. He planted his knee firmly against Bold's chest, leaned over and clamped his powerful jaws on his throat.

Bolden felt the skin break, knew tendons and muscles were being ripped away. Still he fought, twisting, turning, grabbing for any purchase he could find. An oily darkness covered him, a dank miasma that seemed to emanate from the filthy likeness of himself.

Hot blood poured across Bold's chest. He sensed it then, death only moments away. The beast had found the carotid artery. Even now, Bold felt his own heart pumping the blood from his body.

He must not let this thing live—this thing that was more than makáo, was instead the very personification of Evil. His destiny was to save the goddess. He'd already failed Cené.

Mother, help me! She'd not failed him before. Now, even so far away, could his own goddess give him the strength he needed?

Bold felt the blessing bag burning against his chest. Felt his life's blood pouring from his torn throat...felt a massive burst of strength as he lifted the beast away, screaming and struggling in Bold's suddenly superhuman grip.

He bent the body double, his own body, stolen by this foul creature. Bent it double, heard the spine snap. With his last ounce of strength, he dropped the stinking carcass into the fire pit.

A huge wall of flame leapt up, consuming Evil in a fiery blast. Bolden fell beside the pit, his strength gone, the light slowly fading from his eyes. He sensed Cené beside him. Felt her blood on his lips, her hot tears on his chest. He raised his hand, the ebony claws barely extended, and touched the side of her face with the backs of his fingers.

"You're alive," he whispered. "Praise the Mother. I love you. I will always love you. You and the Lady. Both of you. Beautiful. So very, very beautiful."

Suddenly his head lolled to one side. As Cené watched through her tears, the light went out of his beautiful amber eyes. She could make no sound, no cry of grief. Losing Bold went beyond grief, beyond pain. She could only sit and hold his head in her lap, stroke his thick mane between her fingers, and wait for the Lady to return.

* * * * *

She'd not known such exhaustion before. Had never felt this deep, chilling despair, but the makáo were everywhere and she could not fight them all. Her world slipped closer and closer to darkness. Evil grew stronger with each passing moment.

Every emotion, every crying mother, every despairing father, the fear of every victim gave energy and sustenance to Evil. This was so far beyond what she had once contained that she knew something else, something of amazing power must control it.

Black clouds rolled across her oceans and she was powerless to stop them. Lightning struck the tall trees and her forests burned. Her people huddled in fear and asked why their goddess had forsaken them.

I haven't, she wanted to cry. *I'm trying. I'm doing everything I can to save you.*

It wasn't enough. It was never going to be enough. Evil would win and her world would die. Where did that leave one worthless, immortal goddess? Most likely as Evil's prisoner, to do with as he would.

So be it. At least Bolden was safe. She knew she had placed him perfectly on his home world. Knew he was alive when she left him there, close to his home. If only she could have convinced Cené to go with him. Cené, who was as much a part of the goddess as she was of the woman. Evil would not treat her handmaiden well.

She sensed another attack, felt the black fog coming closer, the storm growing stronger. Evil must be planning something big tonight. His final thrust. His death blow.

Calling on her strength, the goddess waited. Makáo surrounded most of her world's villages. Fires burned out of control through her forests. The air was foul with the stink of evil. Maybe, just maybe, if she fought hard enough, long enough, Evil might kill her as well.

Death in battle would be preferable to immortality as a failure.

Suddenly, she sensed a shift, a twist in the way things were. The fog began to dissipate, the sunshine broke through on a littered landscape of tumbled villages and bodies in the streets, but at least it was shining.

The makáo were gone. Every last one of them. She no longer sensed the evil creatures anywhere on her world.

She opened all her senses, searched for the oily stink of Evil that had invaded her world. *Gone? But where?*

Her curiosity growing, she encompassed all of the planet, searching for darkness, for the stink of despair, the barest hint of Evil.

She found only grief. Cené's grief.

Bolden is dead?

No!

In less than a heartbeat she'd entered her temple. Badly injured but still alive, Cené sat on the stone floor cradling Bold's head in her lap. His throat was torn open, his body covered in blood. There was no spark of life about him. Only the faintest essence of his brave and loving spirit still clung to his broken body.

The fire pit smoldered. A dark, oily smoke wafted above the pit and left a sooty stain on the ceiling directly overhead.

She replayed the entire battle as it had happened, saw Bold defeat Evil, heard him call on the Mother, a goddess more powerful than herself, knew he found strength from that kind and generous entity.

Cené suddenly raised her head, sensing her presence. "Save him, my Lady. You must!"

His life force is gone, child. I cannot bring him back, not now. It is too late.

"Give him mine!" She hunched her body over Bold's, protecting him, holding him against her breast. "Give him mine, Lady. I offer it freely, my life force to save him. "

Do you know what you offer? What will happen? You will die, Cené. Bolden may live, but you will die. He will never forgive me. He would not want that from you. Bolden is a man who loves deeply and forever. He would hate me for taking your life to save his.

"Not if you take my body, my Lady. Don't you see?" Cené's emerald eyes glistened with tears, her frustration obvious.

No, I don't. She'd never experienced anything like this, to have a mortal explain things to her as if she were a child.

"Bolden loves both of us, but he loves you more. Give him my life force, take my body to do with as you will. I won't die, goddess. Not really. I'll know I've given a gift of life to a man I love beyond all others. I will also give the gift of love to the goddess I worship. It is a willing gift, my Lady. I beg you. Please do this for me. For us. There's not much time. I sense his spirit. It is anxious to be gone."

There is no greater love...

There was a wrenching tear, a sharp pain beneath her heart. Cené gasped, but she held her cry of pain inside. As her own body slumped to the floor, Bolden's grew warm. His fierce wounds knit, the blood flowed once more through veins and arteries.

Cené hadn't expected to be aware of his recovery, his rebirth. She should be dead. Wasn't her life force now Bolden's?

How? She sensed her goddess nearby, suddenly felt the familiar joining as the Lady slipped comfortably into her body. Once more, Cené knew a sense of joy, of wonder, to feel herself part of the one she served.

You will not die, Cené. By your generous offer, your willingness to sacrifice yourself that another might live, you have earned immortality. Both you and Bolden. There is One more powerful than I...I'm not certain who it is. Possibly the Mother Bolden prays to, as I sense a feminine spirit. A good and loving spirit.

Bolden gave his life to vanquish Evil. You unselfishly gave yours to save Bold, yet you've also promised it to me. I take your gift, my Lady. We, you and I, will forever be one, the consort of Bolden of Three Worlds. This world I have watched over for untold centuries will forever and all time be known as BoldCené.

Chapter Nineteen

Bolden awoke to the indescribable pleasure of being bathed by Cené in the temple pool. She carefully scrubbed away the caked blood that matted the hair on his chest. He felt her slender fingers working through the tangles, rubbing lightly over his sensitive nipples. Would he ever get enough of her touch? His mane had already been shampooed and the thick hair floated behind him in the warm water.

He watched Cené through lowered lids. Praise the Mother, she was still alive. He'd been so certain that thing had killed her. Hadn't her throat been torn? He was sure he'd seen her blood spreading across the floor, the flesh ripped, her body broken.

Now, her neck was as smooth and slender as always, the skin supple and black as velvet. She bathed him gently, singing softly as she washed him. He sensed the goddess in her, stronger than usual though not so overwhelming as when he and the lady had spent their short time alone together. He liked this combination, this sense of an equal division of Cené and her Lady.

Liked it a lot. His cock swelled within its foreskin, growing in size until the covering slipped easily back down to the base. Cené glanced at his erection, smiled briefly, then continued her gentle bathing of his body.

Now, though, she didn't ignore his cock. The soft cloth drifted across the sensitive head, then she dragged the rag down between his legs and gently washed his sac. He leaned his head back and smiled, more than willing to suffer her loving ministrations.

Besides, he needed to get things straight. His mind still felt muddled and confused. He remembered standing in his parents' living room on Earth, surrounded by Tim and Carly Ryan and his mother, his father standing close beside them. He remembered the shift in power, the rush of color and light, then nothing.

His next memory was of coming awake outside the temple. He'd heard Cené's scream, had raced inside...and saw himself, his double leaning over Cené's still form. There'd been a terrible battle, a fight with his twin, a powerful, evil entity that... "That thing killed me! Cené, what the hell is going on? I thought I bled to death. I felt my throat torn out..."

Splashing, floundering in the pool, Bold struggled to sit up. He found a smooth rock at the edge of the pool and caught his balance, then reached up to touch the smooth skin covering what had been a gaping wound in his throat.

"I thought you were dead. I *know* I was dead...or at least dying. What happened?

"You died. But you died bravely." She smiled, almost as if she teased him. It was hard to find any humor in dying, at least right now. "You destroyed Evil. He is gone forever, all because of you, but he fought very hard before you killed him. You fought bravely, Bolden. You have no equal in the bravery you displayed." She paused, took a deep breath. "The goddess brought you back." Cené ducked her head. "There have been changes."

"What kinds of changes?" Bold reached out and tilted her chin up, leaned over and kissed her full lips. She sighed and wrapped her slim arms around his neck.

"Good changes," she whispered, kissing him back. "*Forever* changes. I love you, Bolden of Three Worlds."

"Ah, so it's three worlds, now. I like the sound of that." He stroked her breast, bringing the bright red nipple to a hard point. Then he leaned over and suckled it deep inside his mouth, sucking hard enough that his cheeks hollowed out and his tongue rubbed roughly against the underside.

Cené arched her back and whimpered. "I hope you do," she said, clipping her words off in a soft moan, "...because you'll be hearing it forever."

He recognized the goddess in the dry humor behind Cené's comment. He jerked his head back. Her nipple slipped from between his lips with a loud *pop*.

"Okay. Explain." He pulled her onto his lap, setting her just at the juncture of his thighs so that his erect cock was forced between her legs. It stuck up in front of her with the tip rubbing against her clitoris. She wriggled a bit, finding exactly the right pressure. The warm globes of her bottom rested on his belly.

"You died. The beast tore your throat open and you bled to death before the goddess could get to you. Cené was gravely injured, but still alive when the goddess arrived. She offered up her life force to save you, the goddess saved Cené and the only real change in everything is that you're now an immortal."

"A what?" He couldn't have heard that correctly, that entire litany recited as if she were discussing what went on at the office today. He was still trying to digest the fact Cené had 'offered up her life force' for him. Didn't that mean she'd died so he could live? But Cené was here, sharing her body with her Lady, just as they'd done in the past.

"Immortal." She sighed. "The goddess and Cené are now forever one, which means Cené shares the goddess's immortality. Bolden, by virtue of his bravery and generous sacrifice, gained life through Cené and immortality from an entity even more powerful than the goddess."

Immortality. The one thing that had kept him apart from loving the Lady. "I don't understand. How can I be immortal? I still feel the same. You're not making sense! Who, exactly are you, now? What of Cené?"

"I *am* Cené. I will always *be* Cené, just as you will be known as Bolden of Three Worlds and our planet will now be called BoldCené."

He whipped his head around at the same time he lifted Cené so that she straddled his lap, facing him. His wet mane slapped against his face and flung droplets of water over hers. "What did you say?"

Let your mind go, Bolden. Let it flow into the rocks and trees, into the very air that encircles the world. Feel. Be one with the world. Follow your destiny.

He blinked. Stared into Cené's emerald green eyes and saw the humor in their depths. The love. Their future.

He opened his mind, let his thoughts fly free. It was effortless, really, this ability to become the world. He was the rocks, the trees, the spirits within the birds that flew in great flocks over the oceans. He sensed the winds, the warmth of the sun, even stirred up the clouds over the desert, just to test himself.

When he finally returned his thoughts to the warm pool, the sky was turning dark and Cené slept against his chest. It was a small matter to slip his ready erection into her hot and waiting folds. He lifted her bottom with one hand and directed his cock into her pussy. She was snug, hot and tight and her muscles immediately clung to him. She sighed and settled herself down on his full length, then raised her head and smiled at him with slumberous eyes.

Do you understand now, my love? We are *BoldCené. We are the world and all its rocks and trees, mountains and rivers. Our people have free choice, but they will pray to us. Because of you, because of your bravery, I imagine their prayers will be more of thanks than requests.*

Someday, he thought, *this will all make sense.* Right now, though, all he really needed was Cené, his Lady, his love for all time. She was everything and all things to him...the tenacious little warrior woman he'd stalked through the forest, the regal goddess alone and afraid for her world. No longer afraid, he sensed in her only love, contentment and the deep, spiraling coil of her desire.

He arched his back, driving into her deeper, harder. She met him, thrust for thrust, loving him, her body folding itself around him, holding him for all time.

Immortal? He could live with that, with this woman. Bold watched her face, the full red lips, the closed eyes shaded by lashes darker than night. Her slender fingers gripped his forearms and her legs clamped down on his hips as she rode him.

She might be a goddess, but she was one hot woman. He leaned over and sucked one of her nipples between his lips. She cried out, her body stiffened and he drove into her faster, harder, deeper. Each thrust of his hips took her closer, higher until he felt her climax, felt the tension peak than slowly fade away.

At that moment, that perfect time where her pussy grasped his cock in a tight hot fist, he raised up out of the warm pool, standing tall and holding Cené against him. She came down completely on his hard cock, her body grasping and hot, her legs trembling and mouth wide open in a scream of exultation.

Bold emptied himself into her, filled her with his seed, his hands clasping her buttocks and pressing her closer, giving her all she could take, all she wanted, begged for.

Finally, legs shaking and balls aching, he slipped back down into the hot pool. She looked at him and grinned, an impish smile that in no way looked like the kind of expression one would expect on the face of an immortal. He wondered if he had the same, dopey, love-struck look on his own face?

They dried off with a soft towel Cené had left by the pool, then re-entered the temple. The blood was gone, the area completely clean. "Did you...?"

"There are some things I prefer to handle without getting my hands dirty. Touching anything to do with Evil is way up there on the list." She turned to Bold and grasped both his hands in hers. "I see you wear the blessing bag. Have you thought what you will place inside?"

"As your lifemate, I do have something that seems apropos." He let go of her hands, grabbed a large poker near the fire pit and stirred the cold ashes around. Finally he found what he was looking for.

He knelt beside the pit, reached into the ashes and picked up a perfectly round, black marble, about a half inch in diameter. The surface was pockmarked, as if from great heat, but it was the perfect black of pure obsidian.

Exactly the color of Cené's skin. Bolden held the object in his hand, surprised he felt nothing emanating from it. All that was left of Evil, dead and cold now, melted into a single lump of black glass. He held it out to Cené. When she put it in her hand, it practically disappeared against the matching color.

"To think something this beautiful could have once been so ugly." She looked up at Bolden and smiled. "It is truly the right and proper thing to keep within the bag." She lifted the bag from around his neck, then smiled at him again. "I see the knots have been retied. You have opened it?"

"The bag is what brought me back." Bold clasped her hands once more in his, the bag held between them. "Sending me to an unknown planet went against all protocol on my world. Once they saw the contents of your blessing bag, it was assumed my trip was pre-ordained. My destiny."

He slowly untied the knots and emptied the three items out into the palm of his hand. The claw. The tooth. The amber lion. When Cené took the lion from him, her eyes grew wide. "The heart is beating. Do you see?"

"I don't know how to explain it," he said, "but I sense the life force within the beast. All that has happened was meant to be. You. Me. Somehow, this is our destiny, to be one with this world."

Cené carefully replaced the three items, then added the black bit of glass. Where the goddess had once held Evil captive, she and Bold now held merely the remnant of Evil. There was no life left in this stone.

Bold let Cené tie the blessing bag together and place it once more around his neck. Immediately he felt the power. He couldn't help but wonder who the entity was, the one who had come to his aid, had given him the strength to vanquish Evil.

Someday, maybe he'd find out. For now, though, he was content to hold his Lady in his arms. For now, forever. An odd thought flashed into his head. What did immortality make him? A god?

Shaking his head at his own foolishness, Bold swept Cené up in his arms and carried her to the bed. He was in the process of renewing his acquaintance with her left nipple, when a strange tone interrupted them.

"What the hell?" He slipped off the bed and reached for his pack. His solar receiver beeped, the tone loud and strong.

He flipped it open, saw where someone was trying to contact him. "Hello?"

Bolden? Is that you? Are you all right? Tim's sending this message kinetically, Carly's boosting it and Dad and I are so glad we've figured out how to contact you. Is everything okay?

Laughter bubbled up out of his chest. Bolden sat back on the bed and wrapped his arm around Cené. "Mom," he said, holding his Lady close, laughing even harder, "you're not going to believe what happened..."

About the author:

For over thirty years Kate Douglas has been lucky enough to call writing her profession. She has won three EPPIES, two for Best Contemporary Romance and one for Best Romantic Suspense. Kate occasionally creates cover art and is the winner of EPIC's Quasar Award for outstanding bookcover graphics.

She is multi-published in contemporary romance, both print and electronic formats, as well as her popular futuristic Romantica series: StarQuest. She and her husband of over thirty years live in the northern California wine country where they find more than enough subject material for their shared passion for photography.

Kate welcomes mail from readers. You can write to her c/o Ellora's Cave Publishing at 1337 Commerce Drive, Suite 13, Stow OH 44224.

Why an electronic book?

We live in the Information Age — an exciting time in the history of human civilization in which technology rules supreme and continues to progress in leaps and bounds every minute of every hour of every day. For a multitude of reasons, more and more avid literary fans are opting to purchase e-books instead of paperbacks. The question to those not yet initiated to the world of electronic reading is simply: *why?*

1. *Price.* An electronic title at Ellora's Cave Publishing runs anywhere from 40-75% less than the cover price of the <u>exact same title</u> in paperback format. Why? Cold mathematics. It is less expensive to publish an e-book than it is to publish a paperback, so the savings are passed along to the consumer.

2. *Space.* Running out of room to house your paperback books? That is one worry you will never have with electronic novels. For a low one-time cost, you can purchase a handheld computer designed specifically for e-reading purposes. Many e-readers are larger than the average handheld, giving you plenty of screen room. Better yet, hundreds of titles can be stored within your new library — a single microchip. (Please note that Ellora's Cave does not endorse any specific brands. You can check our website at www.ellorascave.com for customer recommendations we make available to new consumers.)

3. *Mobility.* Because your new library now consists of only a microchip, your entire cache of books can be taken with you wherever you go.

4. *Personal preferences are accounted for.* Are the words you are currently reading too small? Too large? Too...**ANNOYING**? Paperback books cannot be modified according to personal preferences, but e-books can.

5. *Innovation.* The way you read a book is not the only advancement the Information Age has gifted the literary community with. There is also the factor of what you can read. Ellora's Cave Publishing will be introducing a new line of interactive titles that are available in e-book format only.

6. *Instant gratification.* Is it the middle of the night and all the bookstores are closed? Are you tired of waiting days—sometimes weeks—for online and offline bookstores to ship the novels you bought? Ellora's Cave Publishing sells instantaneous downloads 24 hours a day, 7 days a week, 365 days a year. Our e-book delivery system is 100% automated, meaning your order is filled as soon as you pay for it.

Those are a few of the top reasons why electronic novels are displacing paperbacks for many an avid reader. As always, Ellora's Cave Publishing welcomes your questions and comments. We invite you to email us at service@ellorascave.com or write to us directly at: 1337 Commerce Drive, Suite 13, Stow OH 44224.

Discover for yourself why readers can't get enough of the multiple award-winning publisher Ellora's Cave. Whether you prefer e-books or paperbacks, be sure to visit EC on the web at www.ellorascave.com for an erotic reading experience that will leave you breathless.

WWW.ELLORASCAVE.COM